The Wings of the Wind

Books by
RONALD HARDY

The Place of Jackals
A Name Like Herod
Kampong
The Men From the Bush
Act of Destruction
The Iron Snake
The Savages
The Face of Jalanath
Rivers of Darkness
The Wings of the Wind

The Wings of the Wind

RONALD HARDY

G. P. PUTNAM'S SONS / NEW YORK

G. P. Putnam's Sons
Publishers Since 1838
200 Madison Avenue
New York, NY 10016

The author gratefully acknowledges permission from
Alfred A. Knopf, Inc., to reprint lines from
"A Song of Unending Sorrow" from
The Jade Mountain: A Chinese Anthology by Witter Bynner,
copyright 1929 and renewed 1957 by Alfred A. Knopf, Inc.

Library of Congress Cataloging-in-Publication Data

Hardy, Ronald.
The wings of the wind.

I. Title.
PR6058.A676W56   1987   823′.914   86-20545
ISBN 0-399-12986-3

Printed in the United States of America
3 4 5 6 7 8 9 10

This is for Joyce and Ben

Contents

PART ONE

Escape

A thrid-generation medical missionary
in China, on the run from a high rank-
ing security officer, is imprisoned
by the Communists.

This was the second day of their escape and when the light began to fade Lewis Mackenna drove the truck up the rise of the ground to where the camphor trees grew. He positioned the truck so that it would not be seen from the road or from the air and when the engine was switched off he sat for a time immersed in the silence of the wild land. He heard Ellen Mackenna stir beside him and, turning, he watched her awaken. He stroked her cheek. He could see the imprint of exhaustion on her face. They had driven through the previous night and then through the yellow heat of the day. He felt again the onset of fear. What have I done to them? he asked himself; these three lives. He pulled her toward him and their sweating faces slid together. There was movement in the rear and he looked across the crown of her head. But the two boys had not awakened.

"Let them sleep," he said.

He got out of the truck and walked through tree-shadow and into the warmth of the dying sun. Below him the river, a tributary of the Tsien Tang, was touched with its redness. The mountains too were reddening. In this province of Chekiang the ranges ran down at an angle to the coast. The rock was formed into strange shapes. "Like huge bells," his father, Cromer Mackenna, had once described them. Cromer was a fine orator, an evangelist in the family tradition, and he could not restrain the exaggerations. "They were made in God's foundry. And when the wind is in them you can hear them ring." Lewis smiled at the memory of that vibrant voice. There were always voices, Mackenna voices, the voices of forefathers he had never known; protesting, he thought, at this ending to their story. What good did we do? he asked them. In one hundred years what did we, the missionaries, achieve? Where were the Christian converts when the Communists marched in? Wind was gathering, bringing to his nostrils the scent of the camphor trees. This was June of the year 1954. Already the first clouds of the typhoon season reached like barbs from the mountains.

He turned and walked back to the truck.

*   *   *

After they had eaten and darkness now fallen they walked down the slope to the river. Humidity was building and the wind blew warm on the flesh. There had been heavy rains in the north of the province and the river was white with turbulence.

They stripped and, holding hands and the boys between, entered the water. They began to wash, rinsing from their bodies the dust and sweat of the journey. They did not (as in other, sunlit times) laugh or splash joyously. They were silent. Once the headlamps of a vehicle cut channels of light on the road that ran between the river and the trees. They stood unmoving until the sound of the engine died. Lewis felt the fear return. He could see the boys in the shallows, Ellen out deeper and her breasts lifting and her hair writhing on the current. In the darkness their bodies were insubstantial, no more than a white glimmer of flesh. We are already ghosts, he told himself. He felt the undertow tug at his body with a sudden power; as if the river, which was a part of the hostile land, had tried to claim him. He pointed to the bank. "Out now," he said. He could hear the strain in his voice.

When they were dried and the towels fixed around their waists he turned to face the mountains, breathing deeply of the wind. But there was no refreshment in it. For days now it had blown inland from the South China Sea, funneled through the ranges so that it became moist and heated. Soon they would begin to sweat again. Ellen came to his side and leaned her head against his shoulder.

"Shall we make the tea?" Gerard asked.

"Yes."

They watched them, these twins whom they had named Gerard and Joel, moving up the rise to the trees.

"They'll be ten next week," she said.

"My God, yes."

"Had you forgotten?"

He nodded.

"I haven't bought them anything," she said.

He smiled at her guilt.

"There was no time," he murmured. "There were other things. Like running for our lives."

He felt the sudden tension in her body.

"Is it really as bad as that?" she asked.

"For me it is."

She turned to face him.

"And the boys?" she said. "Surely they wouldn't harm the boys?"

He did not answer.

"They're only children," she said.

He kissed her wet hair.

"They won't harm them," he told her. "Why should they?"

But the question lay there, as immovable as the growing fear. Since when was innocence a shield? Mostly it was a provocation. How well do I know these people? he asked himself. After a lifetime spent in China, in medicine and in the priesthood, how much do I understand? No more, perhaps, than a page in a massive book. There had been kindness, humor, sometimes love. Yet the centuries of violence had left their taint and a man with a nose for history, or even a frightened man, could still smell the old barbarities on the air. He himself, as a child, had seen his father tied to a cross and sliced. He felt the woman shiver against him and he whispered: "They won't catch us. I promise you." He put his finger under her chin and lifted her face and smiled into it. "A little luck and we'll be safe across the water."

She moved a pace and began to dry her hair.

"Luck?" she said through the folds of the towel. "That's an odd word for a priest to use."

"Just a word."

She tied the towel into a turban. Everything was pallid in the moonrise and he could see the hollows in her cheeks. She was staring at him.

"With God's help," he said, shrugging. "Is that what you want me to say?"

She did not reply. She stood there like a child betrayed. He felt the self-disgust grow, then anger.

"I'll fall on my knees when we get there," he said. "But not before." The anger surged. "It's the plan that counts. It's Chiang's men being where they should be. It's the bribes I've paid. It's the people that owe me paying a debt. It's the weather and the river and the fuel in the tank." The anger ebbed and left him empty. He smiled faintly. "Of course, I'd be grateful for a bit of divine intervention."

"There is also Chen," she said.

"Yes."

"He's out there somewhere."

"Perhaps."

"He's out there. And he could be near."

The end of the towel disengaged and she uncoiled it and draped it on her shoulders. Then she jerked her long hair back from off her face in her characteristic gesture. He saw it swing across her spine. An old hunger touched him for a moment. In the beginning it was her hair that had excited him, and when the sun struck it had glowed as red as a rowan berry. He had liked to fondle it, brush it, let it fall across his face when she was above him on their bed. But that was a time ago. It had faded, as she too had faded. Now, in the black and silver night, it seemed she was a girl again. He went to her and they embraced and swayed together, unbearably alone in this alien place.

"You were always the better missionary," he said.

She shook her head in denial.

"It's true," he said gently. "Better than I could ever be."

Her head shook again. He could smell the river in her hair. Above them a flower of yellow light quivered in the blackness of the camphor grove.

"I can see the light from the primus," he said, alarmed.

They turned and, hands linked, began the walk up the slope.

"Tell me, Lewis," she said. "Did you ever beat John Chen at chess?"

"Never."

"Then why should you beat him now?"

The question irritated him. He let fall her hand.

"This isn't a game," he said.

But later he awakened in the cicada-singing night and her words came again like the remnant of a dream. Chen, too, was there; and momentarily it seemed that the beautiful lemon face with its nap of cropped blue-black hair hung above him in the camphor branches. I can beat you, he told the face as it dissolved. Because we did not start on equal terms. Because I was warned and there were two priceless days in which to plan escape. So the advantage is as good as the capture of a major piece. He smiled in the darkness. He could not avoid the chess analogies and perhaps for Chen it really was a game. They had first played in the prison camp at Fusan where Chen was the political officer. That was in 1949 after Mao and the Communists had destroyed the old regime and had turned their spite on the missionaries. Then they had played again in the Hangchow mission after his release and at the time when Chen would come to watch and question. Now Chen was a grandmaster, emerging on the world's stages whenever the Politburo decided there was a chance of defeating the Soviets. But there was also another, secret face. It leaned in the darker corners of the Ministry of Public Security across a different kind of chessboard; one on which were arrayed the enemies of the State. John Chen was a hunter.

A faint pallor was growing above the tracery of branches. Lewis rose, shook and folded his blanket and went to the open rear of the truck. They were asleep. Ellen's face was in shadow but he could see the profiles of the two boys, each the replica of the other. The familiar question that he had suffered a thousand times came again into his mind. "How do you tell them apart?" He had learned never to reply, merely to shrug. But he could have answered: "I can tell. Don't ask me how but I can tell. I think it is in the eyes. The eyes truly mirror whatever is within (he could not bring himself to refer to the soul) and since whatever is within is unique to every one of us there must surely be a difference." But he could not use such pompous and priestly words. It was easier to smile and shrug.

He placed the blanket in the truck and picked up a towel, an empty water canteen and his medical case. A single drum of fuel stood behind the driving seat next to the two Long Jing tea chests. The drum contained fuel sufficient for perhaps twelve hours of driving, and the chests contained a collection of antique objects sufficient to provide security for considerably longer. He opened the case. Inside were instruments and drugs, a folded map and a strip of calico that enclosed three cut-throat razors. The razors, like the cherrywood case, had belonged to Jardine Mackenna, the first of the family missionaries, and their ivory handles were stained and pitted with age. Lewis chose one. Then he began the walk down to the river.

Twelve hours. After that the truck was useless. He could not replenish it, and in any event it had become a danger. This was a province of plodding feet, mule or buffalo carts, a million bicycles. Motor transport was rare and therefore conspicuous. An occasional truck might carry produce from the communes to the cities, or a Party car pass with its red triangular flag streaming on the radiator. But that was all. The mission truck had provided a final service. Soon they would make the river assignation.

After he had washed he sat on the bank and, face still wet, shaved off his two-day bristle. He always enjoyed the feel of an open razor. But today there was no such satisfaction. He could also feel the stare of Jardine's accusing eyes. It was Jardine's hand that held the razor, Jardine's haggard cheeks that met its steel. He wiped and closed it. There was an impulse to throw it into the water, divest himself of yet another link with the past. He stood and put it in his pocket. Then he picked up the canteen and went down into the shallows and began to fill it. Crouching above it he watched the first pearly daylight reveal the mountains.

Ellen Mackenna, too, was watching. She stood at the edge of the camphor trees and even at that distance she could see the thinness of his back and the way in which the light sharpened the spinal bones. He was almost as skeletal as the day they had returned him from Fusan. Fusan: the name was like a brand on the mind. It would never heal and there were times at night when he lay beside her jerking in his fearful sleep that those five red and painful letters seemed to throb within her. She saw him screw on the top of the canteen, straighten and stand there for a moment looking at the sky. It had been like that on the day of his release. It was early with the mist still on West Lake and the bicycle bells ringing in the Hangchow boulevards and the children reciting an English verse in the mission school. The car, black with a red pennant, had entered the compound from the Ningpo Avenue entrance. It stopped in the center of the courtyard and a soldier got out and opened a rear door. There was a pause. A sandaled foot emerged. The trouser leg had ridden up and she could see the sores on the ankle-bones and shins. Lewis Mackenna walked slowly from the car to the stone parapet of the little fountain and stood there face raised to the sky and blinking in the sun like a tired child. He put out his hand so that the water splashed on it. She had run from the portico and down the steps and across the paving toward him. But then she had stopped and stared. He was wasted and his life fluttered beneath his ribs like something trapped in a cage. They had found no box or wrapping-paper for his few possessions and they had merely taken them and attached them to his limbs with lengths of jute string. She felt her lips twitch. He was like a badly tied parcel delivered at last to the correct address. But then the engine of the car had cut and she heard his raucous breathing and saw again the life trembling against his rib cage and she went to him and held him as if she would contain it and stop its flight. Now the tears were shooting down her cheeks and she saw John Chen's blurred shape come from the car. He was carrying the medical case and he bent and laid it at their feet.

"What have you done to him?" she whispered.

Chen bowed politely and went back to the car. Rage was rising and she followed him and struck him in the shoulder so that he was turned toward her.

"What have you done?" she shouted.

"I have returned him. Be thankful."

"Thankful?" She pointed at Lewis Mackenna. His head was inclined and he was listening to the children's voices. "Thankful for that?"

Chen nodded and got into the car. He wound down the window and looked up into her face.

"He's the only one," he said.

She did not understand.

"What do you mean?" she said.

"The only one to be freed. Fusan is closed. The prisoners have gone to other camps."

The voices stopped and in the silence she heard some metallic object fall and roll within the buildings.

"How many were there?" she asked.

"About twelve hundred."

The numbers began to register. One out of twelve hundred. A miracle. Chen wound up the window and she looked through the glass into his luminous eyes. They were disconcerting. Be careful of him, she had once been warned; he knows what you are thinking.

"No," Chen said. "Not a miracle. I let him go."

The car left. She went to the fountain and picked up the case and put her arm around him.

"You're home now," she said. "Home."

That was a good word and he had wept when he heard it. He had been born in the mission and except for the years of medical and ordination study he had spent most of his missionary life there. She too had loved the place. The city was one of the oldest in the world and at the end of almost every lane or street there was the haze of the lake and maples standing in the haze and across the lake the hills with their temples and pagodas. There were boats with carved oars and lace-covered seats on which you could sit and watch the prow break through the leaves and flowers of the lotus. The revolutionary committees had not destroyed the past as they had in Peking. Everywhere in Hangchow were the stone and tile features of the old Imperial China. The mission building and its gardens (bought by the defunct Chinese Evangelization Society in those days before such extravagances had sent it bankrupt) were spread across the junction of Ningpo Avenue and Dragon Well Lane and had been the property of an opium-and-tea merchant. It was very old and a section of its enclosing wall was carved into the shape of a dragon so that the head reared above the gates and the body made undulations along the crown of the wall. At night when the wall was in the path of the moon the jaws and spiky ruff cast a monstrous shadow on the courtyard and there were those in the mission who would not walk across it. But in daylight the dragon was a thing of peace; and beyond the wall there were sweetmeat and food shops in the lane and houses with blue painted doors and at certain times of the year bunches of hot red peppers were pinned to the doors for drying in the sun and at a distance they were like Christmas wreaths.

But now she was disrooted. The pain of it was growing and was as bad as the fear. She did not believe that a family with European faces could elude the hunters and cross the mainland and the Formosa Strait to the safety of Taiwan. She had prayed during the two days of their flight because prayer was a habit of life. At first she had prayed for their deliverance but then, as the truck moved through the mountains and was dwarfed by their immensity, the sense of isolation grew. It was as if her prayers had died like echoes in the rock walls. Finally she decided she would not pray for the impossible, merely for an act of mercy when they were caught. Please save the children. They have done nothing. Please save them. Yet the prayer threw an immediate shadow. In this land, so disfigured by the sores of poverty, life had no great value; and in the villages the newborn, who would soon squall for food, were sometimes drowned like unwanted kittens.

She felt a hand slide against her palm. She did not look down; but the hand, she knew, was Joel's. With Joel there was still the need for small acts of affection. Below them Lewis was climbing the slope. They watched him cross the road.

"Will we ever go back?" Joel asked.

She shook her head.

"Never?"

The finality of the word, spoken in his clear meek voice, brought a tremor to her lips.

"We can never go back," she said. "We have to face that."

The fingers tightened.

"We're together," she told him. "That's all that matters."

She bent and kissed him. The words were shallow and not even true. Human love needed places, roots, reminders of the cherished past. She released his fingers. Lewis had stopped in the underbrush and was looking up at them. He smiled and waved. She lifted a hand in response. Love you, she said soundlessly across the separating distance. Love you. Love you. Yet the resentment was there, so intense that she could not look at him without it swelling inside her like a sickness. He had put them in peril, his family, his loved ones. She could not forgive him. He was nearer now, leaning into the slope and the weak sunlight defining the rise and fall of his straining chest. He stopped again, wiped his face with the end of the towel, rubbed his legs. She heard him laugh at his own inadequacy. It was a boyish laugh and her lips trembled at the sound of it. Love, reproach, fear of the day ahead—the emotions were tearing at her and she looked away from him to where the road and the river were lost in mist.

"Why are we running?" Joel asked. "What did he do?"

It was the question again. They had asked it repeatedly; in the mission, in the truck, in every hideaway on the route from Hangchow. It was written on their troubled faces. What did he do? She had heard them ask it of each other when, at night, they whispered together in Cantonese, a dialect that sprang from their child's world of private communication. Why is he running? She had never answered with any truth because she did not now understand them. They were ten years old and therefore children. Yet they were changing rapidly. They were like portraits seen throughout the day in different lights. She stood apart and watched them scamper back and forth from innocence to awareness and she, an accomplished teacher in the mission school, could not find the necessary words. She could not convey to them the pain of a man in conflict with himself. She could not explain that their father, like his kin before him, had given everything a missionary could give, but that he also gave friendship and admiration to the great Marshal Chiang Kai-shek, generalissimo of all the nation's forces, and that because of this his name was added to the list of those who would be punished when the day of liberation came; that when it came and the red flags were raised in Peking and the Communists were in the seats of power and Chiang and his armies had fled to Taiwan they expelled or killed or imprisoned the white missionaries and he, Lewis Mackenna, spent a year in a place called Fusan and that when they released him he was nearly dead and most of the priests had gone and the churches were burned or locked up or emptied of their congregations; that he was stubborn and would not leave and they let him stay because, now, they were contemptuous of the Christian message and did not see it as a threat. She could not show them, these children, the turmoil in his soul, his hatred of the Red Guards who had put their boots into the loving face of Jesus, his rage when the new Chinese government stopped the flow of mission funds so that they sat unreachable in the bank in Hong Kong; could not expect them to understand that he began to see the Reds as the forces of the antichrist and that when Chiang and his army of two million exiles in Taiwan devised their careful plans to invade the mainland and restore the Nationalist regime he had become dangerously and deeply involved. Above all she could not explain to them that the hatred, the rage and the politics had estranged him from his god; that the taking of payment from Chiang's agents for his furtive acts of espionage had made his life a fraud.

"Where is Gerard?" she asked.

"Getting breakfast."

"Then go and help him."

When he had gone back to the truck she moved out from the shadow of the trees and waited for Lewis and held out her hand when he reached her. He stood there quivering from the effort of the climb and she took the towel from his shoulder and hooked it on the branches so that the sun would dry it. She saw his nostrils crinkle at the smell of frying pork.

"Smells good," he said.

"Yes," she said. Then, anxiously: "I hope it isn't dog."

"What did the can say?"

"Nothing. But there was a picture of a pig."

He laughed.

"Could be dog," he said. "But I've eaten worse."

She saw the humor leave his face. Fusan was in his mind, she knew; stews of lizards, rats and snakes. She bent and picked up the water canteen.

"Let's eat and be off," she said abruptly.

After they had eaten and the truck was stowed with their gear and ready for the road Lewis spread the map in the light that was diffused down through the camphor grove. It was a good map and it showed in sufficient detail the provinces of east and southeast China, the offshore group of islands that lay close to Amoy in the province of Fukien, the Strait and Taiwan itself.

He ran his index finger back to where the journey had begun. There was a moment in which his throat thickened with the sense of loss. The lines of bicycles were already moving through the early mists of the Hangchow streets; and Dr. Li, perhaps, was sitting in the little ward of the mission hospital with the night report in his spotted hand. Outside in the courtyards Lin Mei, the cook, would be pouring water into the tree tubs and onto the roots of vines. But morning prayers? They had lost their priest. They had been abandoned and everywhere would be the feel of betrayal. He saw quite clearly in that moment the sun slanting through the windows of the empty church and making the altar cloth yellow where it touched: he heard its awful silence.

Shadow fell across the map.

"Time to go," Ellen said.

He hesitated. Then he rose from the grass and folded the map. Their eyes met. They did not move. The grove enclosed them and there was bird-song in its leaves. It had been their refuge and outside was the bright and perilous day. They were reluctant to leave.

"Come," she said.

They climbed into the truck and he started the engine and reversed out of the grove. Then, making a turn, he took the truck down across the grain of the slope to where it would meet the road.

Chapter 2

When John Chen returned from the International Chess Congress in Peking he went immediately to his apartment. It was on the second floor of a block on the eastern bank of West Lake. He had been absent for four days and there was an accumulation of letters in his box. One of the envelopes bore the distinctive purple stripe of the Ministry of Public Security, but when he opened it he found it contained nothing more than a note of congratulation from the secretary to the minister. This was the first time he had ever received such a note and, he thought, a victory at chess was evidently more praiseworthy than professional success.

This was early morning and when he had bathed and changed he made tea and took the tray out on to the tiny balcony. The block was built on the fringe of Hangchow's central region. It was a drab and graceless region and if he looked to the right his eye would be offended by the flank of a silk embroidery factory and beyond it a mass of workers' houses and industrial chimneys. But ahead and to his left were the waters of the lake, as blue as old porcelain in the summer, and the four small islands that sat in it and above them the rise of Jewel Mountain. Sometimes when rain was near and everything was sharp he could see the tea plantations on the hills and between the hills the distant flats of the Yangtze delta and the strips of feverish green that was the rice. It was a fine view and he always took solace from it and one day, he had resolved, he would fix a trellis on the right of the balcony so that he would not have to look at the factories and the chimneys. He lived alone, because that was his natural condition. By choice he made no friends, believing that friendship was a weakness. He was very fastidious, bathed twice daily and, because the specter of sexual disease haunted the memory of his parents, abstained from the company of women. The telephone (one of the perquisites of high-ranking public servants) began to ring and he hissed with impatience, put down his teacup and went to the receiver.

The call was from his assistant at the Ministry. There had been a message from Dr. Li of the Presbyterian Mission. A matter of urgency required immediate action. It was a written message and there were no details.

"Collect me," Chen said.

The mission lay twelve kilometers from the apartment block and when the car turned from Ningpo Avenue into the front courtyard Dr. Li was waiting on the stone steps that led up into the main building. He was very old and frail; but his mind, now, was apt to stray and it was for this reason that he had taken from its hook Lewis Mackenna's white surgical coat. The hem hung to his ankles and the sleeves touched his fingernails. Chen got out of the car and stared at him. Li had been his informant during the years that Mackenna had been under surveillance. He walked around the fountain. He sensed at once what Li was about to tell him.

"They have gone," Li said.

Chen went up the steps and into the hall. It was very large and it had been used as a counting house when the merchant owned the building. There were gilt-framed portraits on the walls, a high vaulted roof with a pagoda structure. He could hear behind him the tap of Li's tiny feet, rapid and sometimes scuffing like those of a man not quite in balance. He stopped by one of the portraits, a full-length with an ornate frame and a scroll on the base on which was an inscription, and when Dr. Li came lurching toward him he reached out and held him steady.

"When?" Chen asked.

"Yesterday morning."

Chen frowned.

They had left in the truck, Li explained, all four of them. But there was nothing remarkable in this. Often, after morning prayers and the first medical round in the hospital, Dr. Mackenna would put the family into the truck and drive it to the market for provisions or to the depot for the mission fuel allocation. And after that he might visit a patient or a friend and, if time allowed, go up to the gardens on Lonely Hill Island where on occasions the family liked to share a luncheon basket. The piping voice became defensive. Nothing remarkable, Li repeated. It was only at nightfall, when they had not returned, that he felt concern. And it was not until midnight, when Sister Ferguson awoke him to report their continued absence, that he became alarmed. Even then (he shrugged his bony shoulders and the surgical coat slid up and down on his ankles) there was no reason for suspicion. There could have been an accident or a breakdown. So—

"So you went back to sleep."

Li flushed and nodded. In the morning, he said, he had gone with Sister Ferguson to the Mackennas' private quarters. It was obvious that the birds had flown. Most of their clothes and possessions were still there. But certain things were missing; above all the collection.

"Ah," Chen said grimly. "The collection."

A door opened somewhere in the building. Children's voices rose, stumbling on an English verb. "We ran, you ran, they ran—" The door closed.

"But where to?" Chen said softly, as if in answer.

Li shrugged again.

"Time has been wasted."

Li looked down in shame. He could not see his hands and he raised his arms and stared in surprise at the extraordinary length of the sleeves of the coat.

"You should retire," Chen said.

"Yes."

Footsteps sounded in one of the corridors. A woman in a nurse's uniform crossed the hall to them. She was elderly and heavy and the starched apron crackled as she walked. Chen caught her scent of disinfectant.

"Sister Ferguson," Li murmured.

Chen saw the hostility in her face.

"Do you know who I am?" he said in English.

"I can guess."

Chen waited.

"You are a policeman."

He heard her contempt.

"A kind of policeman," he said.

The big chest swelled with aggressiveness. The white apron made a snapping noise. She was like an angry swan, he thought.

"Do you know where the Mackennas have gone?" he asked her.

"No. But if I knew I wouldn't tell you."

"Did you see them leave?"

She did not answer.

"What was in the truck?"

Her lips tightened.

"I could close this mission," Chen said.

"You'll do that anyway."

"Yes," Dr. Li said miserably. "It is finished."

He began to roll back the sleeves of the coat. Sister Ferguson watched him.

"What are you doing in the doctor's coat?" she asked him harshly.

"A mistake."

"Take it off at once."

Li obeyed. She took the coat from him and draped it over her arm. Her face softened and she began to stroke its material as if it was as pleasing to the touch as satin.

"He was a lovely man," she said. "He gave so much. But then all the Mackennas did that." She gestured at the portrait. "They gave their lives, their wives, their children. They are buried in Chinese earth. Do you understand that kind of sacrifice?"

"No," Chen said. Then, with sarcasm: "But of course I am a heathen."

He turned to the portrait. Rev. Jardine Mackenna, FRCS, 1824–1875, the inscription said. Above it, painted in oils on a smooth wooden panel, was the life-size profile of a standing man. He stood very tall and proud against a background of a distant walled city, hills and temples. It was a European face, but the head was shaven and a black pigtail hung to the shoulders. He wore pantaloons that were tucked into white calico stockings, silk shoes with turned-up toes, a black silk gown with full sleeves and patterns of red and blue brocade. Standing there with a pink paper sun-umbrella in his hand he was as imperious as a mandarin.

"He refused to wear Western dress," Sister Ferguson said close behind him. Even her breath smelled of disinfectant. "He said it would make him look like a foreigner." She touched the painting. "So he wore the robes of a teacher. They brought him nearer to the people. He healed them and he taught them." Her voice thinned again with contempt. "How could you understand a man like that? You, a Communist. What do you care for the human soul?"

Chen turned to face her. Immeasurable distance lay between them.

"Go home," he said. "You have no place here."

She shook her head.

"Come," Chen said to Dr. Li. "Take me to Mackenna's quarters."

He followed Li down a corridor. At the end of it he looked back. Sister Ferguson was watching them. He saw her press Lewis Mackenna's coat against her cheek, as if it was something alive in need of comfort. Then the moment passed and she lowered the coat and the white breast puffed and crackled with a sudden anger.

"I hope he gets away," she shouted.

John Chen followed Li's tottering shape past the classrooms, the ward and its dispensary. He had never before entered the mission from the front, and on those occasions when he had visited the Mackennas he had preferred to walk down Dragon Well Lane and through the wooden gateway that led to the gardens and the house. Li led him past the kitchen and out to a walled courtyard, then down a short path. Many old trees shaded the gardens and the branches of one of them, a pear, had already reached out to scratch the house.

It was a small building, at one time no more than a summerhouse retreat for the merchant. Quince and morning glory covered its stone front and curving eaves. Adjoining it and of the same age-eroded stone was the church. Dr. Li walked around the stump of a felled banyan, unlocked the door to the house and stood aside.

Chen entered.

There was no hallway and the living room and kitchen occupied the whole of the ground floor area. A staircase with panels of fretwork Buddhas led to the bedrooms.

"Have you been here before?" Li asked.

"Yes."

Chen stared around the room. It was as he remembered it; a red and turquoise carpet on stone flags, bamboo furniture and bamboo-framed pictures, two bookcases and two display cabinets with latticed doors. The bookcases were full, the cabinets empty. A vase of buddleia stood on the dining table and sunlight from the window touched its yellow and lilac flowers. He crossed the floor to a lacquer side table. Beside it was a wastebasket and, bending, he saw that it was filled with straw. He went to one of the cabinets and opened the doors. Once, he recalled, many rare pieces of porcelain, jade and ivory had been exhibited. He ran a finger along one of the shelves. Now not even the faintest outline of dust remained. He closed the doors and turned. Dr. Li was standing by the table, his lizard-skin face puckered in distress.

"What is the matter?"

"I am ashamed," Li said.

"Of what?"

"Of spying on him."

"No need for shame. It was your duty."

"He was a good man."

"He was an enemy of your country."

Li shook his head.

"An enemy," Chen insisted.

"No," Li said. "He loved this country. He loved its people. If he was an enemy—"

Chen saw the caution touch his eyes.

"Say it," he told him.

"If he was an enemy," Li said, "it was of men like you."

"Men like me defend the State."

Chen went to the table. There were four indentations in the carpet near to the legs and a minute scrap of straw buried in the woollen pile. He bent and plucked it out. Obviously the table had been moved back from the center, then restored to its place after the collection had been wrapped in straw and boxed for transport. He walked slowly around the room. It was very clean and free of dust. Every cushion had been smoothed of its creases. Even the carpet fringes had been combed out so that they lay in perfect alignment on the flags. Ellen Mackenna, that houseproud woman, had made the final celebration of her home with broom and duster and lavender polish—and had left it forever. Chen returned to the table. But she had missed the little particle of straw, he thought. He dropped it into the vase. Dr. Li watched him. He looked very tired and the effort of speech had left a white rim around his lips.

"Sit down," Chen said.

He pulled out one of the dining chairs and Li sat.

"Are you a Christian?" Chen asked.

"Of course."

"And a Judas?"

"Yes."

Chen bent to him.

"I told you," he said. "It was your duty. There is nothing more important than duty."

He walked through into the kitchen, found a tumbler and half-filled it with water. He looked around him. This place too had been meticulously cleaned. Pots and saucepans shone, the floor tiles glowed. A garbage bin, newly washed, stood upside down in the sink. There was a wooden table in the center, so vigorously scrubbed over the years that it was bleached gray. Lotus leaves had been spread on its surface and on them were melons and other fruits, sweet potatoes and green vegetables, mounds of soybeans and unhusked rice; perishables, Chen thought, that she, with her dislike of waste, had placed there so that others might find and eat them before they rotted.

He returned to the living room and handed Dr. Li the water. He watched him sip.

"You spoke of missing things," Chen said.

Li pointed to the side table.

"Over there," he said, "were two framed photographs, one of the children as babies and the other of Ellen Mackenna." The finger moved. "And there on the wall were two pairs of embroidered children's slippers. The first tiny ones, you understand?"

He sipped again.

"What else?" Chen asked.

Li pointed to one of the bookcases.

"Underneath in the cupboard there was always a metal box. He kept his personal documents in it. That too has gone."

Chen went to the bookcase and opened the cupboard. There were bundles of correspondence, mission account books, a clip of receipted bills, children's picture books and boxes of watercolor paints, files containing publications from the China Inland Mission and the Edinburgh Presbyterian Overseas Fellowship, an address book.

"Also things from the church," Li said.

Chen stood and turned.

"What things?"

"Things a priest would value. His vestments. Some altar silver."

"Such as?"

"A crucifix, which was very fine. Ornamental vessels. Candlesticks."

"And what will he do with all this silver?"

"Do?"

"Yes. What will he do with it?"

Li drank more water.

"Wherever he goes," he said, "he will build his church."

Chen smiled.

"He will sell the silver," he said.

"No."

"He will sell it. And the collection too."

Li shook his head.

Chen went to the kitchen. Why do the old become so innocent? he asked himself; as if a mountain of experience had suddenly dissolved.

"Would you like some melon?" he called out.

"No."

Chen cut a slice of melon, put it on a plate and returned to the living room.

"Tell me," he said, eating, "how did he acquire the collection?"

"In the beginning—gifts."

"From grateful patients?"

"Yes."

"And then?"

Li smiled.

"It grew," he said. "A piece here, a piece there. He had become a collector. And that, as you know, is an incurable disease."

"He bought these pieces?"

"Yes."

"Is that what he told you?"

"Yes."

"Was Lewis Mackenna rich?"

"Of course not. Missionaries are poor."

"Yet he was able to purchase works of art?"

"I would not call them works of art."

"I assure you they were."

Chen saw the desperation in his eyes.

"Perhaps they were bargains," Li said.

Chen finished the melon and stood.

"There are no bargains in Chinese markets," he said. "Isn't that what they say?"

He took the plate and its mess of rind and pips out to the kitchen. He had no wish to soil Ellen Mackenna's immaculate garbage bin and he opened the rear door and walked out into the vegetable garden that adjoined it. A much larger bin was standing there but when he looked inside he saw that this too had been scoured clean. He shrugged, scraped the plate with his finger over one of the beds, then went back into the kitchen and rinsed the plate. When he returned to the living room Dr. Li was still sipping water.

Chen sat.

"Tell me," he said, "where is the world's finest collection of Chinese art?"

"In Peking?"

"No. It is not in mainland China at all. It is in Taiwan. Does that surprise you?"

"It does."

"It was removed from Peking by Chiang Kai-shek at the time of the Japanese war. Later, at the time of the liberation when his own defeat was certain, he shipped the best of it to Taiwan. Also his men had systematically looted the country. They were as greedy as rats in sugar cane and there was hardly a museum or palace or temple that was not stripped of its treasures. Imagine it. A nation's heritage stolen."

Chen sat back in his chair. He had learned at the chessboard the dangers of emotion, how it could cloud the intellect. There could be no dejection in defeat, no joy in victory. There was only the mind, cells of infinite capacity. Yet, listening to his own words, he was aware of anger, growing somewhere like a filament of heat; anger against Chiang for the enormity of the theft, anger against Lewis Mackenna for his years of treachery.

"Chiang is planning to invade," he said. "He might succeed. He has the soldiers, the arms, the gold reserves that he stole with the treasures. And he has a network of agents. Mackenna is one of them."

Chen rose and pointed at the empty cabinets.

"As you said, a piece here and a piece there. But they came from Chiang. They were his way of making payment."

Dr. Li looked down and put both hands around the tumbler. Brown spots made a pattern on their backs, as if hospital iodine had splashed across them.

"So who is the Judas?" Chen asked softly.

Li was silent.

"Do you have the church key?"

Li gave it to him.

Chen left the house and walked toward the church. He stopped under the pear tree. He had once played a game of chess with Lewis Mackenna in the shade of the tree. It had been a somnolent afternoon with warmth coming out of the stone of the house and the missionary had smiled up into the branches and murmured some lines from an ancient poem. *Three cups of wine beneath the pear tree, a mat in the shade of willows*— But they had drunk tea, not wine, and there had been no tranquility because Mackenna was under suspicion and the game was really cat and mouse. He had looked into those gray and pleasant eyes and said: "A man must love a country to learn its verse." But Mackenna had merely smiled in answer and there was nothing in the eyes except truth. Yet truth, Chen knew, had long been abandoned. When the game was finished he had said: "I have a phrase in my mind, Lewis."

"A phrase?"

"Yes. The Clandestine Services. Tell me what that means."

"I have no idea."

"I think you do. It is a phrase used by U.S. Intelligence and it refers to covert operations."

"Really?"

"Yes, really. Then there are the initial letters CAT."

"CAT?"

"Yes."

"What kind of cat is that?"

"A cat that flies. Its lair is in Taiwan and it is a favorite of Chiang Kai-shek. CAT. Which means, as well you know, Civil Air Transport. It trades as a commercial airline but is in fact a CIA proprietary corporation. You can buy a scheduled flight but its real business is clandestine air operations. But, as I say, you know all this."

"No."

"Yes. CAT has many secret functions. Overflights of mainland China. Supply drops to guerrillas. It is paramilitary and even now is at work on the logistics of invasion. It uses men like you."

Lewis smiled and shook his head.

"Shall we play another game?" he said.

There had been many such visits, always the verbal fencing, the lies and denials, the glow of sincerity in those honest eyes; every answer as false as the Christian message.

Chen left the shadow of the pear. The church was older than the mission building. A stone tortoise with a stone snake coiled on its carapace sat by the entrance; it was of the kind that was sometimes seen in front of the old Taoist temples. He entered. The church was really a miniature, with a short aisle, five bamboo pews on either side, a stone font that was as small and shallow as a bird bath. Chen walked down the aisle. Even the painted Christ behind the altar was smaller than life-size; much less impressive, he decided, than the painting of Jardine Mackenna in the mission hall. Perhaps they should exchange them?

He sat down on the front pew. He was no stranger to Christian churches. He had been educated for a time in Shanghai at the Society of Jesus School for Boys, entering there in September of 1931, a few months before his twelfth birthday. At first only the Jesuit Fathers knew that he was the son of the warlord General Chen Kuochang. The general was the cruelest of all the warlords. Syphilis was gnawing at his brain and perhaps because of this he had followed a merciless trail as far west as Sinkiang. He, John Chen, had ridden with him during one of his childhood years, watching from the back of a pony the dreadful scars of atrocity that were left behind them on the burning land. But the general was also a baptized Christian, seeing nothing incongruous in the campfire prayers and the lopping of heads. He it was who, in a moment of reverence when the redness left his brain, had given him the saintly name of John. He became John Chen Yuchang; Johnny Chen at the school or, to some of the European boys, Johnny Chink; and then later, when his work had made him too cold and powerful for the warmth of a name like Johnny, a plain John Chen. He had not been received into the Catholic Church; and the Jesuits, uneasy in the shadow of the general and in the knowledge that he, as a child, had seen things that a child should never see, had not pressed him. "God will claim you if he wants you," Father Renaud had told him.

It was very quiet in the church and he could not hear the sounds of the boulevards or of the mission, only the faint whirr of flies in the rafters. He looked around him. Much of it had been built and decorated by the converts. The base of the font had been chiseled into the feet of dragons. There was a carved altar screen depicting a saint in Manchu robes with horseshoe cuffs. A camphorwood chest stood by the vestry door, its panels painted with chrysanthemums and poppies. Even the yellow altar cloth, struck by a shaft of sun, threw a sheen of lemon on the flesh of the Christ. The Mackennas had gone and this was a Chinese place again. It was as if the old gods had returned; like evicted tenants, he thought, creeping back into an empty house.

He stood, went to the chest and lifted the lid. It contained Bibles and prayer books, sheaves of printed hymns, some bamboo offertory plates. How much commission had he taken? Chen wondered. He closed the lid and opened the vestry door. There was a table with nothing on it except a pot of azaleas, two chairs, four clothes hooks on the wall. A straw hat, a walking stick and a surplice hung on the hooks, and when he lifted it he saw that it was old and stained with a mended tear in the linen.

He walked back to the aisle. The pulpit, like everything else in the church, was small, with only two steps. Not much of a stage, he thought, for a priest to thunder from. He climbed up, looked out across its ledge. Not all of the Mackennas had been based in Hangchow, but most of them, self-appointed messengers from Heaven, must have stood here. A Bible with a worn leather binding rested on the ledge. He put his hand on it and said loudly to the upturned faces of the ghosts in the pews: "Thou shalt have no other God but the State. Communism is your faith. It deals with the living of this life, not with a life beyond death." The heresy rang above him in the rafters. He shook his head, resentful of the Western blood that had produced those mocking words. His mother had been part French, a singsong girl and then the housemother in a Shanghai brothel that lay among the wharves of Soochow Creek. At night its name, the Yuk Yin Bathhouse, burned in red neon and could even be seen from the big ships that were anchored in the Whangpoo. She was known as Lisette (although that was not her name) and she had been a favorite of General Chen. Sometimes he could feel her blood surge like a sudden tide within him.

He ran his fingers down the Bible's bruised skin. It seemed very old and when he opened it the gum cracked along its spine. It had been made for the use of preachers and the pages and the type were large. The flyleaves were inscribed by different hands and in different inks and, examining them, he saw that they provided a family record. The entries began with the birth of Jardine Mackenna in 1824 and ended with the arrival of Gerard and Joel 120 years later. They were not the first set of twins to spring from Mackenna loins. Jardine and his wife, Mary, had produced four children— two girls and twin boys James and Sholto. Both the girls had died as children and the boys, after ordination, had returned to China to spread the Gospel; James in Hangchow and Sholto in the town of Tihwa, Sinkiang. Both had been fruitful and James and his wife Margaret had included in their brood the twins Cromer and Stewart. There were sad little notes against some of the names. Died of smallpox. Died of cholera. Died of typhoid. Cromer (Lewis' father) had enjoyed a fine heroic death. Died on the Cross like our Lord, someone had written. Chen let his finger rest on the name Lewis Robert Mackenna. What will they write against it? he wondered. Executed for espionage? Died in prison?

He turned the pages and the spine cracked again with its sound of tiny breaking bones. A sheet of folded paper appeared, and when he spread it he saw that there were four blocks of script; a passage from Saint Matthew in Manchurian, in Mongolian, in Tibetan and in standard Chinese. The script was printed but there was a handwritten sentence along the top of the sheet. "I think this is what you want," the English words said. Underneath were the initials ATC.

Chen closed the Bible and went down from the pulpit to the aisle. He stood there looking up at the ledge, at the faded gold leaf of the Bible's pages that had become bright in the sun shaft. Why had Mackenna left behind him so precious a family memento? Had he forgotten it? He shook his head. Mackenna had come to the church for the silver and the vestments and whatever else had been of value to him. He must have seen the Bible resting there. Value? Wasn't that an explanation? Perhaps, with his God so irretrievably distant, it had come to have no value, not even a sentimental one. Chen sat down again in the pew. That abandoned book—what clearer evidence of defect could there be?

He folded his hands in his lap. He had come here to think, to feel the essence of the man he was about to hunt. This was Mackenna's place. Here he had wielded power. Up there in the pulpit he had spoken quiet words—no need to declaim in so small a church. There by the altar, his white surplice flowing around the blue cotton coolie trousers that he always wore, he would have joined two people in the sacrament of marriage. And over there he had leaned across the font and splashed water from the kitchen over some uncomprehending Chinese face. Why do people like the Mackennas spend their lives in foreign lands? Chen asked himself. Isn't there enough despair and sickness in their own countries?

He closed his eyes, unfolding within his mind the map of east and southeast China. He saw its details with an immediate act of recall; its provinces and railways and major roads, the green of the littoral and behind it the ochers and umbers of the mountain ranges, the course of the rivers, the Formosa Strait and the offshore group of islands that lay close to Amoy in the province of Fukien, and across the Strait the big island of Taiwan where Chiang and his nest of vipers were waiting to strike. The mainland regions were immense, and a fugitive with no other thought than survival might lie up for a lifetime. But Lewis Mackenna was not alone. He was burdened with a family. He would choose a destination and run for it like the flight of an arrow. Yet would he? He was a subtle and intelligent man. He might take his time, weave a complicated trail, do the unexpected or even what was absurdly obvious. There would be friends to harbor him, and always the long lines of intelligence down which Chiang's agents would pass him to safety. He had a twenty-four-hour advantage; time enough, Chen thought, to have already left the country. But that would depend on arrangements, on preparation. He did not think Mackenna had enjoyed sufficient time to plan. A man with time would disperse his loved ones; reasonable acts—the boys to a school in Britain, the wife on a visit to a relative in Hong Kong. And if the shadow of danger was really reaching near he would even go with them. He had been warned, Chen concluded, and he had gone, perhaps with only a few days' notice.

He heard voices outside, something heavy trundling on the path. The door opened and the end of an upright piano appeared. A girl with a flat Mongol face and a teacher's sash guided the piano into the church. Four children of kindergarten size pushed it down the aisle. Chen watched it pass, entrails twanging, to its place by the wall. The children ran out into the sun and the girl bent over the piano and, standing, played a few bars from "Jesus Wants Me for a Sunbeam."

Then she turned.

"Do you want me to go?" Chen asked.

She shook her head.

"It's for tomorrow," she said. "Sunday service."

Chen stared at it. The name of an English maker from somewhere called Bermondsey was inlaid across the lid. It was old, warped by time. How many return journeys had it made down the years, he wondered, from the schoolrooms to the church?

"Will you play it tomorrow?" he asked.

"Perhaps."

"Who usually plays?"

"Madame Mackenna."

"Won't she be here?"

She shrugged. He saw the sorrow in her eyes.

"Who will take the service?"

"I don't know."

"Where have the Mackennas gone?"

"I don't know."

"Where do you think they have gone?"

She looked away from him, fidgeting with unease, around the church, up to the roof. A belfry had been built in one corner and, following her eyes, he saw bats flickering high up in the shadows; clinging there, he thought sardonically, like Mackenna's abandoned souls. The ropes had been tied together so that they hung beyond reach.

"Is the bell still there?" he asked.

"Yes. But the State forbids us to ring it."

"Isn't the State right?"

She did not answer.

"What do you expect?" he said severely. "Christian bells in a Red city?"

She closed the piano lid and walked past him.

"God bless them," she said. He could see the moistness in her eyes. "And lead them to safety."

The door closed.

But where is safety? Chen thought. He shut his eyes again and locked his fingers in his lap. Safety was anywhere beyond the grip of China. But Lewis Mackenna was a committed man. He could not help the Generalissimo from a presbytery in a Scottish village. So the destination, direct or ultimate, was Taiwan. But how to reach it? The nearest exit to the open sea was Hangchow Bay, a few kilometers along the road. Or farther north, a distance of 240 kilometers, was the great port of Shanghai where there were numerous oceangoing foreign ships. Or a fugitive might travel south, attempt the journey of one thousand kilometers to Hong Kong. Or the escape route might cross the five hundred kilometers to Foochow or the seven hundred kilometers down to Amoy. Both were busy ports and faced the Taiwan coast. He would also consider the five small islands that were spread across the channel that led into Amoy harbor and were still in the hands of Chiang Kai-shek. Safety lay in any one of them, and Quemoy, the largest Nationalist island, was only six kilometers out to sea. There were many permutations. But there were also, Chen reminded himself, those four white faces, conspicuous to any Oriental eye, a truck on empty highways that was filled with people and possessions.

He rose, left the church and locked the door. When he entered the house he saw that Dr. Li was asleep at the table, his head supported on his palm. He stood above him, looking down. For Li, he thought, death is never very far from sleep. He dropped the church key onto the table from a height and Li jerked and came back into the world and stared up at him with exhumed eyes.

Chen walked slowly around the room. He opened both the bookcase cupboards, began to search their contents. Li watched him from the table.

"Priests and politics," Chen said with disdain. "The old story."

"Why should a priest stand apart from the affairs of men?" Li asked. "He does not live in a fish bowl."

Chen picked up the address book and, standing, began to turn its pages. The initials on the Saint Matthew translations, ATC, were lodged like a barb in his mind. There were many priests in the book, Anglican and Catholic, Baptists and Methodists. Most of them had been crossed through and the word "gone" written against the names. He found a Rev. Dr. Arthur Cannon at an address on the Shanghai road near to Fengsien. He put down the book on the lacquer side table, looked down at the wastebasket.

"Yes," Dr. Li said with sarcasm, "they always search the wastebaskets."

Chen picked up the basket, took it to the dining table and tipped out its contents. Straw, wood shavings and torn and crumpled paper made a pile in front of Li's hands. Some of it spilled over the edge of the table and onto the carpet. He felt a stab of guilt, as if Ellen Mackenna had suddenly entered the room and was staring accusingly at the mess. He began to sift through the pile, smoothing out the balls and screws of paper. There were some crayon drawings, a market shopping list, a sheet with the numbered headings of a sermon, a temperature chart from the hospital. There were also seven jagged scraps of azure notepaper on some of which were written capital letters. Chen bent and searched the debris on the carpet. He found four more of the little azure pieces.

He took them to the side table and began to assemble them. Some of the tears had ripped the surface of the paper and partially obliterated the writing. The letters FR appeared on the extreme left of the sheet. That, he thought, would be an abbreviation for FATHER. Somewhere would be the name of the priest. There were four other scraps with capital letters: ARD, ON, AG and S. He shuffled them until the first three fitted. AGON-ARD. The word was like the sound of pain, he thought; a good name for a martyred priest. The remaining scrap with the single letter S found an isolated place lower down on the sheet.

"Tell me," he said to Dr. Li, "do you know a Father Agonard?"

Li shook his head. Chen thought he saw amusement touch his lips.

"Have you ever heard that name?"

"No."

Chen opened the address book and riffled through its pages. There was no Agonard. He closed the book. Did any of it have significance? The name of a Catholic priest. Had there been a meeting? And if so, when? There was no date on the notepaper. How long had it lain in the basket?

Was the piecemeal tearing of it deliberate? Chen shrugged. He found an envelope in the drawer and held it against the edge of the table so that he might scoop into it the eleven scraps.

"Let me see it," Dr. Li said.

He came to the side table and bent across it.

"Well?" Chen asked.

"It could be Father Agonard," Li murmured. He bent closer. "Or—"

"Or what?"

"It could be something else." He crooked a clawlike finger above the paper. "The gap between the second and third letters may not be intentional." The claw scratched, moving the two jagged scraps so that the gap was closed. "There, you see? It now becomes one word. FRAGONARD."

He began to laugh.

"Your Roman priest," he said, his thin shoulders heaving, "has now become a great French painter."

He went back to the dining table and sat. The humor of it would not leave him. "A Fragonard," he said. He laughed again, put a handkerchief to his eyes and began to wipe them.

Chen walked past him and out of the house. He stood under the pear, waiting for the anger to subside. Dr. Li had watched him through the folds of the handkerchief and, for a moment, it seemed that mockery had flickered in those rheumy eyes. To his left and beyond the church he could see a glade of azaleas and some leaning gravestones that time had decorated with yellow lichen. When he had regained composure he crossed the courtyard and entered the mission. He heard the laughter of children, the tap-tap-tap of a table tennis ball, a woman singing in the kitchen. Soon it would be empty, with only the ticks in the walls to prick the silence, the wings of bats in the dead church.

Sister Ferguson was in the hall. The doorway to the front was open and she stood there watching his approach, her starched body as hard as armor against the light. She did not stand aside and he stopped and looked into her scrubbed face. The hostility was as palpable as her antiseptic smell. He saw again the graves in the garden and recalled her words.

"I'll bring him back," he said. "He'll get his patch of Chinese earth. That I promise you."

He pushed past her and felt her breast buckle against his shoulder. He went down the steps and got into the waiting car.

When John Chen reached his office in the Ministry block he gave his assistant detailed instructions. All east and southeast ports from Shanghai down to the border with Hong Kong would be alerted. All major inland routes would be kept under strict surveillance. All police departments, army bases and commune committees would be warned. He signed a Closing Order to be executed immediately against the Mackenna mission. The assistant left; and later, a girl entered with a tea tray and yesterday's copy of *The New York Times*. When she had gone he poured his tea and took the cup to the big double window that afforded a view of the square. Below him the fleets of bicycles were weaving patterns around the blue-and-white buses and the Party limousines that were always arriving at or leaving the building. The cherries were in flower and in one corner of the square he could see the eating-house and its pots of red fuchsias and a group of workers sitting outside and nibbling at the edges of steamed pancakes. The eleven pieces of paper were fluttering in his mind like petals in a wind. The letter S. Fragonard. A French name, not necessarily but probably that of the famous painter. Perhaps Ellen Mackenna, who liked to paint pretty watercolors and was certain to teach an art class in the mission, had brought the note from the schoolroom and had later discarded it. Perhaps he too should discard it. Yet instinct would not let him do that.

He walked to his desk, poured some tea and returned to the window. It was a favorite place and like all government men of his particular vocation it was natural for him to watch, from a window or a shadow, those from whom he was set apart. A shower of rain was falling and the motion in the square seemed to stop as the cyclists and the walkers draped themselves in the sheets of scarlet, blue and green plastic that were always carried against the rain. Then the motion began again and the square throbbed with moving color. He remained at the steaming window until the tea was drunk. The door opened and he heard Lin Sheng, his assistant, enter and go to the desk.

Lin was the son of his minister, a young man who had come direct from Peking University and would pause here in this place of secrets and clandestine battles until he was ready for the next step in his predictable ascent. He was clever and efficient. He was also vain and could never resist a mirror or a glance at the reflection that marched beside him in the plate glass of the shop windows. Chen turned and watched him arrange some papers on the desk.

"I shall need a list of ship departures," Chen said.

Lin pointed at the papers.

"Already done," he said.

Chen went to the desk. The major ports were there, from the long Yangtze estuary down to where the Min emptied into the sea at Foochow.

"I shall have Amoy and the others within the hour," Lin said.

Chen examined the schedules. There were merchant and passenger ships, internal and coastal ferries. The sailings began at dawn of the previous day and were projected forward into the following week. Lin had added the flag, the port of registration and in some cases a broad description of the manifest.

"I can't put a firm date to the tramps," Lin said. "They come and go."

The schedules were in alphabetical order. Chen ran a finger down the

Foochow sailings, then those from Hangchow. He pushed them aside. What can they reveal? he asked himself. What more can I do than warn the port authorities? The list for Shanghai was truly formidable. There were many docks and the sea traffic, it seemed, was as heavy as in the days of the old International Settlement. He peered for a moment into his store of memories. The Yuk Yin Bathhouse and all the other singsong houses and the delights they offered were gone by revolutionary decree. Shanghai was purified—or so they said. He slid the sheet away from him, then pulled it back. A name had isolated itself. The *Fragonard,* French, out of Marseille with a cargo of machine parts and sundry manufactures and bound for Taiwan, had cleared Shanghai at eighteen-thirty hours. Yesterday.

John Chen was on the road to Shanghai (obviously the port denoted by the letter S on the scrap of paper) within twenty minutes. He sat in the rear of the car and watched its triangular flag lift in the wind. The little spring of anger was rising again. Father Agonard, that stillborn priest, had become a painter and was now a ship. The Mackennas were aboard her and she was already in waters outside Chinese jurisdiction. At some time today she would berth in Taipei. That should be the end of it. Yet some part of his mind could not accept so abrupt an ending. He did not want to believe in their escape. Certainly there were questions; in Shanghai, in Fengsien at the address of the Reverend Arthur T. Cannon. He began to tap on his knee with frustration. The taste of defeat was bitter. And there would be blame. "You were playing chess in Peking," the minister would say, "while he was sailing off to freedom. He was important, perhaps with knowledge of Chiang's invasion. Why was he not under continuous surveillance?" The voice rang to the rhythm of his tapping finger. "Why? Why? Why?" The red flag made an arc and the car turned from the auto-route toward Fengsien.

Dr. Cannon's address lay beyond Fengsien and near to the coast, a white-painted bungalow in the shadow of the Suei Chang Silk Factory. Flower-beds edged the path and a woman was on her knees with a trowel and a box of plants. She rose painfully when Chen approached, holding her hip like an arthritic. He guessed her identity and showed her his warrant card and said: "Mrs. Cannon?"

He saw alarm in her pale eyes.

"Dr. Cannon," he said. "Where is he?"

She pointed to the factory.

"Inside there?"

"Yes."

The factory was as big as a barn; with benches, a dozen men and women moving around them, walls that were lined with shelves on which were circular flat baskets. There was a sour, vegetable scent. A man with a sun-blotched face and wisps of ginger hair was bent across one of the baskets and Chen saw him take out a handful of mulberry leaves and examine it.

Chen showed his warrant and Dr. Cannon glanced at it and smiled.

"Do you need a doctor?" he asked.

"No."

He proffered the leaves and their quilt of wriggling worms.

"Perhaps some silk?"

Chen heard the mockery in his voice.

"Just information," he said.

"A moment," Dr. Cannon said. He returned the leaves to the basket and brushed off some silkworms from his hand and wrist. Then he slid the basket onto its shelf. There were four long shelves, each with ten baskets and their fillings of leaves and feeding worms.

Chen stared down at the immaculate floor.

"Don't they wriggle off?" he asked.

Dr. Cannon smiled.

"Everyone asks that," he said. "The answer is no. They are like the workers in your beautiful country. Give them enough food and they will be content and stay where they are." He looked into Chen's face. "Does the smell make you sick?"

"A little."

"Let's go outside."

Dr. Cannon led him toward the rear door.

"This used to be the mission," he said. "Once we bred Christians. Now we breed worms."

They went outside. A path followed the flank of the factory to the bungalow. To the right was a building with a reed roof and colored eaves. Through its windows Chen could see seated girls, their fingers fluttering in baskets of silvery shells.

"Cocoons," Dr. Cannon explained. "We have to sort them by weight. Most go off to the silk mill. The rest are retained so they'll hatch into moths and start the cycle all over again." He nodded at the building and warmth glowed for a moment in his sardonic eyes. "At one time it was our little chapel."

They walked down the path.

"After the revolution," Dr. Cannon said, "we were re-educated. We saw the true light. They allowed us to stay. In return we run the silk farm for the State and provide some medical services."

Mrs. Cannon was on her knees again by the flowerbed, pressing plants into the soil. She did not rise and they stood above her and Dr. Cannon put his hand on her thinning gray hair, through which the scalp shone, and said gently: "You shouldn't be doing that." He watched her trowel spacing another row of holes. Then he looked up.

"Well?" he said to Chen. "What can I do for you?"

"When did you last see Lewis Mackenna?"

The trowel stopped.

"Yesterday," Dr. Cannon said.

"At what time?"

"Twelve noon." He looked down again. "Isn't that right, dear?"

"Yes. About twelve."

"And why did he call?"

"No special reason."

"A social call?"

"Yes." Dr. Cannon smiled. "Why not? We were good friends."

Mrs. Cannon dug another hole.

"Where was he going?" Chen asked.

"He didn't say." Dr. Cannon pointed to the sea and the curving bay. "I assume he was going to the big city."

"To Shanghai?"

"Yes."

"Why would he go there?"

"Most people go there, don't they?" Dr. Cannon said. His hand had gone again to Mrs. Cannon's head, stroking it like a man fondling a favorite dog. "A family trip. A bit of shopping. A walk down the Bund."

"And see the ships?"

Mrs. Cannon put down the trowel. Now she was unmoving. Chen could see the tension in her body. She was bent forward over the plants, her furrowed neck exposed; like those he had seen in his father's time, he thought, awaiting a swordstroke.

"Yes, they'd see the ships." Dr. Cannon smiled. "All boys love ships."

Chen heard the strain in his voice. A pigtailed girl came out of the factory, stared at them and went back in. Dr. Cannon put a hand under Mrs. Cannon's armpit. "Let me help you," he said. He pulled her upright, out of her attitude of fear, and Chen heard her hipbone crack. Seabirds were coming in from the bay and she turned her head and listened to their cries.

"Why are you afraid?" Chen asked her.

She did not answer.

"Do you know the penalty for plotting against the State?"

"No," she whispered.

"I assure you there are no sea views."

"What the hell are you talking about?" Dr. Cannon said. His face had paled with anger and the sun-blotches were marked on his cheeks like the red paint of a clown. "Plot against the State?" He slid an arm around her waist. "Why should we plot against the State? We're old. On our last legs. Can't you see that?" He waved a hand at the bay. "This is our home. We're happy here. We hope to die here." He shook his head. "I don't know what Mackenna's done. I give you my Christian word on that." He nodded reflectively. "Yes, it's likely he's on a ship. I think that's very likely."

"Why do you think that?"

"It was nothing he said. But when he left he embraced me. He'd never done that before. I guessed he was going."

Dr. Cannon bent and picked up the trowel.

"A nice family," he said.

"Yes," Mrs. Cannon said tiredly. "Very nice."

Chen turned from them and walked down the path. He looked back from the gate and Dr. Cannon was on his knees bedding the remainder of the plants and Mrs. Cannon continued to watch the seabirds wheeling in the sky.

When he reached the car he opened the door, hesitated, then closed it.

"Wait," he told the driver.

He went down the track that led to the sea and crossed the dunes to the beach. Flotsam from the Shanghai shipping lanes made a fringe on the sand and a man with a basket was scavenging for wood. He began to walk. Out in the mists he could see the distant masts of a wreck and the buoy that was tethered near to it. The intermittent peal of its bell came faintly; like the warning note, he thought, that is sounding so clearly in my mind. He kicked out at a can, then at a melon rind. The mind too was full of flotsam; the accumulations of a lifetime that have no value but refuse to be expelled. Yet amongst it was an object, something he had seen, something of importance, submerged below the surface like the shapes in the tide. He kicked at a tangle of sodden straw.

Straw.

He stopped and picked it up. It was a straw jacket of the kind that sometimes clothes the glass hips of certain wine bottles. He stared at it. The hidden object—a wastebasket with its mouth choked with straw— came to the surface. It sat by the side table in the Mackennas' living room, and in that spotless place it was utterly false. He began to walk. It was easy now to recreate the final farewell scene. Lewis would have understood Ellen Mackenna's need for a few moments of aloneness in that room which had been the center of her life and he would have taken the boys to the waiting truck. Chen saw her clearly; unmoving on the threshold while she imprinted on her memory every detail of her deserted home, this place that, out of love and respect, she had made immaculate. Never, never, he thought, could she have left that overflowing basket.

So the torn note was a plant. That had always been a possibility and he had reserved judgment. But the eleven scraps of paper had been difficult to assemble, so difficult that he had misinterpreted the letters and the absurd Father Agonard had made his brief appearance. And if it had not been for Dr. Li's intervention the anguished priest would never have become a cargo ship. "Let me see it," Li had said, and he had walked to the table and, shifting the two scraps, had effectively pointed him up the road to Shanghai. Was Dr. Li an accomplice? It would seem like it. Sister Ferguson, concerned at the Mackennas' absence, had awakened him at midnight. Yet he had done nothing until morning, a loss to the security services of eight or ten hours. Dr. Li, Chen decided, had earned interrogation.

He dropped the straw jacket into the wind that was coming off the sea. The abandoned Bible now took on a new significance. Old Mackenna ghosts might caper on the flyleaves and, now, mean nothing to a man like Lewis. But the final entry recorded the births of his own dear sons. Even a man of failing faith would prize such a book. He had left it on the pulpit, its gold leaf drawing the eye, so that he, John Chen, would find it, open it, discover the translations and the initials at the head. It was no more than a sacrificial piece in the game they were playing; an early move that led to the address book, to Dr. Cannon and his silk farm. And there, at Fengsien, lay the confirmation that the Mackennas had, indeed, passed that way on the road to the port.

He turned, began the walk back to the car. Was Dr. Cannon involved? he wondered, in the false trail that led to Shanghai? even in Chiang's conspiracy? He had shaken his gingery head in denial. "I give you my Christian word on that," he had said. Yet the Christian word of a missionary who had exchanged his church for a factory was hardly reliable. The Cannons, too, deserved interrogation. Chen felt a fleeting pity, seeing in that moment the ageing woman and her grating hips.

He paused at the car and looked down into the driver's sleeping face. Once again he saw the four white Europeans, the truck and its chests and cases; all to pass through the dock gates and the police and Customs posts and onto the *Fragonard*. The security checks imposed during the Korean War still persisted, even after the armistice of a year ago. Special care world be taken with a foreign ship bound for the Nationalist island of Taiwan. Forged papers and exit permits and substantial bribery? It was possible. Shanghai, once a cesspit, had been cleansed. Yet, as all men knew, the old miasmas of corruption still clung like a sea fog in the alleys of the port. Yes, it was possible. But he shook his head. He reached into the car and smacked the driver's face. The man started out of sleep.

"Turn back," Chen told him. "Back to Hangchow."

It was evening when they left Hangchow. John Chen sat in the passenger seat. Lin Sheng drove. It was a closed truck and in the rear were provisions and bottled water, blankets and camp equipment, some canvas cases with fresh clothing, two handguns and clips, two automatic rifles and magazines. There was also a radio transceiver. When they reached the little bridge that crossed the Sinan River it was nearly nightfall. The first of the Chekiang ranges stood in lakes of darkness but the peaks were still touched with red.

Chapter 3

After they left the camphor grove Lewis drove deeper into Chekiang, the sun now high and the river far below them. Forests of evergreen oak, lacquer and camphor grew where height or steepness made them inaccessible to the axe. But lower were the flayed slopes where the timber had been taken. The slopes ran down the mountains to the river valley and on the farther bank they could see the stacked trunks, some huts, men working.

"I don't see any rafts," Gerard said.

"You will," Lewis said.

The valley opened.

"All the big valleys run down to the sea," Lewis told them. "The rivers are sluggish for most of the time. So they're perfect for rafts. Some of them are built like boats, with a helm and a hut to live in."

"Even a sail," Joel said.

"That's right," Lewis said. "Even a sail."

Ellen Mackenna listened to their voices. Her eyes were closed and when the road turned the sun swung in a red blur across the membranes of the lids.

"I hope you ordered a good one," she said.

"The very best."

"With hot and cold?" Joel asked.

"Every home comfort," Lewis said, smiling.

She heard their laughter. The fears of the night were gone and, now, they were three boys beginning an adventure.

"And electricity," Gerard said.

The truck slowed and she opened her eyes. A line of peasants and mules was passing. Most of the burdens were jute and sugarcane. Some of the women carried bundles of black hair-grass, which they would boil and eat. The last mule passed and the truck accelerated. A few small bunches of grass had fallen to the road. Like human scalps, she thought. The image frightened her. Her mind was full of such images, presenting themselves like omens of their journey. She did not believe in the raft any more than she believed in their deliverance.

"What time did you order the raft?" she asked.

He heard the faint sarcasm in her voice. Or was it merely doubt?

"It isn't a taxi," he said. "It'll be along some time in the afternoon."

"You hope," Joel said.

Gerard laughed softly.

"You better pray it comes," Lewis said. "If it doesn't we're finished."

He saw their faces in the driving mirror, changed abruptly into two identical masks of unease.

"It'll come," he told them. "Chiang won't let us down. It'll come."

They drove in silence. The road was very bad, sometimes crumbling at the lip above the steep fall of the land. There was no cultivation on this side of the river, but across it on the lower slopes they could see where it was terraced for rice. After a time Gerard spoke.

"Why would we be finished?" he asked.

"Because the fuel will be gone."

"Oh, Jesus," Joel said.

"Don't you use that name," Ellen said sharply. "Not like that. When you say it you say it with love. Do you understand?"

"Yes, Mother."

A truck approached.

"Keep low," Lewis warned them. He pulled his wide-brimmed straw hat down across his eyes. The truck passed. There were two men in the front, a mound of barley from the May harvest in the rear. A commune number and a portrait of Mao were stenciled on the side.

Ellen shook her head.

"It could have been army," she said. "Or police."

"Well, it wasn't."

"But it could have been." She stared ahead. The land seemed to smoke in sun. "I don't like this road."

"We have no choice. There's no other road. And we have to reach the river."

The road climbed. The valley was still opening out and there were belts of bamboo along the curl of the river and yellow squares where the rape was in flower. He could feel the humidity in his lungs and when the road turned on a wide traverse he saw that the distant northern peaks were defined very sharp and clear on a sullen sky. The typhoon clouds were moving through the fierce blue light.

"Up there," he said, "they are having some weather."

But they did not turn to look. Ellen's eyes were closed again and the boys were eating dates from a green paper bag. He watched them spitting stones out into the road.

"Don't do that," he said.

"Why not?"

"Because I say so."

Joel spat another stone.

"Good shot, old man," Gerard said.

Lewis felt his hands tremble on the wheel. Now they were grinning. Each face always reflected the other, as if even their emotions worked in unison. It was very hot in the truck and a pulse was beating in his temple.

"I'm not in the mood," he said. "So drop it."

Joel took the stone from his mouth and dropped it to the floor.

"Pick it up."

"But you said drop it."

"Do as I say."

Joel retrieved the stone and put his arm out of the window.

"May I drop it now?"

Gerard laughed.

"Yes," Lewis said. "Drop it." He could hear the strain in his voice. The stone fell and the green bag moved around his ear.

"Have one," Gerard said.

"No."

"They're nice."

"I said no."

The bag touched his cheek. The anger rose and he reached up, took it from the boy's fingers and flung it into the road.

"There," he said. "Let that be a lesson."

Ellen opened her eyes.

"What's going on?"

"They're being saucy."

"Sit quiet," she told them.

They sat quiet. Lewis drove until the tank was nearly empty. Then he stopped the truck and poured in the last of the fuel. It was already past noon. The land quivered in heat but in the north the electric blue of the sky was turning dark. He thought he heard thunder but he could not be sure. He returned to the driving seat. Ellen was staring at the fuel gauge.

"There's enough," he said.

The truck started. She leaned back in her seat. After an hour the road was still climbing. It was filmed with crystalline dust and the glare of it seemed to strike through her eyes and into the bones of her head. She felt the sweat run down her spine. The mission was retreating; that place where her spirit was now imprisoned, that place of stone that was never hot and where the water came up cold from the ancient wells and there was the old enameled bath and the sandalwood soap that came from Canton in the pretty pink-and-red wrappers and the big towel that she would fix around her body before she walked out into the evening peace of the garden. A towel. She sat upright.

"Oh, my God," she said.

"What's up?"

"The towel. I just remembered."

"Towel?"

"Yes, towel. I hung it out to dry this morning. On a tree."

He nodded. "I saw you do it."

"It's still there."

He stopped the truck.

"They'll see it from the road," he said.

"Yes."

"Damn," he said. "Damn, damn."

He got out of the truck.

"Give me a drink," he said to the boys.

Joel gave him a half-empty bottle of mineral water and he took it to the side of the road and stood there looking down at the river. But the anger would not leave him and he drank the water quickly and threw the bottle high into the air and watched it leap down the shale of the slope. Then he went back to the truck.

"How could you?" he said to her. "How could you be so damn careless?"

"I'm sorry."

"Sorry won't help."

"I said I'm sorry."

"A towel," he said bitterly. "A white towel stuck up there on the hill. Why didn't you put a signpost up? They slept here. They came this way. Something like that."

She did not answer.

"They might not see it," Gerard said.

"They'll see it all right."

"Or if they do," Joel said, "how would they know it was ours?"

"How would they know?" Lewis said. "I'll tell you how." He leaned into the truck. "Because the mission's name is on it. In beautiful blue embroidery. There isn't a sheet or a blanket or a towel that that damn woman Ferguson hasn't put our name on."

"Don't talk like that," Ellen said. "Mary Ferguson is a friend. She's fond of you."

He shrugged.

"Yes, fond," she said. "People always get fond of you. And then you hurt them."

"Hurt?"

"Yes."

"Who have I hurt?"

"Us."

She tapped her breast, then gestured at the two boys in the rear. They were listening intently. "Us," she repeated. "You've torn us up by the roots. You've put us in danger. We've lost our home."

"You'd have lost that anyway."

She shook her head.

"Yes," he said. "You'd have lost it. I believe I am the last missionary left in China. So it was only a matter of time."

"We could have stayed."

"No."

"They let the Cannons stay."

"Yes. But they took their church."

"And left them their home."

"Home," he said. "Home. Home. Home. That word. Why do you keep on about it? It isn't everything."

"Nearly everything."

She wiped her face. "It's like a furnace in here." She drank some water. "That's another one you've hurt."

"Who?"

"Arthur Cannon."

"How have I hurt him?"

"You sent John Chen straight to his door."

"Chen can't prove a thing. Arthur's too clever for that."

"But he'll be questioned."

"We bought time," he said. "That was the plan."

Their voices, louder now, echoed in the truck.

"Perhaps not so much," she said.

"How so?"

"Chen might not have gone on to Shanghai."

"He'd have to go. That's his job. He has to investigate."

"Even if he doesn't believe in the ship?"

"I never thought he'd believe in it. But he'd have to go."

She drank more water. Her hand was trembling and some of the water ran down her chin, making lanes through the dust on the skin.

"Yes," she said with contempt. "You bought time—with Arthur Cannon."

"No."

"You threw him away. Like one of your wretched chessmen."

"I told you. There was a plan. It was agreed with Arthur."

Joel put out a hand and touched him.

"Please don't go on like this," he said.

"And then there's Dr. Li," she said. "You've hurt him too."

"Please," Joel said again.

"Dr. Li is one of us," Lewis said. "He knew the risk. Besides, he's a very old man."

"Don't the old feel pain?"

"That isn't what I meant."

"What did you mean?"

He looked away from her. Exhaust fumes were making clouds in the sun.

"Tell me, Lewis."

He reached for the ignition key. She gripped his hand.

"Don't switch it off."

"Why not?"

Her grip tightened.

"Suppose—"

"Suppose what?"

"Suppose it didn't start again."

"Why shouldn't it start again?"

"I don't know. But we'd be alone out here. Marooned."

He felt the depth of her fear in that moment. He got into the truck and pulled her against him, began to rock her as if she were a child in need of comfort. "I'll get you out," he whispered into her hair. They continued to rock. The two boys moved toward them from the rear and, now, Joel's face was against her hair and Gerard's head was pressed across his shoulder. He released her and put his arms around the three of them and drew them close, Ellen weeping and his own eyes flooding. Then the boys moved back and he kissed her and said, smiling: "Crybabies we are." He engaged gear and the truck started forward.

He did not speak again until they reached the escarpment and the road ran level above the bend of the river.

"A towel," he said, dismissing it. "A little towel. Why, up there on the hill it could be anything. A bit of paper blown up on the wind. A tree in flower. Why should anybody bother?"

But, driving and the road beginning its descent, the towel grew bigger. It glared as white as snow in sun. It grew until it enveloped the hillside. He felt the unease return.

It was thirty minutes past noon when the rock wall of the escarpment turned inward to reveal distant and below them the place of assignation. He braked the truck and went to the edge of the road and sat on the parapet. They were still very high and the river ran through a ravine until the land retreated on both sides as if it had been bitten out. Here the river spread to form a lake and it was there, he knew, that the rafts sometimes grouped before they went, singly, into the gorges where the river narrowed. He could see the lake, a small blue lozenge at that distance, and the bamboo that grew on one side of it. Across the width of the lake and poised above the water was the rock outcrop, which, in profile, had a beak for a nose and an undershot jaw. His father, Cromer, whose style of expression came direct from the pictured language of the Chinese, had found the words for that too. "See how it glares like a demon," he once said. "The warlords used to throw their prisoners off it." In the childhood years they had enjoyed many picnics on the demon's head and he could remember flinging orange peel and other debris from the top and wondering if it would settle on the prisoners' bones.

But there was an idea in that memory of sinking things; and when he returned to the truck he drove very slowly down the scarp and watched the terrain from the road. The lake was bigger now, the river near. He stopped and left the truck three times and on the third inspection he found the place. The road curved sharply and there was a parapet of unmortared blocks. Below the parapet the rock fell in steep buttresses. The river had undermined it at its base and he could hear the water sucking in the caverns. Wild clematis was rooted in the rock crevices and the flowers of the lower vines floated on the current. Lewis leaned over the parapet. There was a fall of perhaps eighty feet. He picked up a stone and dropped it. The water was very clear and he watched the stone sink and counted the seconds until it touched the river bed. A depth of about forty feet, he judged.

He returned to the truck.

"What are you up to?" Ellen asked.

"Just an idea."

"You mean a move, don't you?"

"Yes," he said, smiling. "A move."

The road, he knew, would not run to the shores of the lake. It would descend, then rise again and curl inland from the gorges. He drove until the lake was near and the gradients were gentle, left the road and took the truck down the slope and through the scrub to the fringe of the bamboo. He stopped where the trees grew thinly.

"Empty the truck," he told them.

After the truck was emptied and its contents stacked he got back into the driving seat and drove across the scrub and up the slope and regained the road. When he reached the parapet where he had dropped the stone he made a five-point turn, then reversed uphill. Then he put the truck into forward gear and steered it so that the wing struck with a glancing impact at the earth-and-rock hillside from which the road was cut. He did this several times, reversing and striking until he had gouged out a satisfactory scar. He got out, smashed the headlamp glass, wrenched off its metal casing and kicked the fragments so that they lay under the scar. Then he went downhill to the parapet and began to push with the sole of his boot against the blocks. They were heavy and he was gasping with strain before he had made sufficient of a gap and a number of the blocks were in the river.

He walked back to the truck and checked that its nose was pointed at the gap. Then he leaned in and released the handbrake. The truck moved and gained speed and, running behind it across the bend in the road, he saw it break through the gap, balance for a second, then topple. He leaned over. The truck was bounding down the rock in a tangle of torn clematis. He saw it strike the water. It was a very enjoyable splash and he watched it sink and rest, finally, on its roof.

He stood upright. Across the broken parapet he could see the lake. Three small figures were running from the shore to the scrub and toward the road. He felt a surge of alarm. I should have told them, he rebuked himself, told them what I was about to do. He climbed up onto the parapet and shouted and waved. The figures stopped and stared up at the scarp and even at that distance he could feel their relief. He waved again and they waved in response. There was humor in it and he felt his lips stretch. He sat down on the parapet and began to laugh. The figures had turned and were walking back to the bamboo.

He stood and took off his straw hat. It was a favorite hat and he would feel its loss. He fished in his hip pocket and found some currency notes and inserted a total of fifty yuan behind the inner band. Then he leaned across the lip and let the hat fall and watched it slide on the rock wall and lodge halfway down in the clematis.

He turned and began the descent to the lake.

John Chen moved the miniature chessboard into the amber light of the oil lamp so that there would be less shadow on the pieces. Across Lin Sheng's head he could see the range standing in the night like a wall. This was the Shan Pass and the mountains were high on either side and there would be no flush of dawnlight behind those black serrations for at least another hour. It was now almost three o'clock in the morning. After they had crossed the Sinan they had driven through the darkness until, at midnight, the valley road took them to the farm commune at Tekwen. He had summoned the committee members. They were dulled by sleep, sullen because he represented the State and it was the State whose imposts on their produce had made them poorer than in the days of the landlord mandarins. No, there had been no reports of a family of Europeans. They had offered no food, only one of the little cement boxes that lined the plantations and served as houses for the workers. But there were cockroaches in the corners and a fever was flaring in the village. Tekwen was unclean and he had decided to leave and they had driven into the pass, there to spread their blankets and brew their tea and eat a meal.

Chen took Lin Sheng's rook.

Lin sighed.

"Don't sigh like that," Chen said sharply. "It was a deliberate sacrifice. Isn't that so?"

"Yes."

"Then why sigh? That merely insults me."

"I apologize."

"You play like Mackenna. A sacrifice is always obvious."

Lin bowed his head and Chen stood and went to the truck. Lewis Mackenna would not leave his mind. The move that had sent him to the Cannons at Fengsien might yet be decisive. What was his total advantage? To the twenty-four hours presented to him by Dr. Li must now be added the five wasted on that abortive journey. There was also the question of how far Mackenna had driven on the first night of his escape. He opened his case, found a pad and a pen and walked back through the aureole of light that was shed by the lamp and sat. Lin was still studying the little board; preparing, Chen thought, the next transparent ambush. He watched Lin smooth his hair, tap it delicately at the sides and back like a woman arranging a coiffure. He liked Lin, and already he regretted the sharpness of his words. The vanity would pass with the years and the time would come when it would be unbearable to turn his head and see his changing image stalk him like an enemy through the shop windows. There was sadness in the thought and he felt his irritation drain. Lin would surely rise—his father the minister Lin Kiensang would see to that. But he did not know if he would make a good security man. Lin was a child of the light, gentle, an athlete and a fine swimmer. The smell of dungeons would touch him and he would turn away.

Chen drew a rectangle on the pad. The base represented the coast and, moving from right to left, he marked the port of Foochow, the port of Amoy and the smaller port of Swatow. The top of the rectangle he hatched into the continuous range that was formed by the Ta Yuling and the Bohea mountains. The left side of the rectangle was the Han River, which emptied into Swatow; and the right was the Min River, which emptied into Foochow. He also marked the Shan Pass, where they were now camped; and the Liling Pass, which was thirty-five kilometers south of the Shan. Mackenna was somewhere within the box, moving down toward the sea. He did not believe that the missionary would risk the long exposed run through the New Territories and into Hong Kong. He turned the pad and slid it across the blanket.

Lin studied it.

"He must go for the coast," Chen said.

"Yes."

"But which route?"

Lin passed a finger across the diagram.

"A country of many rivers," he said.

"So?"

"So I doubt he'll stay with the truck. At some point there will be a boat."

"I agree."

Chen felt the sweat run suddenly across his scalp. A hot wind was moving through the pass. From now until September the storms would come in from the South China Sea and scour the breathless land.

"Radio all army bases inside that box," he told Lin. "I want an air patrol on every navigable river."

"Yes, sir."

He watched Lin walk through the underbrush to the rear of the truck. A point of red light from the transceiver made an eye in the darkness. He leaned back on his blanket, laced his hands behind his head and stared up at the sky. There was pleasure in the use of power. No one could deny that. He had spoken; and when the first light came the spotter planes and the helicopters would make their runs down the rivers and the waterways. There was no greater power in the nation than that vested in his own Ministry. It sprang from a simple preface to their constitution. *The law of the People's State is a weapon, to be used at any cost to seek out, punish and destroy subversive elements of any kind.* And the cost was truly high. The Ministry of Public Security administered the national police; and the police were supported by the urban and the rural militia and the garrisons of the People's Liberation Army; and the PLA embraced all the forces of land, sea and air; and at the top of the massive edifice were the People's Courts. It was in these courts, at the time of the great treason trials of 1951, that he had worked as a public prosecutor; a time of personal success that had led him from those floodlit arenas to the darker stage of the Ministry.

When Lin returned from the truck there was still no light in the sky.

"We'll leave soon," Chen said.

Lin, too, lay back on his blanket.

"He has to be caught," Chen said. "There are things inside his head. The names of agents. Chiang's invasion plan."

"Will he know that?"

"I cannot say. But if he knows the plan he's in another kind of danger."

"A danger?"

"From Chiang."

"But Chiang is his friend."

"Chiang is a general. He understands the price of victory. He dare not allow Mackenna to be captured. If that seems likely he'll have him killed."

Lin was silent.

"Does that thought disturb you?" Chen asked.

"Yes."

"Then you are in the wrong work."

Chen closed his eyes. He knew he would not sleep. He listened to the sough of wind, the crickets in the scrub. He could sense Lin's disquiet.

What will the years do to him? he wondered; all the acts of the secret life thickening like calluses on that sensitive mind.

"Did you know him well?" Lin asked.

"Mackenna?"

"Yes."

"I knew him."

"What is he like?"

"A mixture. Boy and man would best describe him."

Chen turned on his side. He could confide in no one. He heard Lin's lips part, as if they would frame another question.

"Leave it," Chen said.

They had waited at the edge of the bamboo until the light began to fail. But nothing came down the river, only the lianas and the little floating islands of vegetation that had been torn away upstream. When the light was gone the earth breathed out its heat and mist rose and covered the water and was sour in the throat. They could not see across the lake or the walls of the ravine where the river entered. They stared into the darkness and listened but there was no sign or sound of the raft.

"Will it come?" Ellen whispered.

"Yes," Lewis said. "It'll come."

"I mean at night."

"I don't know. But eventually it will come."

Lightning made a white fork above the mist.

"The big rafts don't stop at night," Joel said.

"How do you know?" Gerard asked.

"I read it. The really big rafts never stop."

"That's 'cause they can't."

"They can stop all right," Lewis said. "Even the big ones."

"Let's be quiet," Ellen said. "Let's listen."

They listened. The lightning made another brilliant fork, revealing for a second the face of the rock outcrop on the opposite shore.

"I don't think it's a demon," Joel said. "More like a witch."

"Why a witch?" Gerard said.

"Because it's a she."

"Why is it a she?"

"You can see it is. An ugly old woman. A hag."

"A demon could be a she."

"No. A demon is a he. Isn't that right, Dad?"

"Could be either," Lewis said seriously. "It doesn't have a sex. Just an evil spirit. And when it's written down out here it's often the same character. Witch, demon, ogre, evil spirit. It's the same."

"Come to that," Gerard said, "you can have a male witch."

Ellen put her hands to her ears.

"Will you stop prattling?" she said nervously. "Just shut up. All of you shut up."

She turned from them and walked along the shore into the darkness and toward the ravine. She heard the boys call out, their clear voices flat in the mist, and Lewis say: "Let her go. Let her be alone." She continued to walk. It was good to be enveloped in the mist, the dark, the silence. Above all the silence and her feet in the sodden grass and the going away from them and their stupidities and the aloneness and the black hem of water that was all she could see of the lake. She walked until the ravine loomed above her. There was a rockfall that had spilled into the water and she sat down on one of the rocks and removed her shoes and socks and put her feet into the current. Then she took off her blouse, soaked her handkerchief and washed her upper body. Let her be alone. He had understood her need. But he did not know how desperate it was. For the first time in her marriage she yearned to be free, to live without love and the fears of love and the responsibilities of love and all its demands and the pain that was its other name. She sat on the rock until the warm wind dried her flesh. The mist was lifting and she could see through its veils across the width of the lake to where the outcrop made a black silhouette against the sky. Stone was twisted down the sides of the head like braids of hair. Joel is right, she thought; definitely a witch.

Later there were footfalls in the grass. She did not turn and she heard his boots on the rocks behind her.

"Want company?" Lewis asked.

"Don't mind."

He sat. She had not replaced her blouse and he smiled at her nakedness and put his arm around her and cupped her breast. They sat for a time. Then she said: "Been having bad thoughts."

"What about?"

"About being free."

"Of me?"

"Of the three of you."

"Don't you love us?"

"You know I do."

"Then how could you leave us?"

"I couldn't. But that doesn't stop me wishing."

She pulled her feet from the water and began to dry them on her blouse.

"I've known people that chose that kind of freedom," Lewis said. "Living inside a shell like a snail. Sticking their heads back in whenever a little Christian love reached out to touch them. It's one way of avoiding hurt. But it isn't the human condition. We have to love and be loved. We have to watch our loved ones in danger. We have to stand aside and see our children grow and be wounded by all the things that will happen to them. And in the end we have to know bereavement."

She turned to face him. Like the dregs of old sermons, she thought; smothering his guilt in words. She gathered up her shoes and socks, draped the blouse across her shoulder and stood. He looked up at her.

"Don't you preach at me," she said.

She crossed the rock spill and began the walk back along the shore. A faint starlight revealed the lake under the shifting mist. The thunderstorm still flickered behind the northern range. She heard his boots padding in the grass but she did not turn. His voice was resounding in her mind. We have to watch our loved ones in danger. And in the end we have to know bereavement. Fear resurged. What was he telling her? The boots came nearer.

"Sweetheart," he called out.

She stopped and turned and he came to her and held her shoulders.

"That's a nice word, Lewis," she said. "But I can't forgive you for what you've done to us."

"You said you loved me."

"Yes."

"Then you have to forgive me."

"I can't."

"But you must. Loving and forgiving are the same. That's what we believe. You have to forgive me if you love me."

"Then perhaps I don't," she said tiredly. "Perhaps it's dying—as I am."

She turned from him and in that moment she heard the sound.

It came from the ravine.

"Listen," she said.

It came again, a splash, then a scraping noise as if something heavy had collided with a rock. They watched the ravine and its throat of darkness and the darker form that was slowly emerging. The form took shape, square and low on the water with a short mast and the figure of a man huddled against it.

"Behold the raft," Lewis said dramatically. Then, laughing: "Your prayers are answered."

The raft passed slowly across their line of vision, borne on the current and keeping parallel to the shore. Lewis shouted but it did not alter course toward them. It was still indistinct in the misty night, the man not moving and his head bent as if he were looking down into the water. Lewis shouted again but there was no response and the raft rode out onto the breast of the lake. Lightning flashed and in that fractional second they saw the raft irradiated and the gallows that had been built on it and the hanged man swaying from the crosstrees and behind the raft the yellow light on the witch's face and the horizontal fissure that was her mouth snarling through the mist that clung like gray bandages to her features. Ellen screamed. The omens, now, were multiplying in her frightened mind: the lolling head, the malignant face, masts that turned into gibbets, the black hair-grasses that were ripped-off scalps lying in the road. She began to run, the shoes falling, then the socks, then the blouse, and he running behind her and her breasts bobbing and the boys running from the bamboo and her screams skating on the waters of the lake. When he caught her he turned her and held her against him until she was emptied of the terror. "There," he murmured. "There, there. It's all right now. Be calm. Calm." The boys came to them and they stood there on the shore in the night and after a time he pushed her from him and wiped the spittle from her chin and kissed her and stroked her cheek. Then he walked back toward the ravine and retrieved the shoes, one sock and the blouse. They did not speak when he rejoined them and they turned and began the walk to the bamboo. The raft had gone from sight.

"A village execution," he told them. "I've seen it once before. There's not much law in some of these places. So if a man does something really bad they'll do the punishing themselves. The raft will lodge somewhere down the river but nobody will touch it. The crows will pick it to the bone and the wood will break up and eventually there'll be nothing left."

She moved away from his side, shaking her head. Now there was another image, ragged black wings on a dead man's face. "No," she said, thrusting it from her. "No."

Lewis took her hand.

"Get some sleep," he said kindly. "Tomorrow we'll be on our way. Sleep."

But none of them could sleep. Lewis rose from his blanket at around midnight. The starlight was stronger and he could see the whole of the lake and the silhouettes of the two boys sitting on a mound near the water. Ellen had spread her blanket between the tea chests and he went to her and looked down. She was half-awake, twisting in the wet heat. Her face had gone haggard with strain. He turned from her and walked down to the shore. He did not go immediately to the boys. He stood, a little apart from them, staring at the lake.

"It's running faster," Joel said.

"Are you sure?"

"Yes. The river's coming in much faster."

He went down to the water's edge. Now he could see the grass islands traveling on the central stream that was the thrust of the river. They passed quickly. Dismay touched him. How heavy had the northern storms been? How much rain was decanting into the river? They would not launch the rafts if the river ran too fast.

"And it's rising," Gerard said. He pointed. "There was a rock down there. Now you can't see it."

Lewis walked back to them and sat on the mound.

"Will it stop the rafts?" Joel asked.

"No."

"It's running pretty fast."

"Yes. But it'll take more than a drop of fast water to stop those fellows. Take it from me. The raft will come."

Now the lake was brightening. But downstream of the bamboo where the river made its exit and would be compressed within the gorges there was white water.

"How is Mummy?" Gerard asked.

"Resting. But she'll be fine."

"She was awfully scared."

"I don't blame her," Joel said. "It couldn't be more scary." He laughed nervously. "That man. Did you see him?" He allowed his head to collapse to one side of his pale stalk of a neck, tongue out above a sagging jaw.

"Never joke about a man's death," Lewis said sharply.

"You said he was bad. A crinimal."

"Criminal."

"Yes, a criminal. Really bad. That's what you said."

"Perhaps he was innocent," Lewis said.

"Innocent?"

He saw the disquiet in their faces.

"Yes," he said. "He could be innocent. The innocent are always suffering. That's the one great question you will ask throughout your lives. Why? Why does God let it happen?"

They watched him intently; like the ones in the pews, he thought, that are always awaiting some shaft of eternal truth.

"I can't give you an answer," he said. "Not even part of an answer. I expect the man was guilty. He was a criminal until he died, and he was a man until he died. But after that—"

He could not finish the sentence with any conviction and he stood and moved a pace down the mound and stared at the creeping lake.

"But after that," the voice said behind him, "he became something more."

He knew at once that the voice was Gerard's. For him their voices were indistinguishable. Yet some sense had told him that the words had come from Gerard. Here on the mound in the darkness above the lake he was aware of a kind of revelation. For the first time in the ten years since their birth he saw their essential difference; in the edge of cruelty to Joel's mimicry of the dangling man, in Gerard's wistful faith. "Yes," he said without turning, "we all hope we shall become something more than what we are." He picked up a stone and lobbed it into the shallows. He was aware also of a growing shame. He had been dishonest with them; about the raft, about Ellen, about the endless night that might be waiting. Why are the young deemed to be too fragile for the truth? he asked himself. Let them be bruised. Let them get used to it. He turned and said to them: "I lied to you. If the river's in flood the raft won't come. I'm very concerned about your mother. She's exhausted in body and in mind and a part of her is still in the mission and it may never come back to us. She's sick with fear, and so am I. I know, and she knows, that we don't have much chance. She prays for us—prayers that I should offer but can't. What has happened to me? What kind of minister is it who can't pray for the safety of his family? Oh, I can still see God. But I've put a distance between him and me. I can feel him there, but at this great distance. Like a father who is so far away that his child can't reach him." He shook his head. The words had a dark sound to them—a man in a prison cell might be as unreachable as that. "So you see I can't say to you the things a priest should say. I can't give you that kind of comfort. I can't reassure you and tell you that the soul of that poor executed man is now in heaven. But then Jesus himself never used such words. Did you know that? He never said our souls will go to heaven when we die. Jesus said he'd give us eternal life, raise us up at the last day if we'd take his flesh and blood and believe in him. But what is eternal life? When is the last day? Can we trust words that other men wrote down long after Jesus died?" He smiled at them. "As you can see I'm in a spiritual mess. Almost an agony. I'm behind walls so thick that my cries can't be heard." He wiped his face. Walls, four walls, it was the cell again. He sat down on the mound, slightly below them. How could they understand? He looked into Gerard's face and said: "Those words of yours were good. A bit pious for a ten-year-old. But good Christian words. After he dies a man becomes something more. I expect I taught you that. But the trouble is they're words, don't you see? There have been so many words. Death and resurrection. The immortality of the soul. Redemption and salvation. Eternal life. Words that run away like sand through the fingers. Words that men have used to conceal their fear that an end may be an end." He watched their faces, pale and solemn in the night. How strange, he thought, that I am talking to them as I have never talked to Ellen; unburdening myself to two children who would rather be spitting date stones into the water. "But I tell you this," he said, "there will always be a great gulf between God and man. How can it be otherwise? Think of God's kingdom and then of our own puny planet. Somehow we have to find a bridge. And if we find it we call it grace." He smiled. "There's another word for you. Grace."

He turned from them. Now he could hear the slap-slap of water in the gorges. Across from him the brightening light had begun to find hollows in the witch's face.

"What a tale it could tell," he said, pointing. "Your great-grandfather, Jardine, mentions it in his diaries."

"Great-great," Joel corrected.

Lewis checked the line of succession on his fingers.

"Yes," he said. "Great-great. And he was also a great-great man. You know that, don't you?"

They nodded.

"In those days it took a very special kind of man to come out to China to spread the Christian message. There were terrible dangers. The mandarins had the power of life and death and a foreign priest was a challenge to them. And outside the cities and the western settlements the warlords were steeping the land in blood. Many priests suffered." He pointed at Joel. "What do we call a minister who goes out into a foreign land to preach?"

Joel shrugged.

"An evangelist," Gerard said.

"Yes, an evangelist. It was easy enough to get ordained and stay at home in a country parish. A lifetime in the arms of Mother Church, a soft bed and a full gut and croquet on the lawn. But Jesus said: Go ye into all the world and preach the Gospel. And that's what men like Jardine did."

"And so did you, Daddy," Gerard said.

"But not very well. I was always a better doctor than I was a priest. A missionary, you see, must have an absolute belief that God has appointed him to convert the heathen. A kind of divine command. But for me the trumpets never really sounded. I used to stand apart from myself, watch myself, listen to myself, ask myself what right I had to interfere with those who led good lives within the teachings of the Buddha or Confucius or Lao-tsze. What right? And perhaps to ask that question was the beginning of doubt." He saw the perplexity in their faces—one day with the passing of the years they might look back and remember his words and understand a little of his turmoil. "For me," he said, "medicine and the priesthood never mixed. All the Mackenna missionaries were doctors. Jesus was a healer and I suppose they'd have said they were following the example of that one perfect man. But I began to see it differently. Set their bones and paint their sores, dangle a crucifix above their grateful eyes and then, lo and behold, there they'd be one Sunday sitting in the Bible class eager for the Word. That seemed to be dishonest." He turned again toward them. "So you see I'm not much of a missionary, not much of a priest. But let me say this. Christ may be distant from me. But that doesn't mean I won't defend him. When the Reds set out to destroy him all over again that's exactly what I did."

He watched a branch with a canopy of leaf sail through the lake. Without doubt the flow was faster.

"I defended him," he told the two intent faces, "by working for Chiang's secret army. There was a part to play and Christian soldiers can't always fight in the light. They had cut off the mission funds and we were desperate for money to run the hospital and buy the drugs and pay the staff. Chiang was in Taiwan and was planning the invasion that must surely come, and when he offered to fund the mission in return for services I agreed." Lewis smiled. "The mission became a very strange place; a radio post, a letter box, a paymaster for the agents, a point on the escape route. People on the run hid in our cellars, sat at our table, even lay in the hospital beds. It was an awful risk, but I had to take it. Chiang had become the only hope. Some say he's vain, ruthless, a relic of the old imperial past. And all that's true. But he's also a believer, a Methodist. He knows what Communism does to the human spirit." Lewis pointed to the sky. "You can look up and almost see the stars turning red. Soon it'll be too late. Only Chiang can change them back again."

Now the river was making small waves against the outcrop. The night was luminous and he could see the spray running like drops of mercury down the stone of the witch's throat.

"You were born in China," he said to them. "You know its people. You know they're not drab and gray. The mandarins have gone but in their hearts they'd rather bow to a peacock robe than a Mao tunic. One tyranny in exchange for another—that's what they got. A mandarin might behead you in the street, but Johnny Chen's men will choke you in a cellar. What hope is there in a godless land?" He shrugged. "I had to do something. But was I right? I'm no longer certain. You see, every lie, every deception made me smaller; as a man and as a priest. I found that out. Perhaps it's less damaging to a man to kill his enemy in the daylight than to plot against him in the shadows. I don't know. But I do know that every priest needs to keep a little bit of innocence and I think I let it die. The acts were done and I pushed Jesus away from me and now I'm running for my life and I've put my lovely family in danger." He reached out and touched their hands. "When you are older I want you to think kindly of me and forgive me."

Along the shore where the camp was he saw Ellen leave the bamboo and walk down to the water's edge. She shook out her hair so that it swung across her back. Her body was thin and childlike in the silver light.

"Your Mummy accused me," he said, "of hurting Dr. Li. But it wasn't like that. It was something he wanted to do. He told me he was old and unwell and had only a few years left and he would give them to us. Do you understand? He made that choice. That was his gift." He saw Joel's eyes blur with tiredness and he said, smiling: "Here endeth the lesson. Or was it confession? Now get some sleep. And kiss me before you go."

They rose and bent to kiss him, each of the small soft mouths the same in shape and texture. He watched them walk along the shore and join hands with Ellen and when the three had gone back into the shadow of the bamboo he turned and stared into the implacable face of the witch and felt the threat of the day that lay ahead.

Soon it would be sunrise.

At sunrise the water from the swelling lake was into the bamboo and the snakes were swimming out of it. Across from the shore Lewis could see where the level had risen nearer to the witch's chin. When the snakes were gone they carried the blankets, the tea chests and the cases and the camping gear out of the grove and up the rising ground to where it was dry and then into the cover of the trees. They could still see the lake and, drinking tea in the first hour of sunlight, they heard the engine of the aircraft and saw it lift out of the walls of the ravine and the red stars on its fuselage. It was a light, slow, piston-driven plane of the kind used for spotting and it crossed the breast of the lake and entered the gorge. The sound faded and was almost gone. Then it resurged and was amplified in the rock walls and the plane came back out of the gorge and made two low circles of the lake. It crossed the bamboo twice, then re-entered the gorge. The sound died.

"So they're searching," Ellen said.

"Yes."

During the morning the plane returned, flying very low across the river terrain and then parallel to the Hangchow road. The current was still fast and there was no traffic on the river, not even a junk or a fishing boat. But at noon, when Lewis walked down to and along the shore, the witch's throat was again exposed. He could see the collar of water-darkened stone that was the measure of the river's fall. He watched the passing tendrils of vegetation. They were much slower now and he knew that the flash floods in the mountains were spent. At two in the afternoon he could no longer see white water where the river broke against the rocks. Hope rose. There were still four or five hours of daylight. He went back to the high ground and told them of the fall and, then, they carried their possessions down again to the edge of the bamboo so that they would be near once more to the shore.

Three hours later the river life awakened; a few sampans, a ferryboat that would trade in the gorge villages and carry people to the coast, a wupan with its two tiny cabins and the oar that thrust against the current from the stern, a junk. Lewis watched it with admiration. He had always loved the junks. They had not changed in two thousand years and some of them were truly beautiful. This one was large but perfect and the mellow light touched the cypress turret of its hull and the painted characters that spelled the name *Shantung* and when it passed across the lake the sky was behind the four-cornered lugsail and he could see the bamboo veins of its construction and the sail was like a brown leaf seen against the sun. "Beautiful," he murmured.

And then, in the sundown hour, the rafts came.

They came from the ravine mists and out onto the breadth of the lake, moving sedately with the current like a line of ships and the forest trees of some of them so tall and heavy in the water that they were built with a crude tiller or a bow sweep. There were men on each of the rafts with the long spars that they would use when the rocks came too close. Joel began to count. The rafts passed; not grouping on the lake so that they might avoid the darkness of the night hours but moving on their undeviating line through the walls of the gorge and out of sight. Perhaps, Lewis thought, there is a full moon tonight. The rafts would not stop, he knew, until they had covered the ninety miles to the sawmills at Pai-shang. Already the raftmen were lighting cooking fires and the hewn ends of the trunks were red wounds in the dying sun.

"Forty-eight," Joel said.

Now the lake was empty.

"And not one of them for us," Ellen said.

But the raft came in the final minutes of the sun. She had walked along the shore so that she might be alone in her despair and, kneeling in the shallows, unpinned her hair and began to rinse out the dust and sweat of the day. Once she immersed her head and opened her eyes and saw the bed of the lake shelving into darkness and she felt the impulse to rise and walk out and be swallowed in the water. But she was on her knees; and because throughout her life that posture had always brought her nearer to her god the despair turned to prayer and she lifted her head from the water and closed her eyes. Please make the raft come for us. Please help us. Please bring us out of the valley of the shadow. Please, please, please. She opened her eyes and, looking through the mesh of dripping hair, saw the raft emerge from between the walls of the ravine and glide out onto the lake. It was a small raft, a puny raft, lopsided in the water with two men to guide it and a large traveling haystack that, as was the custom, would be sold downstream wherever there was a buyer. But this was the shape of deliverance, the sudden answer to a prayer. Thank you, thank you, thank you. She wanted to rise, run back along the shore to Lewis and the boys. But there was no strength in her limbs and the elation left her and a curious peace came in its place and she shifted from her knees so that, sitting now with the water lapping at her breasts, she could stare across the swell.

She saw the raft turn in toward the shore and the men spar-moor it in the shallows between two reefs of rock. One of the men got down and splashed through the water and up onto the grassy strand, the red sun lining his thin brown shinbones. She saw Lewis greet him and heard his voice—high and querulous like the voices of those that live in the lands around the Han. The man held out his palm and Lewis shook his head. Now they were arguing. The man shrugged and turned away and Lewis grasped his arm and pulled him back. The palm lifted again. Their voices rose. She felt the brief tranquility desert her and the anxieties return. She rose and left the shallows and, legs trembling, walked toward them. The sun was nearly gone, only a rim above the range. Another sun, another day. Twenty-four hours lost, given back to Chen. How near was he? The boys ran to her.

"He wants money," Gerard said.

The Han turned when she approached. She saw the cupidity in his eyes.

"He wants money," Lewis said.

"Then give it him."

"Chiang has already paid him. Why should he get it twice?"

"Pay him, Lewis."

"No."

"Aren't we worth a little money?" Now she was afraid again. The raft strained against the spars, the bamboo was bending. She could see its weight striving to move out with the current, away from them.

"Please, Lewis," she said.

"No."

"Just a little money."

"We don't have much cash," he said stubbornly. "And what we have we need."

"Then give him something. Anything." She pointed to his wrist. "Try him with the watch."

He hesitated. Then he removed the watch and offered it. The Han shook his head; he knew cheapness when he saw it, as well as he knew the sight of desperation. He turned away and Ellen moved between him and the swirling water.

"Lewis," she whispered. "Lewis."

He returned the watch to his wrist. An iron sense of propriety in money matters lay within him as it had lain in all the generations of Mackennas, and he was deeply offended by the raftman's greed. Possessions were important and that which a man had earned or was lawfully his belonged to no other. But this was a matter of survival. What good are possessions, he asked himself, if we are abandoned to this lonely place? The raft creaked and struck the rock with the sound of a closing door. "Lewis," she said again. He looked at her, at the wet hair that was matted like seaweed on a drowned face. He saw the edge of terror on which she stood. "Don't fret," he said softly. "I'll find him something."

He went to the black-japanned metal case, unbuckled its leather strap and knelt. It was almost as big as a cabin trunk. Cromer had bought it in the year of his ordination and the scratched white stencils of his name were still legible on its side. He opened the lid. The Han's shadow fell across him. He began to search its contents. There were clothes and vestments, letters and papers and old family diaries, packets of photographs some of which had already spilled out, favorite books and small stuffed toy animals that had once been loved by the children; all that remains, he thought, of our destroyed lives. At the bottom of the case were some items of church silver, each wrapped separately in muslin. Inside the folds of one of his white-linen surplices he found a large envelope that contained a thick sheaf of Imperial Chinese Bonds. He had inherited them on Cromer's death. They were of varying denominations, printed on rice paper that made a satisfying crackle within the fingers. They had the quality of fine engravings and all of them were beautiful. But with the advent of the new China they had ceased to be legal tender, retaining only a tiny stock market value, based on the forlorn hope that Mao's government might eventually redeem them. But certain bonds were very rare and provided their condition was good would fetch a high price in the collectors' market. There were two such bonds in the sheaf, Lewis recalled, both of them 4½-percent Gold Loan of 1898. He extracted the sheaf from the envelope and the Han, drawn by the crackling paper, bent lower. The two Gold Loans, Lewis saw with dismay, lay on the top. They were too valuable to part with. He began to turn the bonds slowly. Most of them, although not rare, would attract a good price from the dealers. In the center of the batch he found a 5-percent Shanghai-Nanking Railway of 1903. Much of the issue was still in existence and the bond had little value. He paused, holding the bond between thumb and index finger. He could smell the fish on the Han's breath. Greed and suspicion go hand in hand, he thought. He transferred the bond to the bottom of the batch. Then he took one of the Gold Loans off the top and proffered it. He felt a momentary guilt. How easy it was to learn deceit. The Han did as predicted, shook his head, bent and took the Shanghai-Nanking from the bottom. Lewis felt the beginning of a smile. "Agreed?" he asked. But the man's eyes had narrowed with distrust. He had never seen notes like these passing in the streets. He dropped the bond into the case and said: "I cannot eat paper." He turned to go and in that moment Ellen's face swung across the case and she tore the bonds from his fingers and scattered them. Her voice spoke unsteadily. "What do you think you're doing?" Then, shouting, so close that her spittle sprayed his lips: "What the devil d'you think you're playing at?"

She plunged her hands into the case, began to snatch out its contents. Clothes and papers and photographs and toys spilled across her feet. The single orange eye of an almost hairless rabbit glinted from the grass. She found one of the muslin-wrapped objects and straightened.

"Put it back," he told her.

She began to unwrap it.

"That belongs to the church," he said.

"You have no church."

The muslin fell. A candlestick rolled down her palm.

"You have no church," she repeated. "You will never have a church. All you have is here. Us. These bits and pieces. There is nothing else."

Now everything was red; their flesh, the water, the silver of the candlestick. She gave it to the Han and he stroked it and weighed it in his hand.

He picked up the strip of muslin and rewound it. Then he nodded and pointed to the raft.

The sun was gone when the raft was loaded and the lake was as gray as slate. They sat with their backs to the haystack and listened to the scuttling sounds inside it and watched the men push off with the bamboo spars. The witch passed astern of them, so near that they seemed to stare into the deep black caves that were her eye sockets. Ahead was the darkening gorge.

Chapter 4

At daybreak Chen and Lin Sheng left the Shan Pass. These were dangerous dirt roads sometimes rising high above ravines where the night mists still hung like gauze. Chen, who was distrustful of all other drivers, had elected to take the truck as far as Kwangtseh. From there a superior and therefore less hazardous road ran down to Nanping and then to the coast at Foochow. Their destination was Army Base Four, which lay eighty kilometers from Kwangtseh and was built on both sides of the railway line. Chen reflected that the pursuit was, for the moment, in a vacuum. But that was inevitable. Instinct and reason had directed him into the provinces of Chekiang and Kiangsi. But even that (for him) formidable mixture could take him no further. He needed the spur of his opponent's move. Without it the game hung suspended; and only luck and efficient communications could renew it. The army bases (there were six in the regions that lay between Hangchow and Canton) sat like spiders in an immense radio web. Each of them was under a First Order Alert, which signified that troops and other forces were searching for some sign of Lewis Mackenna in the towns and villages and communes and the ports, on the rivers and canals. All this activity, Chen thought, must surely reveal some vestige of a trail. The hunted always left a spoor.

And so it was.

At Army Base Four there were two clips of the green sheets on which all forces signals were recorded. They sat in the Radio Office and read them. Outside was the railway track and a locomotive shooting steam up into the clear air and a company of troops embarking. A man brought them tea and a lieutenant fed them with new and supplementary signals. Chen was surprised at the number of Europeans traveling in southeast China. But most of the signals could be discarded; the suspects, on investigation, had proved to be of satisfactory identity. Some were still detained. He turned the sheets slowly; like watching, he thought, a procession of outraged white faces. There were families from the consulates and the banks, journalists, archaeologists from two separate sites where antiquities were being dug, a party from a Swiss film unit, families picnicking, families boating, even a family fishing. One of the sheets referred to a man and his wife and two children arrested twenty kilometers inland from the port of Foochow. The signal had come from Army Base Two. Chen telephoned. The atmospherics were bad and he could not hear clearly the man at the other end. What age are the children? What sex? He had to repeat it. Are they twins? Are they what? Are they identical twins? The answer came faintly. A boy and a girl, one six, one eight. Then release them, and learn to send better signals. Chen put down the telephone. A rainstorm had begun, washing from the windowpanes the grime of a hundred steam trains. He rose and stared through the glass at the parade square. The rain was striking the earth with the force of bullets.

Lin looked up from his clip of signals.

"So far nothing," he said. "A few of these leave questions in the mind. But no more than that."

Chen turned from the window.

"A number of sightings," Lin explained. "Without encounter, you understand." He had dog-eared some of the sheets and he turned back to them. "A truck seen distantly on the brow of a hill. That was in Anhwei. Another truck driving without lights at night on the road to Nanchang. A motor launch on the Kiulung and two white faces in the cabin. A white man filling a canteen from the Tsien Tang." He paused and tapped one of the signals. "Then there are reports of recent bivouacs. Dead fires, litter, cans." He shrugged. "And why not? The weather is good and there will always be harmless campers, or peasants on the march, or a man and a girl from a village." He turned more sheets. "Here we have a towel found by the river bank. Imagine a helicopter patrol alighting, if that is the word, because it has seen something hanging from a tree." Derision touched his voice. "A towel." He went to another sheet. "Listen to this one—"

Chen shook his head and left the window. He had felt a sudden wave of tiredness. "I need a bath and a shave," he said. "Give me thirty minutes." He opened the door. Then he turned on the threshold. For some reason the towel was fluttering like a flag across all the other signals.

"This towel," he said. "Where was it found?"

"By the Liao."

"The Liao."

"Yes. A branch of the Tsien Tang."

Chen walked to the wall map and ran his finger down the course of the big river until he found the branch.

"Only a towel," Lin said, smiling. "As a swimmer, let me tell you, it's easy to lose a towel."

"Yes," Chen said. "But consider the place. The direction. The road that follows the river. It could be significant."

Lin shrugged again.

"Where was the helicopter based?" Chen asked.

"Base Two."

"Does the signal have a map reference?"

"Of course."

"Why of course? Don't forget there is an idiot at Base Two."

"There is an exact reference," Lin said. "Shall I mark it for you?"

"Yes. And mark also the place where the man was seen filling the canteen."

Lin brought the two signals to the wall map and marked the two locations. Chen studied them, then placed his fingertip under the little asterisk on the Tsien Tang. From here, he thought, Mackenna (if in fact it was the missionary who had stopped for water) would make the long drive down to the town of Yungan. At Yungan there was a route through Fukien to the port of Amoy. But, apparently, Amoy was not the destination. A road curled from the town and ran almost parallel to the Liao River, and it was on this thin blue line that the second of the asterisks lay. South of the asterisk was the course of the Han River and the port of Swatow.

"If the towel was left by Mackenna," he said, "then he is making for Swatow."

He took the two signals from Lin's hand and went to the telephone. The atmospherics continued to drown Army Base Two but he recognized the voice of the incompetent. Chen gave him the signal number. It is about the towel that was found on the bank of the Liao River. Towel? Yes, towel. Do you have the signal in front of you? Then get it. The atmospherics came and went like a sea wave on shingle. Chen waited. He was aware that some of Lin's skepticism had entered him. A European bent over a river. A towel. That was all. The noise abated and the man spoke. Do you have the signal and the towel? Good. Examine the towel. Are there any marks on it? No, not dirt marks. Chen saw in that moment the man's rudimentary brain living feebly in its cave of thick bone. Marks of identity, of ownership, a laundry perhaps. A pause. There is something in blue thread. The noise surged again. What does it say? You may have it upside down? Another pause. They are not Chinese characters, the man said. Do you read any English? (What an absurd question.) Then get someone who does. A long pause, then a different voice. What does the blue thread say? They are English capital letters. E P O F. Chen repeated them. The voice said: But I don't know what they mean.

"But I do," Chen said.

It was past noon when they reached the Liao and another hour before they saw the helicopter waiting on the road that ran with the river. A captain and two men were standing in its shadow and they walked forward when Chen and Lin got out of the truck. Chen looked around him; at the swiftly flowing river below the level of the road, at the slope above it and the grove of camphor trees that stood against the sky. The captain gave him a large white bath towel and pointed to the blue thread embroidery in one of the corners.

"Did I speak to you on the telephone?" Chen asked.

"Yes, sir."

"The letters mean Edinburgh Presbyterian Overseas Fellowship."

"Then it was the priest?"

"Yes. Now show me exactly where the towel was found."

The captain spoke to one of the soldiers and the man led them up the rise of the ground to the trees. He pointed to the lower branches.

"Hang it as it was," Chen told him.

The soldier hooked the towel so that it was spread. Chen looked at it, then walked into the shadow of the trees. Lin followed. The grass was flattened and he could see the impressions made by the wheels of the truck. There were two meat cans with some scraps of pork stuck to the insides, a carton that had contained soybeans, date stones lying in the grass like brown chrysalises.

They left the camphor and Chen squatted and, shielding his eyes against the sun, stared down the slope. There were no visible tracks to show the passage of the truck or the points at which it had driven from and returned to the road. The grass, sodden now from the day's early rainfall, must, he reasoned, have been dry and hard when the truck crossed it. So there was still a time disadvantage; a day, perhaps more. Mackenna had planned his escape through this region of Chekiang and to that extent he, Chen, had been proven right. There was satisfaction in that, but already it was evaporating. He straightened and looked again at the towel. Conspicuous, glaring white in the sun, carefully sewn with that identifying thread. Caution, he told himself; the towel is a move, like the ship at Shanghai. Lin, too, was staring at the towel.

"He was here," Chen said. "That is all it tells us. Perhaps it was a mistake. A wet towel hung up to dry and then forgotten. But would a man running for his life be so careless? I doubt it." He pointed at Lin's rear pocket. "Give me the map."

The map was large-scale and informative. The camphor grove lay eighty kilometers from Yungan. Chen put his finger on its approximate position, then drew it slowly down the blue line of the Liao. Itself a tributary of the Tsien Tang, it made many azure scrawls where its waters reached into the surrounding terrain. There were ocher masses where the land rose higher, and at one point the river swelled to form a blue oval that was marked as Ogre Head Lake. From there it ran south to feed the Han. On the coast was Swatow. Chen let his fingertip rest on it. He had once spent a month in Swatow organizing a new security arm. The port was built on a promontory and was on the edge of the tropics. That was where he had caught the malaria that returned at times to plague him. He could recall its granite hills and wet heat, the shape of Double Island in the sea mists and the incomprehensible Fukienese dialect. If this was Mackenna's route then at some point south of the grove the truck must surely be exchanged for a boat. Lin's shadow moved across the map.

"Is he making for Swatow?" Lin asked.

"He wants us to think that."

"So the towel is a trick?"

Chen folded the map and returned it.

"Yes," he said. "I believe he left the towel here, then drove back to Yungan and took the road to Amoy. That would have been at sunrise of yesterday." He went to the trees and pulled the towel from the branches. The tiredness came again. He was still in need of rest and hot water and he had begun to sweat in the sun. He took the towel in both hands and rubbed vigorously at his hair, face and neck. "I cannot be sure," he said into the towel. "Mackenna would know I must suspect it. Trick, bluff, counter-bluff. And so on and so on. Perhaps he is really on the way to Swatow. But I have to respond. I have to make a decision." He threw the towel to the captain and Lin offered him a comb.

"No," Chen said coldly. "I am not like you. I do not comb my hair in public."

He walked down the slope to the truck and got in. The truck was pointed at the road that led to the lake and to Swatow. Lin climbed into the passenger seat and Chen saw from the corner of his eye the offended face turn toward him. Ahead through the windshield he could see the river and road. "He wants me down that road," Chen said. "And I will not go."

He started the truck, reversed and turned it. The journey back to Yungan would take two hours.

It was three in the afternoon when they reached Yungan. At the police depot they washed and shaved and ate. Lin made routine calls to the army bases. There was nothing to report. Exceptional vigilance was ordered on the route to Amoy, in the port itself and in its environs.

Amoy lay nearly two hundred kilometers from Yungan. The railway followed for most of the way the course of the Kiulung. But the land was mountainous and the road, newly cut and still unfinished, rose into the mists of height. Chen was forced to drive in the lowest gear; and when the road began its descent into the hill country the sun was already dipping. Now they could see below them terraced slopes, sugarcane and rice. There was no traffic on the road, only a file of porters carrying tea from Chekiang to the coast.

"Once in Szechuan," Lin said, "I saw a column of men. It was snowing and in the distance you could see the mountains of Tibet. They were carrying brick tea and each man's load was so heavy that he was bent almost double. You could not see the end of the column and I was told that there were more than eighty thousand men. It was very cold and at night they would have to sleep by the road in shelters built from the tea chests."

"So?"

"I tell you this because it was after the liberation."

Chen heard the protest in his voice.

"Five years later," Lin said, "it is still the same."

Chen did not immediately answer. He might have said: "Revolutions change nothing, only those in power." But Lin was a minister's son, closer to the ears of government than he, a man with more than an eggcup of foreign blood, could ever be. Words of cynicism, repeated, could be dangerous. Instead he said carefully: "Be patient. Change is always slow."

Chen stopped the truck at a point fifty kilometers from Amoy so that Lin could make a six o'clock radio contact with the army bases. He went to the side of the road to urinate and watched the great green declivities of the land that swept down to the sea and the last rays of the sun that made the water of the paddies glitter like metal. When he returned to the truck Lin had finished the transmissions. Chen saw the concern in his face. There had been a report, Lin told him. A truck from one of the communes had met and passed another truck at about ten or eleven in the morning of yesterday. This was at a point approximately midway between the clump of camphor trees where the towel was found and Ogre Head Lake on the road to Swatow. There were four whites in the truck; a man and a woman in the front and two young boys in the rear. "It seems," Lin said unnecessarily, "that we are on the wrong road."

Chen nodded and turned his face into the sun. Its heat seemed hostile in that moment. He went back to the edge of the road and unbuttoned the collar of his tunic and wiped his throat. "In every game," he said, "a move is more than it appears to be. That must be so. I made an incorrect response."

But driving back up the mountain road toward Yungan, into the coming darkness, he was aware of tension. Perhaps the game was already lost. Where there was quality in the opposition one error could mean defeat. In this contest time was the major piece. There was a mounting sum; the day stolen from him by Dr. Li's treachery, hours lost on the journey to and from the perimeter of Shanghai, further hours wasted on this the Amoy road. But Mackenna too might have suffered reverses; mishaps, delays, engine problems, failures in the escape route. Anything could happen. The sun was gone and the crags leaned over one side of the fading road. Chen switched on the headlamps and with the sudden brilliance felt the depth of unseen chasms. The missionary would not leave his mind and the grooved but boyish face flickered like a wraith in the forming mist. Where are you now? he said to it. Where?

Ellen Mackenna bent across him. It was dark between the walls of the gorge with only the faintest starlight to touch the raft and the river. The face of a boy, she thought; as if in sleep all the experience has sloughed off to reveal its first innocence. He awakened in that moment and reached up and pulled her down and she lay against him until he had drifted back to sleep. Then she left him and sat up. Behind her the two boys were curled between the tea chests, and behind the chests was the haystack and its garlands of mosquitoes. In front were the raftmen. They stood at opposite corners of the raft. This was deep water. The points of the spars would not find the river bed. They were using paddles and from time to time she saw the broad wooden leaves dip and felt the raft swing into some new tunnel of darkness. This was the strangest journey of her life and she sat there with her fingers in the bark of the tree trunks and felt beneath her the throb of the river's endless life. Sometimes when there was turbulence the raft was lifted and the river struck its underside and came up between the trunks. She was at one with the river, feeling its incalculable age, the presence of those who since the beginning had been borne on it like this; on rafts of trees or bamboo or goat-skins. She watched the river and the rock buttresses coming out of the dark, and did not move. Once she smelled woodsmoke and knew that somewhere in the gorge's alleys men were camped for the night; and, later, when the raft went close to the shore, she saw the body of the executed man, a black shape against a denser blackness. The tiny raft was wedged in the river's teeth so that the gibbet leaned at an angle and the man's legs were stretched in the current as if the river sought to take him. Later still the enclosing rock retreated and the river broadened and was divided by an island and the raft swung to the left of it, so near that she could see the roots of trees standing like mangroves. Then when the raft kept its leftward course and the rock walls moved in again to make the river narrow she knew that they were no longer in the mainstream. It was still very dark and she lay back on the sodden blanket and looked up at the sky above the gorge's towers, joining in the stars (as she had always done as a child) images of animals and gods. Sleep was near. The stars passed. The Chinese called it the River of Heaven. She closed her eyes. Rivers of water and rivers of stars and she and the old river flowing down the palm of the universe: to where?

She slept.

When she awakened the sky was pale with the first light and she saw that they had emerged from the gorge. More mountain ranges lay ahead, but here the river was wider and there was flat land on one side of it. The raftmen were still dipping with the paddles and, lying on her back, she watched their shapes rising and falling with the motion of the raft. She could hear Lewis' deep breathing beside her and she rose and went to the side of the raft so that she could look out across the water-sheeted land. In the middle distance a boy was tending a water buffalo. She had the eye of a painter, although no more than a small talent, and she saw the scene as if it were a picture; everything soft because the night had not yet left it and the buffalo milk-white with stockings of black mud and both the boy and the animal unmoving in the mist. So still and fragile, she thought, faintly brushed on the surface of a pearl. She watched until the river curved and the scene was gone. When she turned she could see ahead of the raft and between the figures of the raftmen. A junk with a brown lugsail was moored in the shadow of a rock outcrop.

"It's the *Shantung*," Lewis said behind her.

There were two hours to midnight when Chen stopped the truck in the yard of the police depot at Yungan. Sleep was now essential. Lin had not awakened and was slumped in the passenger seat and Chen, unwilling to face a straw pallet in the odorous concrete barracks, went to the rear of the truck and lay down on his blanket. Sleep was also a stealer of time; but not, perhaps, for Mackenna. If, as was likely, he had left the motor road for the water then this coming night would give him an immediate advantage. A sailboat might make a hundred kilometers during the hours of darkness, a petrol launch twice that distance. The figures angered him. He resolved to rise early and take the road down to Ogre Head Lake and Swatow before dawn. He had always been able to pre-set an infallible alarm clock in his mind and awaken at a chosen time. He shut his eyes and, as sleep invaded, told himself silently: You will awake at four in the morning. He tried to imagine the little tumblers clicking into place. Four in the morning. Four in the morning.

But it was not the mental clock that jerked him from a dream. It was Lin's arm. The sun, high and climbing, struck into the truck. "Nearly eight," Lin said. Chen left the truck. The anger reclaimed him. Four hours lost. They could be crucial. He stood in the sun and stroked his aching head, as if he might feel beneath his fingers the mechanism that had betrayed him.

When they had washed and drunk tea in the depot Chen walked down the street and bought some apples, pibas and lichees from a fruit vendor. Lin followed in the truck. It was eight-thirty when they left the town. Ahead, between the two steel-gray hills of wolfram ore that fed the tungsten mills, was the Swatow road. Ninety minutes later they passed the camphor grove. From there the road climbed through the river valley with the Liao and its bamboo fringe below them. Here the mountains were rising close to the river and Chen could see their high forests and the lower slopes that were denuded of trees. He could also see men bringing down the trunks, a hut encampment, more men at work on the shore, the shapes of rafts. He stopped the truck, took an apple from its bag and went to the edge of the road. He began to eat. Lin joined him with the lichees. There were fifteen rafts of varying size; twelve of them afloat and moored, three unfinished on the sand of the shore. On the largest a party of men were chaining a rudder in place and building a shelter. They could hear the distant sound of hammers.

"Do the rafts go to the coast?" Chen asked.

"I don't know."

"Then find out."

Lin walked around the truck and Chen heard him searching for an area map. He watched a pair of cormorants fly down the river, the shadows of the wings beating on the water and the beaks like yellow needles in the sun. Lin returned with the map and touched a point on the Han River that was fifty or sixty kilometers from its estuary at Swatow. "Pai-shang," he said. The finger moved to the little ideogram that was drawn against the name. "Sawmills."

Chen threw his apple core over the edge.

"A raft?" Lin asked. "Is that possible?"

"Why not? A raft among rafts in the season of rafts. A convoy of rafts that never stops." Chen climbed into the driving seat. "A raft would be intelligent." He pointed to the rear. "You know what to do." He ate another apple and listened to the transmission that Lin was sending to Army Base Five. Soon all the resources of a Special Alert would be concentrated in and around Pai-shang, on the Liao and the Han, in the port of Swatow and its flanking coasts.

But driving up the escarpment road high above the river Chen could see in his mind only the way this land would be under the shawl of night. In the beginning some great convulsion had twisted it into ravines and canyons, valleys and peaks, pinnacles of rock. In all this the rivers and their countless veins ran. The airplanes and helicopters could not search in the hours of darkness, except in the broadest of channels; and the raft, if raft it was, might very well arrange its journey for the nightfall.

It was three-forty in the afternoon when they saw Ogre Head Lake. The road descended above precipitous drops, the lake so small with distance that they could not see the features of the ogre's face, only an outcrop stretching into the tiny pool like an otter's paw. Now there were stone parapets defining the worst of the bends and, rounding one of them, they saw below and still high on the scarp a group of perhaps a dozen men and a mule cart. Some of the men were standing at the lip of the road and staring down at the river. Chen stopped the truck by the cart. They got out. The cart was piled with rice and there were yokes and bales of rock salt on the road. A man in a cotton head-scarf came forward. There had been an accident. No, they had not seen it happen. He pointed at the lip and a gap in the stone blocks. Bad accident. Chen and Lin followed him to the gap.

The cliff was almost vertical. It fell, ledged and hung with clematis, to where the river washed its base; a drop, Chen thought, of about twenty-five meters. The water was clear and they could see the shape of a vehicle upside down on the bed. It was slightly darkened by depth and the shadow of an overhang. One of the doors was open and a few small fish came out of the interior. The man in the scarf touched his arm and shook his head. Finished. Drowned. There was no pity in his voice or eyes. The river had always claimed. He turned and went to the cart and the men picked up their burdens. Chen heard them shuffle down the road. He continued to study the vehicle. It was plainly a truck. But whose? Had its loss been reported? Was it from a commune or from a town? Or were Mackenna and his family trapped inside? A straw hat, apparently shot from the truck during its fall, was caught halfway down in the flowering vines. Was it Mackenna's? The missionary had always been a man for hats. Straw hats, felt hats, cotton caps and silk caps, even an absurd glengarry that someone had sent to him from Scotland; he had a way of wearing hats so that they were an essential part of him and when he was without one he became noticeably different, like a man with a missing ear.

"Perhaps we could reach it," Lin said.

Chen walked slowly up the curve of the road. Higher where the hillside bulged he found the scar where the truck had struck and below it a mess of earth and rock, glass and metal. He turned and stared downhill to the broken parapet. Such an impact, perhaps at night, might easily snap a steering rod, swing the truck and send it uncontrollable across the road and over the edge. He walked down to the parapet, following the line that the truck would have taken. He could not see Lin. Then he heard a gasp, a scratching sound from somewhere below him. He went to the gap and looked down. Lin was pinned on the cliff face, searching for a hold. Chen watched him move from ledge to ledge, his fingers in the roots of vines and crevices. When he reached the hat he bent and retrieved it and put it on his head. He looked up and laughed, began the climb back.

"That was foolish," Chen said. He reached down and pulled Lin over the parapet and onto the road, took the hat from his head. It was old, with a high weather-stained crown and a broken rim. He turned it and saw that the inner band, rotted by sweat, had been repaired with scraps of snakeskin. He stroked the black-white stripes and, now, he was standing again in the compound at the Fusan camp, the wire near and beyond it the swamp-green hills. I remember. I remember the gaunt face that once was shadowed by this hat and the missionary sitting on the earth, the hat and an improvised bamboo needle in his hands and beside him the skin of the krait cut into strips. The needle had split and he had murmured:

"Difficult stuff, bamboo." And he, Chen, had looked down and said: "You are supposed to stand when you talk to a Chinese officer." But he had known in the moment of speaking that Mackenna was too weak to stand without great effort and he had turned and walked away. Later he had sent him a packet of steel needles and some eggs.

"Well?" Lin asked.

"Yes," Chen said. "It's his."

He stroked the band again. Paper crackled and he opened the band and extracted some currency notes. "Fifty yuan," he said. He went to the lip of the road and stared down again at the water and the truck. The straw hat established its ownership. On the face of it the hat had leaped from the truck during the fall down the cliff. But of course nothing now was obvious. The wastebasket and the torn notepaper, the family Bible left in the church, the towel on the camphor tree—all of these were moves. Their object was delay. The truck too could be a move, the currency notes a sacrifice to disguise it. He folded the notes and put them into his pocket. "They are not our property," he said to Lin. "Remind me to pay them in." But uncertainty was growing. It had all the appearances of a genuine accident; the dangerous nature of the bend, the violence of the hillside impact, the smashed parapet. Fear of pursuit might push a man into unwise speeds. Another question formed. Why should Mackenna confirm the line of his escape route? If I had taken to the river, Chen thought, I would have concealed the truck in the bamboo. He watched the fish making silver darts around the truck. Are you there? he asked silently. He had a fear of drowning. It was rooted in the heart of a sea-wave that had taken him in his childhood years and he would not wish that kind of death even upon an enemy. Fifty yuan. Consider the amount. It was not insignificant, perhaps four weeks' pay for an average worker. But for a European it was small. So the sum became convincing. Hatband money was a reserve; and a larger sum might well be evidence of a trick. So many questions. Would a man of learning, a doctor of theology and of medicine, carry money in his hat like a sailor? Yes, he said, answering himself. If he had been in Fusan, where a prisoner would secrete a thing of value in a boot or a hat, he might not lose that habit.

"Well?" Lin asked again.

"I don't know," Chen said. "If the sum were larger I would suspect it. I would drive on now. I would waste no time." He turned the hat again within his fingers. This old but cherished thing might be more of a sacrifice than the money. He wiped his face. The heat, the special heat that becomes malevolent in the late afternoon, was rebounding off the walls of the escarpment. He could feel it like a cinder inside his head, mists of indecision. I don't know. I don't know. He is stupid, clever, transparent, subtle, over-subtle, he is sailing to freedom, he is dead below me in the water. I cannot decide. He crossed the road and walked around the truck so that he could stand in its shadow. He saw his reflection in one of the windows and on an impulse set the straw hat upon his head. His face was almost totally changed. He heard a footfall and saw amusement in Lin's gentle eyes. He threw the hat into the truck and looked at his watch. It was four-twenty-eight. Within two hours the sun would sink below the peaks. He pointed at the gap in the parapet.

"We have to know if they are down there," he said. "We have to know before nightfall. Get back to Army Base Five. We need a helicopter and a diver."

But when the sun was quartered on the ridge and the first redness was in the sky Chen knew that the helicopter would not come until the morning. Time had been lost on this road above the river. Now they must wait through the hours of darkness. "How can we go on?" he said. "We have to know."

"Yes," Lin said. "We have to know." He went to the rear of the truck and when he emerged from its shadow and walked to the parapet Chen saw that he was undressed. Standing there on the broken lip in his blue underpants he was as slight and lissome as a boy. He bent and found a sliver of stone, tossed it over the lip and watched its fall and its passage through the water to the river bed. He smiled and said: "Easy." Chen felt a sudden alarm. "No," he said. "Don't do it." But Lin was already poised for the dive and Chen, crossing the road, saw the brown rib-sharp body spring outward into a perfect swallow. When he reached the lip Lin had struck the water and there was only a white froth, ripples lapping at the cliff base. He waited, tensed with anxiety and then the beginning of fear, knowing in those seconds of waiting that Lin had become important to him, had touched some arid part of him that he had thought was dead. He waited, waited. Then the water cleared and he could see the truck and Lin ascending and his face, now, smiling up at him from the surface. The voice came faintly up the cliff. "Empty." Lin turned in the water and pointed downstream and Chen watched him begin the swim to the lake. He watched until Lin's head had become a small dark gourd going with the current down the red path of the sun. He felt an unexpected envy. He went to the truck and got in. I have never been young, he told himself; a chessboard instead of a high dive into a wild river, nothing beyond the engines of the mind. He drove down the scarp, carrying the sterile years like a weight.

The road, Chen knew from the map, would leave the Liao at a point above the lake and rise again to mountain height before it fell in steep loops to rejoin the river. He decided to drive through the night to where the rafts ended their voyage at the sawmills. Army Base Five was near to Pai-shang and there was a police post in the town. He collected Lin at the shore and drove up the gradient into the last flare of sunset light. Looking down on the lake it seemed that the ogre's eye-sockets were rimmed with blood.

"Another piece to Mackenna," Chen said. "Another delay." He could see Lin prinking his wet hair with his palms. "But I'm relieved they were not in the truck. The family, you understand? Such a death." Words of compassion, he thought; but not wholly honest. Driving up into the gathering night he wanted to confide in Lin. "Once," he said, "I gave him his life. I returned him to his wife and children. He repaid me with treachery. But I don't want him dead in a river. That would be a kind of escape, wouldn't it?" He shook his head. "He betrayed the State. I want him tried by the State. And I want him punished by the State."

By midmorning the wind in the gorges had died and the *Shantung* would make no headway without the tows. There were fifteen trackers on the junk and when they had climbed from the bow to the shallows and from there to the river bank Lewis Mackenna left the shade of the canvas roof that was rigged outside the stern cabin and walked down the deck to the rope forward rail. Joel and Gerard were already there and he stood behind them and watched the trackers strain against their wooden halters and saw the tow-lines lift from the water and go taut. The junk moved.

"The current is behind us," Joel said. "They could not move her without the current."

"It's not much of a current," Gerard said.

"No. But if the current was against us they could not move her."

"They'd move her all right," Lewis said. "But they'd use more men. On the really big junks I've seen as many as a hundred trackers."

Behind and above them on the turret the junkmaster had begun to beat his drum. The junk moved faster, each forward step synchronized with the beat and the echoes flighting up among the rawboned faces of the gorge and even the breath expelled in unison from the fifteen mouths. There was an illusion that the junk itself was panting like a live thing down the river. "At one time," Lewis told them, "the mandarins would put a man with a whip on the bank. They would not let the junk lose speed and at the end of a trip there'd be empty halters where men had died." He stared down at the line of bent and knotted backs. "Perhaps one day they'll abolish it."

"Like they did with the rickshaws," Gerard said.

"Yes," Lewis said. There had been shame in that too; men running between the shafts, running all the years between boyhood and decrepitude.

"I'm glad they stopped the rickshaw men," Gerard said.

Lewis left them and walked around the turret cabin (which was the master's) and crossed the foredeck to the opposite rail. There were four men on the bow sweep. It had been fashioned from a tree trunk and he stood there for a time and watched them hold the junk against the lateral pull of the trackers. Abaft the mast was the crew shelter; and below the deck were cargo compartments, six separated areas divided by the bulkheads. The hatches were open and, walking down toward the stern, he could smell resinous scents of oil and spices, cotton, salt and grain. Everything was carved from hardwood and the frames of the cabin windows displayed little marquetries that were as graceful as the scrolls of violins. The stern tiller was the lunging neck of a dragon and he stopped and put his hand inside its open redwood jaws. "This boat is a work of art," he said to Ellen with admiration. He pointed at the tholepins, which, serving as oar locks for the sweep, tapered up into the beaks of swans. "Surely she was built for an emperor." He looked around him. "One could live on her forever, sail up and down the great rivers and be at peace."

She nodded. Peace was a word of beauty.

"We're on our way," he said softly. "Well on our way."

Behind her he could see the three steps that led down to the floor level of the cabin. With its two tiers of small mullioned windows it was like the poop of a medieval ship. The cabin doors were hooked back and the engraved glass threw shimmering discs of unstill river light onto the two Long Jing tea chests. He had seen the flicker of interest in the junkmaster's eyes when the chests were brought aboard. "Papers," he had explained. "Books and family things." The lie had come glibly. But the man had plucked a length of straw from under the nailed lid and had put it between his teeth and the eyes became sly with disbelief. How safe are we? Lewis wondered. He went down into the cabin and stared at the chests. The lids were secure but the sides would break under the toe of a boot. There was a fortune nestling in the straw. Most of the pieces were beautiful. He stood with his hand on one of the chests and watched the river through the stern windows.

In the middle afternoon the wind returned and filled the lugsail and the trackers came aboard and lay heaving with exhaustion under the midship shelter. Lewis went again to the bows. The river had narrowed and was compressed between high greenstone cliffs. Sun struck against them so that a luminous green light was shed on the water, the cypress of the junk, the flesh of the hands. This was a world of brooding gorges and sudden bird cries and he felt himself respond to the wildness of the place. Once, when the gorge opened into a cleft, he saw a pagoda on a distant hill. He watched it, gleaming like an ivory chessman, until the gorge closed in again. He could have likened it to any white ivory carving; but he had seen it as a chessman and he knew from this that John Chen, never really absent, had reoccupied his mind.

In the final hour of sunlight the *Shantung* hove to. From its portside rail Lewis could see where the cliffs recessed to form a creek. A man was standing on its farther bank. He was bearded and he wore a turban of emerald silk. It was the posture, as much as the turban, that identified him; the thrust of the beard, the stillness of him that was really alertness, the way in which his round traveling bundle, tied at the neck, was held dangling from his left hand on a loop of plaited string. Shameen. You are the one they call Shameen; and I can see you now on the rise of the hill that day in December of 1941 when we were running from the Japanese occupation of Shanghai. The Fellowship had founded the first of its Chinese missions in that city; but the minister had died and there was no immediate replacement and we had left the Hangchow mission in Dr. Li's speckled hands and had gone, temporarily, up to the city and the little yellow church in Nanking Road. The Japanese were in control of all the areas outside the International Settlement (as, indeed, they controlled Hangchow), but the rivers of commerce continued to run and most of the Europeans stayed and listened to the gunfire and went to the Long Bar and the Shanghai Race Club and watched the English playing cricket. But when, two weeks before that Christmas of 1941, the Nippon planes made their runs above Pearl Harbor the position changed. Japan was now an enemy of America and all those who sheltered under the Allied flags. The scent of danger was in the winds that blew in across the Yangtze and across the port and the city and we, that is Ellen and myself and a party of men and women drawn mainly from Sassoon's and Jardine Matheson and the National City and Chase banks of New York, decided to make the long journey west to Chungking where Chiang Kai-shek and his Kuomintang government had established the capital of Free China. And so it was that, leaving Shanghai, we crossed the Tai Lake to the hills outside the little town of Wu-Hsi. The Japanese were there too and we could see their semaphore lamps flashing in the mountains behind the hills and, walking, we looked up to the rise and you were waiting there, as you are waiting now, with a bundle hanging from your hand; except that the bundle was the head of a Japanese soldier and the string was threaded through the ears and you were holding it away from you fastidiously, as you are holding the bundle now, so that it would not stain your leg and you were as still as a sculpture, as still as you are now, and, then, you came down the rise and laid the head at our feet as if it were an offering and we knew from this that you were not an enemy. You were called Shameen, you told us. This was not your true name but was really the name of the tiny island with the shape of a ship and an avenue of flame trees that lay off the Canton mainland and you had been sent there as a small boy from your home in the north because, you told us, your entire family, from the youngest to the eldest, had been sentenced to burial alive, which was the old punishment for subversion. So the family name died in the choking earth and you, the survivor, could never use that name again and became Shameen. But you never told us where your home had been. It would be somewhere in Turkestan and, we thought, with your sharp Tartar face and hook nose, curling brown beard and Moslem faith, you were probably a Tungan. Certainly on that journey of 850 miles there was a Tartar fierceness in the way in which you lopped the heads and garotted the throats of Japanese soldiers, Ching Shan bandits and Nationalist deserters. You were a young man then but you had been born with these dark and secret skills and we were uneasy in your presence. But you led us to Chungking and we were grateful. Later you became one of the Generalissimo's guards and then, because you were exceptional, his only guard; and I can recall those years of friendship with Chiang when he and I played chess and talked of politics and Methodism and you were always near to the presidential palace; sometimes a shadow on a blind or a shape seen and then not seen among the Buddhas on the terrace or a green turban glowing for a moment in the evergreen darkness of the thickets; so alert that you would turn at the fall of a leaf or the lifting of a bird's wing. I remember you, Shameen.

They did not speak when Shameen came aboard. He was a devout Moslem and this, the twilight hour, was one of the times for prayer and Lewis saw him walk on his soft goatskin shoes to the bow and sit on the little area of foredeck that was partly concealed by the jutting flank of the master's cabin. He removed his shoes, opened the bundle and took from it a purification jar. Then, kneeling now, he uncorked the jar and sprinkled water on his face, hands, arms and feet. When the prayer was finished he raised his hands and touched the backs of his ears, bowed toward Mecca, rose and bowed again. Lewis waited until he had returned the jar to the bundle. Then he walked along the deck to the bow and Shameen turned and Lewis saw that there was gray in his beard, that the years had made grooves down his cinnamon jaws. He had not seen him since early 1949 and a few months later Chungking was in flames and Mao's men were in the palace and Chiang and his generals had fled to Taiwan. Yet there was still unease in his presence, still the same feel of supple menace. A gold brooch was pinned in his rough camel-hair waistcoat. It was in the shape of a stake with a head impaled on it and had been, Lewis knew, a rare and personal gift from Chiang. He pointed at it and said: "Do you still guard the president?"

"Yes."

"Is he well?"

"Yes."

"And Madame Chiang?"

"Well."

"Did he send you to protect us?"

"Yes."

"That's good," Lewis said. "Very, very good."

He turned and walked back to the stern. Ellen was at the rail and he put his arm around her and smiled into her face and said: "Be thankful."

"For Shameen?"

"Yes. He's here to guard us."

"One man?"

"One special man."

After nightfall the junk was taken slowly by oar through the darkness of the gorge. This was the time for food and the master and most of the crew were under the deck shelter. Ellen sat with her back to the doorjamb of the stern cabin. They had given her two bowls, one of stew and one of rice. Behind her in the cabin she could hear the voices of Lewis and the boys. The food was good. There was an iron plate set in the deck planks and before sundown they had built fires with dried reeds and wood and had hung above them three caldrons and into the largest they had put water, mutton, vegetables and spices. Shameen sat apart in a well of shadow at the extreme of the shelter, not speaking except, once, to ask the master in his soft and sonorous Mandarin for an assurance that there was no part of a pig in the stew. She watched the scene through the steam that rose from the bowls, seeing it (as she had seen the boy and the water buffalo in the light of the dawn) as if it were a picture. If we get to Taiwan, she thought, I could try to paint it. If? That was an unexpected word, surfacing from all the despair of the last few days. Yet she could feel a rekindling of hope. They had been utterly alone. But, then, the raft had come; and then the junk; and then Shameen. Above all Shameen. The president had sent them his own incomparable bodyguard, across the Strait, across country to this lonely place. Shameen would lead them to Taiwan as he had once led them to Chungking. She finished the food and a man came and took the two bowls and gave her a glass of white rice brandy and she sipped it and felt its crudeness burn her tongue. Behind her Joel (or was it Gerard?) tapped his bowl and said: "It's jolly good. But what is it?" And Lewis laughed and said: "It's Mongolian Hotpot." "Really?" "Yes, really." And all three laughed and she too smiled and stared across the rim of the glass and tried to imagine the painting it might make. It was too vivid for the pale washes of a watercolor or the ink-on-silk that the Chinese masters used, which, with its spidery lines and faint pink and white lusters, always seemed as delicate as a rose petal. It needed the texture of oil on canvas, vibrant color moving through the night. See how the light from the glass chimneys of the oil lamps touches the ring of dark and meditative faces and the edge of the sail; how that hand is foreshortened as it reaches toward the brass bowl so that the fingertips are broad and spatulate above an unseen palm; the way in which the breeze fans the embers and makes the hot deck-plate go momentarily pink and how the lampshine touches the old earthenware oil jars and turns their hips orange and is reflected on the dried-biltong face of the old man who is breaking bits of brick tea into a kettle; and how it reaches further into darkness to the glass of water that, freshened with a fig, sits in thin strangler's fingers and rebounds from the glass to the head of a gold pin and up to that Tungan face and the lines in it that are as deep as claw marks and higher still to make a sliver of green in the turban and then faintly glows on the black wall of the gorge so that the feldspar crystals shine for a second like a necklace hung on the rock. And beyond the junk the night as black as a Bible. If you were good enough that is how the painting would look. And if you were a Rembrandt and understood the use and mystery of light and darkness all the detail of the foreground would fade and one face, that assassin's face lurking in the depth of shadow, would remain to trouble the mind.

Later in the night Lewis awakened. It was very hot in the cabin and he rose from the blanket that was spread on the floor and went up onto the deck. There was no breeze in the sail and he could hear the creak and splash of the oars. He walked to the bow and leaned across the rail so that he might find some movement of air from where the hull parted the river. A diffused moonlight touched the arch of the bow and the shape that had been painted on it. He had seen it from a distance on boarding the junk and had thought that it was the usual eye that, symbolically, would watch for danger. But now, near to it and looking down, he saw that it was the stylized diagram of a fish. It was painted in a continuous line, beginning at the point of the head and forming the curve of the body and the square-ended tail, then recrossing under the tail and returning along the opposing curve to meet the point of origin. He stared at it. He had once drawn such a fish; in exactly that shape, in exactly that way. He stood there for a time with the fish turning silver in the light. Then he left the rail and lay down on the deck and closed his eyes. But sleep would not come and he felt himself enter the jade gate of memory and, now, the fish grew and swam on a concrete wall in the glare of sun.

Chapter 5

From the first line of prisoners Lewis Mackenna watched the bamboo cane rapping on the head of the fish. I forgot to draw its eye, he thought. Without the eye it does not have the expression of a fish. Teng Hua, Commander of the Fusan penal camp, had begun to pace with short urgent steps up and down the flank wall of the execution shed, scratching with the cane at the charcoal outline of the fish, rapping so that the sounds rang across the silent compound. The three guards shuffled. Teng stopped and turned, his eyes so narrowed against the strong sun that they were like stitches.

"It was done during the night," he said. "One of you drew this fish." He had been a teacher at the American School in Shanghai before the revolution took him into the People's Liberation Army and here in Compound One, where there were many Europeans and Americans, he always addressed them in clear and accurate English. He bent and picked up a charred stick and held it out toward them. "And it was done with this." He threw the stick to the ground. Then he pointed with the cane and moved it slowly so that it described an arc. "Which of you did it?"

There was no answer.

"I am waiting."

There was still no answer and Teng swished the air with the cane, then pointed with it to where a frail and elderly man was leaning on a stick.

"Father Methuen," he said, "is the oldest man in the camp. If the culprit does not own up I will have the Father beaten."

Lewis stepped forward.

"You again, Dr. Mackenna?"

"Yes."

"Come here."

Lewis crossed the space between the line and the shed. His legs were weak and he could hear his feet dragging on the earth.

"Are you ill?" Teng asked.

"All of us are ill."

"All?"

"All the whites. We cannot live on a few grains of rice."

"Are you not alive?"

"Just."

"Then be grateful." Teng rapped again on the wall. "Do you admit to drawing this fish?"

"Fish?"

"Yes, fish."

"I don't think that's a fish, Commander."

"Then what is it?"

Lewis stared at the charcoal shape. Behind the wall was the place where Father Tsai had been put to death. They had come for him at midnight and every man in the compound had known and waited and listened. But there had been no sound to indicate the manner of his dying; only the sounds of a door closing and the shooting of a bolt and boots marching away into the night. Later, when the camp was silent, he had left the hut and walked to the shed and, standing in the moon-bars, had offered a prayer for the soul of that kind and gentle man. Tsai had been the sole remaining priest in the church behind the Rice Market in Hangchow; and although it was the Church of Rome and therefore a rival he, Lewis, had known and loved Tsai for many years and he had often gone there and listened to him preach and minister in his strange mixture of Latin and Chinese. After the service he would sometimes walk to the garden at the rear where there were willows and evening primroses and wait on one of the stone seats and, soon, Tsai would join him and his face would be flushed and dewy from the fervor of the preaching. Seated and talking his hand would always toy with the tiny silver-filigree fish that hung on a chain from his neck to glint on the blackness of his cassock. He was asked constantly why he wore a fish instead of a crucifix and he would smile and say: "At one time it meant the same." But the Red Guards had come for him and accused him of seditious sermons and they had built a fire outside the church and burned his Bibles and hymn sheets and missals and then they had put the wax saints and angels into the flames so that they writhed like early martyrs and then dissolved into rivers of colored wax running down the flags. Standing by the shed it was the little fish that emerged from all the grief and he had gone to the embers of one of the cooking-fires and found a length of charred kindling and, returning to the wall, had drawn the immense outline of the fish.

"Well?" Teng asked.

"I don't know. It could be anything."

"But you drew it, did you not?"

"Yes."

"If you drew it you must know what it is."

Lewis shook his head. He could see the pulse beating in Teng's temple.

Teng was dangerous, a man inflamed by sudden rages. Like most of the prisoners he was afraid of Teng; and it was fear, he now knew, that had crept into his fingers and made him draw the fish. It had seemed a sufficient gesture in the small hours of the night; clever too because only he and the dead priest would understand it. But here in the light of day in a place from which God was banished it did not seem to be much of an epitaph. He shook his head again: it was like a denial of Father Tsai himself.

"It is a fish," Teng said. He struck the wall with the cane. "That is the head. That is the body. And that is the tail."

"No."

"Yes. It is plainly a fish." He turned from the wall. "But of course it is much more than a fish. Do you take me for a fool? I have a knowledge of history. Of Romans and Christians." He scratched the cane through the length of the fish. "This is an ancient symbol of Christianity. Do you know that?"

"Yes."

"Tell the truth and own up." Now it was the schoolmaster speaking. "Isn't that why you drew it?"

"Yes."

Teng walked behind him and the cane lashed very hard across his thighs. The pain was so intense that his bowels, already weakened by the dysentery, voided themselves and his legs collapsed and he fell to his knees. Teng beat him until his arm was tired and when the beating was finished Lewis opened his eyes. They were wet with tears and, still kneeling and looking at the wall, it seemed through the tears that the fish was flickering in water. He heard Teng turn on his heel to face the prisoners and the high nasal voice crossing the compound. "I warned you that in this camp there is no Christ, no God, no Holy Ghost. I warned you that I would not permit any kind of Christian worship. No prayers. No hymns. No Bibles. No Communions. No Masses. No requiems for the dead. I warned you that you would not be permitted to carry a crucifix or make a sign of the Cross—" Faintness made him sway and Teng's voice retreated. But the words echoed in his mind. The sign of the Cross. He could see the piece of charred stick and he reached out and picked it up, then rose and went to the wall. He drew a long perpendicular, crossed it with a short transverse stroke. Teng was still speaking. "I warned you. You are not permitted an immortal soul. There is no divine law, only the law of the State. You will obey it—" Now the guards were pointing and Teng stopped and turned and stared at the wall. Lewis drew a circle to represent a head, a serrated line for the crown of thorns, the hanging stick-limbs of the crucified Christ.

"Last night," Lewis said in the silence, "you murdered a man. A good man. A saintly man. He was a priest. There are many priests in this camp. Yet you did not give him the comfort of a priest and he did not hear a final sacrament. But he was not alone. God was with him."

"You will not use that word," Teng said.

One of the guards dug a furrow in the earth with the point of his bayonet. Lewis saw the sun reflect from the steel. He was afraid again. He wanted to repeat the word but it would not come and he stood there in the glare in the stench of his own soiling and heard in the silence the claws of a lizard scuttling on the wall. He could see the challenge in Teng's bright angry eyes. "Not that word," Teng said softly. He waited but Lewis did not speak. The lizard moved down the charcoal Cross. Teng smiled and put his hand into his pocket and took something out and held out the hand and when the fingers opened Father Tsai's silver fish swung on its chain and Lewis saw in that moment the priest's commiserative face above the fish and he was released from the fear and said loudly so that the prisoners should hear: "God was with him." And Father Methuen looked up from where the knuckles of his hands were bunched on the handle of his stick and raised his head and cried out in his age-thin voice: "God was with him." And, then, the men in the compound began to mutter the words and the muttering swelled into a chant with every man crying out in unison. "God was with him. God was with him. God was with him."

These had been heady moments of defiance and for a time it was even possible to understand those men of the past, some of them saints, who had suffered the fire or other torments because they would not deny their faith. But of course the elation did not last. He had not yet been punished; and Teng Hua, despite his rages, knew the value of anticipation. They did not come for him during that day, and he lay awake on his bunk for most of the night and listened to the sounds of the hut, sounds that had become so familiar that he hardly noticed them. Gottlieb Roth was whimpering in his sleep and, above him on the second tier, Pastor Irwin snored and bubbled through his flattened nose. Somewhere in the darkness a man was weeping and, soon, Ed Gallagher would once again relive his beatings and growl and twist until the spasms of his limbs jerked him from his dreams. The door of the hut was never locked and when the mosquitoes and the humidity were bad men would sometimes sleep on the ground outside. In the hour before dawn Lewis rose and left the hut and crossed the compound to the wire fence.

There had been a rainfall and the drops hung on the barbs and made little points of brilliance in the starshine. He hated barbed wire and for him it was now and always would be a symbol of captivity. From here at the fence he could see some of the other compounds and the roofs of huts, the yellow lights of the barracks and, beyond it all, the belt of high bamboo that ringed the camp. Fusan lay in a bowl in the Tsing-hai region of western China. It had been built in the late 1930s for those senior Japanese prisoners of war who, for one reason or another, had not been chopped; and from that beginning it had grown. Now there were six compounds, each separated from the others by a wire rectangle, each containing around two hundred men. Some of the Japanese were still there. Most were political prisoners, dissidents or active enemies of the new regime; and perhaps a third were believers, lay or ordained, who were not content to whisper the Christian message. Some, like himself, had openly supported the deposed Chiang Kai-shek or were connected to him by blood or allegiance. And there were those, like Father Tsai, who had been sentenced by the People's Courts and had come to Fusan for execution. There were many grave-digging parties and sometimes when the spades struck deep enough they would expose the remains of stone walls and foundations and there would be fragments of pottery and terra cotta shards in the soil. Father Methuen (whose fourth passion after the Trinity was archaeology) had told him that here under their feet there had once been a seventeenth-century settlement. But he was not impressed. The past could easily be found under China's antique skin and, because he had been brought to the camp in the night hours and had never left it during his nine months' imprisonment, he was more interested in what lay beyond it. East of the camp, Methuen explained, were the waters of the Huang Ho; and if you walked to the west to the crown of the bamboo hills it was possible to see the snows of the distant Kun-lun mountains. The land, rising to the north over many hundreds of miles, was as rich as a carpet and fat with grass and it was there that they were developing the great hide export industry. It was said that during the summer before the Mongolian cold came down you might see half a million head of cattle. There was a little oasis farming but mostly it was pastures, beasts and the communes that tended them. These grasslands began no more than a few miles from the camp and surely, Methuen asked, you must have heard a distant lowing when the wind changed? After that he had listened for the lowing and had even heard it once or twice and, then, the visions came; beef so near to starving men, beef in such incredible quantity that the merest fraction of it would help to cure the beriberi and other nutritional diseases with which they were afflicted.

He heard feet shuffling across the compound. The camp was a place of shuffling feet but he knew at once that they were Gallagher's. The American, like many in Fusan, suffered from a recurrent dengue. Some called it breakbone fever and it was conveyed by the bite of the little mosquito (known to Lewis by its family name of *aedes aegypti*) that during the hot months was their constant companion. It had involved his knee joints so that, shuffling from weakness, he also limped from pain. His approach was so distinctive that Lewis did not turn, and when he reached the wire he put out a hand to support himself and the barbs shed their raindrops. A wind was gathering and they stood there listening to its sighs as it clawed around the huts.

"Did you hear that?" Lewis asked.

"The wind?"

"No. Not the wind."

Gallagher smiled. "The beef again?"

"I thought I heard it."

Gallagher shook his head. "I don't hear any cattle." Then, seriously: "You have more to worry about than an empty gut, Lewis."

"I know."

"That Teng is a bad one. He's going to come for you."

"Yes."

"Funny how bookworms can be such bastards."

"Yes, funny."

Gallagher turned and Lewis saw the anxiety in his face. It was a good face but gaunt and prematurely aged by imprisonment. He had once been a flier and he had come to China in 1942 with the U.S. Army's Fourteenth Air Force. From then until the end of the war he had flown military freight through the Himalayan passes that lay between India and Yunnan. But he had not gone home with his unit and he had taken his discharge in China and remained to fly for the next four years for Generalissimo Chiang and after the defeat the ones now in power had remembered and they had arrested him and sent him without trial to Fusan. He was forgotten and Lewis did not think he would ever be charged or even that he would be strong enough to fly again.

"Why did you do it?" Gallagher asked. "All that Hallelujah stuff. Drawing things on walls. God was with him. What good does it do?" He smiled. "Oh, I joined in the chorus—even though I don't believe it. But you remember this, Lewis. Old Teng has the power. He can do whatever he likes. And lifting up your voice to the Lord and all that crap don't do one little bit of good. Not for you or for us." He shook his head. "Why the hell did they put me in a camp with a gang of Jesus-jumpers?" He raised his face to the sky. "More rain, I think."

"Yes."

"Goodnight, Lewis."

"Goodnight, Ed."

Lewis watched him cross the compound. He stopped once and half-turned his head and said: "Even Saint Peter kept his mouth shut."

The guards came for him at first light but he was not taken to some place of punishment but to the concrete wall. There was a bucket of water at its base and one of the guards gave him a bristle brush and pointed at the wall. He scrubbed until the fish and the crucified Christ were no more than faint gray smears. Then they returned him to the hut and he spent the day with the hope rising hour by hour. Was that all? He had already had a beating and perhaps Teng considered that sufficient. But at midnight he heard the sound of a truck and a tailgate falling and some sharp commands and he left the hut and stared across the compound. The truck faced the entrance to the execution shed and the channels of light from its headlamps struck the opened door. Shapes were moving in the darkness at the rear of the truck and, then, the silhouettes of six men with bound wrists crossed the light and entered the shed. Soldiers followed, a man in a civilian suit. Then Teng's squat body stood for a moment between the lamps and his arm pointed in the direction of the hut and Lewis watched two of the soldiers walk toward him.

Inside the shed the walls were wet with condensation. The six prisoners were seated on a wooden bench. All of them were Chinese. One of the soldiers pinioned his wrists behind him, then pushed him down onto the bench so that he was seventh in the line and the nearest to the doorway. There were four oil lamps on iron brackets but none was lighted and it was the beams from the truck that illuminated the interior of the shed. A scaffold with five steps was built at the end. Above it in the roof there was a concrete joist into which was set an iron plate and an iron hook. A rope with a noose hung from the hook and a man in a dirty white singlet was waxing where the knot would run. The soldiers lined the walls and the civilian unfolded a sheet of foolscap and ran his finger down its length. Teng spoke to him, then moved behind the bench and toward the door so that Lewis, looking down, saw the putteed calves and the end of the bamboo cane stop beside him. He closed his eyes and he heard the civilian read out the first of the names. "Fu Jen-chang. Enemy of the State. By directive of the People's Court—" Boots were scuffing down the shed. The steps creaked and, now, the boots were on the scaffold and making hollow echoes in the well beneath. "Open your eyes," Teng said. He did not open them and he heard the crash of the trap and the gasp from the soldiers. Then pain shot through his right ear and into his head and Teng bent and, still pushing into the ear with the point of the cane, said: "You watch." He watched. Men were under the scaffold now and he saw their hands reaching up from the well and the rope lose its tautness and the man in the singlet remove the noose from the first of the broken necks, then adjust the knot. The trap closed. "The next is a priest," Teng whispered. "A Catholic." The civilian was reading again. "Peng Teh-huai. Enemy of the State—" The boots scuffed, the steps bent. He tried to look away but the cane pressed into the ear so that his face was turned to the scaffold. The trap fell. "Tell me," Teng said softly. "Was God with him?"

"Yes."

"I ask you again. Was God with him?"

"Yes."

The third prisoner rose from the bench and the little party went down the length of the shed to the steps. "Lu Hsun. Enemy of the State—" The man mounted the scaffold and stood by the swaying rope. Lewis stared. The light from the headlamps drove down the shed in brilliant channels and, striking the scaffold, projected its shapes and figures onto the wall behind as if on a screen. Everything was enlarged and made grotesque, the profiles swelling and shrinking, the rope as broad as a tree. Even the insects that whirled across the truck outside in the night were thrown on the wall to swoop and climb as big as birds. Teng too was staring at the wall and he held out his hands into the paths of light, creating patterns so that immense banana-fingers fluttered above the head of the victim. Now the soldiers were laughing. The trap fell. Shadow rushed. The rope tree swung. The fourth man rose. "Fu Chin-kuei. Enemy of the State—" Teng bent low and Lewis looked into his face, so near that he could see the corners of the pigmented eyes and the tiny red veins that had been engorged by frequent tempers. "Another priest," Teng said. They watched him die. Teng straightened, began to tap with the cane against his puttees. "Was God with him?" he asked.

"Yes."

The cane thrust again into his ear and tears of pain blurred the tableau on the wall. Birds were shooting down a cliff of black-ringed light. Another name was read. Boots clattered. Figures moved on the scaffold. The trap crashed.

"One to go," Teng said. "As you can see he too is a priest."

The man rose. He was still in a torn soutane and the skirts touched his ankles. The civilian scratched a fingernail on the foolscap. "Tung Pi-wu. Enemy of the State—" The priest went with the soldiers. His legs had collapsed and his black skirts dragged on the concrete. Teng bent again. "When he is dead," he said, "I am going to repeat that question. If you do not change your answer you will follow him. Do you believe me?"

Lewis felt the utter emptiness of the bench. There was a patch of wetness on the wood where one of the prisoners had urinated from fear. He too could feel the weakness of fear.

"Do you believe me?"

"I believe you."

The cane pressed.

"You watch," Teng said.

The priest dropped and the trap flung echoes to the roof. The soldiers returned and waited by the bench. More soldiers were arranging the six bodies on the floor by the scaffold.

"Stand," Teng said.

Lewis stood.

"Tell me," Teng said. "Was God with him?"

Lewis did not answer. His mouth had dried and he could not take his eyes from the shadow of the rope and the insect shapes that palpitated around it. Teng smiled and moved his hands into the headlamp beams and crooked the fingers so that immense black talons clawed the wall. The civilian folded the foolscap and slid it into his pocket and said, as if he were still reading from the list: "Lewis Robert Mackenna. Enemy of the State—" The hangman fondled the lever.

"Was God with him?" Teng asked again.

"No."

"Say it in full."

"God was not with him."

Teng cupped his ear. "You are whispering. I can't hear you."

"God was not with him."

"Louder."

"God was not with him."

One of the soldiers laughed and Teng smiled and pointed into the night.

"Go," he said.

Crossing the compound the reaction brought him spewing to his knees. Father Methuen, Gallagher and Kazumi, the Japanese major, were waiting by the wire. He rose but did not join them. The nausea gave way to a paroxysm of weeping and he walked to the angle that was formed by the fence and stood there with his hands on the barbs and his shoulders jerking. He did not know at first why he should weep with such intensity. Tears were easy in Fusan and relief at his deliverance from the rope had brought them coursing. Thank you, God, for saving me—the words had trembled on his lips as he crossed the headlamps into darkness. Yet the words were a mockery, not even logical. It was not the hand of God that had pulled him back from the scaffold: he had saved himself by his own act of denial. Standing by the wire with the points in his palms he knew that the self-disgust had grown into anger, that it was anger that was racking him. He began to shake again and he compressed his fingers until the barbs broke the flesh. He heard their feet behind him and Father Methuen's fluttering lungs.

"Have they hurt you?" Methuen asked with concern.

Lewis turned.

"Not like that," he said.

"Tell us, Lewis."

He told them.

"It's your pride that's hurt," Methuen said. "Teng had his way with you. He made you say something. But what does it matter? Say this or say that. God was with him. God was not with him. The difference is a tiny word of three letters. Why should you die for it?"

"That's right," Gallagher said. "One tiny word."

"Some words are important," Methuen said. "And some are just sounds." He reached out and lifted Lewis' hand and held it. "I don't think God loves martyrs. I used to think so but now I'm not so sure. He'd rather you lived to serve." He let fall the hand and said kindly: "We need you here, Lewis."

"That's right," Gallagher said again. "We need you. We don't need priests. Who does? But we do need doctors." He bent and began to massage his painful knees. "You can't beat Teng. I keep telling you that. He's one of the new breed. All the old gods have gone, yours included. And every time you hit him on the head with the Holy Bible he's going to hit you back. So keep quiet. He can't touch what's inside you." He flexed his right leg, then the left. "Christ, these knees. They're real bad. You think it's the weather?"

Lewis did not reply.

"The humidity," Methuen said, nodding. He rubbed his hip. "I get it too."

"In both hips?"

"Yes, both."

"Of course," Gallagher said, shrugging, "once the joints have gone—"

"You should get a stick, Ed."

Lewis listened to them; intent now on their eroded bones, offering him nothing except caution. But Kazumi had not spoken and he turned to him, this man who was his friend, and looked into his wasted face. Only the black agate eyes gave it life. Kazumi shook his head and said: "I can't help you, Lewis."

"But you can."

"No."

Lewis waited. The anger had left him and he wiped his nose and eyes with the back of his hand like a weary child and Kazumi, watching the gesture, said gently: "You were brave."

"But not brave enough?"

"How can I say? We are east and west, Lewis. A world apart."

"Say it."

"Nothing to say. You heard the Holy Father. The words were unimportant. You are both Christians. You have to believe him."

"But what do you believe, Kazumi?"

The Japanese turned to go but Lewis touched his arm.

"Very well," Kazumi said. "You allowed Teng to humble you. You are less now than you were."

"Pride," Father Methuen said with disapproval. "Just pride. Stupid Shinto pride."

Kazumi walked into darkness.

"And don't call me Holy Father," Methuen cried out after him in his piping voice. "I am not the Pope."

But back in the hut Major Kazumi's voice continued to reproach him. You are less now than you were. Kazumi had answered him, not with cruelty but with truth. He lay there listening to the lizards on the roof. You are less now than you were. The words seemed to throb like a wound. He could feel the anger returning and he left the bunk and went out into the compound. The night was still dark. Watches were as rare as Bibles in Fusan and he did not know the time. But somewhere beyond the barracks boots were marching on the road and he knew that the two o'clock picket was making its circuit. He crossed the compound to the execution shed. The flank wall was in effect a part of the perimeter fence and he stood in front of it and murmured a prayer for Father Tsai and the six men who had gone to the noose. How many priests, Christian or Buddhist or of other creeds, had died in this place since the revolution? It was now a hallowed place and he reached out and touched the wall. Then he walked to the remains of the evening's cooking-fires and chose several lengths of blackened kindling.

When he returned to the wall he stood in front of it and felt his courage ebb. It was the death of the sixth man, the soutaned priest, that remained with him and he could see clearly the skirts lifting up and spreading when the trap fell so that they were like the wings of a blackbird. But there was also Kazumi. You are less now than you were. Perhaps he could excise those bitter words. He drew a large Christ in the center of the wall, giving the figure a lolling head and upstretched arms that were suspending weight, a ribcage, a loincloth, joined feet. He added the thorns, then the outline of the Cross behind the figure. He stepped back to examine it. In the faint pallor that came from the night sky it was barely visible. Not one of the great religious murals, he thought, smiling. The amusement left him and he knew that he was standing again on the edge of fear. But the drawing seemed incomplete. He re-examined it. Somewhere in the camp a door was slamming as if in wind and, listening to the staccato sounds, he saw in that moment the centurion's hammer and heard its awful thuds and he went to the wall and raised the stump of kindling and with three strong strokes drove the nails down the wall into the hands and feet. A few words were needed to sanctify the shed and he reached up and drew in the best classical style a length of partly unrolled parchment and wrote across it in capital letters HIC LOCUS SANCTUS.

"This is a Holy Place," Teng translated. He turned from the wall and stared through the sun glare at the lines of prisoners and asked: "Your work, Dr. Mackenna?"

"Yes."

"Come forward."

He came forward. He had expected rage and, perhaps, an immediate lashing with the cane. But Teng did not speak. There was a curious weakness in his face, a change; and, looking at him, Lewis saw the droop in the right corner of his mouth and a bead of spittle and knew that during the night he had suffered a stroke. Teng wiped away the bead, then turned and, using his cane as a stick, went to the guards and said something. The lieutenant of the guard nodded and pointed at Lewis, then at the gateway in the wire and the entrance to the shed. Lewis began to walk. This time Father Methuen and the other prisoners were silent. They watched, as still as mourners at a graveside. When he reached the shed the lieutenant unlocked the door, pushed him inside and closed it. He stood there alone in the shed and heard the key turn behind him.

A window was set high in the flank walls on either side of the scaffold. The early sun sent a shaft through one of them and touched the rope so that a part of its length hung like a yellow wand in the gloom. He sat down on the bench and stared at it. How long would it be before the man in the white singlet came? Not long perhaps. There were things to be whispered, faces of loved ones to be resurrected from where they lived within him and given light and substance and held there and held there and held there and never fading until his own light died. He could feel the coldness of the concrete floor (or was it fear?) and he stood and walked down the shed to the scaffold. Standing at the side of it he could see the shadowed well below the platform, the bruises on the wooden supports where the trap struck. A scrap of black material was caught on a wood splinter and he plucked it off and put it on his palm. Had it come from Father Tsai's soutane? Time was passing. They might come at any moment. He did not kneel for the prayer and he leaned against the wood and closed his eyes. The three faces formed as if they were floating in the scaffold well, Ellen in the center and a twin on either side, smiling at him like the triptych photograph that had always sat on the chest in the mission bedroom. But he could not form the ritual words as easily as the faces. The Scriptures and the prayer books were filled with majestic words that would have come fluently at any other time. He could only whisper like any dying man afraid for his family: "Please God look after Ellen and Joel and Gerard. Please look after them." The faces dissolved and he turned and went back to the bench and lay there half-sleeping until the heat of the day began to build in the shed.

He sat up. The sun shaft had gone from the window and the rope, no longer yellowed by it, hung quivering from the roof. Quivering? He stared at it, then rose and went to the foot of the scaffold. White ants were descending from the hook to the noose and he watched them making ravenous clusters on the hangman's wax. Nausea rose. Why had they not come? He could feel the weakness in his legs and he wondered if he would find the strength to climb the steps. He put a foot on the first, then moved to the second and then to the third. The trap and the lever were very near. So was the thought of self-destruction. It would be simple to stand on the trap near to the side, adjust the noose, then kick the lever out of the teeth of the ratchet. Was that the reason he had been left alone in the shed? Was Teng as subtle as that? Seeking victory in an act of damnation that for a minister would be spit in the face of Jesus? It was possible. He shook his head and descended the steps, walked back to the bench and sat.

The sun had made an arc around the shed and was slanting through the opposite window when the door opened. The lieutenant and two soldiers entered. But the man in the singlet was not with them. "Come with us," the lieutenant said kindly. Lewis heard the compassion in his voice and it was this unexpected low tone that sent the fear leaping through him. He had prepared himself for his brief union with the hangman; but not for pity. Pity meant something worse. He turned and looked with a kind of longing at the rope and the lieutenant watched him and said: "Too late now for that." He stood and went out with them into the afternoon sun and they walked down the road that led past the barracks. A squad of soldiers was sprawled on the steps, some without caps, some with trailing puttees. They did not acknowledge the lieutenant. "There is no longer respect for officers," he said severely. They turned left at the barracks and onto a path. "Soon," the lieutenant said, "they plan to abolish the officer class. There will be no military ranks, no badges, no insignia." He turned a worried face. "How will they know who is commanding them?" There was a bamboo hut at the end of the path and when they reached it the lieutenant stopped and pointed at the half-open door and touched his arm and said: "Go in."

He went in and the door closed behind him. There was nothing in the hut except an iron bed-frame with a spring and three lengths of rope laid across it, two men with shaved Mongol heads. He stood with his hands pressed back against the door. The men did not speak or move. His heart began to pound.

On the second night of his time of trial he saw the hut from afar and he was walking away from it and over the dark brows of the land toward a distant hill shrine and he knew he was released forever from the body on the bed-frame. But it was sleep, not release; and he awakened into the night of the hut and he saw again the silver window in the wall and the men returned and hung a lamp and began again. This time it was worse, the two pigskin skulls swinging in and out of the flare of orange lamplight and his body arched and the skulls low and nuzzling into him and even a cheek pressed against his own. Once he heard the cattle lowing out in the grasslands and the lowing so loud that it filled his head and became his own uplifted voice. Sometimes soldiers from the night picket came into the hut and watched what the men were doing and sipped their tea from mess cans and went out again into the camp. And sometimes the two men left him and there was only the blur of the lamp and the translucent bodies of the lizards flickering on the walls. But the men always returned and began again and it did not stop until the silver square went pale with the early sunrise. Another day, the heat crackling in the bamboo, he alone on the frame, the lieutenant's commiserative face bent across him and some water splashing on his lips, the dusk. The third night was worse than the second. Give up the ghost—that was the Biblical phrase. Give it up. Let it go. But it would not go. Frantic though it was it would not go. It stayed there, imprisoned in its dark glass, and the men came and went throughout the night and the orange skulls bobbed around him and eyes watched over the rims of cans and the cattle bellowed in the pastures of the night. Finally it escaped and this time it was no falseness of a dream from which he would be torn but a true release and he was striding again up the rise of the land into the scented day and there was light and sweet cold air, everything cold and even the clouds like frozen eddies of water. But, then, the darkness closed as swift as a shutter and the fetid smell of the hut was in his nostrils and the lamp was burning on its nail and the two men were coming out of the shadows like the creatures of the night they really were, the skulls leaning across him and pinpricks of orange light reflected in the orbits and the hands searching and the frame leaping and the springs jangling and the sound of them and other sounds filling the hut and the hands not leaving him until the window paled on the wall. The lamp left its nail. He lay there and watched the window growing bright. The door was open behind the head of the bed-frame and he could feel the winds of morning in his hair.

Later he heard boots on the path, boots in the hut, the lieutenant's voice murmuring in respectful tones, another voice he did not recognize. Someone moved behind him. A face bent down. The face was inverted from where he lay and he could not register its details. Their eyes met. Then the face moved back.

"Release him," the man said.

The voice, Lewis learned from Gallagher, had been that of John Chen Yuchang. Teng, paralyzed by a series of strokes, had gone; and Chen was his replacement. Not a soldier, Gallagher said, but a new breed from the Communist stud that was known as a political officer. Now that the land battles were won the power was moving from the Army to the presidiums, to the men in suits. The camps were filled with subversives and potential enemies of the new regime and it would be the task of the political officers to reassess them; a word, Gallagher said wryly, that could mean anything. But Chen, it seemed, was a very odd horse indeed. The sensitive Lieutenant Pu had gathered some facts and perhaps a little hearsay. It was said that Chen was not a pure Chinese—as if such a thing existed; that there was a taint of European blood; that he was the bastard of a crazy warlord, a chess prodigy in the years before the Japanese invasion, a pupil in a Catholic college. "A very rum horse," Gallagher said. Then, smiling and looking down at Lewis on the bunk: "But he let you go."

"Yes."

"Still hurting?"

Lewis nodded.

"Bad?"

"Yes."

"It's been a week now. Let's try a walk."

"No."

"You can't lie here forever. Try, Lewis."

He tried; and in the days that followed and limping between the arms of Gallagher and Kazumi he felt some strength return. It was still very hot and he could not bear to look at the blistered sky. But the time of the serious rains was near and there were always falls during the night hours and when the day came the craters in the compound steamed. The drawing on the wall of the shed had not been removed, but each night it was made fainter by the rain and by the time he was able to walk unaided around the four sides of the compound the charcoal Christ and the Latin legend were gone. Once he saw Chen on the barracks road in the center of a party of officers, too indistinct at that distance to be more than a silhouette against an evening sun; and again when, sitting on the earth with Pastor Irwin and bent across a chessboard, he heard feet and voices and looked up, pawn in hand, to see Chen, two guards, Lieutenant Pu.

"This is the commander," the lieutenant said. "You should stand."

But Chen shook his head and pointed at the board. They continued to play. Time passed. The sun dipped. Irwin, disconcerted as always by the prospect of defeat, began to strike his forehead in exasperation whenever he lost a piece. The lieutenant and the guards shuffled with impatience but Chen did not move. His shadow lay elongated by the board. It did not sway or shift. He had the gift of stillness and it was not until the game was finished that the shadow leaped and Chen bent and picked up a knight and examined it. The piece was crudely carved, stained red with the juice of the berries that grew around the camp.

"Who made this set?" Chen asked in English.

"I did," Lewis said. He looked up. Chen, he thought, was a man of about thirty years. Standing there in the regulation cap and dark gray suit with the tunic collar that had become the uniform of those in authority in the public service he seemed, like all such men, anonymous. Yet he had poise. He wore the cheap clothes with elegance. There was a sense of power in his trim slight body. And the eyes had knowledge; too much, Lewis decided, for a man still young. Chen returned the piece to Irwin's small group of captures and said to him: "How can you win if you are always angry?"

Chen sent for Lewis on the following morning. The administration and officers' buildings lay opposite the barracks. The road ran between. Chen's office was entered through an orderly room in which were a row of filing cabinets and two tables. A major sat at one of them, Pu at the other. The lieutenant was a man perpetually worried by the paper of bureaucracy and, passing, Lewis saw his hands darting like nervous yellow fish in a depth of forms and dockets. But there was no disorder in the room in which Chen waited; nothing on the metal desk except a manila file, not a scrap of correspondence or a teacup or a tobacco tin or even a paper-clip. Chen sat there stiffly with his cap pulled down squarely on his head and his hands aligned exactly to the file, as if he too were a visitor. He pointed with his chin and Lewis sat. The blades of a fan revolved on the ceiling and he could hear the hum of a generator. A window made a square behind Chen's head and through the bamboo slats of the blind there was a view of a grass area and a timber bungalow. Tree peonies and davidias shaded its veranda; and it was there, Lewis knew, that the camp commanders were always quartered.

"Shall we talk in English?" Chen asked.

Lewis nodded and Chen took a gold pen from an inner pocket and laid it on the file. "This is your dossier," he said. "We shall examine it together. But first let me make my own position clear. I am, as you know, John Chen Yuchang. I don't like the smell of prisons. I am a political animal, not a jailer. But there are fifteen men in this camp whose dossiers deserve a further scrutiny. You are one of them. While I am here I have to assume the responsibilities of commander. But not much will change. Men will still be punished if they misbehave. Men will still come here with execution warrants." His voice became sardonic. "Perhaps we'll try some political education."

"Of the sick and dying?"

"Are there so many?"

"Every day there are burials," Lewis said. "The camp is full of fevers and dysenteries. Fly infections. Skin infections. Hookworm. Diseases I don't even recognize. We need medicines and drugs. Penicillin. Dressings. Anesthetics. I could give you a list."

Chen smiled.

"Then there are the empty stomachs," Lewis said. "Some men are too weak to walk. I could show you most of the nutritional diseases. Especially beriberi. At one time we had a little meat and vegetables, salt, even fish. Now it's mainly rice. We can't survive on rice, Commander."

"Should you eat better than the peasants?"

"No. But we need something different. Rice isn't enough. It would help if we could have the husks."

Chen shook his head.

"The rice comes here already polished," he said. He unscrewed the cap of his pen. "Anything else?"

"We need soap. And a lot more water. There's a danger of dirt diseases. Many of the men have lice."

"Lice?"

"Yes."

"Do you have lice, Dr. Mackenna?"

Lewis heard the anxiety in his voice.

"Not yet," he said.

"Lice are bad," Chen said with disgust. "Do you recall what Chairman Mao said about lice?"

"No."

"He said that if a man hasn't had lice he can't understand China."

Lewis smiled.

"Why do you smile?"

"I sometimes think the Chairman has said something about everything."

Chen stared.

"Careful," he said. "Your tongue has already got you into trouble." He looked at his wristwatch. "We are wasting time. I have many questions."

He opened the dossier.

"Somewhere in the world," Lewis said tiredly, "there is always an inquisition."

"Yes," Chen said. "And let us begin on yours."

Chen sent for him again in the afternoon. The generator had failed and the blades of the fan hung motionless on the ceiling. Chen made no concessions to the heat. He sat rigid in his chair, the cap still square upon his head and the tunic collar hooked tight around his neck. He was now halfway through the dossier. He read aloud, asked questions, listened intently with his head on one side as if he would catch every inflexion of deceit, annotated the pages with his expensive pen. How incongruous it was, Lewis thought; gleaming there below the sleeve of the cheap suit. There was movement by the bungalow veranda. A bare-chested man in army trousers had begun to tie back the bracts of one of the davidias. The flowers hung like white pocket-handkerchiefs across the rail. A pleasant scene, Lewis thought, not much more than two hundred paces from the wire and the camp of starving men. Chen followed his eyes.

"Teng Hua is dead," he said. "Does that please you?"

"No."

"Why not? He was cruel to you."

"No pleasure in another man's death."

Chen smiled.

"Will you forgive him?" he asked.

Lewis watched the soldier sweeping leaves. Forgive Teng? He had not yet asked himself that question. It was easy enough to tell others to forgive. Nothing was unforgivable—that was the Christian ethic. But Teng and the anguish in the hut? Perhaps, he thought, I have never before in my life had so powerful a reason for not forgiving. Chen was still smiling. The generator whined into life and the fan began to throw moving bars of shadow and if there was mockery in the smile he could not see it.

"I don't know," he said. "I am still in pain. And I think I'm still afraid. Perhaps in time. I don't know."

＊　　＊　　＊

There were two more visits to the office before Chen closed the covers of the dossier. Each of its pages was examined with meticulous care, the afternoon heat still thick in the office and the sky darkening outside with the impending rains and the fan failing and reviving and failing again and he, Lewis, stuck with sweat to the seat of the metal chair. There was never any water on the desk, never an interruption from the orderly room; only Chen's quiet voice like a probe inside the head, the whirr of flies. Sometimes Chen sat bent across a page in one of his strange periods of absolute stillness so that there was not a movement of a finger or a lip or even the rise and fall of his chest in the airless heat, bent and concentrated as if each word was as significant as a chess piece. It was always the gaps and omissions that interested him. We have the date of your medical degree, but not the place. Where was that? Edinburgh. There is then a missing year. What were you doing? Further studies. Of what? Tropical diseases. Where? London. There is another two-year gap before you embark for Hangchow. What were you doing? Theological college. In Edinburgh? No, Dundee. We have the date of your marriage, but not the place. Where? Hangchow. In the mission church? Yes. What was your wife's maiden name? Shirecliff. Ellen Mary Shirecliff? Yes. Where did you meet her? In Kiangsi. What was she doing in Kiangsi? She was working in the Methodist missionary hospital. As a nurse? As a nurse and a teacher. Where were your children born? In Hangchow. In the mission hospital? Yes. Why are you crying? Can't help it. Your family is safe. No one has harmed them. I assure you of that. No need for tears. But this is a place of tears, Commander. We try not to think of homes and families: but you mentioned them, the mission, that day in Kiangsi. Will you please wipe your nose, I am a fastidious man. Fastidious? You should try being fastidious on the other side of the wire. What were you doing in Kiangsi? You are not a Methodist. What were you doing there? They were in need of some vaccine. I took it there. And there she was? Yes, there she was.

She was still there when Lieutenant Pu escorted him from the building. The sun was low, red on the bamboo stems. As red as her hair. That hair. That hair. Kiangsi. Walking with Pu he saw her again, coming toward him down the path that led through the vegetable garden from the little thatch-roof hospital. Plainly she was off duty for her hair was unpinned and hung very long and the crown of it glowed where the sun struck and when she reached him she smiled and said "Ellen Shirecliff" and in that moment a hornet alighted on her head and, feeling it, she shook her hair to dislodge it and the hair swung so violently that it came like a cascade near to his face and he reached out and grasped it and with his other hand swept off the hornet. He did not release the hair and it hung across his wrist and the moment was as sensuous and intimate as if he had reached out to hold her breast. This was the beginning of their marriage. He had touched her like a lover and she had known it and later whenever he thought about beginnings it seemed that the holding of her hair, the weight and texture of it in his palm and on his wrist, was as voluptuous a moment as when he had first put his hand inside her fertile sweetness.

"Do you have a handkerchief?" Pu asked.

"No."

"Take this."

He took the lieutenant's handkerchief and wiped his eyes and nose. Two soldiers were filling potholes in the road outside the barracks, bent low across their shovels. There was something familiar in the two prickly scalps; and when they passed the men looked up and the shaven heads swung together and became skulls turning in the lamplight and he stopped and felt the fear invade him.

"What is the matter?" Pu asked.

"Those men."

Pu stared at them and understood.

"Ah," he said sadly. "Those men."

When they reached the gate in the wire Lewis looked back. The men had finished their task and were walking down the road with the shovels sloped like rifles on their shoulders; two soldiers, he thought, going somewhere for a cigarette and a can of tea. Were these really the shapes of terror that had leaned across him in the hut?

Later he came from sleep and there was a second in which he saw Chen's shapely hands on the dossier. Unease was growing. That agile mind had prowled around the gaps in his record, always searching. Nothing was left unexplored. Yet his friendship with Chiang Kai-shek, that friendship that had marked him as a suspect and brought him to Fusan, had produced no more than a few superficial questions. How curious that was. Chen, he decided, had closed the covers of the dossier, but not the interrogation. They would return for him.

They returned.

Walking through the eight o'clock darkness of the following day toward the barracks and the path that led to the hut, Pu on one side of him and a guard on the other, he felt the fear reinvade. The lieutenant sensed it and held his arm for a moment and said: "No, not down there." They turned right opposite the barracks and onto the earth path that skirted the administration building. Ahead was the timber bungalow. A lighted oil lamp hung on one of the veranda posts and another light burned inside. But they did not mount the steps. Pu took him to a shed that stood near to the flank of the bungalow, pushed open the door and pointed.

He entered. It was a bare place. An oil lamp, nailed above a wall mirror, shed light. There was a wooden table, on it a bucket with a curl of steam, a cake of soap, a pair of scissors. A wooden chair stood in the corner. A coarse towel was folded on the back of it and a singlet and some khaki shorts were on the seat. He stood there in surprise. Then he smiled with understanding. "I am a fastidious man," Chen had said. He stripped off his torn and dirty clothing, picked up the scissors and went to the mirror. He had not looked in a mirror since his entry to the camp and he was shocked at the fleshless creature that looked back at him. There was a hollow under his breastbone that would have admitted most of his fist. If you were a patient, he said to the reflection, I would give you an unenthusiastic prognosis. He cut off the hair from his head, chest, armpits and pubis. Then he held the cuttings up against the light. He could not see any obvious infestations and he went to the bucket and began to soap his head. When the whole of his body was cleansed he put on the shorts and singlet and went outside. Pu had gone but the guard was there and the red point of his cigarette gestured toward the veranda.

Crossing the boards of the veranda he caught the scent of incense, and when he entered the lighted room he saw the bronze burner that stood on a camphorwood chest. The room occupied the whole of the frontage of the bungalow. It was comfortably furnished. There were a fringed carpet, a rattan chaise longue, rattan chairs with cushions, a variety of redwood cabinets and tables. There was no sign of John Chen. He walked around the room. The dossier, a writing pad and the gold pen lay on one of the tables, some covered food dishes on another. The smallest of the tables had a marquetry surface the inlay of which formed the squares of a chessboard. The pieces were arranged for combat and when he bent he saw that they were intricately carved from jade. The walls were bare. He heard the wands crackle faintly in the burner and he examined it and touched the bronze serpent that coiled its hips and in that moment Chen came from an inner room.

Lewis turned. This was a different Chen, no longer the austere man in the Mao cap and tunic. He wore a blue silk robe that was wide-sleeved and sashed like a kimono, white silk trousers and black silk slippers. He seemed to shimmer when he crossed the room. He pointed at the burner and said: "A lovely thing."

"Yes. Very fine."

"It was dug up in the camp. Did you know there was an ancient settlement here?"

Lewis nodded.

"I dislike incense," Chen said. "But it's better than the smell of the camp. Sometimes when the wind changes, you understand?"

Lewis smiled. "You are a fastidious man, Commander."

"I am indeed." Chen stared at him. "Are you clean now, Dr. Mackenna?"

"Spotless."

"And hungry?"

"Always."

Chen gestured at the food dishes.

"Please eat," he said.

Lewis sat at the table and removed the lids. There was a mix of cold meat and chicken, some apples, a dish of dried apricots that had been macerated in water, a mound of bran that sat in a lake of jujube juice. He began to eat. Chen sat at another of the tables and watched him. Lewis was aware again of his quality of total stillness. Like a learned discipline, he thought; so that even the coins and slivers of reflected light lie unmoving on his silken clothes. He looked up once and saw that there was beauty in the lemon face. His hair was cropped so that it was no more than a blue-black shadow, and his head was as shapely as his hands. He ate frugally until he felt the first protest in his shrunken stomach.

"No more?" Chen asked.

"No. But if I could have the apples?"

"Take them when you go."

Wind was gathering and the veranda door swung. Chen rose and hooked it back.

"The rain is near," he said.

Now the davidias were scraping on the rail.

"I saw your family," Chen said. He returned to his chair. "Twice at the mission. Once at the time of your arrest. And again six months later."

"Were they well?"

"Safe and well."

"Why the second visit?"

"Questions. There are always more questions. Your sons are very intelligent."

"You mean you questioned them?"

"Of course."

"But they are only children."

"Children observe. Children listen. Young or old, every human mind is a storehouse. One has only to search."

"And what did you find?"

Chen rose and went to the chessboard table.

"I thought we might play a game or two," he said.

But there were five games. After the first of them Lewis knew that the months in the camp and its deprivations had robbed him of his mental energy, knew also that even at his best he would never defeat John Chen. "At the age of eight," Chen told him, "I was a chess prodigy. And at fourteen I was playing the best in the land." The words seemed distant. The unaccustomed food had produced a nausea in his stomach. He could not concentrate and sometimes Chen made a tut-tutting noise and said gently: "Make that move again." At the end of the third game his face was suffused with heat and his senses were drowning in waves of fatigue. He closed his eyes and heard Chen say: "I used to play four-handed chess. A stupid game. Four minds in conflict with each other." Now the waves were engulfing him. "Wake up, Dr. Mackenna." He opened his eyes. "Would you like a drink?" "Yes, please." He saw the blue robe bend to one of the cabinets. A bottle of *maotai* and two tumblers appeared on the table. Then the robe shimmered across the room like a kingfisher's wing and went into the inner room and he saw the edge of a bed and the mosquito net that hung in billows from the ceiling. Chen returned and a bottle of citrus cordial with a Canton label was set down on the table. "What would you like?" Lewis pointed at the *maotai*. But the spirit was a mistake. The raw vodkalike flavor dried his mouth and brought a new spasm of nausea. He began to sweat. "You are not going to be sick, are you?" Chen's voice said severely. "I would not like that." Lewis rose. "If I could get some air?" Chen nodded. "Go out on the veranda."

On the veranda he stood by the rail and breathed deeply of the night air and smelled the fragrance of the tree peonies. When he returned to the room he saw that Chen had arranged the pieces.

"I can't play another game," Lewis said. "I am very tired."

"Sit."

"I told you. I'm tired. I can't give you a proper game."

Chen picked up one of his bishops and dropped it into its box.

"There," he said. "I'll give you that. Now sit."

"No. I have to rest."

"Sit and play."

Lewis sat. They began to play. The jade pieces shuddered, Chen's right hand came and went in the orbit of the lamplight, the silk sleeve rustled. What time was it? The casualties from his little army were mounting. If only I could sleep.

"Wake up, Dr. Mackenna."

In the endgame of this the fifth contest he heard the distant scuff of marching boots. He looked up from the board and listened.

"Yes," Chen said. "The midnight picket."

"Midnight?"

"Yes." Chen pushed his pieces into the center of the board. "Let us finish. You have no chance."

Lewis stood. He felt his body sway with exhaustion.

"May I go now?" he asked.

"Not yet."

"Please. I have to sleep."

Chen shook his head.

"There is work to do," he said.

"Work?"

Chen rose and went to the table where the dossier lay.

"Bring up a chair," he said.

They sat and Chen opened the dossier and turned some pages.

"I'm too tired to help you," Lewis said wearily. "Can't think. Can't remember." Sleep was near again. Chen's face blurred. "Can't possibly remember things."

"You can and will remember."

"No."

Chen touched his temple.

"As I told you," he said, "everything is here. All here on the tablets of memory."

Lewis closed his eyes. Sleep came abruptly. The tablets of memory. Seek and ye shall find. The tablets, standing like inscribed gravestones, began to slide inside his head, clattering against the bones of his skull. Skull. Two skulls. Now he was back inside the hut, the lamp burning on its nail and the skulls of the two men bent across him and their hands searching for his secret life.

"Wake up. Wake up."

That was Chen's voice.

"Wake up."

He opened his eyes.

"I didn't thank you," he said thickly.

"For what?"

"For saving me from Teng."

"Do you accuse me of compassion?"

Accuse. A strange word. Had he heard a note of irony? For Chen and his kind, Lewis thought, compassion might indeed be a weakness.

"If you need a motive," Chen said, "it is because I cannot search a dead man's mind." He turned another page. "Let us get on."

Later he heard the two o'clock picket. Boots, wind, rustling leaves, Chen's voice as sharp as a chisel, Chen's voice soft and murmurous, Chen's mind inside his own, *he knows what I'm thinking, I swear he knows,* incense sick in the stomach and Chiang's presence there in the room, that shaven olive-brown nut of a head lurking on the fringe of lamplight, listening. The Peanut. That was how the American general, Joseph Stilwell, had with contempt always referred to him during the war. I have to meet with the Peanut today. Would you believe I have to decorate the Peanut with the Legion of Merit? Chen's voice again. I want to talk to you about the Americans. Americans? *Why has he suddenly mentioned Americans? Could he have seen Stilwell's vulturine face peering from my mind?* Yes, Americans. They are the key to the present situation in Taiwan. They are with Chiang, advising him, planning his return. Tell me this, Dr. Mackenna. In the four years since the end of the war have you had any contact with Americans? Yes, I know lots of Americans. The pad and the pen moved across the table. I want you to write down the names and descriptions of all the Americans you have met during, say, the six months prior to your arrest. Open your eyes. Keep awake. Please let me go to bed. Write them down. Now. You may go when you have written them down.

The first light was in the sky when he put down the pen. Chen had sat unmoving.

"May I go now?"

"Yes."

He went out onto the veranda. Chen followed and they stood there in the fresh dawn wind. The boards and rail were filmed with fine sand and Chen put out a hand to the rail and made a track through the sand with his finger.

"The wind brings it from the deserts of the Gobi," he said. "All that way."

Lewis went to the steps.

"Wait," Chen said.

He walked from the veranda to the room and Lewis heard a drawer open, the crackle of paper. When he returned he was carrying a filled paper bag.

"You forgot your apples," Chen said.

At eight o'clock in the evening of that day Lieutenant Pu took him again to the bungalow. There was the same unvarying ritual; the soap and hot water in the shed and the laundered shorts and singlet, the moments in which he stood alone in the living room and awaited Chen's entry, Chen shimmering from the bedroom (this time in a robe of scarlet silk), the same anxious question "Are you clean?" food and drink and Chen watching him without sound or movement from a rattan chair and, when he had had sufficient, the finger pointing at the chess table.

There were changes in the room. Some painted figurines of acrobats and jugglers now stood on one of the chests. Above them on the wall was a pair of blanc-de-chine porcelain pictures of Yellow River scenes. A palm-leaf fan with an ornamental brass handle lay by the dossier and a carved Tibetan prayer wheel had been set in the corner. It was as if, Lewis thought, Chen had decided to reveal a little of himself by exposing to the view a few personal possessions. What would appear tomorrow?

After three long games he felt himself sink again into depths of tiredness. Chen, now, had begun to comment on his moves and tactics, speaking in a quiet didactic voice as if he were a pupil. No, no, no, you must not passively await events. Passive play is hopeless. The voice came faintly. Remember the old concept—pawns are the soul of chess. He drank some cordial and rubbed his eyes. It is your move, Dr. Mackenna. Is it? Yes, your move. The wind was rising. They played for a time and a shower of rain made beads on the veranda rail. No, no, you have castled too soon. Try to think. I am too tired to think. Boots on the road. Is that the two o'clock picket? No, it is midnight. We have several more games. Please concentrate. Those last three moves were very primitive. I don't expect you to beat me, but I expect you to learn. A strange hiatus in the night in which he could hear no wind or rain or marching boots or scratching flower bracts. Wake up. Wake up. Think. Move. Ah, how careless that was. Your rook was ideally placed to attack my pawns from behind. I have a very bad headache. I cannot go on. Now the headache was a pain, the tumblers of his mind grinding, he thought fancifully, like unlubricated engine parts. Your brain is an engine, the voice said distantly: the most complex engine in the world. Use it. *God! Why did he say engine? How did he see that word form within my mind?* Boots approaching on the road. Yes, that is the two o'clock guard. Leave the game. Let us sit at the table and discuss your American friends and the Generalissimo.

At the table Chen opened the dossier.

"I had several years of education in England," he said. "And during that time I once played chess in Edinburgh. A tournament."

"Did you win?"

"Yes." Chen held up his gold pen. "They gave me this."

"It's very nice."

"Yes, very nice." He handed Lewis the pen. "There's an inscription."

Lewis examined it. The need for sleep had blurred his vision and he could not decipher the engraved letters.

"The university found me a room on the Lawnmarket," Chen said. "Do you know it?"

"Of course."

"A beautiful city," Chen said. Then, sardonically: "A great exporter of Christianity."

"Yes, always."

"What would the burghers say if we built a Buddhist temple on Princes Street?"

Lewis smiled.

"Would they permit it?"

"I doubt it."

Sleep closed his eyes. He felt Chen take the pen from his fingers.

"A beautiful city," Chen said again. The voice was distant. "But perplexing."

"Perplexing?"

"The streets. Some of them change their names. The Royal Mile is an example."

"Four times," Lewis said.

"Four is it?"

"Yes."

He heard Chen turning pages.

"A president and a missionary," Chen said. "A strange friendship."

"Not so strange. Chiang is a Christian."

"United in Christ?"

"Something like that."

"And against the Reds?"

"Of course."

"Where did you first meet Chiang?"

"At Nanking. The Wesley Church."

"Why there?"

"The minister was a friend. I was invited to the reconsecration."

Chen looked up.

"Why should it be reconsecrated?"

"Because the Japanese had used it as a brothel."

Chen smiled.

"At least it was useful," he said.

The sardonic note again, Lewis thought. That kind of humor was hardly a Chinese trait. Was it true about the European blood? He closed his eyes. Beyond the mists of sleep he heard the nib of Chen's pen, then some murmured words. "You were wrong about the Royal Mile."

He awakened.

"What did you say?"

"I said you were wrong about the Royal Mile."

"Wrong?"

"Yes. There are five changes of name. Not four."

"Does it matter?"

"Accuracy always matters. So I want you to make an effort of recall. I want you to start walking."

"Walking?"

"Down the Royal Mile. Start at the Holyrood end."

He felt his head sag.

"Wake up."

Fingers pressed underneath his chin. He lifted his head.

"Now," Chen said. "Imagine you are walking. Watch the blocks. Read the names."

He closed his eyes.

"Are you walking?"

"Yes."

Pavements, old tenements, one block, two blocks, a nameplate, painted beams, medieval shops. There was an illusion that Chen walked beside him. Now we are passing Clarinda's—tea and cakes in the afternoon. Remember? More blocks, road junctions. I can see the top of the Scott Monument. Two hundred and eighty-seven steps to the top. I could never climb it. Too tired. Too tired. There is the Castle. Nearly there.

"Where are you now?"

That was Chen's voice.

"At the Lawnmarket. Outside Glen's."

"The bagpipe makers?"

"Yes."

"Did you count?"

"Yes."

"How many changes?"

"Five."

"Are you sure?"

"Yes, five. You were right."

Chen nodded approval.

"It was there in your memory," he said. "You had only to make the effort." He took a sheet of paper from within the cover of the dossier. "This is your list of American contacts." He placed a finger under the first of the names. "You are going to make another effort. You are going to recall the details of every man and woman on the list."

He slid the sheet to the center of the table. Outside a bloom of gray daylight was growing on the sky.

"Bagpipes," Chen said with distaste. "All those years of British domination. China, like other places, has heard the sound of bagpipes."

John Chen's strategy remained unchanging. It was effective enough, Lewis thought. First the lethargies that followed food and drink, then the chess games that sapped his strength and, through defeat, seemed to admit Chen to every recess of his mind, then the questions and the desperate need for sleep and the questions and the lustrous eyes watching him like a cat's and growing larger as the night passed and always the questions and, finally, Chen roaming in his head and excavating every buried sound and thought and image. Personal objects continued to appear in the room, as if drawn cautiously from some private store. On the third visit he saw that two paintings had been hung; one depicting small girls in a poppy field, the other presenting a section of the Grand Canal at Tientsin. On the fourth visit a shortbread tin now sat on one of the camphorwood chests. Its faded lid exhibited an Edinburgh view of the Castle and Princes Street Gardens and Chen went to it from time to time and took from it the incense sticks that fed the burner. On the following night he found that eight French novels, all of them detective stories, were stacked on the cushion of a chair. This was the night when, in the small hours of that fifth visit to the bungalow, the veil of exhaustion fell across him and the chessmen blurred and became the rippling red-and-white hides of cattle and he heard them lowing in the distant grasslands and he slipped from the chair to the floor and, now, Chen was bending across him and he looked up into his face and said wearily: "Why do we have to go through all this? I have nothing to hide. I was born in this country. So were my children. I've given it all I have to give. I liked Chiang and I supported him. But you'd expect that, wouldn't you? You'd expect a Christian minister to support a Christian head of state. The Church was safe with Chiang. But it isn't safe now, so of course I want him back. But that doesn't mean I've been involved in plots and politics. Ask me the questions and I'll answer. And always with truth. You don't have to wear me down. You don't have to attack my mind."

On the sixth visit he saw that a framed sepia photograph had been set down next to the shortbread tin. He bent to it. A young black-haired woman smiled from a pool of sun under the branches of a ginkgo tree. She had a Western face, a Western skirt and blouse. Who was she? He waited in the sickly incense smell and when Chen made his entrance, rustling in from the bedroom and exotic in the kingfisher robe and lips parting to frame the usual question, Lewis smiled and said: "Yes, I assure you I am scrupulously clean."

But this night there was a change in Chen. Some of the innate stillness was gone. He was restless and Lewis, seated, watched him cross the room to the veranda door, toy with his sash, go to the rail and hold his hand out into the rain-spitting dark. Then he returned, walked around the room, picked up one of the novels. "I prefer the *roman policier,*" he said. "The best of them are so well organized." He dropped the book, inspected the incense burner, rearranged the group of figurines, picked up the book again and riffled its pages.

"May I borrow one?" Lewis asked.

Chen put down the book.

"No," he said. "Books are easily soiled." He gestured to where the camp huts would be. "I could not return to a book if it had been out there."

He went again to the veranda door, stood there listening to the beat of rain. Then, turning, he pointed to the food dishes.

"Aren't you going to eat?" he asked.

"No."

"Not hungry?"

"Of course."

"Then eat."

"No food," Lewis said. "No drink. No chess. No answers."

"But I have no questions."

"You mean you believe me?"

"I mean I have no further questions."

Chen bent to one of the cabinets, took out a bottle and two glasses. "Perhaps a drink," he said. He turned the bottle so that Lewis should see its label. It was a Jim Beam whiskey.

"A bourbon," Chen said, pouring. "I have no scotch." He put a glass into Lewis' hand. Then he touched his silk robe. "Like this, like everything else that makes life less drab in our puritan country, it comes from Hong Kong."

He crossed to the window, stared out at the water that was spilling from the eaves.

"No reason not to eat," he said.

Lewis went to the table, ate a little of the fruit and meat. The bourbon was good and he sipped it and watched Chen move from the window, pace around the room, touch the frame of the photograph.

"They tell me she's dying," Chen said.

"Who is she?"

"My mother."

"Shouldn't you go to her?"

"Not possible."

"Why not?"

"The State requires me here."

"Surely they would let you go?"

"No. We do not make journeys of compassion."

Lewis ate some of the hot-pepper bread.

"Where is she?" he asked.

"Shanghai."

"The hospital?"

"Yes."

"What is wrong?"

Chen hesitated.

"A disease," he said.

He proffered the whiskey bottle.

"Some more Jim?"

"Please."

Chen refilled both glasses, then sat on the chaise longue.

"She was a strange woman," he said. "As you can see she was pretty in her youth. Her father was a French consular official in Shanghai. He kept a Chinese mistress in a house in Bubbling Well Road. And at the end of his service he stayed in Shanghai and married her. But that's all I know about them. My mother was born in that house." He smiled. "Mixed blood—as I am. But nothing remarkable in that. Shanghai was always as foreign as it was Chinese. Foreign blood, foreign money, foreign armies." He nodded at the woman in the photograph. "Her name was Ophélie. She had a yearning for France, a country she had never seen. And because of that she spoke to me in French, read to me in French, sang to me in French. I can hear her now. Of course she never got to France. Her parents died and so did the dream. Later she worked in a variety of respectable jobs. For the Asiatic Petroleum Company. For Shell. For Standard Oil. All this was before I was born. She was well-paid and intelligent. Yet there must have been something perverse in her. She hated the respectability. She wanted to escape. The last of the dignified jobs was with Jardine's. But finance was as dull as the oil companies. She left them and went to work at Farren's."

Rain, now, was roaring in the thatch.

"As you know," Chen said, "Farren's was a gambling house. Exclusive.

Expensive. One could dine and dance there. But its real business was roulette. Soon Ophélie had learned all the secrets of the wheel. She earned good money. She was popular. But she had restless feet. She moved on from Farren's to the night clubs. Places like Roxy's and the Blue Lagoon. And from there to the cabarets at Casanova's and Del Monte where the girls, usually Russian, sat at tables and were paid a percentage of the amounts a customer had spent. It was a long way from the sedate offices of the oil companies. A decline, of course. Yet the Shanghai of those days burned away on the bank of the Whangpoo in a kind of fever. Like a ruby in the night, a poet called it. But people caught its fever. Their lives were changed. Ophélie went happily from the cabarets to the dancehalls to the bars to the pimps in the wharfside flats. Eventually she became a singsong girl in a place in Soochow Creek that was named for some reason the Yuk Yin Bathhouse. They changed her name from Ophélie to Lisette, which was thought to be more enticing. And it was there that she met the general."

Chen rose and picked up the whiskey bottle.

"More?"

"Yes."

Chen poured.

"I have to tell you," he said, "that whiskey affects me. It makes me talkative."

Lewis watched him return to the chaise longue, lift his legs on its cushions. Was Chen a lonely man? The rainstorm was fiercer and Chen lay back and sipped the bourbon.

"So let me talk about General Chen Kuochang," he said. "A name you may recognize. The name of a warlord. The name of a man with a power of life and death over vast populations. What a strange era that was, those years between the two world wars. Savage men raising great armies, pouring across the land from east to west, ruling provinces. They called themselves generals. But they were neither generals nor lords. They were bandits. But like all scavengers they had their value. They hated the Communists, fought them, killed them. And because of this they were given arms and money by Chiang, by the Japanese, even by the Western powers." Chen shrugged. "All this is history. But it explains how General Chen grew rich. He had his hand in three fat purses. Then, when the Second World War ended in 1945, the United Nations began to pour money into China. It was supposed to be for the relief of refugees. But of course it was yet another purse for the warlords to dip their hands in." Chen smiled. "The general had need of a well-filled purse. He had expensive tastes. In his early days he used to come into Shanghai on the first-class train. Always with his lieutenants, always dressed as severely as a banker. You would not know he had come fresh from some bloody massacre. I am told he would put up at the best hotel, spend his time at the racecourse and the gaming tables, eat trout and lobster at Fiaker's. In the afternoon you might find him playing Liar Dice in the Wing On Gardens. He also had an appetite for women. But like many men who can afford the company of the chic, the well-bred and the elegant he found his satisfaction elsewhere. In the evening he would leave the Gardens and walk through the wharves to the Yuk Yin, spend an hour there with a girl. Understandable, I suppose. I first went there as a boy to see my mother and I can still smell those crude sexual scents. Even the curtains breathed perfume when they moved. Pleasure for sale—yes, I can see why that would stir a man. It was there that he met Lisette. And after that he would have no other girl. Always Lisette. Finally he wanted her exclusively for himself. He took her out of the bathhouse, leased one of the fine houses in Rue Molière in the French Concession and installed her in it. Two years later I was born there." Chen smiled again. "Of course it was never the same for the general. Lisette now had money for gowns, jewelry, servants. She became respectable again, the kind of woman the general had always despised. His passions cooled. He yearned for the excitements of the brothel. He solved the problem by buying the Yuk Yin Bathhouse and putting Lisette back in it. Not as a singsong girl—that would have been too lowly—but as the house mother. She had charge of the establishment and its fifteen girls. The general went away from time to time on his murderous campaigns, returned on the train and visited the brothel and lay in Lisette's perfumed arms. Perhaps he paid her. I do not know. I remained in Rue Molière and spent my childhood in the care of the servants and an Indian *ayah*."

Chen held out his glass.

"Will you fill it, please?"

Lewis filled it. A voice called out beyond the veranda and, turning, he saw through the trembling curtains of rain the face of Lieutenant Pu sunk in the collar of a glistening cape. Chen waved him away.

"The general was a Catholic Christian," Chen said. "He had caught that particular disease in a mission school and for the rest of his life he read nothing but the lives of the saints and the New Testament. He had also caught another disease, which was the syphilis." Chen tapped his head. "He was going slowly mad. Toward the end he'd come into Shanghai on the train as always. But now there might be a bandolier of shells slung across his somber suiting, even a cutlass hanging on his thigh. But people never laughed. They were too afraid of him for that. When I was nine he took me with him on one of the campaigns. I remember it so well. The train out of the city, then smaller trains out into the wild country, a railway halt with a water tower and a party of waiting horsemen and a beautiful shaggy pony that was his gift to me. And after that the ferocious army flowing west and burning and killing as if the old Tartar hordes had ridden out of the past. This was the time when Mao and Chu Teh were forming the first Red Army. The general wheeled his own forces south to Hunan to meet it. His hatred of the Communists was now an obsession. God had given him a holy task and he set about destroying them. Even then he was inflamed by the sight of the color red. And later, my mother told me, the insanity of it became so bad that he would kill a man if he was wearing a red scarf or carrying a red handkerchief and once when he saw from the hills a valley of red poppy fields he led the army back and forth through the valley until the hated color was trampled into the earth. But he was always devout. There were evening prayers by the campfire and he would read aloud from the Gospels and proclaim Jesus' gentle message and behind his voice you could hear the cries of prisoners being chopped."

Chen was silent for a time.

"John Chen," he said. "John. Do you know how I got that name? It was on that campaign. The general had been cut down the ribs by a sword stroke and the bleeding would not stop and the bandage was wet. It was night and he was lying by the fire and reading from the Book of John. Perhaps he thought he was dying. He was very calm and serious and he stopped the reading and looked up and said to me: 'Come here.' I went to him and he put his fingers on the bandage and then traced in blood the sign of the Cross on my forehead and said: 'I baptize thee in the name of the Father and of the Son and of the Holy Ghost. I name thee John.' " Chen smiled faintly. "It didn't sound like the Christian sacrament but it was all he could remember of it and later, on my blanket, I could feel his blood on my face and I wept. I think I was fond of him. There is always a bond between father and son, isn't there? Yet now, when I think of that poisoned blood on my flesh, I shudder. He was cruel, the cruelest of them all, utterly merciless. He smelled of tobacco and opium, leather and steel and old blood. But yes, I was fond of him. Years later, when the pox was disfiguring him and he could no longer endure it, he asked one of his captains to shoot him. And he did."

Chen put down his glass on the floor and closed his eyes. The lamp was flickering and the room was unstill with tongues of light and shadow. Then the lamp died and there was only the diffused glow from the veranda light. Lewis waited. There was more to come, he knew. Chen was using him, as priests were always used; priests were listeners; priests could be shown the wounds of the past. Here in this warm lamplit cell of a room, in the incense smell, enclosed by the roaring night, it would be easy to confide, even confess.

"I was sent to the Jesuit School," Chen said. "But I got nothing from it. I was already winning the important chess tournaments and that was all that interested me. The Fathers knew that, knew also that I was the son of General Chen. In their eyes there was no place for me. Some of them tried to beat me at chess but they could never do so. One of them, a Father Renaud, would try again and again. He could not accept defeat at the hands of a schoolboy. He read all the books, studied the masters' games, learned the gambits. But I could defeat him with only half my mind.

Eventually I let him win. He was a perceptive man and he knew what I had done. Intellectual arrogance, he called it. He became my enemy. He was a sinister man, burning with moral fire, always peering out from the Jesuit walls at Shanghai and what he called the surrounding moat of sin. Wherever he walked he carried with him a catechism book and he would stop boys and ask them questions from it. A wrong answer meant a punishment. With his ugly wrinkled face and the soutane that flapped as he hurried along he was like a bat. In those days in the school every boy carried a pink card so that he could record on it the commission of a sin. There was a black circle in the center of the card. If it was merely a venial sin a boy would make a hole with a pin anywhere outside the circle. But if it was a mortal sin the pin would be pricked inside the circle. I remember one day when Renaud asked to see my card. I gave it to him and he held it up against the light. There was not a pinprick in it and he asked sarcastically: 'A week without sin?' And I answered: 'No, Father. I lost my pin.' The other boys laughed and the laughter made him shake with anger and that evening he gave me a beating." Chen opened his eyes and turned his head. "There was a time," he said, "when I might easily have entered the Church of Rome. The first few terms with the Society of Jesus were good. There was a young Alsace priest—his name was Roussel—who took an interest in me, talked to me, made me see things. I think he would have led me into the Church. But he left. And Father Renaud's shadow fell across me. Christ disappeared and all I could see was that carnivorous little face. A hypocrite. An empty man with nothing in him but secondhand phrases. He had three that he used incessantly. The mysteries of Creation. The journey to God. The ascent of man." Chen relaxed again on the cushion and shut his eyes. The rainstorm was passing and the thatch no longer roared. Lewis took an apple from the dish and began to eat it. Chen did not move or speak. Was he asleep? Lewis finished the apple, stoppered the Jim Beam bottle. Then Chen said wearily: "The ascent of man. Now we don't ascend anywhere. We go sideways on endless journeys to the next commune."

Lieutenant Pu appeared again outside the veranda. Chen stood.

"Go now," he said.

Lewis went to the door.

"Wait," Chen said.

He took something from the pocket of his gown and put it into Lewis' hand. It was Father Tsai's silver fish and chain.

"You know the camp rule," Chen said. "If you wear it I shall have to punish you."

Lewis left.

Walking with Pu down the bungalow path he heard Chen's voice speak softly from the veranda. "Goodnight, Lewis." He did not turn. The rain had stopped and the earth steamed. When they reached the compound he saw that a truck was standing in front of the execution shed and that its headlamps threw beams of light inside its open doors. Guards were shouting and men came from the truck and into the beams. One of them paused and looked up at the hot full moon.

In the morning one of the Americans in Compound Four reported to Lieutenant Pu that three men were seriously ill. There were two huts in the compound in each of which slept a hundred men. The three cases were all in one hut. Pu went into the hut and bent across the men. When he was satisfied of the gravity of their condition he walked through the system of wire fences to Compound One. Once there had been six medical doctors (four of them missionaries) in Fusan. But four had died and of the remaining two only Lewis Mackenna was effective.

Lewis listened to Pu. Then he went back with him to Compound Four. One of the sick was American, a man named Schumacher. The other two were Chinese Nationalists. Inside the hut there was the usual odor of dirt and disease. The two Chinese were on the floor. Schumacher lay on his face in one of the bottom bunks. Lewis turned him over, touched his forehead. It was suffused with fever.

"How long have you been ill?" Lewis asked.

"Three, four days."

"What do you complain of?"

"Headache. Sick. Can't stand."

"Let me see you get up."

"No, no. Can't get up."

"Try."

Schumacher raised himself onto his left elbow, dropped a leg over the wooden tier of the bunk, then the other.

"Now stand up."

Schumacher grasped the edge of the overhead bunk and began to pull himself upright. The muscles of his stomach contracted and he vomited and fell back on the bunk. Lewis looked down into his congested face.

"Put out your tongue," he said.

Schumacher did so.

"I see," Lewis said. He opened the shirt, pulled down the shorts. There was a rash on the abdomen, on the inner aspects of the arms and on the chest. He examined the palms of the hands, the soles of the feet. Then he went to the two Chinese. The signs were the same. One of them, an old man with a wisp of sweat-wet beard, had convulsions in the legs.

Lewis left the hut and Pu followed.

"Well?" Pu said.

"I don't know. It could be anything. Headaches, nausea, rashes—probably from scratching. Fevers are much alike in the early stages."

The next day Pu reported that the three men in Compound Four were now delirious. There were six new cases in the hut, three in the adjacent hut and twelve in the other compounds. Lewis returned to the hut in Compound Four. Schumacher's tongue and the tongues of the two Chinese were coated, as brown as leather. The American's temperature was as high as 104 and the rashes on all three were brighter and more extensive. The expressions were stuporous and there were now roseolas mottling the palms of the hands and the soles of the feet. Lewis studied Schumacher for a time. Then, on impulse, he pushed his head to one side and looked closely at the base of the hair. There was a fine comb in his medical bag and he passed it lightly through the neck-hair, then went outside and held it up to the sunlight. Lice moved across the comb's teeth. He threw it to the ground and beckoned to Pu.

"I want to see every other case," he said.

There were twelve huts in the six compounds and it was noon when they left the last of them.

"I must speak to the commander," he told Pu.

But Chen did not summon him to the admin office or to the bungalow. He came to the wire and stood ten paces from it and spoke across the intervening space. This was a different Chen. Gone were the colored silks and the graceful body. He stood there in his crude Mao tunic and heavy boots and the cheap red-starred cap that sat squarely on his head and even the beauty of his face was gone. Pu waited behind him.

"What are you afraid of, Dr. Mackenna?" Chen asked.

"I'm not certain. Many men are dangerously ill."

"Perhaps the dysentery?"

"No."

"Then what?"

"Could be measles. Cerebrospinal fever. Typhoid or paratyphoid."

"But you don't think so?"

"No. Some of them have roseolas on the palms and feet. You don't get that in typhoid."

"Please come to the point. What do you suspect?"

"It may be a form of typhus."

"Typhus!"

Lewis saw the shadow of unease in Chen's eyes.

"I warned you about dirt diseases," he said. "Men are living here in filth. No soap and not much water. Heads alive with lice. That might point to typhus."

"Have you ever seen a case of typhus?"

"I have."

He knew the question that would follow.

"How contagious is it?" Chen asked anxiously.

"That depends on the form."

"In what way?"

"There is an epidemic typhus. It is transmitted by the louse."

"How?"

"Through its feces. Men inoculate themselves by scratching."

He saw Chen's lips tighten in disgust. Soon, he thought, his fear of anything unclean will cause an itch. He watched Chen's fingers wander down his sleeve, begin to scratch the wrist.

"But you may not be entirely safe outside the wire," Lewis said.

"Why not?"

"Infected feces can be blown on the wind."

"And?"

"You could inhale them." He smiled. "You had better keep your mouth shut, Commander."

A breeze crossed the camp and Chen turned his face from it. He waited until the air was still. Then he said: "If it is an epidemic typhus how serious would that be?"

"You mean deaths?"

"Yes."

"With weak and undernourished men I would expect a fifty percent mortality."

"As high as that?"

"Yes."

"We cannot have an epidemic, Doctor. It could spread beyond the camp."

"Yes, easily."

"Surely there are drugs or serums?"

"Nothing satisfactory."

"Then what is the treatment?"

"There is no specific. Good nursing is considered essential."

"Good nursing," Chen repeated.

"Yes."

"Are you trying to be funny?"

Pu smiled. His thin shoulders shook gently.

"Firstly," Lewis said, "we have to determine whether or not it's typhus. And if it is what form. But I have no facilities for that. I can take some blood samples. You have to get them immediately to whatever hospital or laboratory can examine them."

"And how long will it take?"

"To filter a virus—perhaps five days."

"And in the meantime?"

"Louse prophylaxis. We have to destroy them. Hot water. Naphthaline soap. Head powders. Insecticidal liquids. Cresol baths. Burn the clothes. Paint the huts with creosote."

Chen nodded.

"Your own men must be examined."

"Yes."
"And a quarantine for those already sick."
Chen scratched again.
"It's all very disturbing," he said.
"Very. Shall we play chess tonight?"

They did not play chess that night or, indeed, on any other night of his time in Fusan. In the week that followed they waited for the supplies that might relieve them; but nothing came, no soap or disinfectants or medicines. Additional water was made available. But that was all. There were more than fifty new cases, seven of them in the barracks. Lewis did not need a laboratory confirmation that the outbreak was epidemic typhus. And when it came on the seventh day from Chungking (the report identified *Rickettsia prowazeki* or exanthematic typhus) they had already buried twelve infected prisoners. The report was delivered in an army helicopter by two government men. They were medical officers of a high rank. They walked with him through the compounds and inside the huts and studied the sick and held handkerchiefs to their mouths and noses, sometimes retched in the stench. John Chen did not enter the compounds and Lewis saw him pacing in the barbed-wire alleys with a disinfected white mask tied around his face. The two scientists went back to the admin wing and Chen spoke to him, voice muffled, from beyond the fence. "They are blaming me for what has happened. But I am not responsible for conditions. Teng Hua was the commander."

The next day trucks came from the perimeter road and into the camp. They brought bundles of calico shorts and trousers and shirts, boots and sandals, cases of naphthaline soap, insecticidal powders, drums of army cresol, creosote paint, various chemical and medical sundries, twelve large metal containers of the kind normally used for the cooking of food in army field kitchens. Then they departed; and when they were gone the guards put two of the containers in each of the compounds and filled them with a cold water cresol solution. Then they built pyramids of kindling and wood in the centers and stacked the new calico garments and footwear against the fences. Then they set fire to the pyramids and when they were blazing they brought from inside and outside the huts all the prisoners, even the sick and the dying, and with them their scraps of clothing and blankets and their books and other possessions. Lewis walked through the camp and watched. Palls of smoke were rising against the early sun and the black shadows of it crossed the compounds. Lines of men, naked now, approached the fires, clutching blankets, reluctant to part. Everything was cast into the flames. Gray faces blossomed into roseate life, grayed again as the columns shuffled past. He felt his throat go thick with pity for them. He had not realized how emaciated they were. He had the feeling that if the wind gathered it would scatter them like withered grasses.

When the burning was finished and the black ashes from it were falling from the sky the prisoners were arranged again in columns or lay prostrate on the earth. Pu gave a signal and the columns advanced and men climbed into the containers and lowered themselves, ducked in the cresol water, climbed out. Chen and the two scientists watched from outside the wire. "Every man must be submerged," Chen ordered. Lewis walked through the heat of the fires to the little groups of prostrate men, looked down at the big heads and pipestem limbs. He heard Chen shout: "Their heads. Their heads. They must go right under." Dripping men were going now to the fence, choosing fresh clothes, pulling on boots. The fires were still exploding fragments on the sky. Chen's voice came again: "That man there. That one. He never went right under." Now the guards were going to the bundles on the ground. Lewis went to Chen and said: "Some of these men are dying. You can't duck them in cold water."

"Every man goes under."

"The shock will kill them."

"And so will the typhus."

Chen tightened his face mask. Lewis saw the loathing in his eyes.

"Every man," Chen said.

In the next seven days the trucks came to the camp with more supplies of army cresol, water tanks and hoses for the spraying of the huts, hair clippers and soap, new blankets. A mechanical excavator came on one of the trucks and began to move about the compounds, digging great pits for the burial of the dead. Its steel body was shaped like that of a mantis and at night it stood in the shadows with its head raised to the sky. Every day the prisoners bathed in the containers. Every day men fell sick, recovered, died. The two government men took their samples, diagnosed, reported, watched the typhus smolder. The weather was changing, colder at night; and the Kun-lun mountains, Pu told them, were thick with early snow. The huge and multiplying herds were already moving down from the high ground and soon, they knew, they would hear again their distant lowing. Lewis waited. There was an incubation period of anything from four to fourteen days. For many men the onset was still to come. Predictably the typhus flared and, once more, the huts filled with the fevers and the rose-spots, the tremors and the earthy blue faces. In Compound One thirty-eight men died within a day and the mantis came and began to tear at the rain-soft crust with its green voracious jaws. When the pit was dug the mantis scuttled backward and waited with its head uplifted and the raw earth streaked redly down its jowls and the men of the burial party moved forward between the mounds and stared down, as prisoners always did, into the new grave. In the base of it they could see the remains of a stone wall and the place where it made an angle with another wall, a litter of shards and iron shapes, skulls and other bones. Father Methuen pointed down and said to Lewis: "I told you, didn't I? There was once a settlement here. Give me a hand." Lewis held his arm and Methuen clambered down. "You'll never get up again, Father," Gallagher said. And Methuen looked up and smiled and tapped his aged body and said: "Well, it won't be long before they put me here, will it?" He began to move through the length of the pit, bending stiffly, pushing with his boot into the earth, exposing skeletons. "An old burial place," he said. He held up a femur, brushed soil from its pitted surface. "A child, this one." His face was flushed now with his archaeologist's passion. The mantis moved nearer and its shadow fell across him. "Better come up now," Lewis said.

When the burying was done and Father Methuen had sanctified it with the appropriate words they watched the mantis gobble at the mounds, regurgitate earth until the pit was filled. Methuen looked across the camp to the slopes of the bowl and the trees that edged it and the rising hills.

"Such good land," he said. "Pastures, fertile soil, water." He took a piece of pottery from his pocket and gestured with it at the burial site. "Three hundred years ago. A community. I wonder why they left."

He was soon to know.

In the next two weeks there was no new case of typhus. The scientists returned to Chungking. Lewis, enfevered by recurring dysentery, watched his bones grow sharper. Chen, seldom seen during that time, emerged from the bungalow without his face-mask. One hundred and seventy men had died from typhus and other causes and because the reduction in numbers offended the Ministry bureaucrats the equivalent was transferred to Fusan from an overflowing camp in Shansi. Among them was an American named Lyndon Nathanson, an epidemiologist who had been studying the protozoal diseases in Peking when he was arrested and charged with harboring a fugitive from the forces of the revolution. He was known to Lewis by reputation and it was to Nathanson that he went when Father Methuen fell ill. Nathanson was in Compound Four, a crop-haired man in steel-rimmed spectacles with cracked lenses, still plump despite the privations of three months in Shansi.

"Why come to me?" he asked. "Don't you know what's wrong with him?"

"No."

"You've had the typhus here. Could it be that?"

"I doubt it."

"Why do you doubt it, Doctor?"

Lewis hesitated.

"There's a very high fever," he said. "And other similarities. There are also skin eruptions. Yes, I thought the typhus might be back."

"But now you don't think so?"

"No. It isn't a typhus rash."

"How would you describe it?"

"Pustules."

Nathanson walked back with him to Compound One.

"Three months I did in Shansi," he said. "A cruel lot."

Inside the hut he examined Father Methuen.

"I don't give him long," he said.

"No, not long."

Nathanson bent again, looked into the groin and armpits.

"No buboes," he said.

"No. I considered bubonic. But I'm sure it isn't."

"Early days, though."

"Yes."

"Do you have rats in the camp?"

"Of course."

"Then it could be bubonic."

"It's possible."

Nathanson held out his hands.

"Is there some disinfectant?"

"Over there."

Nathanson went to the bucket and plunged his hands.

"I agree with you," he said. "Those abscesses and pustules don't suggest bubonic."

He went to Father Methuen.

"A nice old man," he said with pity.

"Yes. Awfully nice."

"But don't touch him. Don't let anybody touch him."

Outside the hut Nathanson removed the cracked spectacles and rubbed his watering eyes.

"These are no damn good."

"We have a box," Lewis said. "When people die we never throw away their glasses. You're welcome to look."

"I'll do that."

In the morning Nathanson searched the box and found a pair of spectacles that would assist his myopic eyes. Then he went again to the hut and bent across Father Methuen.

"How are the specs?" Lewis asked.

"Quite good." He pointed to Methuen's hand. "Good enough to see this."

Lewis bent.

"A partially healed cut," Nathanson said. "Do you know how he got it?"

"No."

Nathanson examined the tongue, then the feet.

"What do you think?" Lewis asked.

"I don't know."

Outside in the compound Nathanson stared at the mound of earth that stood proud of the burial pit.

"Mass grave?" he asked.

"Yes."

"The answer could be there. Maybe there are typhus cases that weren't typhus."

Wind came, bringing with it the faint sound of lowing. Nathanson turned his head and listened.

"Did I hear cattle?"

Lewis smiled.

"You heard roast beef," he said.

"I'm not joking," Nathanson said sharply.

"Yes, there are cattle. Enormous herds."

The lowing came again.

"Let's have another look," Nathanson said.

Inside the hut he bent very low across Father Methuen, examined each eruption, turned him, lifted his arms. He pointed to the large malignant abscess on the inside of the left forearm.

"Have a look," he said.

Lewis bent.

"You see that coal-black center?" Nathanson asked.

"I see it."

"Come outside."

They went out.

"I know what it is," Nathanson said. "I heard those cows and I knew at once."

A light rain was falling.

"Do you mind the rain?" Nathanson asked.

Lewis shook his head.

"Then let's walk."

Walking through the shadow of the wire fences, faces wet in the warm rain, Nathanson said: "Have you ever heard of Camp Detrick?"

"No."

"But you've heard of Porton, England?"

"Oh, yes."

"One of its functions was the study of biological weapons."

"I know."

"That was in 1940. We began a similar thing in '43. At Camp Detrick, Maryland. I was a member of the team. Field experiments with live microorganisms. Plague, smallpox, anthrax and a dozen others. Could they be dropped in bombs and survive explosions? What would be the mortality rates in cities? A filthy business."

"Yes, filthy."

"We were especially interested in bacterial diseases that could be transmitted through the air. That way you could hit the big populations. So we concentrated on anthrax. Have you ever seen a case?"

"Only in animals."

"The bacterium proved to be a tough little bastard. Very infectious. Very lethal. And a real survivor. Nobody knows how long he lives."

"Centuries, they say."

"Centuries for sure. You talk of animals, Doctor. Well, we killed plenty of animals. I recall we filled a four-pint bottle with anthrax gruel and blew it up on the top of a gantry. We had a thousand sheep tethered around it and that evil little cloud of spores drifted across them and killed the lot. You could do the same with people."

Major Kazumi walked toward them.

"How is the Holy Father?" he asked.

Lewis shook his head.

"No hope?"

"No."

"Is the typhus back?"

"He has anthrax," Nathanson said. "Don't go near him. And you'd better seal that hut."

He took Lewis' arm and they began to walk.

"Are you sure?" Lewis asked.

"Almost. There'll have to be tests. But I'm pretty sure. It's my old companion. *Bacillus anthracis* is around again. Who's in command of this place?"

"A man named Chen."

"Then I have to speak with him."

Chen listened and when Nathanson was finished he went to the wire and stood there looking through its strands at the camp. Then he turned and Lewis saw the agitation in his face.

"This is very serious."

"Yes," Nathanson said. "You'll have to tell your government, Mr. Chen."

"But can you be certain?"

"Not without tests. But I think they'll confirm it."

"How did it get here, Doctor? Can you tell me that?"

"No," Nathanson said. "But we don't have to look far, do we?" He pointed to the hills. "It's a splenic fever of sheep and cattle. And from what they tell me you have considerable herds right nearby."

"We do indeed."

"Your people will have to check them. My guess is they'll find infected beasts. You see, Mr. Chen, there are two forms of anthrax. Father Methuen has one of them. We call it cutaneous—of the skin."

"And the other?"

"Ah, much more dangerous."

"Why?"

"Because it's airborne. Inhale the spores and a man will get a pulmonary anthrax. He'll probably die. We are talking now of epidemics."

"Man and beast?"

"Yes."

"A disaster."

"But it can be contained," Lewis said. "The camp is isolated. There's not a village or a town within thirty kilometers. Our concern is with twelve hundred men."

Chen turned again and looked out across the huts to the hill-line.

"And with half a million cattle," he said.

The next day a line of vehicles crossed the horizon above the east perimeter road and moved down into the camp. There were trucks, cars, a heavy earth-mover and a large enclosed van that was tall and painted white. This time the two scientists were part of a team. The team was led by Dr. Cao Hai, a bacteriologist with a wide experience of anthrax in Mongolia. Soon men in protective clothing, gloved and hooded and booted, were moving through the camp. Every prisoner was examined. Blood and skin samples were collected. Father Methuen (who had died at first light) was taken to the white van for dissection. At first it seemed that his was the only identifiable case. Then in the late afternoon seven prisoners collapsed with the high fever, coughing lungs and cyanosed faces that were the signs of pulmonary anthrax. The old pestilence had risen. The earth-mover went through the compounds and tore open the ground and the graves of all those who had died and in Compound One Lewis and Nathanson and Cao Hai watched it break through the high mound, then burrow down until the newly buried and the stones and bones of the old settlement were exposed. Soil samples were placed in bags, numbered according to site and sent to the white van. Quarantines were established in the center of the camp in Compound Three and the infected and the suspects sealed inside. Then, when this was done, the guards and army personnel were clinically examined. Meanwhile, outside the camp, more than a hundred men from the government veterinary service moved slowly up the long rise of the land and through the feeding herds.

But there were no signs of anthrax. "It seemed an obvious source," Dr. Cao said. "A dead animal. A bird, then, picking at the carcass and carrying the spores down to the camp. But the obvious is not always the truth. The transmission of disease is one of the mysteries of mankind and I have learned to always look further than what is in front of me. I have also learned never to drown my instinct in a sea of science. I believe that the camp itself is contaminated. I hope to prove it."

Dr. Cao proved it two days later. Eight lambs brought from Chungking in two of the enclosed trucks and sealed in aerated compartments had been exposed to the soil samples. Three were now dead. Lewis and Nathanson followed Dr. Cao to the pit in Compound One. They stood on the lip between the excavated mounds and looked down. "The soil came out of here," Cao said. He pointed at the broken skeletons. "They died three hundred years ago. As you know there was a village. Then disease came and the survivors fled. In those days they would have called it the plague. But it was really anthrax. I am always astounded at the bacterium's capacity for survival. When you reopened the old grave, Dr. Mackenna, you exposed it to the air. It formed spores. And when your friend—what was his name?"

"Father Methuen."

"When Father Methuen climbed down to explore he touched the soil or even a bone and became infected through a cut in his hand. Now we have airborne spores and dying men. How incredible it is. All those long years ago. Corrupt flesh planted deep in the ground and now"—he waved a hand sadly at the camp—"this dark harvest."

John Chen was waiting for them outside the wire. When they were within five paces he held up a hand and they stopped.

"No nearer," Chen said. His voice was thick within the antiseptic mask. "Please report."

Dr. Cao reported.

"Are you telling me," Chen said, "that the anthrax originated here?"

"Yes."

"And not with the cattle?"

"No."

"Are the cattle safe?"

Dr. Cao hesitated.

"They are moving them to higher ground," he said.

"I asked if they are safe."

"Nothing can be certain," Nathanson said. "They may be safe. But we are dealing with airborne spores."

Chen stared at the unmoving trees and the unmoving flag on the pole by the barracks.

"No wind," he said.

"And that's good," Nathanson said.

"And the converse? Is there danger in the wind?"

"Perhaps."

"Could a wind cross the camp and carry the spores to the herds?"

"It could."

"Let's talk of men," Lewis said coldly. "Men in danger. Men needing treatment."

Chen pointed at the hills.

"Out there," he said, "is an industry. A new one. Meat. Hides. Exports.

Important to the nation. Let's talk of that, shall we?" Revulsion touched his voice. "All at risk from this filthy pest-hole."

Later that day before sundown a car came to the camp. A Red Army star was painted on the side and two army officers got out. Lewis saw them walking with Chen and Lieutenant Pu in the distance on the perimeter road. Sometimes they stopped and talked and pointed down into the bowl where the camp lay. Then after nightfall he came awake in the darkness of the hut and heard the boots of marching squads, tailboards crashing, engines. He rose and went out into the compound. Headlamps were moving through the night, out of the camp, throwing pale yellow on the slopes. He listened until the sound of engines was gone.

In the morning there was the feel of emptiness in the camp, no pickets thudding down the roads, no smoke from the kitchen chimneys. A few guards stood in shadow. But that was all. The high white van was gone and with it the earth-mover and the trucks and most of the cars. At noon a little food and water was put inside each of the compound gates. One of the garrison trucks came from the direction of Chen's bungalow and he saw under the edge of the tarpaulin the angles of redwood chests, rattan furniture. Then at six in the evening Pu came to the hut.

"Gather your possessions," he said.

"My possessions?"

"Yes. Get them."

He knelt on the floor and pulled them out from under the bunk. There were some cardboard boxes that contained a surplice and clerical bands and the bamboo chessmen, a chessboard, clothing and sandals, a metal plate and messcan, the brown paper parcel in which were a Bible and the Book of Common Prayer whose language had sustained him throughout the months in the camp, his medical case. He picked them up and went with Pu from the compound and out onto the road. An open truck passed. It was filled with soldiers in full marching order.

"What is happening?" Lewis asked. "Why are the soldiers leaving?"

Pu did not answer.

"Where are you taking me?"

"Don't ask questions," Pu said roughly. "Just be thankful."

The parcel fell and Pu bent and retrieved it. There was a tear in the paper and he touched the gold-edged leaves of the Bible. "Teng would have beaten you for keeping this," he said.

Pu led him to a room in the admin wing. Dr. Cao was waiting and he smiled and pointed at a bench and said: "Remove your clothes and get on there." Cao examined him with great care, took a blood sample, listened again to his heart and lungs. "You are very weak," he said kindly. "But your lungs sound clear and I doubt if you have the anthrax. It could of course be incubating. So I'm going to give you some antibiotics and anti-serum."

Another truck passed the window. Soldiers waved.

"Why are they leaving?" Lewis asked.

Dr. Cao completed the injections and washed his hands.

"Dress," he said.

Lewis dressed.

"You must wait here," Pu told him. "I'll come for you."

He left and Dr. Cao took off his white coat and draped it over his arm. At the door he paused and turned. There was shame in his eyes and he looked away. Lewis felt the first foreboding. It touched him, as cold as shadow.

"Try to understand," Cao said miserably. "It is for the greater good."

After he had gone Lewis sat on the bench. For the greater good. What did that mean? Be thankful, Pu had said. The building was very quiet. He listened but he could hear no sound. Thankful for what? He rose and went out into the corridor and walked along it. The orderly room was bare. The filing cabinets and the tables had gone and there was not even a ball of crumpled paper on the floor. He went through into Chen's office. That too was bare. He stood there in the silence. Then he returned to the medical inspection room and sat again on the bench.

The sun was sinking when Lieutenant Pu came for him. Pu drove the small black car down the main camp road toward the gates. A single truck with a mounted machine gun stood outside the guard room. There were eight soldiers inside the truck and one of them was seated behind the gun and watched the compounds. The gates were unguarded and open and Pu took the car out of the camp and onto the perimeter road that encircled the camp and all its huts and buildings and then, leaving the perimeter, drove up the road that was cut out of the side of the bowl and rose steeply to its crest. There were belts of bamboo and, higher, forest trees against the sky. Another road followed the crest and along one side of it was a line of stationary army trucks and cars. Pu did not stop. Passing, Lewis saw Chen's face look at him through the window of one of the cars. Guards and soldiers from the camp stood by the road or leaned against the trucks, smoked and talked; men waiting. Below in the bowl he could see the camp. The compounds were filled with men; not sitting or sprawling in the shade or disposed in listless twos and threes, but tightly grouped in the dying sun. Even from height he sensed their agitation. They too were waiting.

The road descended. Pu stopped the car at a point below the crest where the land opened out into rising undulations. Very distant in the shadowing valleys were the dark and endless lines of the moving herds.

"Get out," Pu said.

He got out and Pu pointed at the copse that lay beyond the road.

"Go in there," Pu said. "I want your word that you will remain until I come for you."

"You have it."

He watched Pu turn the car and drive back to the crest. Then he walked through underbrush and into the copse and sat down within the fork of an exposed tree root and leaned back against the bole. Above him, seen through the tree canopies, was the pink sky. The copse was silent. He had spent nearly a year in Fusan and this place of unreachable peace with its thick green moss and soil that would run through the fingers and leaves that made fragile skeletons against the light would normally have healed him. But there was only tension, a swelling fear. What was about to happen? Why had Pu shut him in the copse and bound him with his word? You have to keep it, he told himself. A small red spider, suspended on a thread, began to descend. He touched it and in that moment the light went from the sky as the hem of darkness brushed across the land. You gave him your word. He shook his head and rose. Honor was a coin of little value in this impending night. He went to the edge of the copse and looked up the rise of the road. A hundred paces higher a soldier stood in silhouette, a rifle cradled in his arms.

Lewis retreated into the copse, walked through it and down the fall of the land until the trees thinned. Then, moving across the grain of the slope, he regained the crest and its fringe of thicket. Below was the bowl and the huts and the night already filling it like dark rising water. To his left he could see the line of trucks and soldiers. Every man was standing on the edge and staring down. Chen and Pu stood talking at the side of one of the cars. Voices came faintly. Then Chen held up a hand and the voices stopped. Heads turned to listen. Lewis heard a distant rumble. He waited. The sound died. The night had almost flooded the bowl and only the head of the mantis (abandoned in the corner of Compound One) rose from the lake of darkness. The rumbling sound came again, much nearer. Lewis listened. He had heard once before that awful sound of power. They were tanks. He heard their iron tramp.

The first shape came out of blackness and onto the perimeter road, and when the column was fully revealed there were eight of the shapes spaced at intervals around the camp. The guns, each of them with strange bulbous snouts, were pointed inward so that the whole of the camp was within their field of fire. Now the compounds and the crest above them and the tanks were silent. A flight of homing birds crossed the sky and their wings beat echoes into the bowl. The echoes died. Then a solitary bird crossed and was gone with its forlorn and fading cry. Silence again. Lewis stared down. All light was lost now in the impenetrable dark and even the neck and head of the mantis had sunk from sight. Then a sound rose; voices joined in some part of the camp, swelling, louder now, rising up the walls of the bowl. It was like a hymn, yet not one that he could recognize. It had all the sorrowing of some Jewish chant. Louder, louder. It seemed that every throat was singing. Then it stopped. There was a second's silence. Then a lone voice raised itself in a long despairing cry, as forlorn as the cry of the straggling bird. It eddied and flowed away into the night as if one man had lifted up his voice to express their terror of the ending. A whistle blew. Flame leapt from the eight snouts and the night turned brilliant. In that moment Lewis saw the camp revealed; its roofs and fences and tiny scampering figures, black in the heart of brilliance. Another burst. This time the waves of flame seemed to collide. The camp exploded. Lewis shut his eyes. He could not bear to look. He could hear the roar when the flame was thrown, the different roar of the burning huts. Once he opened his eyes and there was a fireball rolling in the bowl below him and the slopes too were burning and the firestorm was growing and the huts were gone and only the mantis stood in the sea of fire and stretched its neck to the sky like a thing in pain. He looked away, upward to where the clouds were splitting in the rising heat. Again the burst, then another. He turned and went back through the thicket and down across the slope and into the copse. He lowered himself trembling into the vee of the tree root and lay down. It was dark in the copse but above it there were red reflections in the night sky. There were no emotions left and he could not weep or pray for the men and there was only exhaustion drawing him into sleep. His thoughts became formless and unrelated. He turned over within the root and slid his hand under his cheek as he had always done as a child.

Later (how much later?) he heard John Chen's voice and, sitting up, saw his silhouette on the edge of the copse. He rose and followed Chen to the road. A car was waiting, Lieutenant Pu at the wheel. His possessions were piled on the rear seat. The red glow was still on the sky, showing through the low black clouds like veins of copper. Chen opened the rear door, then turned. Lewis saw the change in him. The strain had gone. His face was soft in the faint light. The camp and all its foulness had been burned clean in the fire and he too was cleansed.

"I like you, Lewis," Chen said. "But you are Chiang's man. You were always Chiang's man. Deeply involved." He reached out and touched Lewis' temple. "There are still a few secret things locked in here. We shall talk again."

He pointed into the car and Lewis climbed in.

"I am taking you home," Chen said.

Home. That word of beauty. That word of love. The word would not leave him. He heard it when the helicopter circled and he saw below him the bowl glowing like a coal in the blackness, heard it when the Kun-lun peaks fell behind him, heard it as the light aircraft flew into the paling day and across plains and the curl of rivers. And above all he heard it when the Party car with the red pennant drove through early mists and he saw the haze of West Lake and the Hangchow boulevards and the lake again and island temples and Dragon Well Lane and the little houses with painted doors. Home is there, here now, near to you, behind that courtyard wall.

Chapter 6

The wind was strong in the gorge and continually behind the *Shantung* and there were now eight men on the forward sweep. The walls of the gorge were very high, leaning across a sun-white sky. From the top, Ellen Mackenna thought, the junk would be like a painted toy on the enamel river. On the left of the foredeck she could see Shameen, sitting cross-legged and with his back toward them. Lewis lay beside her, eyes closed, under the canvas roof that fronted the stern cabin. The two boys were bent across the rope rail higher up near to the turret cabin. She watched them spit little flecks of saliva down into the racing water.

"You can stop that spitting," she said sharply.

Lewis opened his eyes.

"They're spitting," she said.

"Dirty little devils."

"Yes," she said, smiling. "Do you know what day it is?"

He shook his head. At first every hour gained and every hour lost had seemed crucial. But now, on the old river whose flow had shaped the rock through ages past, he had lost the sense of time.

"It's their birthday," she told him.

He sat up.

"Ten today," she said. "You forgot."

"Yes," he said. "I did forget, God bless them."

He called to them and when they came he said: "We know what a special day this is. Ten. At last in double figures." He rose and kissed their heads. "I'm afraid we have no gifts. But you have our love."

They grimaced.

"Yes," he said, laughing. "Not as good as a wristwatch. But it's all we have."

The junk rode out from the shadow of the overhangs, into sun. Shameen's turban became an emerald.

"He hardly ever moves," Joel said.

"Perhaps he's asleep," Gerard said.

They watched the camel-hair back.

"He's not asleep," Lewis said.

"How do you know?"

"When he sits like that he's not asleep."

"Why not?"

"Because," Joel said, "if he was asleep his head would fall forward."

"It might not," Gerard said.

"It would."

"Why?"

"Because as soon as he fell asleep the muscles of his neck would go. Isn't that right, Daddy?"

"Not always. A man like Shameen would always have control."

"Even when asleep?"

"Yes."

"Is he really Chiang's bodyguard?"

"He is."

"And now he's ours?"

"Yes."

"He's not guarding us now," Joel said. "He's watching the river."

"That's where the danger is," Lewis said.

Spray from the sweep sparkled above the turban.

"He makes me shiver," Ellen said. "A killer of people. That's his trade. That's all he is."

"No, he's more than that. He protects the president. And that's a very important job. Now he's protecting us. If he has to kill then that's his simple duty."

"I wonder how he kills them?" Gerard said to Joel.

"Be quiet," Ellen said. "I'll have no more talk of killing."

"You can't see a gun."

"No."

"Or a knife."

"No."

"I said be quiet."

"It could be in his boot."

"He's not wearing boots. Not high boots."

Ellen rose and went to the rail.

"Just shut up," Lewis said. "You're upsetting her. So shut up." He saw the hurt in their faces. "Look," he said kindly, "killing is a dark and nasty business. But sometimes it can be a Christian business. Certainly Shameen will kill our enemies. But he'll also lay down his life to defend us. Remember that. Shameen is different from us. Think of a leopard, the way it sees and hears and stalks and moves. That's the way Shameen is. He was born like that and perhaps he should live his life alone in a forest and be as fierce and beautiful as all the other leopards." He pointed at Shameen's back. "He has the most marvelous instincts." He touched Joel's ear. "Listen."

"What to?"

"Sound. The boat. The river. The crew. Listen to the sound of it all."

They listened; to the groaning of the tree-trunk sweep, the boom when the water struck it, the creak of the junk's timber, the chatter of the trackers. Two men were lowering water pails into the river so that the metal sound threw echoes into the gorge. The rattan sail whipped in wind.

"Pretty noisy, eh?" Lewis said.

"Yes."

"Take off your shoes," he said to Joel.

Joel removed them.

"There is Shameen," Lewis said, pointing. "His back is toward you. But you could not reach him without he heard you."

"You want to bet?"

"You have nothing to bet with. Now try."

They watched the boy creep along the deck, very slow, the naked feet poised, meeting the boards, parting from them, poised again, all with enormous care. A man was singing on the turret. Now the boy was within six steps of the unmoving figure.

"Nearly there," Gerard whispered.

Another step, then another. Shameen turned swiftly and there was a moment in which they saw and felt the tensile spring that his body had become. Then the Tungan turned again to where the bows thrust. Joel ran laughing to the stern.

"How did he do that?" Gerard asked.

"He could not tell you," Lewis said. "He could not put it into words. It would be something to do with the pattern of sound. Innocent sound. But when he heard your feet he heard the sound of stealth."

By noonday the wind had abated. The junk slowed. Ellen was in the cabin, Lewis on the deck by the stern tiller. He could see the silhouettes of the boys and the junkmaster on the turret. They were throwing dice and he walked up deck and climbed the turret stairway and watched them for a time. Ahead of the bows the river was broadening and the gorge no longer towered. One of the dice struck his foot and he bent to retrieve it. In that moment he heard the putter of an engine. The junkmaster stood. To his left and below him he saw Shameen's turban move into the point of the bows. The two boys came to his side. They watched the river. The engine sound grew louder. A launch came from behind the turning shoulder of the gorge and out onto the breast of the river. It showed a red pennant and a red star. He counted eight men with rifles seated in its open rear. The junkmaster touched his arm and pointed to the stern and he went with the boys to the cabin. Ellen was standing, hairbrush in hand, at the foot of the three interior steps. She too was listening to the engine. He saw the fear in her face.

"Soldiers," he said.

"How many?"

"Eight."

They felt the junk heave to. A voice called from somewhere on the river. Ellen looked around her, at the boys and at the doors. There was desperation in her eyes.

"Nowhere to hide," he told her.

Red-starred caps and rifle barrels glided past the mullioned windows. Wood bumped on wood. A rope ladder splashed. Then a turbaned figure stood above them in the doorway, black against the glaring sky. Shameen unhooked the doors, came down the steps into the cabin, then turned and closed the doors and secured them with the two brass bolts. The glass of the doors was heavily and intricately engraved so that, looking through it, they could see the perspective of the deck stretching from the shade cast by the canvas roof into sun. Everything was slightly blurred by the vines and flowers and foliage that had been patterned on the glass. The junkmaster and an army officer, their outlines disjointed as if seen through water, were talking by the mast. Three soldiers stood behind the officer and two more soldiers were descending into the hold. The officer began to gesticulate. The junkmaster spread his hands. Their voices rose. The junk swung gently on the swell. The officer shook his head and the junkmaster put his hand into his pocket and transferred something to the officer's palm. A coin fell and made a minute glint of gold on the deck. The officer bent and picked it up. Again the shake of the head. More coins passed and the officer's voice came angrily. "No, no, no, no." The junkmaster shrugged. The officer said something. Then he and the three soldiers turned and stared down the deck to the stern cabin.

Shameen turned from the doors so that his back was to the deck. He took a step into the cabin. Now he was facing them. Across his shoulder they could see the approach of the officer and the soldiers. The junkmaster followed behind them. Shameen advanced another step, so near now that Lewis could have reached out and touched him. The officer and the junkmaster had stopped by the cabin doors. They were arguing again and he heard the officer say: "It is not enough." A palm pushed against the glass and the doors rattled. Shameen's hand slid down inside his sash and then, partially emerging, revealed the haft of a knife within the fist. Lewis saw the change in his eyes. They were as yellow and implacable as those of a springing cat. He heard Ellen gasp behind him. The palm moved from the glass and, now, was held out cupped and a pouch appeared and decanted golden coins. The officer nodded and pocketed the coins and he and the junkmaster and the soldiers turned and walked back along the deck to the hatches. Shameen listened to the retreating boots. The hand went again inside of the sash and came out empty. He unbolted the doors and climbed the steps and hooked back the doors and Lewis watched him pad away on his goatskinned feet. The river breeze entered the cabin and was cold against his sweating face. When he turned he saw that Ellen was seated on the bed with her face in her hands and that the boys were huddled against her as if they too had sensed the menace that had stood in the cabin, and shared her fear.

He went to them and pulled her head against his chest. He stood there poised on the sway of the junk and listened to the voices on the deck and the bumping of the launch. Then the engine started into life and they did not move until the sound of it was lost in the reaches of the river. He drew her hands from off her face and she looked up at him.

"Did you see his eyes?" she whispered.

"Yes."

"He was ready to kill you."

Later in the stern and the dusk blurring the shores he stood by the rail and watched the dark groove in the back water that was made as the junk moved faster. The gorge was narrowing into greenstone cliffs and there were dams of porphyry at the bases with white water where the river pressed. There was beauty, even peace, in the scene; but he could see only the Tungan and the haft of the knife and the feral eyes. He remained by the rail with the breath of the river rising until the moonrise came. He heard a movement behind him and, turning, saw that it was the steersman. He was holding a food bowl and he dipped into it and ate a morsel and said politely: "I greet you with respect."

"I greet you too."

The steersman wiped a finger around the bowl, then sucked it.

"Is it true you are a minister?" he asked.

"Yes."

"Of which church?"

"Presbyterian."

"Is that of Rome?"

"No. It is a free church."

The finger wiped again.

"I am a Catholic," the steersman said. He smiled. "But we are both Christians, are we not?"

"We are."

"It is as a Christian that I speak to you. It is my duty."

Lewis waited. The junk rolled and the steersman went from the stern to the port rail and looked down at the river.

"It is becoming strong," he said. "At this point the cliffs make a funnel. Lower down the water will rise and will be very strong."

Lewis joined him. Across the man's shoulder he could see to the foredeck and the pattern of moon and shadow where Shameen sat.

"A savage," the steersman said.

"Yes."

"A great slitter of throats."

"I know that."

"This is why I speak to you. You are in danger."

"I know that too."

"I mean from Shameen. Do you understand?"

"I am beginning to."

"He is your guard. Chiang has sent him to protect you. But if he cannot protect you from your enemies he will not let them take you. I have seen it happen."

"On this boat?"

"Yes. A general of the Kuomintang. His head, they say, was filled with secrets. And the boat that waited at the river bend was filled with soldiers. So Shameen killed him and dropped him over."

They listened to the booming of the river on the bows. The steersman tapped his head.

"Do you have such secrets?" he asked.

"I do."

"Then you must prepare to defend yourself."

"Against Shameen? I would have no chance."

"You would need a gun."

A voice shouted from the bows.

"I have to go," the steersman said. He turned from the rail. He began to walk up deck. Words came on the wind. "May Jesus help you."

Now she was distraught. He watched her pace the cabin, her swift steps.

"I felt safe," she said. "With Shameen there was hope."

The boys entered.

"Leave us," Lewis said.

They went.

"You told us he'd guard us," she said.

"Yes."

"Lay down his life for us. That's what you said."

"I know."

She wiped her cheeks and left the cabin. He followed her to the rail and stood behind her and held her and felt the shudder in her body. Daybreak was near.

"Can we be certain?" she asked.

"Yes."

She turned to face him.

"There was murder in his eyes," she said. "And his hand was on the knife. I know that. But perhaps it was for the soldiers."

"It was for us. If the officer had entered the cabin he'd have used it."

Birds crossed the junk.

"Seabirds already," he said. "Not too far to go."

River light, reflected from the cabin windows, quivered on her pallid face. Now there was not even fear in it, only emptiness. The birds came crying once again. She turned and walked slowly alongside the rail.

"Ellen," he said.

She stopped and he went to her.

"You still don't understand," he said.

"I understand."

"No, you don't. Shameen would have killed us all."

She shook her head, disbelieving.

"Yes. Me. You. The boys."

"The boys know nothing."

"Children observe. Children listen. Young or old every human mind is a storehouse. One has only to search." He stared down into the water. "Those are not my words. They are Chen's."

She was silent.

"That doesn't mean I'm going to lie down and wait for it," he said. "Tomorrow night we leave the junk and go overland to the coast. Shameen will be with us until we reach Taiwan. All that time we'll be in danger from him. Here on the river. On the land. On the sea." He put his arm around her. "I was never meek. So I'll defend you. You and the boys." His arm tightened. "My beloved family. But to do that I'll need a gun."

At noon he went up deck and called to the junkmaster and when the man came down he drew him to the rail and said: "Do you keep a gun aboard?"

"Of course."

"Will you lend it?"

"No."

"Will you sell it?"

The man stared.

"A strange request from a priest," he said.

"Will you sell me the gun?"

"Why do you want it?"

"For protection."

The junkmaster pointed at the foredeck and Shameen's unmoving figure.

"You have a protector," he said.

"Perhaps."

"Have you ever owned a gun?"

"No."

"Fired one?"

"Never."

The junkmaster laughed. "I think we shall all need protection."

"The gun," Lewis said.

"What would you pay?"

"A good price."

"Gold?"

"No. And I have very little cash."

"Then what would you pay with? A blessing?"

"With valuables."

The junkmaster nodded in understanding.

"Ah," he said. "The tea chests."

"Yes. I'd give you some valuable things. They'd fetch a very high price."

The junkmaster looked again at Shameen.

"I know why you want the gun," he said.

"Then you'll sell it?"

"No. It would not be worth the risk. Chiang has a long arm. It would reach across the sea."

"An exceptional price," Lewis offered.

"No."

"Please."

The junkmaster went to the stairs that led to the turret. He turned on the second step.

"You are not much of a priest," he said with contempt.

"No," Lewis said. "I know that."

The sun was low when they heard again the putter of an engine. The river was high and wild and the junk plunged and three men held the bow sweep against its power. From the stern window they saw the army launch appear within the rock walls and approach along the wake. "The soldiers," Ellen said. "They're back." Her hand gripped his arm. A klaxon sounded and the launch gained and moved out from the wake to overtake. There were eight rifle barrels, a different officer. Behind the klaxon they heard the cabin doors close and, turning, watched Shameen shoot the bolts. This time he stood with his face to the engraved glass and his eyes intent on the deck. They stared at the camel-hair back and the sash where the knife was held and the hand that hung beside it. Ellen took the two boys to the angle made by the cabin walls, then moved in front of them. The rifle barrels slid past the mullioned windows on the starboard, lifted on the river waves, sank into the trough, appeared again. They heard the junk-master shout: "No, no. Cannot stop." The launch passed. The shout came again on the wind: "No, no, no. Too rough." The klaxon threw its echoes in the gorge. The launch, somewhere near the bow, bumped once, then twice, then collided. They felt the impact run through the hull. A man screamed. Then the rifle barrels, thrust up in disarray, reappeared. The launch fell back into the wake and, turning, they watched it through the stern window. It had taken on water and was low on one side and the officer was clapping his hands in anger. It grew smaller. Then the river curved and it was gone from sight.

What now? Sitting by the tiller with his dish of rice and fish, the sun dipping and the sail russet against it and the junk carved from old glowing wood, Lewis could see Shameen in his place on the foredeck. Higher, on the conning deck beyond the turret cabin, was the junkmaster. Waiting for the night, he thought, as they all were; for the safety of the darkness. Already the cumulus made darkening ramparts above the river. It was wider now, growing ever calmer. He ate some of the salted fish. How could a family of four escape from Shameen within the confines of a junk? The soldiers would return and that turbaned head would swing down from the deck and into the cabin. This time, the third time, the fearful thing could happen. What to do? Bribery? Or the awful alternative that already hovered on the edge of the mind and would not go? Bribery was no solution. Shameen was incorruptible and in any event would place no value on possessions. For him, as with Chen, duty was all. So what was left? The shadow, the unthinkable act, crept nearer like something coming from the night. I have to face it. *He has to be killed.* The words, once formed, would not leave him. *He has to be killed.* He could not sit there with their terrifying echoes and he stood and walked to the cook and gave him his dish and spoon. He could see Ellen and the boys in the stern. They were sitting in the partial shadow of the cabin, very close together and a band of wan sunlight softening their faces. God, how I love you all. She looked up and smiled at him. Love you all. I'll do anything to save you. Anything. He felt a sudden, terrible confusion. Love and the murderous intent that now possessed his mind—how could such things live together?

He went back to the tiller and watched the sun sink behind the hills and the twilight of the river. Everything was turning gray. Shameen still sat motionless with his calves tucked beneath him; a man, it seemed, in perpetual meditation. With his grace and savagery and instinctive gifts he had likened him to a leopard. How did one set about killing a leopard? He had no hunter's rifle, no handgun, no weapon of any kind except a razor or the scalpel in his case. He could not get near to the leopard without that strange antenna sensing danger. For such a creature was there ever an unguarded moment? In sleep? No, not even in sleep. Every instinct would be preternaturally sharp. Follow the leopard, watch it move, a shadow among shadows and the hammer of the sun gone and the night closing and the heat of the day still thick and coming off the earth and the rocks and the tongue and the membranes of the throat so dry that the smell of a stream or a river would draw it through cavities of silence and out from cover and onto the bank and, now, the shoulders hunched and the chest low and the head low and the tongue curling round the water. Even then the yellow eyes must watch; but there might be a moment in the first slaking of the thirst when the sensuous pleasure of the water would close the eyes so that there was only the sound and flavor of the water and in that moment an enemy could strike.

Lewis moved from the tiller. The leopard crept away into those imagined thickets. The light was nearly gone and, up deck, he saw Shameen preparing for his twilight prayer. He watched him kneel barefoot, sprinkle water from a purification jar onto his face, hands, arms and feet, then lean forward and down until his lips brushed the deck. He remained there briefly in silent prayer. Then he touched the backs of his ears, lifted his head and bowed toward Mecca, rose to his feet and bowed again. Lewis turned and went to the rail and stared at the water and the distant wooded banks. The image of that submissive body bent in prayer would not leave him. The drinking leopard, he thought, stretched low across the shallows, exposed. The mottled head reformed into the folds of an emerald turban and he saw quite clearly the two unguarded moments of Shameen's day.

That night he slept on a mat outside the cabin. He awakened before dawn. The sky had not yet begun to pale and the shores were lost in darkness. These were always the quiet hours in the *Shantung* with the crew and the trackers asleep under the central shelter or in the holds and only a few men holding the sweep against the river and the bow steersman to keep a watch. He sat up. He could see the faint perspective of the deck planks and in the foredeck the area of deep shadow that was made by the flank of the junkmaster's cabin. He could not see Shameen but he knew that the Tungan lay enfolded in his blanket somewhere within the shadow. He stood and draped his own blanket around his shoulders and crossed to the deck that was to the right of the lugsail and stood by the rail. There was still no glimmer of daylight. He looked around him. Then he went to the little sampan that was kept on the deck and tied to the stanchions and bent to it and eased one of the tholepins from out its socket. It was carved from hard cypress wood and rimmed with iron and it hung heavy in his hand. He concealed it under the blanket and walked up deck to the bow and to the rope rail that fronted the cabin. Below the rail on the lower level were the sweep and the steersman and three men. The jutting edge of the cabin obscured the left foredeck and he still could not see Shameen, only the protruding ear of a striped blanket. Shameen, he knew, must have heard his approach; the scuff of sandals to join the other sounds of the junk, the creak of the sweep, the stertorous breathing of the master inside the cabin. Footfalls might or might not portend danger. But Shameen, now, would be listening. He decided to call down to the steersman so that Shameen would hear and recognize his voice. When he spoke the words were strained with tension.

"There is not much wind."

The steersman looked up.

"There is enough."

The steersman turned again to the bows. Lewis moved further to the left, stepped back a pace from the rail. The edge of the cabin was very near. Nausea was rising and he could feel his hand sweating on the tholepin. He stood there watching the dark sky and the lift of the bows and feeling the cold of the river's night against his heated face. Go back to your cabin, he told himself. Don't do it. But he did not move and he knew he would do it if he could and was committed. He searched the sky. There was gray now in the nearest shore and he thought he saw the fleck of white water where the river touched it. He waited. A bird cawed and when he turned toward the sound he saw a luminous gleam, faintly pink, and a silhouette of distant trees.

The blanket moved and was drawn along the deck. Shameen, too, had seen the gleam of breaking day and was stirring. Lewis listened. He heard the soft tap-tap when the goatskin shoes were placed on the deck, the little rasp as the mouth of the bundle opened on its drawstring. He let the blanket fall from his shoulders and gripped tightly on the tholepin. He heard the sound of the cork coming from the neck of the purification jar. He waited. Shameen, now, would be sprinkling water. Give him ten seconds to complete the sprinkling, recork the jar, set it down, lean down and forward to the deck and begin his prayer. He counted to ten. Then he stepped around the angle of the cabin and raised the tholepin and Shameen was there prone on the deck and he brought the tholepin down with awful force on the nape of the neck and there was no cry and the body slid so that the left cheek was against the deck.

Lewis looked about him. Nothing moved on the deck. He heard the junkmaster yawn in the cabin. The pink light was creeping and already the lugsail was turning russet. He bent to Shameen and pulled him across the deck and under the rope rail. Then he pushed with his foot and the body went over the side and he heard it splash. Shameen's gold brooch glinted on the deck. He picked it up and, straightening, he saw a figure standing by the stern cabin. It was Ellen and she was watching him. There was a moment in which they stared across the length of the intervening deck. Then he went to the rail and looked down to the water and Ellen too went to the rail and they watched the river and the body twisting in the turbulence that was left by the junk. The turban was unraveling and the silk stretched on the current as bright as seaweed. They watched until the green was gone.

Evening was near when the *Shantung* swung from the river and around an island of village huts and into a waterway that was known by all (the steersman said) as the River Shih. This too was the name of the village.

It was a fishing village and Ellen Mackenna could see the jetties and the flat-bottomed boats that were moored or were drawn back on the shores. The two boys were drinking tea under the deck shelter and Lewis stood alone by the rail to the right of the turret cabin. They had not spoken since the sunrise and even then, after the body was gone from sight, he had held up his palms as if to keep her at a distance and had said no more than: "Leave me be." So she had left him in his aloneness and with his guilt and the day had passed and because of her own terrible conflict there were no words she could say or comfort she could give. She had not seen what had happened. The first gleam of daylight had struck the engraved glass of the cabin doors and she had risen and gone out onto the deck and filled her lungs with the river air and, turning, she saw him on the foredeck and Shameen's unmoving body poised on the edge beneath the rail and he, Lewis, pressing with his foot against the Tungan's ribs and she saw the body slide and plunge to the water and she had gone to the rail and watched it pass and sink into the night-dark trough behind the junk. She did not go to him or speak and when he had kicked Shameen's bundle, shoes and blanket over the side he turned and walked from sight across the front of the master's cabin and when he reappeared his own blanket was draped around his shoulders. He had gone, then, to the sampan that lay on the right deck and there was an object in his hand and he bent to the little boat and when he walked away from it to the bows his hand was empty. She watched the light grow stronger. Then she went to the sampan and stared down at the gunwale. One of the tholepins glistened and she reached out and touched it and turned her fingers into the sun. They were wet with blood.

But now, at the day's end, there were still no words. The act had been done, the taking of a human life, and could not be reversed. The enormity of it would not leave her mind. She could sense his own inner turmoil. She saw him bend lower on the rail, straighten and square his shoulders like a man easing a burden on his back. Then he turned and crossed the deck and went down into the cabin. She listened. There was a scraping sound, like something dragging on the cabin floor. She went to the head of the steps and Joel came to her side.

"Where is Shameen?" he asked.

"He left the boat."

"Left it?"

"Yes. Now go away."

How devious that answer was, she thought. Words of truth with a fearful double meaning. She went down the steps and closed the doors behind her. The big black-japanned metal case was on the floor in the center of the cabin. The lid was open and he was on his knees and his hands were in its contents. She watched him pulling out his vestments.

"What are you doing?"

He stood, picked up the vestments. One of the lawn sleeves hung to his knee and he gathered it and laid it in the crook of his arm.

"What are you doing?" she said again.

"Getting rid of things."

She shook her head.

"Yes," he said. "I have to."

"No."

"I have to."

"Put them back, Lewis."

He moved toward the step.

"I know what you're suffering," she said. "It hurts me too. But it wasn't murder. It wasn't a sin."

"I think it was."

"You were defending us. Shameen had his orders. That's what you said. He'd've killed us."

"If he had to."

"Yes, if he had to. But you had no choice either."

They heard the boys laughing on the deck.

"Do you hear that?" she asked.

"I hear it."

"You made them safe."

"Let me pass, Ellen."

She put her hand on the vestments.

"Don't do it," she said.

"I must."

"Over the side?"

"Yes."

"Throwing them into the river won't absolve you."

She saw him wince.

"You said it wasn't a sin," he said.

They were silent. They heard the steersman call.

"We're miles apart," he said slowly. "Not talking of the same thing." Her hand was still on the vestments and he knocked it off. "Why don't you understand? You saw me kill him."

"No."

"But you were standing there."

"I saw you push him over."

"And that was all?"

"Yes."

"I see. I see."

He went to the center of the cabin and closed the lid of the metal case. Then, without turning, he said: "I must tell you—"

"Yes, Lewis."

"I struck him—"

He could not get the words out.

"Tell me," she said gently.

"He was praying."

"Praying."

"Yes." He turned to her. "I killed a man at prayer."

She did not answer.

"What could be worse?" he said. Now he was crying. He held up the vestments. "I can never wear them again. You must see that?"

"Yes, I see it."

"It's finished."

"Yes."

He stroked the vestments.

"They have a kind of innocence," he said.

"Yes."

"I always felt that. I could put them on and feel the change. Like being a child again." He held them against his chest. "But no more."

She went to him.

"Just once more," she said.

He stared.

"Wear them?"

"For me, my love."

"That's silly."

"Put them on. Let me see you as you were."

She saw the words wound him. Something was ending. He dropped the vestments onto the case. Then he bent and chose a surplice and bands and dressed himself. He smiled at her and the light from the mullioned windows touched his face and made the surplice pearly white. He turned from her and she put her arms around him so that her face was in his back. She could feel his body bucking with the tears. "You're a good man," she whispered into the stuff of the surplice. "What more could you give? When people called you went to them. Always. A good, good man."

After he had thrown the vestments from the stern they watched them float and sink and the clerical bands writhe in the wake like the silk of Shameen's turban. "Leave me alone now," she told him; and when he had walked up deck to the bows she sat on the deck with her back to the cabin's timbers. For him, she thought, it had finished long before the killing. The espionage had taken him down dark paths that could never emerge into light. She had feared this and known this from the commission of the first secret act. At the lakeside she had seen him bargaining with the Han Chinese and clinging to the candlestick as if a bit of church silver could keep his faith intact, still believing in another ministry, another altar to put the silver on. "You have no church," she'd said. "You will never have a church." She had seen it clearly then. Now perhaps, she thought with fear, there is nothing behind the trappings: it has become an empty house with pale spaces on the walls where the rich pictures were. She looked up to the sky. It was shot with sunset lights. You, she said to her god in a sudden anger, you up there in your stained-glass attic, why have you let this happen to him? Why have you done this to us? We are your children, your special children. She could not yet weep as he had wept. Perhaps the currents of anger ran too strongly. The two boys came laughing from the deck. "Clear off," she said. When they were gone she rose and went to the rail and gripped its rope and watched the scene. Its beauty calmed her. The anger died. There were fishing boats on the river. They were using cormorants, as many as ten birds to a boat and each bird with a little collar, so tight that it could not swallow the fish. There were infants on some of the boats and she could see the blocks of bamboo that were tied to their bodies and would keep them afloat when they fell into the water. It became a painting. Paint it with your mind. Everything fragile; the boats slender and ready to break and the fishermen skeletal and burned to the bone by sun and the single oars like splinters and the necks and legs of the cormorants as thin as wire; and beyond the river that field and the starved boy with the plough and a yellow bull, pockets of gray-green darkness in the mountain valleys where the night was reaching. A warm fine rain had begun to fall. Ahead two women, one old and one young, were walking along the shore, away from the village to where the river ran back into little creeks and sandbanks. The young woman was carrying something that was held against her breasts. They turned and went from the shore and up onto the banks. They stopped and the old woman placed a square of silk on the sand and the young woman bent and put a small doll, so small that it was no larger than her hands, down onto the silk. The junk passed. The doll, Ellen knew, was a stillborn child. The old woman scattered rice seeds on it. Then they turned and walked from the sandbanks to the shore and toward the village. She watched until they were gone from sight and there was only the dead child, alone by the river and christened by rain.

When the river looped and she could not see the child she crossed the deck and sat again by the cabin and leaned so that her cheek was against the timber. The unshed tears were pressing and she covered her face with her hands and let them come.

It was past midnight when the *Shantung* hove to. The river was wide and the moonrise revealed sandbars and the water bright between them. Here, the junkmaster told them, they must go ashore and wait. Chiang's men would come, or were already there, and they would be taken down to Swatow. Soon, he said, they would be safe in Taiwan and sitting at the president's table. They stood on the deck above the rope ladder that hung down to where the sampan floated and watched the crewmen bring their possessions from the cabin. When the cases and loose clothes and the two

Long Jing tea chests were arranged on the deck they climbed down into the sampan and the junkmaster bent over the rail and said: "It's a very small boat. We have to make two journeys." The sampan was low in the water when it was loaded and only the tea chests remained on the junk. The boatman pushed off and the junkmaster took a wisp of straw from one of the chests and began to chew it. "You be very careful of them, d'you hear me?" Lewis called up to him. The junkmaster smiled. "As if they were my own," he said.

When the sandbars were negotiated and they were ashore the sampan began its return. Torchlights were moving through the tree-dark slope that rose beyond the shore. They heard men's voices. "They're here," Lewis said with relief. He put his arm around her. "Feel better now?" She nodded. The torches died. Three men came out from the trees. Lewis walked to meet them. He felt a hand plucking at his sleeve and he stopped and looked down into Joel's face. The boy pointed at the river and he turned and stared. The sampan was tied at the stern and he saw the securing rope lift from the water and go taut. There were a few clouds in the moony sky and they were moving slowly behind the lugsail. Or were they? The junk swung and the silhouette changed its shape. "She's going," Lewis whispered. Then, shouting: "She's going."

He ran down the shore and into the water, over a sandbar, into water again. The junk was gliding down the moonpath. "You come back," he cried. The water touched his thighs. He heard the junkmaster laugh. Another sandbar. He fell across it and the river closed above him. When he rose the junk was in profile and he could see the tea chests and the junkmaster bent across them and coughing with laughter at the comedy of it. He ran out farther. "I'll have you punished," he shouted. He fell again, rose. "I'll tell Chiang." Even the crew were laughing. Now the water was at his throat. The junk went on its unreachable way, grew smaller. Rage shook him. "I'll have you chopped,' he cried. The word echoed like the snick of an axe. When the *Shantung* was gone around the loop of the river he turned and walked slowly to the shore. Ellen and the boys and the three men were standing in a group, watching him. He did not speak and he passed them and went up the rise of the shore and into the trees and stood there shivering.

Pai-shang, the sawmill town, was built around a large basin on the Han River. When John Chen and Lin drove through its ornamental archway it was somnolent with afternoon heat. Skirting the basin they could see the multitude of floating rafts. It was a place of giant cranes, chains, concrete dormitories, gaunt mills standing against a ring of brown soft hillocks; and everywhere the trunks of the forest and the dust from the sawing adrift in the air like yellow pollen. But Pai-shang had not always been a sawmill town. Now it lived on timber. But it was very old, and the police post lay in the old quarter where there were merchants and artisans, streets of shops and stalls. Driving to the post Chen wondered if the Mackennas had come this far. If it were a large raft it could not stop until it reached the basin.

Inside the post they were greeted by a young captain with a yellow patent-leather belt and an air of self-importance. But he was vigilant; and from the mass of reports that had been generated by the Special Alert he had assembled ten that might have some significance. He gave them tea and then, sitting, discussed each of the reports. Chen shook his head as the folios turned. Only one of them stirred his hunter's instinct.

"A candlestick?" he said.

The report, the captain told him, had come this morning from a shop in Ropemaker's Alley. The shop was of a general nature; merchandise, money-changing, pawnbroking, silversmith. The proprietor had been offered a silver candlestick by a raftman recently arrived in the town. He had demanded a high price and the proprietor had asked for time to consider. The raftman had agreed to return later that day and he had left, taking the candlestick with him. Then, because the candlestick was of a good weight and artistry and therefore too valuable to be in the ownership of a poor raftman, the proprietor had (as he was bound to do by local law) informed the police. A man had been placed in the rear of the shop and would arrest the raftman when he returned.

"But he may not return," Lin said.

"No."

"Tell me," Chen said to the captain, "why do you think the candlestick has importance?"

"Because it is not Oriental."

"And?"

"We are looking for a priest. Perhaps it is of a sacred nature."

Ropemaker's Alley had remained in another century. There were sidewalks and a narrow road of beaten earth. Chen, walking down it, stared from sun into the gloom of shops, at stalls and shacks, at street vendors, at sidewalk benches where tailors and barbers worked and men trod goat hair into felt. In some of the shops he could see clerks reckoning totals on an abacus, buyers and sellers agreeing a price by putting a finger up the other party's sleeve. Yesterday's ways, he thought with exasperation. Do they not know there has been a revolution? In one of the little courtyards a woman was holding a duck with a slit throat and a child was catching in a cup the blood that would make rich gravy. He stopped outside a boiling-water shop where there were stoves with steaming kettles and people with teapots buying the hot water to make their tea. Opposite was a double-fronted shop. Like most of the shops it exhibited a colored banner on which was painted a symbol that denoted the trade or craft that was carried on within. This one showed, among others, the sign of the pawnbroker.

Chen crossed the road and entered the shop. An old man with a face that was freckled with the scars of an old smallpox was seated at a money-lender's tray. He stood when Chen approached and Chen showed his identification and said: "Candlestick."

"Ah, yes."

"Will he return?"

"Who can say?"

"Was he from these parts?"

"Yes. A Han."

"You say that the candlestick is not Oriental?"

"In my opinion, no."

"Do you know its origin?"

"No."

"European?"

"Perhaps."

"Did you not examine it?"

"I weighed it. Here we buy silver. It is always melted down."

Chen walked into the rear of the shop. The bamboo curtain fell behind him. A policeman was smoking a cheroot in the corner and a woman, bent over a stove, was making chitterling soup. A man worked at a furnace that was set near to a bench and behind the furnace the double doors that formed the back wall of the shop were open so that the heat and fumes would escape. Chen watched. The man poured molten silver into a crucible, then returned to the shaping and weighing of a number of silver blocks. In the old towns and villages, Chen knew, where nothing ever changed, lump silver was still a currency. Each of the little blocks was known as a *tael* and would be used for transactions and sometimes when the giving of change was necessary tiny chips would be chiseled from the block. He shook his head with disapproval. It was at times like this when the doubts came. How could such a nation, its feet so firmly in the feudal past, walk into the future? He watched the silversmith, drank soup, drank tea, listened to the traffic in the shop, sweated in the heat and drank more tea until the evening sun turned red and the proprietor ran his hand along the curtain and made the bamboo joints shiver. This was their arranged signal and Chen and the policeman walked through into the shop.

A man was standing by some bales of merchandise and he was holding a muslin-wrapped object. The policeman moved behind him and Chen took the object from his hand. He removed the muslin. Then he held up the candlestick and asked: "Where did you get it?"

The Han was silent.

"Did you steal it?"

"No."

"Find it?"

"No."

"A gift?"

"No."

Chen went to the entrance and turned the candlestick into the light. The proprietor followed.

"There are a million candlesticks in China," the old man said.

"But not like this one."

Chen pointed to its base.

"Do you recognize this mark?"

"No."

"It is the hallmark of an English assay office."

The old man peered at it.

"It denotes silver," Chen said.

He returned to the Han.

"Was it payment for a service?" he asked.

Silence.

"It is a matter of State security," Chen said. "You must answer."

No answer.

"Did you bring a white family down the river on a raft?"

"No."

"Are you an agent for Chiang Kai-shek?"

"No."

"Truth is easy," Chen said. "The other way is hard."

Back in the police post, the Han manacled and Lin silent in a corner, Chen said to the captain: "Do you understand the importance of this?"

"I do."

"Whatever he knows we must know."

"Yes."

"Get the truth."

The captain and two policemen took the Han to the door. Outside was a truck.

"You too," Chen said to Lin.

Lin shook his head.

"Go with them."

"No."

"Go."

"I would rather not."

"But you have to," Chen said. "This is your work. The safety of the State. What is one man's pain compared to that?"

Lin did not move.

"Go," Chen said.

When he was gone and the sound of the truck had died Chen went down again to Ropemaker's Alley and sat on the bench of one of the sidewalk barbers. There was time to waste and he had his hair (already cropped) cropped shorter. Then he walked through the throngs of people and out of the alley and through the town until he stood on the fringe of the basin. Yellow lights burned in the sawmills and he could hear the sound of the steam traction-engines that were dragging trunks from the water. The candlestick made a silver glow within his mind. Was it as it seemed? Or had Lewis Mackenna moved yet another piece across the board? Without doubt the candlestick had once stood in the mission church. Yet it was a part of a sequence. First the cunningly prepared scraps of paper in the wastebasket and the ship in Shanghai, then the white towel on the camphor tree, then the hat caught on the river cliff and the drowned truck below; and now the Han raftman stepping onto the stage in this place where the rafts ended their voyage. Was it even certain that he was a raftman? Yes, Chen decided; that face ravaged by sun, wind and rain, those callused hands, those calves that were scarred by trunk and rock. He was one of the river people. He was a raftman. But an agent of Chiang? Anything was possible. But to accept such risks a man would need a deep political belief or a devouring greed. Chen shook his head. A man born to work and die on the wild rivers was concerned with survival, not with governments. Greed was the motive. For a payment such a man would ferry a fugitive from one point to another. He turned from the basin and walked back through the town and Ropemaker's Alley. The banners swayed in wind. There was not, it seemed, a shop where rope was made.

It was past midnight when the captain and Lin returned to the post. The captain was carrying a folded map. Lin did not speak. He walked through to the washroom and Chen saw him bend shuddering above the basin.

"Soft," the captain said with disdain.

"No," Chen said. "Not soft. But he'll find his strength in other work."

The captain spread the map on the table. A thick line had been drawn across a section of it. The line began at Ogre Head Lake, followed the Liao River, diverged from the mainstream into the Shih, then left it to curl inland and stop abruptly in the ocher tints that indicated higher ground. The captain ran his finger along the line.

"Mackenna's route," he said.

All that morning the track had climbed. In the beginning, when the track wound on the shoulders of the hills, they saw below them the bend of the river. Then the hills closed behind them and they could no longer see the river. Walking at the rear Lewis Mackenna could see the swinging tails of the three mules and the Hakka tribesman in the lead and behind him the two Fukienese and all three holding to the rope bridles of the mules and the two boys with the Hakka and Ellen and her sweat-dark shirt on the inside of the track and next to the center mule. Cases and bundles and panniers were tied to the mules but he could see, also, the two stolen tea chests. The anger would not leave him. They should be there, he thought, roped above me on those swaying backs. Rare and beautiful things, payment for the risks I took and the home I lost and the church I lost. Gone. Our security, a house in Taiwan, an education for the twins. All gone. Now he could hear the mocking laughter of the junkmaster and the echoes of his own shouted threat. *I'll have you chopped.* Those savage words. Did you mean them? he asked himself. Be honest with yourself. Yes, at that moment I would have had him chopped. I would have had his head rolling on the deck. And now? If at this moment you could lift your hand and have him chopped would you do it? The laughter crossed the water and he saw the junk slide away into the night. The anger surged. The intensity of it made him lift up his hand. He saw Ellen staring down at him. She stopped and let the column pass until he was level with her. Then she turned and, their steps synchronized, resumed the climb.

"What's the matter?" she asked.

"Nothing."

"Yes there is. I saw it in your face. You were in a rage."

"No."

"Yes. In a rage."

"All right, I was in a rage."

"What was it? The chests?"

"Yes."

The mule went sideways and the white tail flicked their faces.

"I know you, Lewis," she said wearily. "Know you so well. You were robbed. And you'll never forget it."

"That's right."

"All your life," she said, "you'll be two tea chests short."

"They were all we had."

She put an arm around him.

"Call it a payment," she said. "Something we paid for freedom."

"Not free yet."

"But near."

"Yes, near."

She pointed uptrack to where a ridge crossed the sky.

"From there," she said, "we'll see the sea."

But there was no sea when they reached the ridge, only ravines and granite walls and another, higher ridge and beyond it the indigo slope of a mountain. They stood on the shale where the track ended and looked down to where they must go before the land rose again. The Hakka pointed. They began the descent.

When the helicopter came from Army Base Five it brought with it a report. John Chen, Lin and two soldiers boarded; and while the helicopter was refueling Chen took the report from its envelope and read it. The *Shantung* (the junk named under interrogation by the Han raftman) had been impounded by a river patrol and its master arrested. *It is confirmed* (the report continued) *that the Mackenna family was berthed on the junk and disembarked at a point twenty kilometers down the River Shih. Included in the cargo were two chests containing Chinese antiquities. The master denies that he was engaged in the illegal transportation of antiquities and claims that the chests were brought aboard by Mackenna and were retained by way of payment for the passage. The master is still under interrogation and a further report will follow.* Chen laughed. By way of theft would be more accurate. Was it a crime to rob a spy? He laughed again and Lin said: "May I share the joke?"

Chen gave him the report. The helicopter lifted. The amusement lingered and he saw again the living room in the Hangchow mission and the cabinets and the empty shelves where the collection, accumulated during those years of danger, was once displayed. There was, it seemed, some natural justice after all. The treasures, stolen by Chiang Kai-shek and dropped into the palm of a traitor, would now return to the State. Yes, there was justice in that. The sawmills passed beneath him. He closed his eyes. He was on his way, as straight as an arrow to the missionary's trail.

The trail was no longer discernible. The Hakka led the column on a rising traverse, the bed of the ravine below them and the shadow of the mountain sometimes dark across the water. The Hakkas, Lewis knew, were mountain people, true aborigines who would not willingly live in the heat of the lowlands. Yet the man was not a primitive. He had talked with him across the back of the lead mule and listened to the careful and grammatical speech and the Hakka had read his thoughts and said: "I have had an education."

"I know that."

"Three years at a mission."

Lewis smiled.

"What better?" he said. "How many characters can you write?"

"Eight thousand."

"As many as that?"

"Yes, eight thousand."

"Then you are indeed an educated man."

The Hakka grunted with pleasure; and later he leaned across the skillet of boiling tea and said through the steam: "I have the gun."

"Good."

"Are you sure you want it?"

"Yes."

The Hakka rose and went to one of the mules. When he returned he was holding a magazine pistol.

"It is ready to fire," he said.

Lewis took it.

"Do you understand this gun?" the man asked.

"No."

"Do you understand any gun?"

"No."

"It is no good at distance. No more than eight paces."

Lewis nodded.

"Carry it inside your belt."

Lewis wedged the gun between belt and hip.

"Good," the Hakka said. "But remember the safety catch. When you are wearing the gun like that you must keep it safe."

One of the Fukienese laughed.

"You must kill Reds," the Hakka said, smiling. "Not your big toe."

"I'll remember."

The Hakka poured tea.

"Forgive me," he said. "I should not have spoken in that way. About the knowing of guns. About killing. You are a priest."

Lewis shook his head.

"Not a priest?"

"No."

"I was told you are a priest."

"Not now."

They were silent. The Hakka watched him over the tea can. A mule whinnied. Lewis threw his tea dregs into the fire. Rising, he heard the sound of an engine in the sky. Ellen and the boys came from tree-shadow. The sound was distant and they listened until it faded and was gone. The two Fukienese led the mules into the cover of the trees and the Hakka emptied the skillet onto the fire and when it was was dead he pointed and Lewis and the boys and Ellen went with him into cover. Now they could see the long gradient of shale that was spilled from the mountain and a ribbon of water in the gully and at the end of the gully the glare of white sky where the granite cliffs opened. The sound returned, still faint, and they saw a helicopter cross the patch of glare and disappear. "Do not move," the Hakka said. This time the helicopter came out of the glare and between the cliffs and down the gully toward them and its clattering echoes closed around them and they watched its red star above the tree canopy. When it was gone and the sound had died the Hakka led them out of cover and down into the passes of the granite land.

Chapter 7

From the helicopter John Chen searched the strange granite landscape that twisted below. Even here in the air and turning the shoulder of the mountain he felt its melancholy. Later the evening mists would fill the ravines. But how much later? He looked at his watch. There were two more hours of daylight. They had systematically quartered the terrain but they had not seen the Mackennas. Nothing at all had moved except their own shadow scuttling like a crab across the granite. But I know you are there, he whispered, looking down. It would take time to climb from the river, up the long rise and across the granite and you would not attempt the exposed run to the coast until the nightfall. So you are still there. I know. I can feel you there. The anxiety, now, was gnawing at him. In Pai-shang an arrest had seemed certain. Lewis Mackenna's escape route had been precisely located in these crags above the Shih. A fingertip placed on the map could easily cover them and that same finger could slide south to the sea with hardly a movement. How could the family avoid capture with all the resources of police and army concentrated in so small a box? Yet this was wilderness; canyons, cliffs of black rock, stands of fir, ridgwoods, mist and shadow. From height he could see where the granite ended as if shorn off, great declivities of scrub, a distant line of low hills that were hunched and tawny like sleeping lions. And beyond the hills would be the communes, valleys, terraces of rice, plantations of sugarcane and bananas. And then Swatow and its littoral. The port lay almost on the same latitude as Hong Kong, half asleep now in the wet heats of tropical summer. That too could be a factor; police and troops drowsing at their posts. He felt suddenly uncertain. The pilot touched his arm and tapped the fuel gauge. He nodded. Fuel must be conserved. The helicopter descended through the firs and alighted on a table of rock. The engine stopped.

They heard the engine stop.

"It's near," Ellen said.

The Hakka put a finger on his lips. They listened. There was only the sound of the stream.

"I'm sure it's near," she said.

"Maybe not so near," Lewis said.

"I think it's near," Joel said.

They listened again.

"Can't really tell," Gerard said. He pointed to the rock faces. "Echoes travel."

"That's right," Lewis said. "It could be anywhere."

Ellen turned to the Hakka.

"Did they see us?" she asked.

"No. They could not have seen us."

"We must move out," she said urgently. "Now."

"No," the Hakka said. "We do not know where they are. If we move we could move toward them." He looked up at the sun. "We stay here. We wait for darkness. Then we cross, over and down. You will meet Sister Tai. She will take you through to Swatow."

After he had washed in one of the ravine's rock pools John Chen sat with his feet in the water. Farther down, where the watercourse widened, he could see Lin splashing through the shallows. He watched him until he was out of sight. The sun was low and he must make a decision before it sank behind the summit ridge. The phase of the full moon had passed and the dark night was in Mackenna's favor and under its cover he must cross the ninety kilometers to Swatow. Rough tracks began where the scrub ended and these led into the pattern of dirt roads that served the communes and the plantations. Somewhere there would be a rendezvous. What transport would they use? Mule, horse, horse and cart? He shook his head. Too far and too slow. The railway? A line ran the forty kilometers from Chaochow down to the port. A journey in a freight wagon would be audacious, but unlikely. A train was a trap, easily searched, difficult to leave unobserved—especially for four white faces. So it would be a motor truck. The family would be driven through some devious route that could be any one of a hundred permutations of the roads and tracks that interlaced the cultivated lands.

Chen stood, crossed from the pool to the shallows and sat again and immersed his feet so that he might enjoy the flow of the water against his anklebones. I made a mistake, he told himself. By searching this isolated place so meticulously and then landing the helicopter I revealed myself, my knowledge of their presence. Now they will be vigilant. Times, routes, even destination could be altered. He could see the pilot staring up at the sky and the granite walls and spires that ringed them like a girdle. He sensed the man's unease. This was a dangerous place. Already there were a few drifts of mist. A moonless night would trap him. And by sunrise the

Mackennas might, if they evaded the roadblocks, be in Swatow. He decided to fly out before the light died. How much fuel remained? He beckoned to the pilot.

Standing above him on the bank of the stream she watched him fill the canteen.

"They know we're here," Ellen said.

"Yes."

"They would not search like that unless they knew."

"That's right."

"Is it Chen?"

"Could be."

"He'll never rest until he gets you."

"No."

Downstream she could see the boy Joel. He bent, picked up a pebble and sent it skating on the rock slabs.

"How far to Swatow?" she asked.

"Fifty or sixty miles."

"Who is this Sister Tai?"

"I don't know."

"A nun?"

"Perhaps."

"Or a missionary?"

"I don't know." He sealed the canteen, put it down, lowered another into the water. "A friend," he said. "A friend who will risk her neck."

She watched Joel walk slowly down the bank of the stream.

"Don't you go too far," she called.

The boy waved.

"It's real goodness," she said softly.

"What is?"

"People helping us. Taking risks."

"Some get paid."

"But not all."

"That damn junkmaster got paid," he said. "He got paid all right."

She heard the bitterness in his voice.

"Perhaps he too has paid," she said.

"How so?"

"Chen knew we were here."

He looked up at her.

"Someone must have talked," she said.

"Yes," he said, laughing. "Maybe they questioned him."

"Does that please you, Lewis?"

"Not really." He sealed the canteen and stood. "After all," he said, "I know what that means, don't I?"

"Yes."

"I wouldn't wish that on any man."

"I know that."

She held his face and kissed him. Then, knowing that her lips were cold and lifeless, she pushed him away.

"I can't kiss you properly," she said. "I'm too afraid."

"It'll pass."

"It's as if I'm dead. I keep thinking of those old graves in the mission garden."

"You'll come alive."

"No."

"Yes. We'll make you come alive. There'll be a house, another garden. No speckled old graves. Just flowers and light." He kissed her hair. "You'll love me properly then."

They began the walk from the stream to the camp.

"What will you do, Lewis?" she asked.

"In Taiwan?"

"Yes."

"There's always work for a doctor."

"Yes, always."

"We'll need money, of course. But Chiang will look after us."

"Are you certain?"

"Yes, certain."

"Put not your trust in princes," she said bleakly.

He stopped. His face had hardened.

"Don't you quote the book at me," he said. "You keep that black old book closed, d'you hear me?"

He left her and she watched him tie the canteens to one of the mules. If only it were here, she thought, that black old book, the weight of it in my hands, in my possession so that one day I might write in it the name of a grandchild. Now it lay abandoned on the pulpit in the empty church and only the shadows of the bats to touch it. That black old book.

She turned and looked back and down to the stream. She could not see Joel.

The boy felt the ravine close around him. There was pleasure in the walk through this brooding place; to be alone and apart for a time from his parents and his twin. He would not walk far; down the curve of the stream and around the edge of that leaning wall and through its shadow. What lay beyond? He followed the stream, this stream that would become a river, even a torrent, when the typhoon rains came. He emerged from the shadow. The stream was wider now, curving again under yet another jutting spur. He would walk around the spur, no farther. Then he must return. He rounded the spur. The walls were high and he could not see the mountain, only slopes of fir and a group of three granite crags reaching up from the fir like broken fingers. There were caves in the walls, so deep that the sun would never penetrate. Everything was bathed in a pink and luminous light from the setting sun and he could see the red leaves of the wild rhubarb that grew along the stream. He felt excitement. This was a special place, he knew; one of those places that, once discovered, would be kept secret and returned to again and again until another person found it and took away its mystery. He stood there without moving. Now the place had only sadness. He would never see it again. He listened to the stream, which was its voice, watched it ripen in the strange mystical light. He turned away with regret.

It was then that he saw the eagle.

At first it was no more than a movement on the highest of the fingers, a shadow shifting on the granite. Then the shadow fell and opened into wings. He sighed with wonder. He had never seen such an eagle, such wings, such grace and power. It came, heavy and beautiful, down the crag and across the fir, so close that he could see its black pinions, the sun on its amber beak. It went from sight behind the tree line. He waited but it did not reappear. Nothing moved except the stream. He felt a growing sense of loss. He could not fully understand his yearning for the eagle; only that it had come swiftly out of height to touch him with its shadow, into this magical place, *his* place. It was the spirit of the place, perhaps its guardian, and now it was gone from him and he had to see it again, had to. He turned and began to walk deeper into the ravine. Somewhere behind the fir on the climbing rock would be the eagle's sunlit eye.

Lin too had seen the eagle. Here, walking through the deep silences of the firs and the scent of resin in the nostrils, he was at peace. He liked the feel of his naked feet in the needles and the way in which the sun slanted through the trees and made the bark red. He would have to return before the sun was gone and he left the trees and began the walk down the ribs of rock that fell to the stream. Above him were the three strange pinnacles that from this aspect were like claws hooked on the sky. He stepped into the stream and bent and rolled up his trousers to the knee and as he straightened he saw a shape move on one of the granite faces and unfurl itself and fall in a long black-winged dive through the evening mists. He watched it soar out of the fall, glide and fall again behind the trees. Only an eagle would have a wingspread like that, he thought. He felt an affinity with the eagle; to dive from height like that—into mist or into water it was the same free and beautiful fall through chasms of light and air. Yes, he knew that feeling. He wanted to see the eagle once more and he walked farther down the stream, stopping from time to time so that he might search the unfolding scene of fir and granite. When the eagle came again he saw that its talons had caught up lichen from a tree.

*   *   *

The boy saw the eagle on the sun, black on the red with something long like a braid hanging from its right foot. It crossed the stream and the silhouette took detail and he could see its pinions and heard the wingbeat flighting in the rock. It went from sight behind the spur. Then it returned and flew low and parallel to the course of the stream and when it was above him the braid came loose and fell and draped itself on the bank. He went to it and picked it up and saw that the braid was a length of green and yellow lichen. It was attached to a piece of broken bark and there were deep wounds in the bark from the grip of the eagle's talons. He ran his fingers down the bark, put it to his nose and smelled it. He felt again the swelling of emotion. It was as if the eagle, *his* eagle, had dropped a gift almost at his feet. He could not throw away the lichen and he wound it around his waist and fixed the ends inside his belt. He waited, searched the crags and trees. But the eagle did not return. The sun was low and he must regain the camp. He heard a sound, a splashing of water, and, turning, saw a man standing in the stream.

The man was watching him. He was young, with a pleasant face and neat hair and an unbuttoned tunic. One of those in the helicopter, the boy thought. He was not afraid and he did not run. No man who paddled in a stream with rolled-up trousers and his boots tied by the laces and slung around his neck could be a threat. The man walked toward him through the water and smiled and said in English: "Which one are you?"

"Joel."

"My name is Lin Sheng."

The boy nodded and the man pointed at the lichen.

"It was an eagle," he said.

"Yes."

"The best I ever saw."

"Yes."

"A king of all the birds."

"Yes," the boy said. "A king."

"Did you follow it?"

"Yes."

"So did I."

The man reached out and grasped his arm.

"You must come with me," he said gently.

Walking quickly through the ravine, the sun low and the nightfall near, Lewis Mackenna felt the fear grow. Where was Joel? Soon this wild place would be buried in darkness. Where? He passed into the shadow of a large rock buttress. Then, emerging, he saw the two figures, the man and the boy, standing in the stream. They were quite near and the man was wearing a Mao tunic and he was bending over Joel and pulling at his arm. Relief, fear, anger—he felt them tearing at him and without hesitation he pulled the pistol from his belt and flicked off the safety and when he was within a few paces of them he leveled the pistol and fired three times and the sound of the shots went in great detonations through the rock walls and birds exploded upward from the firs and a wet red furrow appeared on the man's right temple and he fell so that now he was lying on the bank and his head was hanging to the water. "Run," Lewis said to the boy. "Back to the camp." The boy was staring down at the man and did not move and Lewis took him by the shoulder and shook him and said urgently: "Run. Run fast." He turned him and watched him run along the bank and past the buttress.

Running, the boy felt his legs weaken with the shock. I liked him, liked him so much, his nice face and he smiling down at me, his nice soft voice, in that minute of talking of the bird I liked him and took to him and I did not mind sharing the eagle with him and now Oh God he is lying on the bank and shot and don't let him be dead, don't let him. He stumbled and the sun swam behind the stone fingers. He began to pant with the terror of it all.

Lewis bent across the injured man. It was a young face with good features, already wan from shock and loss of blood. The pulse was weak. He pulled him from the lip of the bank and propped him upright in the rocks so that he would not hemorrhage so freely. He could hear voices and he turned and ran toward the buttress. When he reached it he stopped and looked back. Downstream, beyond where the young man sat, he saw movement and two men came out of the shadow of an overhang. One of them was John Chen. Their eyes met across the separating distance and there was a moment of recognition in which they stared through the fiery light. A soldier came from behind the overhang and the star on the cap glowed as red as a poppy and he pointed the pistol at the star and fired and saw the man flinch from the rock splinters. He pushed the pistol down behind his belt. Then he turned and stepped back behind the buttress and began the run to the camp.

Chen listened to the running feet and when the sound of them was gone he went to Lin and bent to him. He was unconscious and he could not find a pulse and he made a pad from his handkerchief and placed it on the wound so that it might stanch the flow of blood and the helicopter pilot took the bandanna from his neck and tied the pad in place.

"I think he is dying," the pilot said.

"Perhaps."

"He will need the hospital."

"Yes."

"And the light is going."

Chen looked at the sun. Only its rim was visible.

"We must hurry," the pilot said.

Chen turned to him.

"Be very clear," he said. "The State comes first. If it were an hour earlier I would follow him and I would leave Lin Sheng down here. That is my duty. But we cannot find him in the darkness."

The rim sank behind the crags. Now there was only the reflection flung across the sky.

"So it is Swatow," the pilot said.

"Yes. Swatow."

Looking back from the open rear of the truck Lewis saw the mountain and the long reef of granite integrate with darkness.

"This is a commune truck," Sister Tai said from the driving seat. She had the humped back of old age and when she turned her head her profile made a sharp-boned line on the windshield. She laughed. "Yes, we are part of a commune now. Once we were a mission. Our Order owned a thousand hectares of land. Then the liberation came and the State took most of it." She was driving without lights and from time to time she peered from the side window at the sloping scrub. "One by one our people left. The Order died. Now there are only four of us." She laughed again. It was the clear laughter of a young girl and it came strangely from her scrawny throat. "Four old girls. We have three hundred hectares and the revolutionary committee has given us some field workers and we keep a little of the produce for our needs and the rest goes to the commune. They're becoming much more subtle, you see. No violence. No cruelty. We are very old and they will wait for us to die and in time no one will know the mission ever existed."

"Some will remember," Lewis said.

"Perhaps," Sister Tai said softly. "Perhaps."

The truck turned from the scrub onto a dirt road.

"There are patrols on some of the roads," Sister Tai said. "But I know how to avoid them."

Later, the night still dark, they felt the heat that was coming off the coast. The two boys were moving restlessly on the metal floor.

"Don't fidget," Ellen said sharply.

"If they feel a call of nature," Sister Tai said, "I can stop."

"Please," Gerard said.

"Yes," Joel said.

When the truck was stopped the boys got down from the tail and ran through darkness to where a clump of trees grew. Standing there and straining for height they watched the two streams strike the trunk, rise, then fall.

"I won," Gerard said.

"You drank more."

"Makes no difference."

"Must do."

Gerard turned from the tree and touched the lichen that girdled Joel's waist.

"What's it for?" he asked.

Joel shook his head.

"Tell me."

Joel did not answer and Gerard shrugged and loped away to where the truck would be. Joel watched him go. He stroked the lichen. The eagle was still swooping through his mind. The eagle was secret. He could not tell Gerard. He had shared with Lin Sheng but he could not share with Gerard. For the first time in his life he could not share a secret with his twin. He felt the sadness of it and his lip was trembling and he did not understand. He called out into the darkness: "Gerard. Gerard." There was no reply. He felt suddenly alone.

The sky was lighter when they reached the first of the plantations. The tattered leaves of bananas edged the road and scraped the truck. Sister Tai drove from road to track, from track to field. Sometimes they saw the gleam of paddies. The heat, now, was intense. "At this time of the year," Sister Tai said, "it becomes unbearable." She took the truck through a pattern of irrigation ditches. "Not long now," she said. Ahead and running endlessly through starlight were the erect spikes of aloe flowers.

It was an hour to midnight when the aloe ended. They could see where the sugar began. Sister Tai stopped the truck, switched off the engine and listened. There was no sound in the night. "There's a roadblock ahead," she said. She turned her sweating face and smiled. "So we go straight through the sugarcane." She started the engine. "Hold your hats."

The truck accelerated and then, at speed, swung off the road and into the high wall of cane. There was a moment in which the truck faltered in the breaking wall. Then it gathered speed again and they sat enclosed in the noise of the engine and the tunnel of jointed stems. The cane lashed the truck and looking back Lewis could see the swathe they had cut through it. "Don't worry," Sister Tai said, laughing again. "It isn't our sugar."

"In the morning," Gerard said, "there'll be a great big trail."

"Of course," Sister Tai agreed. "Of course there will. But it won't lead them to us."

The truck broke out of the cane and onto a narrow plantation track.

"Now we double back," Sister Tai said.

The truck turned inland again. The cane, high above them, hemmed both sides of the track. Sister Tai drove until the sugar ended. Now there were rice paddies, fields of cereal and vegetable crops. The truck turned right, then right again, stopped by an entrance gate.

"Please get out," Sister Tai said.

They got out. A drive, fringed with shrubs, ran from the road and curved toward a cluster of low buildings. A single light burned in one of the buildings and a church flèche made a black silhouette on the night sky.

Sister Tai pointed to the road that passed the gate. It was straight and long and it climbed to where three palms grew on the brow.

"Up there," she said.

They began the walk. Lewis looked back once and Sister Tai was standing by the truck. When they were near to the palms Ellen held up a hand and said: "Listen." They stopped and listened. The sound of waves came faintly, surged and died and surged again. The boys ran ahead and when they were through the palms they turned and beckoned and Lewis and Ellen ran up and under the fronds of the palms and out onto the brow. Below them was the beach and the breaking waves and the sea. The lights of Swatow, its town and port and Double Island, threw an amber glow on the sky. They did not speak and they stood in the perfumed night and looked out across the sea to where the horizon was lost in mist and darkness.

Lewis rose at first light. The room with its small high window and white-washed walls was like a cell. The night had droned with mosquitoes and his face was lumpy from the bites. There were faintly marked rectangles on the walls where, perhaps, religious texts or pictures of biblical scenes had hung and, opposite the bed, an empty niche that had once accommodated a plaster Virgin. A basin and an ewer of water and a towel had been placed in a corner and when he had washed he went out into the corridor and walked through the building. There were empty rooms, a bare dining hall with a few chairs and a refectory table. Dust lay everywhere and the painted walls, peeling in the damp, were as scabrous as a rotting cheek. He passed through the entrance hall and stood for a moment on the threshold. He had seen no sign that the building had ever known the devotions of a religious Order. The smell of worm and fungus touched the nostrils; or perhaps, he thought wryly, spiritual decay had its own elusive scent.

He went out into sun. The path led to the church and he walked inside. There was nothing in it except four bentwood chairs arranged in a row, a little side table, and at the end of a paved aisle a bamboo altar. There were no cloths or ornaments on it and he could see the splintered holes in the floor around it where the rails had been wrenched out. Above him was the empty belfry and the timbers of the flèche; and behind and above the altar was another of the dirt-marked shapes that revealed where the crucified Christ had been. He went to the side table and opened the drawer. There was no Bible or prayer book inside, only an age-speckled card with the printed heading SWATOW CENTRAL MISSION. He heard footsteps and, turning, saw that it was Sister Tai. She came toward him.

"We are ashamed," she said.

"Of what, Sister?"

She gestured at the church.

"Of this," she said. "Of the mission. Of what it has become."

He closed the drawer.

"We are not defeated, Dr. Mackenna. Merely old."

"I understand."

"They will not permit the commune workers to help us with the buildings. So it's all too much for us. We can't repair them, can't keep them clean."

She led him to the door.

"It's still a house of God," she said. "But only we know it. Once it was beautiful, a true celebration of our Lord's glory. But they forbade all Christian things. At first we resisted. So they beat one of the Sisters for wearing a crucifix. A week later they returned and beat a Sister for concealing a Testament in her robe. And so it went on; punishments for praying for the sick, for keeping a confessional, for lighting a candle, for using Christ's name in the school." She pointed again at the denuded church. "Sometimes we sit on those chairs, the four of us, and we make a deliberate act of remembrance. We close our eyes and, lo, it is all restored and the altar gleams with silver and there are stained-glass saints in the windows and Jesus looks down on us from that wall." She turned to him. "But of course that costs us nothing. The truth is that we stopped being brave."

"I think you're brave."

"No."

"You are helping us. I call that brave."

She led him through the doorway and past a wired chicken run and two tethered goats and onto a path that rose between unkempt borders to the white sky where the sea would be. When they reached the brow he saw that the mission was built on the same promontory as the port, so near to the docks and quays and derricks that he could read the names of the nearest ships and catch on the sea breeze the smells of oil and fish. The town curved behind them and a few miles distant he could see Double Island and the masts of junks pricking the early mist like needles. The sun had not yet sucked the mist from the horizon or from the line of Breaker Point. Swatow (like Shanghai and Amoy and other east-coast harbors) had once been a Treaty Port. In those days there had been illegal trades in opium and coolies and over there on Double Island, he knew, were the houses of the old Western settlement and the merchants who had grown rich in that vanished age. One of the derricks moved a few feet down its steel tracks, revealing the stern of a ship.

"Well I'm damned," he said.

"What is it?"

He pointed at the painted letters on the stern.

"It's the *Fragonard*," he said.

"Yes," Sister Tai said. "Of Marseille. Do you know the ship?"

"In a way," he said, smiling.

She looked at him.

"A private joke, Sister—between me and me."

A kind of joke, he thought; that this ship the *Fragonard*, chosen at random from the list of Shanghai/Taipei sailings as a ruse to send Chen in the wrong direction, had returned to the China mainland to appear here in front of him in a Swatow berth.

"There are two items of news," Sister Tai said. "Chen is in Swatow." She pointed seaward to the shrouding mist. "And during the night a gunboat was placed out there."

"A gunboat," he said with dismay.

"Yes, a gunboat. You must be a very important man, Doctor."

"How will we cross the Strait?"

"I don't know. Father Jethro will decide."

"Father Jethro?"

"He lives at To-kuei. That's a village six kilometers down the coast. Like us he no longer has a church. But he does have a boat."

They turned and walked down the slope. The three Sisters were behind the chicken-wire; two of them sprinkling feed, the other gathering eggs in a wicker basket. They came to the wire and smiled and bowed and gave their names.They were very old with dried and tea-brown faces into which time and hardship had sewn innumerable pleats.

"I regret," Sister Tai said sadly, "that for breakfast we can only offer eggs."

After they had eaten they followed Sister Tai out onto the mission compound. Two Peking carts were waiting, each of them with a shaft mule. Their cases and other possessions had already been brought out and were lying by the carts. Lewis examined them. They were of the kind once used in the north by rich families, light in weight with a bamboo frame and a cover of dark blue cotton cloth. They were old and dilapidated but at one time, he knew, the wheels would have been gay with scarlet paint and varnish. The three Sisters came from the mission. One of them climbed into the driving seat of the leading cart.

"Do we go to To-kuei now?" Ellen asked.

"Yes."

"In daylight?"

"You'll be safe, madame. Every Wednesday we go to the Father for the Mass." She pointed at the carts. "They are a familiar sight. No one will stop us."

Ellen put some clothes into the cart and Joel and Gerard bent to the black-japanned metal case.

"Not yet," Lewis told them. "Take it to the church and put it down by the altar." He gave his arm to Sister Tai. "Come with me, Sister."

They followed the boys into the church and when they had placed the case by the altar he said: "Leave us." He watched them go. Then he knelt by the case and opened it and removed its contents so that the muslin-wrapped silver in the base was exposed. Sister Tai stood above him.

"What is this?" she asked.

He stripped the muslin from one of the candlesticks and gestured with it at the empty altar.

"Time to be brave again," he said.

She shook her head.

"Take it, Sister. Take all of it."

"No. You'll need it. For your church."

"I have no church."

"You will have."

"No."

He put the candlestick into her hand.

"Take it."

She hesitated, then placed the candlestick on the altar. He unwrapped more silver and handed her the remaining candlestick, a salver, some plates and vessels, finally the large wall-crucifix that had been made for his father by a Hangchow silversmith. Now there was nothing in the case except Father Tsai's silver fish. He picked it up and let it swing on its chain.

"I'll keep this," he said softly.

"A fish?" she asked.

"Yes."

"A Christian fish?"

"Yes. It belonged to a friend."

"Then wear it."

"No."

"Please. Wear it for me."

"Not even for you, Sister."

He returned the fish to the case and she put her hand on his shoulder so that he could not rise.

"Stay there," she said.

He looked up at her and sensed her purpose.

"I'm kneeling by a case," he said. "Not by an altar."

"Then turn toward it."

He shook his head.

"I know you're troubled," she said kindly. "Is it a crisis of faith?"

He did not answer.

"We all have times of doubt," she said. "A blind faith is not a faith at all."

"I don't doubt He's somewhere, Sister."

"Then wait for Him."

The hand left his shoulder.

"Time to go," she said.

After the case was repacked he went to the door and called to the boys and when they had taken the case outside he walked back down the aisle. Sister Tai was still standing by the altar and he saw her reach out and touch it.

"We'll make it nice again," she said.

"Yes."

"Embroider a new cloth." She turned to him. "I remember when the first cloth was made. I was a girl then and I worked on it with five other novices. It was a thing of great complexity, more like a tapestry. We called it our Christmas cloth because there was a Nativity scene in each corner and we embroidered a procession of manger animals around the hem. But in those days I was very mischievous."

He saw the amusement in her filmy eyes.

"What did you do?" he asked.

"I gave one of the oxen five legs."

"Did they find out?"

"Yes." She began to laugh. It was the girl's laugh again, as clear as it was in those distant times. "They gave me a little punishment but the Mother was secretly amused and she allowed it to stay as it was." She wiped her eyes. "A long time ago."

A lizard scratched in one of the empty window apertures and she pointed at it and then at the naked walls.

"There is so much to do," she said. "Perhaps there are a few Christian souls in the town who will help."

"Sure to be."

"And I know where there's a piano."

He laughed.

"We had a piano," he said. "My wife used to play it for the mission children. On Sundays they had to wheel it from the schoolhouse to the church. You never heard such a noise. Jangle and twang. I can hear it now. It was all very funny and of course they did it on purpose."

Now both of them were laughing. Then the laughter died and they stood in silence.

"Things of the past," she said. "In the end they always hurt."

He put an arm around her thin humped back.

"Yes," he said. "That's always the way of it."

Outside and standing by the church door he saw that the carts were loaded and the Sisters were in the driving seats. The blue cotton coverings had been drawn like curtains and he could not see Ellen and the boys. He gave Sister Tai his arm and they began to walk down toward the compound. Beyond the compound was the drive and the gates that opened onto the road. Something moved behind the iron of the gates and the sunlight glinted suddenly on the handlebars of a bicycle. It had stopped and there was a moment in which the rider, a man in a wide straw hat, stared up the drive. Then he mounted and the bicycle passed from sight.

"He saw you," Sister Tai said.

"Do you know him?"

"He's the commune leader."

"Will he report it?"

"Of course."

He saw the fear in her face.

"Are you sure he saw you?" Father Jethro asked.

"He saw me," Lewis said.

"And the carts? Could he see the carts from the gate?"

"Yes."

"What about the road from Swatow? Were you seen?"

"Yes," Sister Tai said. "There were two soldiers standing in the shade of a tree. We waved at them as we passed."

"And what did they do?"

"They waved back."

One of the Sisters laughed.

"It's no laughing matter, Sister."

Jethro turned again toward the sea and raised his binoculars and studied the white shape of the gunboat that lay out in the mists of the bay. He wore only shorts and he had a thick body and powerful thighs and the dark body hair that curled across his chest grew over his shoulders and down across the blades. He lowered the binoculars and pointed at the gunboat.

"How do we get past that, Mackenna?"

"At night?"

"Can't wait till night." He turned to them. "You must understand how serious this is. The commune leader saw Dr. Mackenna and he saw the carts. He's certain to report. The soldiers will be questioned and they'll remember the carts. And the road leads here."

"We are sorry, Father," Sister Tai said. "We were careless and we have put you in danger."

"Danger?" Jethro smiled. "Five years I've lived with danger." He studied the gunboat again. "She was there at first light," he said. "And she hasn't moved."

He handed Lewis the binoculars and he raised them and turned the focus wheel. They were standing in the cover of the palms and tamarinds that made a fringe between the shore and the garden of the house. Beyond the trees he could see dunes of sand and tussock grass, the sea, a scattering of small yellow-headed buoys. To-kuei (Sister Tai had told him) lived off fish and the sale of seaweed. The seaweed had a medicinal value and the algae was grown on the ropes that ran through the deep from the buoys to the shore. It was a pretty scene, she said, at the time of the harvest and all the boats went out and the ropes were dragged in and the sea became bright green with the glistening braids and the men pulling and singing and the shore turning green so that you could not see its sand and later, when all the harvest was in, the girls of the village would bathe in the evening sea, always separated from the men and each girl in a pink-and-white hat and the red sun touching the hats and the sea and the green shore and even the wings of the wheeling gulls red in it. A pretty scene, she had told him in the confines of the Peking cart; one, perhaps, that she would not see again. Lewis focused on the gunboat, so clear now that he could see two men polishing the stern gun, the rust stain on the whiteness of the paint, the red flag and the numeral on the bow. There were a few fishing boats in the bay, a drift of smoke from a distant ship. He heard Jethro say: "If you will please go into the house, ladies, for our last Communion." He turned. Sister Tai nodded in obedience. He thought he saw disapproval in her eyes; as if she could not reconcile this hairy and half-naked man with the priest who would shortly put the wafer in her lips. The four Sisters walked toward the house. It stood behind an immense banyan and Ellen and the boys were sitting in its shade. The house, perhaps at one time the property of a merchant, was enclosed by vegetable gardens and on one side was the shell of a burned building. The vines and blue flowers of convolvulus climbed in the charred timbers. The church, he thought. They burned his church. He raised the binoculars. Across from the house were the huts and barns of the village, in front of it a rocky cove and a little fleet of crude wooden boats. A path led from the house to the cove and where the path ended he could see the mast and cabin roof of a small motor-sailer. He moved the lenses seaward again, out to Breaker Point and past the gunboat. The port of Swatow came into vision. It was very near and clear (a direct line across the water, he estimated, of no more than two miles) and he could even distinguish the tricolor flag of the *Fragonard* and the mission flèche on the brow above the cranes. The priest's words had remained in his mind and he turned to Jethro and said: "What did you mean? Our last Communion?"

The two boys came running from the banyan.

"You must keep out of sight," Jethro told them. He watched them return to the tree. Then he took Lewis' arm and said: "Walk with me."

The path led through vegetable beds to the flank of the house. Jethro pointed down. "Asparagus," he said. He bent to the bed and grasped a handful of soil and let it sift through his fingers. "Food for a king," he said. "Yet, as you know, the Chinese won't eat it. They'll turn any old bitter weed into a tasty dish. But asparagus?" He shook his head. "No."

A pile of chopped tamarisk roots lay by the kitchen door and as they approached a girl came out and bowed to them, then gathered some of the roots and took them back in. She was dark-skinned with thin arms and a blue silk head-scarf, perhaps sixteen or seventeen years of age. Passing the open door Lewis saw her feeding tamarisk into the cooking stove.

"Malay," Jethro said.

The path stopped at the ruined church. Lizards ran. A bell was caught in the blackened upper timbers and a small green snake was entwined around the clapper. Below it fragments of stained glass made colored lights in the weed.

"So much has been destroyed," Jethro said. "Churches, people, books, belief."

Jethro led him to the harbor path. Steps had been cut in the rock and they stood on the first of them and looked down on the motor-sailer. The boat was old but its brass was bright and its deck clean and the cabin housing and the name *Justine* were newly painted.

"You asked me a question," Jethro said. "So I'll answer you." He pointed to the sea. "I've made maybe twenty trips across the Strait with men like you." The finger moved to the burned church. "And each time I've come back to that. To a dead bell. To a dead mission. To a dead life. I knew that one day they'd come for me. So I kept the boat ready, stored with food, water, fuel." He rubbed his stomach. "I do a lot of fishing, Mackenna. Not for souls, now, but for the frying pan. And many a time when I've been out there I've wanted to keep going. But I never did. There was always some poor devil waiting for a trip." He took the binoculars from Lewis' hands and focused on the gunboat. "Perhaps she'll go," Jethro said. "And perhaps we'll escape. But if we do escape I can't return. One way or the other it's over."

Ellen joined them. Behind her the four Sisters were walking to the house. Sister Tai stopped at the porch and looked back.

"I'll be with you," Jethro called.

"Will we take them with us?" Ellen asked.

"No."

"Why not? The boat's big enough."

"They wouldn't come."

"How do you know?"

"Because we've discussed it, Mrs. Mackenna. What would we do if arrest was certain? I said I would leave. They said they would stay."

"Try them again."

"It would do no good."

"Try," Lewis said.

"Run and be caught?" Jethro shook his head. "That isn't their style. Shall I tell you what they'll do? They'll get into their ridiculous carts and go back to the church and they'll sit down on those four chairs and fold their hands in their laps—and wait."

John Chen walked into the empty church and heard his heels send echoes through the silence. There were four chairs aligned in a row on one side of the aisle and he stopped and put his hand on the back of one of them and looked around him. Jagged windows, dirty walls, spider webs filming the roof; was this the abode of the Christian god? It was sour with the smell of worm and dust. But silver glowed on the altar and he went to it. There was no cloth and the bamboo was stained and splintered. Strange that sacramental silver, not even arranged, should be left in this forsaken place. But the candlestick was instantly recognizable. It was one of a pair and he had seen its twin in the shop in Ropemaker's Alley. He picked it up and examined its base and saw its English assay mark. He put it down. You were here, he whispered to Lewis Mackenna's face.

He returned to the row of chairs and sat. His old malarial fever, contracted years ago in Swatow, was awakening. The first of the bone pains had announced itself when, in the hospital, he had bent across Lin Sheng's unconscious body. Then, standing, a wave of heat had swept across his chest. That too was strange; that the parasite should stir again in the very port in which it had first invaded. Would Lin recover? The physician had given him a bottle of mepacrine tablets for the malaria and, capping the bottle, had said: "The young man is near to death. I do not know if we can save him. His father, the minister, is flying down." But it was the missionary's face that occupied his mind. Sunlight from one of the vacant windows was striating the floor and making stars on the candlestick. He did not believe in the candlestick. He rose and walked to the altar and stared again at the silver. He examined it piece by piece. It was all Chinese and therefore told him nothing. But the candlestick? It was the second to appear. The first had led him to the River Shih and up to the granite mountains and the confrontation with Mackenna; a trail that was true and no more than the gift of fortune. But this? He picked it up again. Its silver features winked in sun. Silver—but as base as lead. He set it down and went back to the chair. Nausea was swelling in his stomach and already he had a full and bounding pulse. He could not think clearly. He closed his eyes. Think. Consider the facts. This derelict place is occupied by four old women, the survivors of a proscribed religious Order. Early today a commune leader is passing the entrance gates on his bicycle and observes that two Peking carts, draped and ready for the road, are standing on the compound and that two people, one of them a Sister Tai and the other a European man, are walking down from the church toward the waiting carts. He dismounts, watches for a time, then resumes his journey. On the coastal road, running west of the port, the carts overtake and pass him. Some hours later (inertia being the curse of the Fukienese) he reports to the police; and at noon here I am, predictably, and in front of me is the proof that the European was Lewis Mackenna. A piece of silver, a piece moved across a board. Two covered carts, two more pieces moving. He felt his face flush with fever. The candlestick shone with reflected light. I do not believe in your innocence, he said to it. Now he could see Mackenna's mocking eyes. And where is the proof, he said to him, that you and your family were behind the drapes of the Peking carts? Sweat was streaming. Within the ache and the head-noises a question was forming. How could the missionary rely on the commune leader to be there at the gates at that particular time, to observe and then report? The man, he concluded, was either bribed or a Chiang agent. He stood and walked to the door. His legs were weak and there was a need to vomit. He would have to end the game before the malaria put him on his back. When he reached the doorway he stopped and looked back. Everything was blurred and Mackenna's face, now, had moved up into the dark space in the roof where the flèche was built. "I will not follow the carts down the coast," he said aloud. "That is what you want. I will not do it. You are still here, here in the port, here in Swatow." He decided to walk up the rise to the edge of the sea and confirm that the gunboat lay on guard.

When he reached the brow he stood in the warm wind that was coming off the sea until the nausea had abated and his eyes were clear. He had not realized how near the docks were to the mission land. Masts and derricks loomed above him and he could smell the smoke from the funnel of the French steamer that was moving out into the roads. The gunboat lay anchored in a satisfactory position out in the bay; well placed, he thought, to cover the port exits and the wide curve of coast. Below and to his right he could see moving cranes, cargo tractors, currents of brown and yellow faces, a police post and the harbormaster's office. A white police launch was moored at the quay that was adjacent to the post and soldiers or police stood at each of the dock gates. He watched the steamer point to the Double Island sea lane. The stern swung so that its white-painted letters were revealed. *Fragonard.* He read it again. *Fragonard.* The shock brought the bile welling to his mouth. That name again. That ship. He saw in that moment the scraps of azure paper and the name and the letter S. Waves of heat rose and the letters on the stern ran and became a blur. *They are on that ship.* The pulse throbbed like a piston and a sudden pain struck within his head. It was as if a chain of reason, begun in the mission living room, had snapped and whipped against his enfevered brain. He put his hands to his head and held them there across the pain. S for Shanghai, but also S for Swatow. *The Mackennas are on that ship.* The nausea rode up and bent him and he vomited and when he straightened his flesh was cold. The ship shuddered on the water. I have to stop her. He stood there trembling until the sickness passed. Then he turned and walked quickly down to the compound and the waiting car.

In the car, descending and then moving onto the road that would bring it to the dockyard gates, he leaned back in the rear seat and closed his eyes. Fool, he told himself; to see a trick that was never there, subtlety where none existed. Imbecile; to see deceit in the bottom of a wastebasket because, choked with straw and paper, it had been left behind in Ellen Mackenna's spotless home. Swatow had always been the destination, the *Fragonard* the ship that, prearranged, would wait and smuggle them aboard and take them off. Sweat was running once again and he wiped his face. So much for the years of chess; to so condition a man's mind that nothing was ever as it seemed.

When he entered the harbormaster's office he saw that the seaward side of it was glassed. There was a view of Double Island and the open bay and in the central panel the *Fragonard* was growing smaller. To the east and distant was the gunboat. There were three men in the office; a radio operator seated at the shore-to-ship radio, a pilot and the harbormaster. Chen went to the radio operator and bent close behind his back and laid his arm across his shoulder so that it was parallel to his cheek and pointed at the gunboat. Then he moved the arm slowly until his finger pointed at the ship.

"I want her stopped," he said.

From the tamarinds Lewis Mackenna watched the *Fragonard,* now a small black profile off Breaker Point. Then, moving the binoculars, he saw the sudden froth of water at the gunboat's stern. The anchor had been raised and he waited and the bows began to glide and, now, the froth was a long and widening wake. "She's moving," he called out. He turned. Ellen and the Sisters were under the banyan and there was orange peel on the grass where the boys had thrown it and at the side of the house the boys were holding open the mouths of sacks and Jethro was digging in the asparagus beds and lifting balls of soil and roots and dropping them into the sacks. "She's moving," Lewis cried out again; and Jethro and the boys and Ellen came running and the Sisters came sedately and they stood in the tree-shadow and one of them lifted her eyes and murmured thanks and Jethro took the binoculars from Lewis and watched the sharp white bows of the gunboat and the course she was on. "She's after that ship," he said. He returned the binoculars and Lewis refocused them and studied the gunboat and the *Fragonard.* "I do believe she is," he said. A police launch appeared on the lenses, heading out from the quays and curving through the roads so that she too was pointing at the steamer. There were police and soldiers in the launch and he saw John Chen's face move behind the aligned barrels of the rifles and in that moment he understood. A more distinguished player than Chen had taken a piece that was carved like a ship and placed it in the port of Swatow. He began to laugh and Jethro stared and now the laughter would not stop and he walked away from them and he wanted to sit down on the grass and laugh at the richness of it. He wiped his eyes and the laughter heaved again. Now he could see the room in the bungalow in the Fusan camp and Chen's superior face and Chen's superior hand poised above his superior army and hear Chen's superior voice. Rich. How could a man lose if the Lord was at his elbow? He turned and, still laughing, walked back to them.

"Later," Jethro said, "you must tell us the joke. But right now it's time to leave." He turned to Joel and Gerard. "Finish the sacks and bring them down to the boat."

The boys ran.

"And pick up that orange peel," Ellen called after them.

"Never mind the peel," Jethro said. "Please get into the boat." He pointed at the house. "In the meantime I have a goodbye to say."

"And so do I," Lewis said.

Ellen watched the priest walk to the house. A goodbye? Who was in the house? Lewis left her side and went to the four Sisters and she heard his murmuring voice and saw him reach out and touch Sister Tai's cheek and now all the Sisters were smiling and Sister Tai gave her little trill of girlish laughter and the four beautiful old faces were nodding in the sun as brown and wrinkled as decaying apples. "Thank you, thank you, thank you," she said to them. "God keep you safe." But she could not leave the litter under the banyan and she went to it and picked up the orange peel and walked down the path to the house and Joel passed her with a sack of asparagus roots. "Get into the boat," she told him. "And stay there." Gerard was still lifting roots. She went into the kitchen. There was no one in it and she put the peel into a bin and came outside again and said to Gerard: "Go to the boat. Hurry." When he had gone with the sack she walked farther down the flank of the house. She could not see Jethro and she called out: "Are you there, Father? We have to hurry." There was no answer. An uprooted notice board with a rotten base and a worm-eaten shaft was on its side against the trunk of a shrub. Most of the lettering, written in Chinese and English, was so weathered that she could not read it. *MISSION OF THE MACAO FATHERS* (it began) *Conducted by Rev. Father Frank Jethro;* and underneath: *Confessions after all Mission Masses.* There was a window toward the rear of the house and she stopped and looked through it. Jethro and a young woman were standing in the center of the room. His back was toward the window and he was holding her hands. She was thin, brown of face but not Chinese, and her black hair was bound up into a blue scarf. She was weeping but her grief did not contort her eyes or mouth and her body was still and only the wetness on her face revealed the grief. She saw Jethro kiss her forehead, then unbutton her dress and draw it down from the shoulders and bend to her and press his mouth to the nipple of her right breast and the girl put her hand under the heavy dark curls on the nape of his neck and held him there and pressed against her and then he moved his lips to the nipple of the other breast and she held him there and they began to rock gently. There was no sensual passion in it and they were drawing comfort from it and it was like an act of affection long known to both of them. But Ellen, watching, felt the outrage rise, and she rapped on the window and shouted: "Hurry. You know we have to hurry."

She turned and walked trembling along the side of the house and through the beds and down the harbor path to where the rock steps led to the boat. She stood there in the sea breeze and waited and when she heard his feet on the path she turned to him. They stared and she saw amusement in his eyes.

"Don't expect me to call you Father," she said.

The breeze had strengthened when they cleared the harbor. Jethro, using the motor, took the *Justine* out through the seaweed ropes and the puttering sound made echoes in the rocks. The people of To-kuei knew, inexplicably, that he was leaving and would not return and six of the fishing boats followed in the wake so that the brown mainsail of the *Justine* would, when it was rigged, be less conspicuous among the brown lateen sails of the fishing boats. They had done this out of affection for him and many of them were waving from the shore. Ellen watched from the stern, looking down the wake to the dunes and the tussock grass and the house. The girl in the scarf was nowhere to be seen but the four Sisters were standing in sunlight away from the tamarinds, their creased and warty faces smiling with love. When they reached the buoys she could see the thick growth of the algae, not bright green as Sister Tai had described it but tawny where the sun struck down through the water onto it and dark green where the ropes sank into depth. She did not turn from the stern until the land was indistinct. The fishing boats were leaving and would work until sundown and she watched them trolling down the current and becoming smaller.

But when the sundown came and was red behind the mainsail she could not see the fishing boats or the China mainland. There was only sea. The boat, driven by the wind and the engine silent, had no grace. A misbegotten craft, Jethro had told them. The *Justine* had spent her youth in Macao (where he had bought her) and the engine was added later, and then the jib. But like many unprepossessing females she was reliable. "How fast will she go?" Gerard had asked, and Jethro answered: "Maybe ten." Ellen stood and held on to one of the mast stays and watched the sea for a time. Ten. Ten miles an hour. That meant they could be forty miles out. The island of Taiwan was ninety miles from the China coast at the nearest point. But their own course lay much farther south. Kaohsiung, one of the island's deep-water ports, was more than two hundred miles from Swatow. Tomorrow, God willing, they might make the landfall. She smiled. Strange how easily the nautical terms formed on the tongue. But the fear was still there and would revive whenever a pillar of smoke broke the line of the horizon. There were no national limits in these waters, Jethro had warned; or at least none that were observed. Any ship could be an enemy, even close in to the Taiwan shores. The night is near, she thought, will be a cover and a respite from the fear. She turned to the stern and watched the red that was on the sea. Out there beyond the mists of distance is the unseen land where my home is, where my parents are buried, where my children were born and played in Dragon Well Lane and rowed the boats on West Lake. That is where I am still. She heard Jethro say to the boys: "The first ships sailed before the wind, as we are now. Do you know the word for that? No? We call it running. They had a square sail, those early craft. Square-rigged is the term. And the big ones could cross an ocean on the trade winds. But later, much later, there was another kind of rig. Can you tell me what it was? No? You must have seen the Arab dhows. You saw the fishing boats that came out with us. They have a fore-and-aft rig. You, Gerard, tell me what you think that is." A silence. Then: "I am Joel." And Jethro's deep laugh. "Well, I have to believe you. A fore-and-aft rig is when the forward edge of the sail is fixed to the mast and can be made to pivot according to the wind. Like this one. Interesting, isn't it, that a boat can sail against the very force that is driving it?"

Ellen turned.

Jethro was seated swiveled on the steering stool, the two boys at his feet on the deck. Lewis was sleeping, head sunk onto his chest, on the seat that made a top to the gasoline tanks. Jethro was shirtless again. Some priest, she thought. A Mass for the four old Sisters, offering Christ, pronouncing over the bread and wine. *This is my body, this is the Chalice of my blood.* Then off with the vestments and snuff out the candles and the slobbering over a young girl's teats. The anger would not leave her. She sat down on the deck next to the engine hatch. The two asparagus sacks were beside the hatch. One of them was torn and earth and root had spilled.

Jethro stood.

"Would you like to steer her?" he said to the boys.

They rose.

"Take it in turns. Keep her on two-one-five."

Jethro came to the hatch, opened it and secured it back. She watched him reach down into the motors, feel the cylinders, adjust the grease cups. "She's been stalling," he said. He closed the hatch. He was very near to her and she could see his hard pectoral muscles and the black hair that curled on them and smell the sweat of him. He knelt to the torn sack and began to scoop up the roots and return them to the sack. Then, cupping a hand and brushing with the other, he cleaned the deck of the spilled soil and dropped it into the sack. Now she could smell the sweat and the hessian of the sack and the dark brown earth, all commingling into one strong and primal scent. He tied the mouth of the sack. Then, turning on his knee, he reached across her and propped both the sacks against the hatch and there was a second in which she felt the pressure of his hard bare thigh. He stood and looked down at her and she thought she saw again the flicker of amusement. Then he left her and went to the boys and checked the compass and looked at the waves and the little swallow-tailed burgee on the masthead so that he might assess the direction of the wind. Watching him and the power of him and his heavy-muscled back that was reddish in the sunset light she felt the stirring of a forgotten want. It touched her and then was gone.

Across from the jib Lewis could see through the darkness to where, north of them, the Pescadores made little points of distant light. There were more than sixty islands in the archipelago. Soon the lights would be gone into the night of the sea and the *Justine,* swift now in the quartering wind, would pass into the Pescadores Channel. Two-thirds of the way across the Strait, he judged. Yet there was no elation, only an emptiness and Shameen floating down the river and a young man with a bloodied head and the faces of those who had given to him that he might be two-thirds of the way to safety and four chairs in a desecrated church. He looked across the deck to where Ellen sat with her hair lifting in the wind. She too showed no elation. Why are we all so apart? he asked himself. Over there is the valise with the gun and the length of lichen in it and I have not talked to her of the shooting or talked to Joel of it and the boy has not spoken to any of us about it or of the meaning of the lichen and we are each of us alone and perhaps it always comes to that: aloneness. Jethro was silent now, his face bent into the glow of the binnacle light. They had listened to his rich and vibrant voice, murmuring about his early days in the Church and the thread of destiny that was drawing him now to another place and another life. He had been born in Macao to an English mother and a Portuguese gambler whose love in life was the breeding of horses for the trotting races. They had lived almost in the shadow of the Sáo Domingos church and the tolling of its bells was his earliest recollected sound. There were also the sounds of the casinos, of roulette and baccarat and even the jingling of coins under the fantan cup—that cunning game that he had played as a child with the coolies. But it was the bells that won, he said, laughing. Both his parents were devout Roman Catholics and they had sent him for his education to a church school in Hong Kong. Like the Macao Fathers and other affiliated colonial missions the school was administered from Lisbon. The seed was sprouting and at the school he had come under the influence of a very distinguished theologian who had advised him to study for the priesthood. But that would come later. The torrents of youth were flowing hotly through his veins and he could not dam them back and he had returned to Macao where for some years there would be horses and cards and good living and the discovery of sailing and (he laughed again) other less innocent pursuits.

"He means women," Ellen said coldly.

But it was the sudden death of his father, he told them, that had returned him to the arms of the Church. It affected him deeply and left a void that he could not fill. The sailing was still good and would always be good and was as important to him as the trotting had been to his father. But away from the sea he was as cold as a dead fire. He entered the seminary in Lisbon. He was twenty-five and the war in Europe had just begun. For a time all went well. This was his vocation and despite his human frailties would remain so. But wartime Lisbon was a feverish place for a seedling priest. The shock of his father's death began to fade. The sea was near and sometimes its humid airs lay on the city and were perfumed and touched the senses. There were lapses. Eventually and near to the time of his ordination one of the preceptors warned him and talked to him of temptation. "Don't you know," the preceptor asked, "that the Devil hides under a woman's skirts?" And he had answered: "Yes, Father. But are we not taught to challenge the Devil wherever we may find him?" Jethro smiled at the memory. An example, he told them, of the irreverence that would forever be his curse. After his ordination he returned to Macao. He borrowed some money from his mother and bought and refitted the *Justine*. For a month or two there was the sea, the boat, the fishing. He waited like a good soldier of Christ for a posting. The war had ended and the mission fields beckoned. They sent him to many places; to Lourenço in Mozambique, to St. Paul de Loanda in Angola, to Principé in the Gulf of Guinea where they had great need of a priest and to Goa in Portuguese India where the Goanese were Roman Catholics to a man and there was no one to convert. Then he had gone to Timor. And it was there that he met Ajang.

"Ajang?" Lewis asked.

"The girl," Ellen said with disdain. "The Malay girl. The one with the dress that unbuttons."

Lewis stared at her, not understanding. But Jethro laughed and his warm dark eyes went wet with merriment. The powers had not approved, he said. So they sent him back to Macao. There would be another posting and because, obviously, he would need a housekeeper (this with a chuckle) he had taken the girl with him. For a time he concealed her on the *Justine*. Then he was told that the missioner at To-kuei, a village in the Swatow region, had died and that he would replace him. He could not bear to part from the boat, or from Ajang, and they decided to sail her up the coast. Six months after they arrived Chiang and his armies were defeated and the Red Guards came. They burned his church. There were executions in the village. Christ was banished and the priests were leaving. He too made plans to leave. After all there was little for a priest to do. The Chinese Christians were afraid and he did not see his ministry in terms of secret Masses in a barn at night. But then the Reds began to give Sister Tai and the Sisterhood a very bad time. It enraged him. And when he was approached by a Kuomintang agent and asked to ferry an elderly priest across the Strait he agreed. There was an enormous satisfaction when he saw the red and green blinker lights on the Taiwan coast and knew that the priest was safe. This was one they would not get. So it continued. Priests, fugitives, enemies of Mao—he sailed them all to safety. Jethro's face had turned, then, from the compass. "It was a victory," he said. "A small victory. But why has it come to taste so bitter? Can you tell me that, Dr. Mackenna? Why?"

Lewis was silent.

"Dr. Mackenna?"

"I wish I knew," Lewis said.

Ellen awakened. She could feel the hardness of the deck against her hipbone and, turning in the sleeping bag, she opened her eyes and saw Lewis' face above her. He was smiling. There was a little rain, enough to make his temples shine, and above him was the morning sky and clouds flowing down it like gray herds. "Come," he said. He opened the sleeping bag and lifted her to her feet. Jethro and the two boys were standing in the bows and they went to them and stood behind them. They did not turn or speak. Ahead was the sea mist and the swell of the sea dark within it and bright in places where the sun struck through. He put his arm around her and, still not speaking, they watched the mist open. Now she could catch on the warm wind the faint flowery scent of the land. They could not yet see the land, only the parting mist and once, when a veil of it dissolved, the sail of a fishing boat and the white of the gulls that were circling it. Then the mist closed again and they waited, the boat gone and listening to the distant cries of the gulls, and Jethro left them and moved away to the stern so that he might leave them alone as a family with their moment of the journey's end. When it came and the long low line of the coast revealed itself she felt his arm tighten around her waist. Rain was falling.

PART TWO

Haven

Chapter 8

From the table on the hotel terrace Ellen could see the curve of Sun Moon
Lake and the mountains of the Niitaka Chain. The lake lay very high in
the approximate center of Taiwan and was a reservoir. It was also beautiful
and was therefore a tourist resort and already in this the early day there
were rowing boats out on the lake and a group of people at the end of the
terrace who had come up from the heat of Taipei. She would sit here, she
decided, until Lewis returned; here in the peace of the lake and without
the fear in the stomach and watch the white herons flying down the shores
and the fishermen and drink tea and eat pineapple and move into shade
when the sun got hot and reflect how good it was not to have the fear.
Below the terrace she could see Joel and Gerard in the orange trees and
walking down to the shore and the wooden jetty and eating from the
bunches of longans that they were holding in their hands. Out on the lake
and across from the jetty there was a bamboo raft with a grass hut built
on it that would serve as a shelter and the raft went very slowly and she
watched the fisherman lower the boom into the water from time to time
so that the net would catch the tiny surface fish that the hotels would buy
for the flavoring of soups. When the boys and the raft were gone from
sight she turned on her seat and looked up and over the roof of the hotel
to where there were forested slopes of camphor and cryptomeria and above
the line of the forests the peaks of mountains. Somewhere up there would
be the president's retreat. The eyrie (as Chiang liked to call it) lay, remote
and guarded, at the end of the mountain road. There was an opening in
the trees high up where the road climbed and she saw the jeep cross the
opening and then disappear. He was in that jeep, sitting in the passenger
seat next to the president's aide and dressed in the white borrowed suit
that was too short in the sleeves and trousers; on his way, she thought, to
test the gratitude of princes.

*   *   *

The aide pointed to the little temple that stood in the garden in the shade of trees away from the house and said: "You must wait. The president and Madame Chiang are at prayer." He touched one of the garden chairs. "Sit." Lewis sat and the aide said severely: "The early morning is always set aside for prayers and meditation. They must never be disturbed." He turned and walked toward the house with his leather military boots ringing on the path. The house was built on a spur of rock and its upturned scarlet eaves seemed to reach into cloud and mountain mist. But the temple had once been Buddhist. Now a bronze Christian Cross, gone green with time, was set in the wall. This was a quiet place with no sound from the house or the temple and only bird-song and the faint murmur of an unseen spring to accent the silence.

Lewis waited thirty minutes. Then a woman came from the temple and smiled and beckoned. He rose and went to her. Mei-ling, the president's wife, was still dark of hair and handsome and she took his hand and said in English: "We are relieved to see you safe." She pointed to the interior and he bowed and walked inside. The Buddhas were long since gone. Chiang had always been an austere man and there was little furniture in the temple, only some unpainted screens, rush mats, a plain table and three hard chairs. A prayer book, a hymnal and an open Bible lay on the table and the walls were bare except for a small area where there were some black-framed photographs and a reproduction of a Raphael Christ. He went to the photographs. The Generalissimo appeared in all of them; the younger Chiang as the commandant of the Whampoa Military Academy, as lithe and dangerous as a hungry cat and those cruel and arrogant eyes staring out from under the peak of his army cap; Chiang standing in the archway entrance to the Ming Tombs in Nanking and as somber as a monk in his ankle-length cloak and a stiletto of light across his temples as if the mark of high destiny was already stamped upon him; Chiang in a flower garden with the beautiful Mei-ling at his side and his ripe-brown oiled nut of a head glowing in the sun; Chiang in the war years, older now, receiving the Legion of Merit from Lieutenant-General Stilwell and the American's face haughty with dislike; and, then, Chiang with his shaven head as white as a rime of frost and in the company of the great ones, with Roosevelt, with Churchill, with Marshal Stalin. The door to an inner room opened and Chiang entered. He stood there unsmiling and his eyes went to the photographs. Then he sat and his thin hand went out to the Bible and closed it and remained for a moment on its cover. Lewis walked to the table and, looking down on Chiang's averted head and the sharp cranial bones that made a pattern under the nap of white bristle, saw that he had aged. Chiang looked up and smiled and said in Mandarin: "Good to see you, Lewis. Are you well?"

"Yes, Mr. President."

"And your family?"

"Yes. All well."

"A difficult journey?"

"At times."

"But you are safe now."

"Yes, Mr. President. And for that we thank you."

Chiang stood.

"I find it cold in here," he said. "Let us walk in the sun."

He picked up the Bible and cradled it in his left hand and led Lewis from the temple. Mei-ling had gone but there were guards on one of the paths and the gleam of a helmet in the foliage. The path wound around the house and under trees. Chiang walked softly with the Bible pressed to his hip and head bowed, as meek as a preacher in a graveyard. They emerged from the trees above the waters of Sun Moon Lake. Chiang stopped and pointed down. "It's a reservoir," he said. "Most of the island's light and power is provided from it. The hydroelectric plants are on a lower level and therefore you cannot see them from up here. The Americans bombed them during the war. Did you know that? Oh, yes. The Japanese were in control then. They were very successful raids and all the transformers were destroyed." They began to walk. "We have two retreats," Chiang said. "This one and another north of Taipei in the mountains at Tsaoshan. But we prefer it here. There are hot springs at Tsaoshan and it always smells of sulphur." The path wound. Chiang talked in his sharp and toneless voice; always in Mandarin for he had no English and his second language was Japanese. Taiwan, he said, was now a garrison. There was martial law and the island was fat with American money, filled with American advisers and American planes and guns and military equipment. At the time of his exile (he did not refer to his defeat) he had brought with him from the mainland a million of the finest Chinese troops and the best of the officer corps. They were invincible. Lewis heard the old arrogance entering his voice. The U.S.A. wanted the Communists out of China, knew that he, Chiang Kai-shek, was the only man who could rout Mao's armies. Soon the invasion would begin. Soon the two Chinas would be one. Chiang stopped and turned and his eyes burned with fervor. He tapped the spine of the Bible. "That's work for a Christian general, is it not?"

"It is indeed."

The lake revealed itself again and Chiang pointed down to the hotels on the shore.

"Which is your hotel?" he asked.

"The one with the blue awnings."

"Are you comfortable?"

"Very."

"What are your plans, Lewis?"

"That depends."

"On what?"

"On you, sir."

"Tell me what you need."

"Money."

"Money?"

"Yes."

Chiang frowned.

"But you are rich, Lewis."

"No. I have nothing."

"You have the antiquities. They were your payment. Have you seen the prices on the London art market?"

"Not lately."

"I assure you they are very high."

"I don't have the antiquities. They were stolen from me."

"Stolen?"

"Yes. During my escape."

"Was that my fault?"

"No. But you still have a responsibility."

"In what way?"

"Because I served you. A year in a camp, another four in constant danger. Now I stand before you with nothing."

"You have your life."

"Yes."

"Your freedom."

"Yes."

"And your family."

He could see the change in Chiang. The meekness and the preacher's stoop were gone. Anger was growing and this was no longer the ageing general sitting frail and cold in the warmth of the temple. Chiang turned and took a dozen rapid paces up the path with his shoulders squared and his heels stamping as hard as a sentry's and when he turned again it was the pitiless face of the war campaigns that came back through bars of sun.

"I will not pay twice, Lewis."

"I need a house. And some cash."

"A house and cash."

"Yes. Surely you owe me that?"

Chiang shook his head.

"We have to live. And we have to educate our sons."

"I will not pay twice."

Chiang turned away. Farther up the path Mei-ling was cutting flowers and beyond her the aide waited in a pool of shadow.

"I thought we were friends," Lewis said.

Chiang smiled.

"Friendship is for equals," he said.

He began to walk and Lewis felt his own dormant anger rise and he put his hand in his pocket and took out Shameen's brooch.

"You'd better have this," he called out.

Chiang stopped and Lewis went to him and held out his closed fist and dropped the brooch into Chiang's right palm. Chiang stared down at it. He was disconcerted and he gave Lewis the Bible so that his left hand would be free and the fingers stroked the brooch, then ran gently up the slender shaft to the gold head that was impaled on it.

"This is Shameen's," he said.

"Yes."

"How did you get it? It was my gift."

"I took it from him."

"From Shameen?"

"From his body."

"Shameen is dead?"

"Yes."

He saw no grief in the Generalissimo's eyes. For him there had been too many deaths.

"How did he die?" Chiang asked.

"I killed him."

They heard Mei-ling speak, the aide's respectful voice.

"You killed him?" Chiang said.

"Yes."

"Why?"

"To protect my family."

Chiang frowned.

"But he was your guard," he said. "Not your enemy."

"I know."

"I sent him to you. My own faithful guard. His orders were to bring you here."

"There were other orders."

"Other orders?"

"Yes, as well you know."

He saw the caution in Chiang's face.

"His orders," Lewis said, "were to kill us if it seemed we would be captured."

Chiang shook his head.

"Yes," Lewis said. "They were his orders. Don't deny it."

"But I do deny it."

Across Chiang's shoulder he saw a flower fall from Mei-ling's hand and the aide bend and retrieve it and place it in her basket.

"Such an order would be prudent," Chiang said. "But I did not give it. That is the truth. Have I ever lied to you?"

Lewis did not answer.

"Have I?"

"No."

Chiang pointed to the Bible.

"Would I place my hand on that and lie?"

"No."

"Hold it out."

Lewis held out the Bible and Chiang put his hand on it and said softly: "I swear on this holy book that I gave no such order, neither direct nor implied." He took the Bible from Lewis' grasp and opened it and placed the brooch there reverently as if it might be sanctified within the pages. "Shameen," he whispered. "Shameen. He was a remarkable man with strange and wonderful talents. The best of all my men. I shall mourn him." He looked up. "I am shocked," he said. "Shocked that you, Lewis, a minister, a man of God, could do this thing." He closed the Bible on the brooch, as gently as a child pressing a wild flower. "I shall forget the pain in time. But you, Lewis? Will you forget?" He turned away and walked up the path to where Mei-ling and the aide were standing. They began to talk and the warmth went from Mei-ling's face and the aide's lip jutted with anger. Then Chiang and Mei-ling went toward the house and the aide came down the path.

"You must leave," he said.

Driving down the slope the aide said: "You will not see the president again. You are no longer welcome. You may remain on the island and you will receive a permit of employment." He stopped the jeep at the hotel entrance. They got out.

"Wait here," the aide said.

He went inside; and when he returned he showed Lewis a receipt and said: "We have paid your account. But you cannot stay here. It is far too expensive. We have arranged for you to go to a modest hotel in Taipei. You may stay there at the State's expense for no more than two weeks. During that time you must obtain employment." He smiled with insolence. "If, that is, you can find a mission that will employ a murderous priest. Do you understand?"

"Yes."

The aide took some currency notes from his pocket and put them into Lewis' hand.

"A gift from Madame Chiang," he said. "She has no wish to see your family without cash."

Lewis counted the notes.

"It isn't very much,' he said.

"No," the aide said. "But even a little charity is a beautiful thing." He got into the jeep. "If you are careful," he said derisively, "you may have enough to buy a suit."

*   *   *

But he did not buy a suit or replace any of their water-damaged clothes. There was a need for aloneness, to put himself at a distance from Ellen and the chatter of the twins. In the early light of the following day and the noise of Taipei city already building in the plaza outside the hotel he put his razors and a towel and soap and clean garments into a traveling bag and took a blanket from a cupboard and folded it into the bag and said to her: "I have to be alone for a day or two." She nodded and did not ask a question and he gave her two-thirds of the money.

Down in the reception he asked the clerk where he might hire a car cheaply and the man wrote down an address and pointed through the windows to the plaza and the waiting pedicabs. Outside from the forecourt he could see, opposite, the red-brick building that was the military headquarters and in front of it a company of white-vested Nationalist soldiers. The white chests bent and jerked to the rhythm of tai-chi exercises. There were many private cars, mostly American makes, people in brightly colored clothes; a scene, he thought, he would not see on the mainland where there would be a mass of workers' bicycles and faded Mao jackets and gray trousers, all of them dressed drably from the same State warehouse. He watched for a minute. Then he beckoned to a pedicab.

The address lay in a street two blocks off the plaza. The city, apparently, had inherited a fine legacy of wartime jeeps. This one, the dealer told him, had once been used by the great General MacArthur and, therefore, had historic value. Lewis paid a deposit. He did not know if the general had ever come to Taiwan, but the rate of hire was cheap and there was a good canvas roof and the dealer gave him a road map on which he had drawn a route that would circumscribe the island.

Driving northeast to Chilung, the spine of mountains always high above the road and the road climbing from the valleys toward the island's tip, he saw the distant city vanish in the mist and the Tanshui River, the rice paddies that were turning green with the second season's crop and above them the terraces of tea and orange. Ilha Formosa (Beautiful Island) the Portuguese had named it, and watching it unfold he felt a sudden yearning for that other land of beauty that lay unreachably behind him. When the lowland and its stands of bamboo and paddies were gone he stopped the jeep. A cigar butt rolled out from under the throttle and between his feet (was it a relic of the great general?) and he picked it up and threw it out. He sat there for a time and listened to the cicadas and breathed on the wind the scent of the evergreen forests and the camphor laurel that were thick on the mountains. Then he opened the map.

The island, shaped like a fish, was perhaps 250 miles from head to tail and, at its maximum, 80 miles wide. The dealer's route, he saw, was unreliable. No road encircled the island; and at Hualienchiang, which lay one-third of the distance down the eastern coast, the highway finished and only a rail track ran south. He decided to keep within this upper third. Climbing again he watched the terrain change with height. Now there were cedars, juniper and maples, and above them where it would be colder the coniferous forests. For the first time since Hangchow he felt the strain leave him. This road in the morning sun was freedom. He had shed the weight of fear like a discarded garment. Later in the night there would be the other enemies that lived within and he did not know if they would ever go; but now there was only the sunlight and the road ahead.

When the sun was high he stopped the jeep at an inn that was built on a spur of rock at the summit of the road. Here the conifers made a dark skirt around the base of the peaks. The inn was placed so that it would command a view from the rear and he walked around its flank and sat at a table. It was a pleasant place with rhododendrons and wild lilies in the rocks. Far below him the plains floated in heat haze. He could see the confluence of the Tanshui and Chilung rivers, the port of Chilung and the sea. Rice fields glittered as bright as tin. There were two stalls on the terrace, stocked with tourist goods. He rose and went over to them. There were hats, marble ornaments, coral jewelry, racks of seashell earrings. He examined the hats. He had left his collection in Hangchow and he felt incomplete without one. He chose a hat made from woven grass and put it on and a man came from inside the inn and laughed and clapped his hands. "One U.S. dollar," he said and Lewis gave him one of his Bank of Taiwan notes. The man had tribal tattoos on the forehead and the chin. Up in the mountains, Jethro had told him, there were no Chinese races, only the aboriginals, who were usually Taiyals. The man laughed again and showed the spaces in his teeth where the incisors had been drawn in some childhood ritual.

After he had eaten a dish of venison and rice and bamboo sprouts he pulled his chair into the shade and tipped down the hat across his eyes and drifted into sleep. He was awakened by the slamming of car doors, voices and laughter. Three men and three women came through onto the terrace. They spoke with Australian accents and the men had cameras and red thighs and one wore a singlet with the Sydney Harbor bridge making a span across the chest. Lewis watched them search the stalls, buy souvenirs and beer and, finally, six hats of woven grass. He felt the anger rise. The peace was gone. Now they were posing for pictures in the funny hats. After they had left he went to the edge of the terrace and took off his own hat of woven grass and flung it over and the Taiyal came out and clucked with disapproval and clambered down the slope and retrieved it and, regaining the terrace, brushed the hat and held it out. Lewis, laughing now, put it on. He had no right to resent them and, after all, there was not much laughter in Mao's grim China and you would not find parties of beer-belly Diggers driving freely up a mountain road.

Later the Taiyal brought two brass-ringed bamboo pipes out onto the terrace so that they might share a smoke and sat and filled the bowls. During that somnolent afternoon they smoked and drank tea and sat in reflective silence and sometimes talked. Lewis pointed at the tattoos and the Taiyal touched the mark on his chin.

"A head," he said.

"A head?"

"Yes. Such a mark signifies the taking of a head."

"In the war?"

"Yes. For me it was in the war. Japanese soldiers."

"How many heads?"

"Thirty-five."

Lewis heard the pride in his voice.

"Thirty-five," the man repeated.

"You are a great warrior."

Pleasure touched the Taiyal's eyes. He stood.

"Come," he said.

Lewis followed him from the terrace to the flank of the inn and through a bead curtain and into a small room that had colored paper panels on the walls and cushions on the floor. Above the panels on one of the walls there was a row of wooden hat-pegs and on each of the pegs a Japanese Army cap. The caps were old and stained. Lewis stared at them. It was as if, he thought, a platoon of soldiers had hung their caps in a cloakroom. He took one of the caps off its peg and examined it, turned it so that he saw its greasy band. He could not resist the wearing of this unusual piece of headgear and he put it on. The Taiyal smiled.

"You may keep it," he said.

"No."

"Yes, keep it."

"But it's a trophy."

"Keep it."

They walked back to the terrace.

"Sadly," the Taiyal said, "all the Japanese have gone. There will be no more heads."

"There are always the Australian tourists."

When he had paid for the meal and some citrus drinks he stood and held out his hand. The Taiyal took it.

"There is a bed here," he said.

"No."

"Where will you go?"

Lewis pointed.

"Up the mountain?"

"Yes."

"And then?"

"East."

The Taiyal showed him a map and slid his finger on it. Higher, on the right hand, there was a track that the jeep could negotiate and which was used by the mule carts to carry camphor chips down the mountain. There was a very fine waterfall and as secret a place as a man could wish for. Lewis smiled at his perceptiveness. The track, he said, would descend and find the road that led to Chiaochi and the sea.

Driving from the inn he looked back once and the Taiyal was standing in the sun in the road and watching him and his red sleeveless blouse and bright blue shorts were glowing and it was difficult to accept that he had taken thirty-five heads. The woven grass hat lay on the passenger seat and this together with the army cap would be the beginning of another hat collection and he would wear the cap occasionally for his friend the Japanese Major Kazumi who had died in the fireball at the Fusan camp. An estate wagon was approaching and it slowed on the narrow road when it reached him and the faces of the Australians turned toward him and they were laughing and waving and he too laughed and waved until the wagon was gone from the driving mirror.

But the good humor left him when the nightfall came. He had braked the jeep off the track on the rock shelves that were near to the waterfall and sitting on the blanket away from the jeep and above the pool below the fall he watched the water turn white in the rising moon and the pale light moving into the fringe of the camphor. There had been a camphor grove that second night of their escape when they had stood above the river and still damp from it and the scent of the camphor on the wind he had talked of the luck they would need to get them safe across the water and Ellen had resented the word because for her there was no luck, good or bad, only God's will or a favorable answer to a prayer and he had grown angry, perhaps out of guilt, and he had told her: "I'll fall on my knees when we get there, but not before." Perhaps he had meant it at the time; but of course you could not make such a bargain—bring us to safety and I promise to return to you—and in any event too much had happened since that night. There were now the two accusing faces, that of Shameen and that of the young security policeman (had he died?) and the faces refused to fade and were in possession and because of them he could not say a prayer of thanksgiving for their deliverance or pray for forgiveness for the killing or the life of the policeman. He could not even believe that he could be absolved for what he had done. Perhaps he was truly alone. The espionage was a form of corruption; and there were those that believed that when corruption entered the soul it would leave and could never return. And if that was true he was dead even before the killing. He felt himself shiver and he lay down on the blanket and pulled it across him and closed his eyes and listened to the fall of water.

At sunrise he went down the rocks through the spray to the pool and washed and shaved. Then he drove to the inn. The Taiyal had gone to the markets in Taipei and a woman with tattoos that ran in black bands from the mouth to each ear gave him a bowl of meat and rice and a dish of green tea. He sat for a time on the terrace and watched the plains and the feverish green of the paddies showing through the mist. Then, rising and paying the woman, he asked what the tattoos represented and she smiled and followed the bands with her forefingers and said: "They are my marriage marks." After he had refueled the jeep—how good it was to be free to buy a tank of gasoline—he drove back up the mountain. There were more Taiyals in the underbrush by the road. They were gathering giant snails and most of them wore tribal marks and a woman offered him her basket and all of them smiled. Marks for marriage, marks for taking heads; he too had marks, invisible but there forever.

At noon he reached the rim of the escarpment on the eastern coast. He could see below him the plain and, distant, the Pacific and the island of Kueishan, which lay in the ocean like a turtle. This was the tail of the Taiwan wet season and when he turned onto the road that would lead to Chilung the rain came with such intensity that he could not see the ocean or the island, only the tree ferns bending under the rain and the cedar forests on the mountains turning black. In the port and the rain still heavy he bought a supply of food and drink and sat in a waterfront bar and drank coffee and talked to an American geologist and when the rain had stopped he drove back up the road to the escarpment and onto the road that led to Suao. Everything steamed in heat and there were paper mills outside the town and a railhead and now the plain had gone and the mountains ran down to the edge of the sea and after Suao the road was cut very high across the grain of the mountain. It was a dramatic road with great depths always to his left and south of Suao he saw the little harbortown of Nanfangao. Mist covered it and he could not see its details; but it was here, Jethro had told him, that the Macao Fathers began one of the earliest of their missions.

After Nanfangao the road was dangerous and therefore slow. He reached the Tachingshui Cliff in the late afternoon and the sun already low and sat on one of the concrete blocks that edged the road and drank an orange juice and watched the sea turning mauve below the precipice. Back in the jeep he studied the map and saw that five miles on the Taroko River ran inland into the mountain chain.

At the bridge he left the coast highway and made a turn onto the road that ran with the river. Ahead were the lower slopes and patches of sweet potato and above them the forests and the true heights of the mountains. He drove until the road became a track and ended in a stand of bamboo. He concealed the jeep in its cover and took from it his bag and the jute basket that contained his provisions.

He would follow the river.

*   *   *

Lewis Mackenna spent three nights in the Taroko Gorge. This was a wilderness and during those two complete days he walked from sunrise to sunset. Four months of rain had sent the river wild. He was never away from the sound of rushing water. It entered him and made torrents within his head and at first it seemed that solitude and physical exhaustion had freed him from his bodyguard of ghosts. But the gorge was itself a haunted place. Ghosts lived there easily and soon there were other faces, Mackenna faces, to join those of Shameen and the policeman; old Jardine stepping down from his portrait in the mission hall—rectitude dressed up in a pigtail and pantaloons; James and Stewart and Sholto with his suffering eyes and Chinese whiskers; Cromer so near at night that he could smell the blood of his martyred body. Why was a man's dead father always standing at his side? On the second dawn he went into the shallows and bathed and sat on the bank and soaped his face and opened the calico strip that contained the three razors. At one time there would have been a set of seven; one for each day of the week. And the ivory handles of these three survivors were still faintly marked with abbreviations for Tuesday, Thursday and Sunday. Once before, by another river, there had been an impulse to discard them. This time he would do it. He shaved, using the Sunday razor as a tribute to the saintly men whose beards it had cut. Then he stood and hurled them high above the river and watched them sink.

Perhaps his accusers had drowned with the razors, for they did not invade his dreams on that third and final night in the gorge. But now there was another face; and in those moments between sleeping and waking he saw the junkmaster on the moon-pale deck and the wisp of straw in his teeth and the junk and the Long Jing tea chests going into the night, his fortune, his capital, his future all lost to him and now the ineradicable anger, as strong as the guilt, was rising and he saw the two chests standing on the rock and he went to them and levered open the lids and removed the upper thicknesses of straw and then with loving care took out objects and arranged them on the rock; an Imari vase with red-blue patterns of birds and flowers; a Ming enamel box with a decoration on the upper lid of two parrots on a peach branch; a Tang silver stem-cup with the Persian hunting scenes flowing around its curves; another Imari vase to make the pair; a jade monkey with its young and the peach in the monkey's hands that represented immortality; a bronze dragon with the fiery glow in its jaws that came from twenty small rubies; a Tang earthenware vase with the necks of dragons to form the handles and the heads curved inward over the lip as if they were sipping from the vase; a Tang porcelain of horse and rider— ah, see the rarity of the small monkey on the saddle, that is what gives it value; and a variety of plates and bowls and animals and tomb furniture and the bronze ritual *kuei* with the beautiful green patination that came from three thousand years in the earth and jades and lacquers and pottery and gilt-bronze bears—he watched the collection grow on the rock in the moonlight and somewhere out on the river the buyers at the auction were nodding and signaling with excitement as each of the pieces was revealed. He awakened with the anger still in his hands and his fingers gripped and the anger did not leave him until, at dawn, he plunged into the river and felt its coldness on his flesh.

When the light had strengthened he ate and began the walk back to the jeep. There was the spoor of a deer by one of the pools. In these mountains, the Taiyal had told him, there were panthers and bears and wild boars; but he had seen no living thing except the high-wheeling birds in the towers of the gorge and, once, a tribesman crouched by a stream and panning for gold. It was past noon when he reached the bamboo stand and brought out the jeep; and when he turned onto the coast road that would lead him north to Taipei the rain clouds were gathering and at Tachingshui Cliff the rain was heavy and he could not see the ocean.

At Nanfangao the mist had gone. He stopped the jeep and looked down on the town. Hills sheltered it from the Pacific typhoons and a channel ran from the sea to a breakwater and the harbor and the broad man-made canal on either side of which were the port buildings. There were many fishing boats in the harbor and in the channels and on the beaches and on some of the prows there were painted eyes. A church with a white-painted wooden spire faced the harbor and a familiar figure, small from the height of the mountain road, was crossing the quay to one of the jetties. Jethro's face turned into the sun. A motor-sailer was moored at the jetty. This too was familiar. It was the *Justine*.

Jethro pointed at the white spire.

"Our church," he said. "The Mission of St. Paul at Corinth. A nice name, isn't it?"

They walked from the quay toward the church.

"Taiwan," Jethro said, smiling, "is sinking under the weight of piety. Sometimes I think every priest in China fled here. Walk the city streets and you'll find as many friars as temple monks. Would you believe that apart from the mosques and the Buddhist and Taoist temples there are fifteen hundred Protestant and Catholic churches? They say that when the bells ring on holy days the rocks fall down the mountains. Priests are ten to the dollar. A surplice, you might say." He laughed richly at his own joke. "You'll find it difficult to get a job, Lewis."

"Maybe."

"There's a Canadian Presbyterian Mission. They might help you."

"No."

"Or the Church of Scotland."

Lewis shook his head.

"What will you do? Go home?"

"Home is Hangchow."

"But gone forever."

"Yes, gone."

"Will you stay here?"

"Yes."

"As a priest?"

"As a doctor."

They reached the church.

"Medicine is good Christian work," Jethro said. "But it isn't why you were ordained."

"I had two vocations. Now I have one."

"You won't escape that easily."

"Escape?"

"From what you are."

Above him was the spire. He could see the patches where the white ant had devoured the wood.

"I knew you were troubled, Lewis."

"That's what Sister Tai said."

Jethro smiled.

"A lovely woman, that," he said.

"Yes, lovely."

"Do you want to talk to me about it?"

"About what?"

"About your trouble."

"First heal thyself."

Jethro laughed.

"Yes," he said. "I have a problem."

He led Lewis through the shade of oleanders to a rectangle of newly dug earth. A spade was stuck in it and he pulled out the spade and sloped it on his shoulder like a rifle.

"Not a grave," he said. "Asparagus."

"The roots?"

"Yes. It's good soil and maybe we'll be lucky." He turned the blade of the spade to his nostrils and then to his lips and there was a moment in which it seemed his tongue might flicker into the granules of soil. "But I doubt it. Some things you can't uproot." He smiled. "It's like you, Lewis. It may not take."

Lewis watched the cloud-shadow moving through the mountains. Up there he had savored the taste of freedom and found it good.

"I'll take," he said. "I'll take."

Water splashed and, turning, he saw that a young girl in a shirt and a scarlet skirt had begun to wash the ground-floor window that was near to the porch. There was an area of brown skin above the waist of the skirt where the shirt had ridden out.

"Another problem?" he asked.

Jethro laughed.

"Not yet," he said. Then, seriously: "I can help you, Lewis."

"With a girl?"

"With a job. Two years ago I brought a man here from the mainland. An eminent Shanghai surgeon who had become a fugitive from Mao. His name is Dr. Wei."

Lewis nodded.

"You know him?"

"By reputation."

"Dr. Wei," Jethro said, "is now the director of one of the Taipei hospitals. You and he have much in common. I'll speak to him and I'm sure he'll listen."

Dr. Wei gestured at the microscopes that were poised above the operating table and Lewis Mackenna bent and looked down through one of the lenses. The nerve, enlarged, was like a pale white straw. "One day," Dr. Wei's soft voice said behind him, "the rejoining of severed limbs will be a commonplace. Now it is all experiment. We get many failures and a few successes. This young man is the victim of a sawmill accident. Success is achieved if the limb is restored to its natural functions and, if the gods smile, he may yet play again for his handball team. But it's very exhausting work. Some of the vessels and the nerves are so small that you cannot stitch them without a microscope and even the thread is thinner than a human hair. I have stood here for six hours and now I must ask my assistant to complete."

Lewis followed him from the theater and into a six-bed ward. Dr. Wei removed his cap and dragged some wisps of white hair down across his ears. He stopped by the first of the beds and murmured to the patient, then pointed to the man's hand. It was like a lobster's claw with only an index finger and a big toe where the thumb had been. "Yes," Dr. Wei said, "I have given him a claw. It will never be pretty but now he will learn to make a grip." There was a dark discoloration on the tip of the toe-thumb and Lewis bent across it.

"Is that gangrene?" he asked.

"Smell it and see."

Lewis bent nearer. There was no odor.

"Not gangrene," Dr. Wei said. "All is well." He took a needle from a dish and pricked the tip and the man grimaced.

"You see?" Dr. Wei said, smiling. "All alive-o." Then to the man: "In a month you will be lifting your teacup." He led Lewis around the ward. "Tea is a good idea," he said. He looked very tired and he licked his drying lips. In one of the beds a man lay sleeping with bandaged hands spread on the cover. Outside the door Dr. Wei shook his head and said sadly:

"A radiologist. The radium burns have left him with a single finger. I am trying some transplants of the two central toes from each foot. But I am not optimistic. If the tissues are affected there can be no healing."

Dr. Wei's office was on the ground floor. From the window there was a view of a section of the gardens and some flowering cherries, a boundary wall, the rear of a factory and the rise of the mountain chain. Drinking tea and slumped with exhaustion and sometimes near to sleep Dr. Wei began to talk. Kodaki's Hospital, he explained, had been built in 1895 at the time when Formosa had been ceded by China to Japan. It still retained its Japanese name but much had changed since those early days. The single story had grown to five, its twenty beds to more than two hundred. There were four specialist departments and a path lab that served the three other major hospitals. And above all it had become a teaching hospital. Students came from many different countries; some to study general medicine and some (this with modesty) to learn the new transplant techniques. "Every qualified member of staff is expected to teach," Dr. Wei said. "That is our rule and if you come to us, Dr. Mackenna, you will take your turn. Is that understood?"

"Yes."

Dr. Wei reached for a medical directory, opened it at a bookmark and ran a finger down the page.

"You are an Edinburgh man," he said. "And for us that is good enough. And of course the Mackenna name is a reference in itself."

He closed the directory and went to the window. Two nurses were walking on the path that bisected the garden and one of them stopped by a hibiscus and plucked a flower and put it in her cap. Rain came and the nurses ran and Dr. Wei laughed and turned and said: "We are a foundation and our funds come from the government, from charities and from commercial benefactors." He pointed at the factory. "The American motorcar factory is one of them. We don't have unlimited money and in fact we are fully staffed. We can't pay high salaries, you understand?"

"I understand."

Dr. Wei sat and yawned and hovered again on the edge of sleep. "I find it embarrassing to discuss money," he said kindly, "so I'll write your salary down and you shall tell me if it's acceptable." He scrawled the figure, folded the scrap of paper and gave it to Lewis, averted his eyes.

"It's pretty low," Lewis said.

"Less than the mission paid?"

"Yes, much less."

"I'm afraid that's our limit."

His eyes were still averted and Lewis returned the paper and said: "Don't apologize, Doctor. I'm grateful and I thank you."

"Then you accept?"

"I accept."

Chapter 9

In accepting (Ellen Mackenna wrote to her sister in Fort William, Inverness-shire, Scotland) *he put the Church behind him. That was two months ago and since then he's worked very hard at Kodaki's. They begin the day early with exercises on the lawns, everyone arriving on duty has to join in, and after that it's medicine and minor surgery and quite a bit of teaching. Mostly the students are first-year nurses who come from all over the place and Lewis has forgotten a lot of the academic stuff and has to read it up on the night before his lectures. But it's all very different from mission doctoring. No more tooth-drawing and obstetrics and appendectomies in bamboo huts! But will it work? Father Frank Jethro, the Roman priest who got us out of the mainland on his boat, says that no matter what burdens a priest carries in his soul and no matter what he's done or hasn't done he cannot throw back at God the marvelous gift of his ordination, only if he's become wicked and beyond redemption could he do a thing like that. Lewis is a good man, he says, who has suffered imprisonment and cruelty and like many fugitives he has had to do violent and uncharacteristic things in order to survive and one day, perhaps through some personal act of atonement, he will again see the face of our Savior and it will never never leave him.*

Now for our other news. The twins are on their way to Edinburgh and as I write they are already on the Hong Kong/London plane. I feel wretched, yet relieved. As I told you in my last letter we've had to consider their education and there was also the worry, fear really, that one of them might be snatched and taken to the mainland. This island is crawling with Mao's agents and what better way could there be of getting Lewis back for trial? These are the things that come into the mind at night and maybe it's all imagination and one has to remember that according to Mao there are a million or so traitors from Chiang Kai-shek downward hiding in Taiwan. We haven't yet heard of anyone being kidnaped and, come to think of it, Lewis is a small fish compared to some of them. Anyway the boys have gone. We had planned that they would be educated either in Taiwan or in

Hong Kong so that they would keep their Chinese fluent and I'm afraid they won't hear much Mandarin and Cantonese spoken over the tea and scones in Scotland! It was the Fellowship that made it possible. They offered to make themselves responsible for the costs and to put them into a boarding prep school and from there into the Academy. Perhaps they think they'll get two more Mackenna missionaries. But they've been generous, and they've also sent us some accumulated back pay from the last year in the Hangchow mission. Not a large sum but enough to set us up in a little house in Crooked Pond, that's one of the market areas of Taipei, although there is no pond, crooked or otherwise, only a pool on the fringe of the market, which is really a muddy wallow and where the water buffalo would at one time cool themselves off after ploughing the rice fields. We also bought a jeep so that we can get around. But we're going to be hard up, no doubt of that. Like almost everything else here the rent is high and Lewis is not earning very much. But we're free and safe, thank our Lord, and we have to build a new life.

Ellen put down the pen. Later in the afternoon she would finish the letter. There was no real impulse or obligation to write to her sister or indeed to anyone else. But there was novelty in it. She had written many letters since the escape and still there was the pleasure of sitting here at one of the rattan tables outside Mandy's Bar with a coffee or a Coca-Cola and a notepad and writing freely and mailing it freely and knowing that it would go freely to its destination. In the People's Republic there had been no such freedom and a letter, written only if it was of the first importance, would travel secretly through the New Territories and into Hong Kong for redirection. Even the Coca-Cola was a novelty and on the mainland, where they called it *Kekou-Kele,* the drink was banned because there was caffeine in it and, far worse, it was a product of the corrupted West.

She addressed the envelope and pushed the unfinished letter under its flap. She heard his footsteps on the road and she did not turn her head and when the boots mounted the wooden sidewalk and his shadow bent across the table she knew what he would say.

"Fort William?" Lewis said.

"Yes."

"That's only one hundred and fifty miles from Edinburgh."

"So?"

"The boys will be in Edinburgh before that letter. They could have taken it with them, posted it when they got there."

"Yes," she agreed. "They could have."

"Well, why not?" Lewis asked. "The stamp from here is expensive."

She did not answer and the shadow left the table and she watched him walk up the road.

"I've had two Cokes," she cried out in anger. "Think of it. The expense. Two whole Cokes."

He did not turn.

"And I'm going to have another one."

Still he did not turn and she saw him step aside from the path of a buffalo cart and the spurts of orange dust that came up from the hooves. Joe Mandy's voice spoke from inside the bar.

"You want something?"

"No."

"I thought you said two Cokes."

"We can't afford it."

"Then have one with me."

Pouring and looking across her he asked: "Why does he wear that Jap Army cap?"

"He has a passion for unusual hats."

"Nothing unusual in it. When the Japs got beat they left all their kit behind. Every shop sold those caps and at one time all the young fellows wore them."

She smiled and the anger left her. So much for the trophy and its decapitated owner.

"Could you get me one, Joe?"

"A Jap cap?"

"Yes."

"I can try, Mrs. Mackenna."

He went back inside the bar and she sipped the drink and watched the motorcycles and the buffaloes competing in the narrow road. The rains had passed and would not return until November and Taipei was still a green city but the dirt roads had turned to dust and she could see Lewis at the junction where the road led to the hospital and there was dust in the sun shafts and now he had been joined by a group of student nurses and some of them were buying sweetmeats from a stall. Most of the group were known to her and had come to the house at one time or another for tea or medical discussion hours and some she had met at the hospital or at Dr. Wei's hillside garden. She saw the Cantonese girl Hsu Yu (whose name meant Happy Rain) dipping with her long and elegant fingers into the green sweetmeat bag and at her side Sun Ai-hua, the one who was always buying flowers and then presenting a single bloom to each of her companions; Elizabeth South, the English girl from Penang; and Sui-Teh, whose name was pronounced Sweet Hay by certain of the Europeans and was even written like that on the duty rosters; Tan Su-ching who was seventeen and as fragile as the shape of her own breaking shadow—a giggler that one, Ellen thought, always giggling and blushing, too shy and vulnerable to make a competent nurse; Emmy Kwan from Djakarta who turned her head so that you would not see the marks of smallpox on her other cheek and Lan Ping (whose name meant Blue Apple) and Sing-hai the little gymnast from Peking whose name was a joke to those Westerners who did not know or care that jokes that were made around the phonetic sounds of names were offensive to the Chinese; all of them, she guessed, had come to Kodaki's to see the work of the famous Dr. Wei: and when the doctor approached, perched on his powerful Japanese motorcycle, the group parted and smiled and waved or bowed and Sun Ai-hua took a flower from her posy and held it out and Dr. Wei reached out and grasped it and put the stalk between his teeth.

When the doctor was gone down the hospital road, the nurses following through the dust that was thrown from the wheels and Lewis tall in the center of them, Ellen felt the somnolent afternoon heat engulf her and the drift into sleep. When she awakened the cola was warm in the glass and she pushed it away from her and picked up her pen.

The house (she wrote) *is in a narrow road and there are the usual laundry poles fixed to all the houses and crossing the road and full of washing. It's a quaint old place sandwiched between two shops, one selling fruit and wine, the other a herbalist. It has a ground floor and the bedroom floor, which is reached by wooden steps at the rear. There is a nice garden leading to some vegetable farms and we have three big plum trees in the garden. The plum, they say, is about to become the national flower. Sometimes we catch a lovely scent from the shops, wine and figs and spices. But I'm afraid there's another scent that's not so pleasant. We think that at one time the house was a stable and that the upstairs was the loft. The ground floor is laid with broken marble flagstones, a common thing here because there is enough marble in the Taroko Gorge to build a city. But at certain times there's a faint smell of urine that comes up through the cracks and they say that where there has been cattle or horses this smell always remains and will never go. Ah well, our Lord began his life in a stable, and here in what was once a stable our own new life begins. Did I tell you that I've begun to paint again? There's a shop here in Crooked Pond that's run by an Austrian named Erich Brandt. It sells all sorts of things, curios and carvings and silks, but because there are a lot of painters in Taiwan—they come for the light and the marvelous landscapes—there's a corner in the shop for artists' materials. I'm learning to paint in oils but so far without much success.*

The writing, now, was an effort in the thickening heat. She would complete it in the evening. She rose and dropped the notepaper, the envelope and the pen into the straw shopping bag that was propped against the table leg. There were two canvas stretchers in the bag.

She decided to walk through the lanes to Brandt's shop.

The shop lay at the center of the market where the five lanes converged. A tourist with an airline bag was at the counter and she watched Brandt hold a macramé necklace to her throat and the woman's fingertips glide down the delicate knotwork. "Or you can have one for the hair," Brandt said. He pinned it to her crown so that the adornment hung to her neck.

"With Chinese macramé," he told her, "there are thirteen basic knots. Each knot has a name and a special meaning." He laid both the pieces on the counter and brought out more from a drawer and arranged them and Ellen turned away to the cedar tables on which a variety of stock was always exhibited. There were curios, jewelry, figurines in old porcelain and soapstone, lanterns and festival masks. On one of the tables there was a collection of scrimshaw—those prized pieces of ivory or whale's tooth that early seamen had carved into wondrous shapes. She walked from table to table. Behind her the woman crooned with admiration and she heard Brandt say: "Yes, that one is exceptionally beautiful. This knot signifies double happiness, and this one is the character for immortality." The woman laughed and said: "If that's what I get for the money it's cheap and I'll buy it." Ellen went to another of the tables. On it were a dozen name chops—signature seals of great age that had stamped the documents of all the offices of the imperial past. She heard the rustle of notes and the woman passed and stepped out into the lane and Brandt came from the counter and stood, smiling, in a lance of sunlight so that his heavily veined nose glowed and his beard was as amber as the straw of her shopping bag.

Brandt pointed at the bag and the canvas stretchers that protruded.

"Do you have something for me?"

"Yes."

She gave him the canvases and he held them into the light and studied them. She saw the disapproval purse his lips. He touched one of the canvases.

"Where is this, Mrs. Mackenna?"

"Our mission."

"In Hangchow?"

"Yes."

He touched the other canvas.

"And this?"

"West Lake."

"Hangchow?"

"Yes."

"Why paint Hangchow? You don't live there now."

"In a way I do."

Brandt held out the canvases again, one in each hand.

"They're very bad."

"I know," she said. "But I'll improve. Oil paint is difficult."

"I'm not talking about technique or the medium you use. It's the approach that's wrong." He pointed with his beard at the West Lake scene. "It's Chinese painting, isn't it?"

"Is it?"

"Yes. Just look at it." Contempt touched his voice. "Still water. Pretty trees. Leaves that will never move. Pale grays and pinks. Everything dreaming in mist. And that figure in the distance, so tiny that you cannot see if it is man or woman. Nature first, human life second. Oh, yes, this is Chinese painting, all right. And that's what you did in Hangchow, did you not?"

"Yes."

"On paper or silk?"

"Silk."

"How delicate." The contempt was still there. "I can see it clearly. The little brush, the little cake of solid ink, the little stone slab to grind it on, a little discreet pigment. And a little green tea at your elbow, drunk from a fragile cup."

He returned the pictures and, anger rising, she dropped them to the floor and poised her heel.

"I'll destroy them," she said.

"No. Don't do that. Canvas is expensive. I can size them over for you. That way you'll get a new surface."

He went to the door.

"Come outside."

Outside he said: "I had to make you angry. Now you can start again. Forget Hangchow. Forget the pretty pictures." He pointed above the market and the flowering canopies of trees to the hills and the mountain ridges. "This is a sensuous land. As succulent as a plum. You could squeeze the color and the richness out of it as if you had a tube of rainbow paint." The finger moved down to the market and its lanes and the alleys that left the lanes, down through the stalls and shops and traders and the mass of bicycles and people. "But don't do landscapes. Stay with Crooked Pond. Here in the market you'll find everything you need. Wander in it. Feel its life. And remember this. You are drawing in color. Color alone is not enough. If you cannot draw you cannot paint." He took her arm and turned her and pointed to where a street trader sat among his wares. "You see the old man? The one who is selling snakeskins?"

"I see him."

"Walk over. Look at him. Then come back."

She walked to the mud-and-dung wall where the old man squatted and stopped and smiled down at him. There were many skins, on the ground and pinned to the wall. Each skin was coiled around the four spokes of a small wooden cross so that it formed a wheel. The man looked up and she saw his mottled face and famished cheeks, lips of leather that were parted by one long brown tooth. She gave him a coin and returned to Brandt.

"Well?" Brandt asked.

"An interesting face."

"Could you paint it?"

"I could try."

"How would you paint it?"

"How?"

"Yes, how. Would it be a portrait? A canvas full of face?"

She looked back at the old man.

"It would have to be more than that," she said. "You would have to paint the whole scene."

"Why?"

"To show what he is."

"Is that important?"

"Yes. With him it is. He's a seller of snakeskins. He's nothing else. You can't separate him from what he does."

Brandt nodded.

"So you'll paint him crouching by the wall and the skins all around him and the shadow of the wall on the bright ground and some of the skins in the sunlight and that thin hand scratching at his anklebone?"

"Yes."

"What else?"

"What else is there?"

"Look again."

She stared across the road and the old man turned his head and smiled.

"Do you see the skin that is near to his right foot?" Brandt asked.

"I see it."

"It has a pattern. Brown diamonds on yellow."

"Yes."

"Now look at the man's face. Describe its coloring."

"Like old parchment."

"Yellowish?"

"In parts."

"And?"

"Age has marked it with dark brown blotches."

"A pattern?"

"Yes," she agreed. "A pattern."

The old man turned again and the single tooth gleamed.

Brandt smiled.

"Yes," she said. "I see what you mean. His skin is like the snake's."

"And the tooth?"

"Like a fang."

"A serpent's fang?"

"Yes."

"And how would you put all this on canvas?"

She felt a surge of excitement.

"I'd paint the snakeskin so that it was the only one that was touched by sun. The old man's face would also be in light. The eye would be drawn to the snakeskin and the face. It would at once see the similarity."

"Good."

"And the light would also touch the tooth. One would think of fangs and venom."

Brandt laughed.

"And when this famous picture is hanging in the gallery what will the viewer know?" he asked.

"He'll know that all his life the old man has gone up into the mountains to catch the snakes and there have been so many years that he has come to look like one."

Brandt laughed again.

"If I were that good," she said.

"Yes," Brandt said seriously. "If you were that good you would have become more than a camera. Isn't that what painting is about?"

He went into the shop, retrieved her shopping bag and gave it to her.

"I'd better have some of that paint," she said.

"Which paint?"

"The rainbow paint."

Brandt smiled and pointed at the market.

"Remember," he said. "Explore. Observe."

She turned to go.

"But not at night," Brandt said. "It's no place for a missionary's wife."

A missionary's wife. The words had remained like an irritant and would not leave her; and now, two days later and she sitting under one of the plum trees at the rear of the house and Lewis and the student nurses grouped on the grass in the shade of the other two plums, the words reformed. A missionary's wife. Why should I resent them? she asked herself. Proud words. Proud years in which I stood at his side since that day in Kiangsi at the Methodist hospital when first we met and the hornet was on my hair and the hair flicked across his face and he held it in his hand and did not release it so that it became a caress; all those years, the sickness and the cruelty and the indifference to the weak, the wounds and the epidemics that had taken them to the villages and those who could not understand why anyone in the pitiless land should want to help them, the war, the Japanese, the second civil war and a million Red troops crossing the Yangtze and Mao's armies at the mission gates and a way of life dying like the people in the streets, Fusan and the captivity and the awful fear, the espionage and another kind of fear and the face of Jesus now indistinct; all those years, a missionary's wife, that old phrase that she had heard so many times as if she and women like her were saintly creatures whose sensibilities must be protected, I have seen a few things, my goodness the things I've seen, I could tell them and they would not think I need protection against the night of Crooked Pond. Why am I changing? Why do I want to be someone else? She watched a pair of yoked oxen crossing the fields of the vegetable farm and the deep scar the plough left. Then, turning her head, she stared at the tutorial group. Lewis was tapping the spread pages of a medical manual and speaking gently to Tan Su-ching's upturned face.

"Tell me, Su-ching, did you study the chapter on helminthic infections?"

"Yes, Doctor."

"But not very well, I think. Reading is not the same as studying."

"No, Doctor."

"And that's what you did. You read it quickly, didn't you?"

"Yes, Doctor."

Ellen saw the girl's lip tremble.

"But I'm not cross with you," Lewis said kindly. "It's in English and I know that's not easy. So we'll start again. We are studying one particular infection. Bilharzia. What is the intermediary host?"

"A snail," Su-ching said.

"What kind of snail?"

"Freshwater."

"Then you should say so. Be exact. How many varieties of freshwater snail are host to the infection?"

"Three."

Lewis nodded and took a colored diagram plate from the back of the manual and passed it to her.

"Which of the bilharzias are we discussing?"

"Eastern."

"Yes, Eastern. Where do you come from, Su-ching?"

"Hunan."

"Then you should know all about it. It's endemic in Hunan, isn't it?"

"Yes."

"Tell me, what is its name?"

"Name?"

"Yes. It is of the East. But it has a name."

Su-ching shook her head and Lewis turned to Sweet Hay.

"Do you know, Sweet Hay?"

"It is bilharzia japonica."

"Yes. That's very good. Is the infection confined to man?"

"No, Doctor. It infects domestic animals."

"Any other animals?"

"Horses and cattle."

"Any immunities?"

"Native cows."

"Yes. Thank you, Sweet Hay."

Stupid name, Ellen thought. She watched Lewis turn again to Su-ching.

"Now, Su-ching, there are three snails illustrated on that plate. Which one carries B. japonica?"

Su-ching pointed.

"Wrong. It is quite distinct from other snails. It is the bottom of the three. A long narrow shape. Do you see it?"

"Yes."

"You'll have to work harder."

Su-ching looked down at her hands and Lewis reached out and put a finger under her chin and lifted her face.

"No need for tears," he said, smiling. "This is how we learn. Question and answer. It's the best way. You'll never forget this old snail, will you?"

"No, Doctor."

"And you won't go putting those pretty little feet into the rivers and the ponds?"

Now she was laughing.

"No, Doctor. I promise."

Ellen stood.

"I'll make some tea," she called to him. Walking to the house she heard him say: "Now let's consider the clinical features." In the kitchen the urine scent touched her nostrils. Su-ching was laughing again. The sound came distantly. Trilling like a lark, she thought, and a feather brain to match. She felt an immediate shame. In Hangchow so unchristian a sentiment could never have surfaced. She stared out of the window at the heat haze and the minaret of the mosque that was shimmering in it like a breaking chimney and the violet ridges. Sensuous, Brandt had described the island. As succulent as a plum. Certainly there was a ripeness about it that stroked the senses. She had felt it from the beginning and during the heavy rains it seemed she could taste its fertility and so intense was the feeling that it was like a faint ache in the womb as if her own body was about to flower.

When the tea was brewed and the seven cups and saucers placed on two trays she walked from the kitchen toward the plum trees. The discussion hour was apparently ended and Su-ching was lying on her back and watching the clouds above the branches and Lewis had closed the manual. Elizabeth South was speaking in her soft burred voice: "—and I was born in Devon and I can tell you that sweet hay had a meaning."

"What meaning?" Sweet Hay asked.

"Yes, do tell us," Emmy Kwan said.

"Isn't it obvious?" Lewis said. "It would mean hay that was ripe and ready for cutting."

"It has another meaning," Elizabeth South said. She smiled. "A special meaning."

They waited.

"Sweet hay is made when sweethearts plait some hay into a ring and the boy and the girl stand on either side of it and kiss through the center."

"You have just made it up."

"I tell you it's true. That is how sweet hay is made."

"It's a very nice way to make hay."

Ellen beckoned to Sun Ai-hua.

"Will you help me with the trays, please?"

Ai-hua followed her into the kitchen.

"There is bilharzia in the south of this island," Ellen told her. "Did you know that?"

"No, madame."

"Some of the places are marked with warnings. But not all of them. So be careful."

They picked up the trays and walked toward the plums. Sing-hai, the gymnast, was standing on her hands, so controlled and motionless that there was not even a tremor in her shadow.

Ellen stopped.

Su-ching was coming from where there was underbrush near to the perimeter fence. She was walking slowly and there were some lengths of long swamp grass in her hands and her fingers were working in the grass and when she reached the group under the trees Ellen saw that she had fashioned a ring. She padded softly until she was standing behind Lewis' back. She did not speak and she held up the ring of plaited grass so that her face was framed in it. Now the group was smiling and Sing-hai rolled and stood upright and she too began to smile and the smiles became laughter and Lewis stared at them.

"May I share the joke?"

Emmy Kwan pointed and Lewis turned. Su-ching's delicate shoulders shook with merriment. Her lips pouted through the ring. Ellen saw him frown, then smile and nod with understanding. The lips pouted again.

"Make hay?" Lewis asked gravely.

"Please."

He bent down toward the ring and kissed her and the nurses laughed and clapped their hands and Lewis took the grass from her fingers and placed it on the crown of her head.

Ellen put down the tray at Ai-hua's feet.

"Send Su-ching to me," she said.

In the kitchen she drank tea and waited and when Su-ching's feet tapped gently on the threshold she turned and saw that the grass was still fixed like a coronet in her hair.

"Take it off," she said.

The girl removed it and placed it on the table and Ellen picked it up and tore it out of shape, then dropped it into the wastecan.

"Do you know the English word flirt?" she asked.

"Flirt?"

"Yes, flirt."

"No, madame. What is flirt?"

"It's what you are."

"Please?"

"A flirt is a woman who provokes men for her own amusement. Do you understand?"

"I think so."

"But of course you are not a woman." The anger was returning. "You are a girl. Seventeen, isn't it?"

"Yes, madame."

"A silly giggling girl. Tears, giggles, pranks. Weep one minute, laugh the next. Nursing is very serious work. Humor is fine and good for the patient. But never silliness. How much training have you had?"

"Three months, madame."

"Three months. That's not very long. I spent all my working life as a nurse and I tell you this, Su-ching, you'll have to change."

"I will try, madame."

"Do you have parents?"

"A father."

"No mother?"

"Dead."

"Is your father here in Taipei?"

"Yes."

"How old were you when your mother died?"

"One hour."

Ellen saw her eyes brim. Tears for this one were easy. Yet perhaps these sprang from an enduring sense of loss. The shame re-entered her. She had been too harsh. Su-ching wiped her cheeks. She had a small oval face edged with sleek black hair that fell from a central parting, the defenseless eyes of a child; like one of those olive-skinned wax Madonnas, Ellen thought, that the Chinese Catholics always painted for their churches.

"Forgive me," she said. "I was unkind."

"It is nothing, madame."

"Leave now."

Su-ching turned in the doorway and bowed. The sun was low behind her and there was a moment in which her head glowed with a halo of light. Ellen laughed. Now the painting was complete.

"And no more of the sweet hay," she said. "Not in my garden and not with my husband."

When the girl was gone she drank more tea. Then she looked in the larder and in her purse. There was a little food and not much money. Ai-hua entered with a tray in each hand and a wildflower in her teeth. She put the trays on the table and presented the gift of the flower.

"Thank you, dear," Ellen said.

She went into the living room and sat there for a time and when she heard his boots in the kitchen she returned.

"What did you say to her?" Lewis asked.

"To Su-ching?"

"Yes. She was upset."

"I told her she was silly, a flirt, and a rotten nurse."

"That was a bit hard, wasn't it?"

"It was. I also told her there'll be no more making hay."

Lewis smiled.

"Don't you know the proverb?" he asked.

"I do. But for you, Lewis, the sun has now stopped shining."

Ellen put the wildflower in water.

"I'm on duty at six," Lewis said.

"All night?"

"Yes."

He went to her and kissed her.

"Were you jealous?" he asked, laughing.

"Of that child?"

"She's seventeen. Out here that's an age for marriage." Now he was teasing her. "She's very pretty."

He turned to the door.

"Lewis."

"Yes?"

"I'm short of money."

"But you had your house allowance."

"It wasn't enough. It never is."

"I know that. I wish I could increase it. But they don't pay me very much. And the rent is due."

"I too have bills."

"Bills?"

"Yes."

"What bills?"

She did not answer.

"Do you owe money?"

"Yes. In the market."

Dismay touched his eyes.

"I don't like that," he said. "You shouldn't ask for credit."

"Lose face?"

"Yes."

"What else can I do?"

"Make economies."

Emmy Kwan came to the door.

"We are going now," she said. "Thank you for the tea, madame."

She left.

"What economies?" Ellen asked.

"There must be something."

"Like tea for the nurses?"

"That isn't what I meant."

"Then what did you mean?"

He was silent.

"A coffee or a Coke in Mandy's?" she asked. "I could cut that out."

"Don't be sarcastic."

"Then tell me what you meant."

She saw him glance at the corner where her easel and six canvas stretchers stood. There was a table by the easel and on it a palette and a palette knife, a maulstick, tubes of pigment, oil bottles, a jar of brushes. She felt the anger growing.

"Do you call that waste?" she asked.

"It all costs money."

"I have to have something, Lewis. Some interest of my own. So much has been lost. The home, the ministry, the children."

"And the collection," he said. "Don't forget the collection."

"I try to."

"Well, I don't. I'll never forget it."

He took a wallet from his pocket and placed a few banknotes on the table. The two tea chests were always there, she thought; carried around with him like an inseparable burden.

"You and your precious collection," she said with scorn.

"Precious is the word," he agreed. He was recounting the notes. "I made an inquiry. You wouldn't believe the prices the market will pay for Chinese antiquities. One of those pieces alone would have made us rich."

"We're rich now."

"Are we?"

"Yes. Alive. Safe. Free."

He nodded.

"Riches of a kind. I know that. But money is important." He pushed the notes across the table. "Otherwise you wouldn't be frowning at these."

"It isn't enough."

He turned to the door and she swept the notes from the table.

"I have to pay the bills," she said.

He went out into sunlight.

"What shall I do?" she called after him.

"You could always sell a painting."

She had not seen his face when, walking down the path, the words were spoken. Perhaps he had smiled and the words were not a gibe. But they had hurt and, restless now, she went out into the garden to the fence and watched the sun sink and the ranges turning dark. "There are those who create and those who do not," Erich Brandt had once said to her. "And the uncreative ones will never understand you." There was also resentment; springing as always from the constant disputes over money. She picked a sprig of plum blossom and returned to the house and put the blossom into the vase with Ai-hua's wildflower. The house was silent and the horse-smell was invading the living room. She bathed and changed. Then she walked though the dusk to Mandy's Bar.

This, the fifteenth day of the seventh moon, was the festival of the Month of Ghosts and already the roads were filled with people. From the sidewalk table she could see into the bar and across the brass-rimmed counter and a group of Merchant Navy officers to the kitchen at the rear where the American Joe Mandy was shaving. She watched his arms turning under the light bulb and the tattoos on the biceps that, inexpertly done, were like the red-mauve disfigurements of old burns. He came to her, wiping soap from his earlobes, and asked: "You want a Coke, Mrs. Mackenna?"

"Not tonight. Do you have any limes?"

"Yes."

"Bring me some. And a large London gin."

"A large gin?"

"Yes, Joe."

She saw him look from the table to the lanes that led to the heart of Crooked Pond and the reflected lantern light that threw color on the sky.

"Are you alone?"

"I am."

When he returned he put a tray on the table. On it were a tall glass, a bottle of gin, a saucer of limes and a Japanese Army cap.

"I hope it fits," he said.

She picked it up and examined it. The band was sweat-stained and some numerals were written inside.

"I seen a lot of those," he said. "Some with brains in."

"Yes, you told me."

He had served in the Pacific war, she knew; and there had been many landings and battles and, finally, a wound. But after his discharge and a time in a veteran's hospital and then the homecoming he had suffered the lash of two Pennsylvania winters. Perhaps they had not been as intolerable as he believed. But he had known the islands and the warm seas and, now, they lay like an enticement in the mind. He returned to the Philippines and opened a bar in Manila; and later, when the regime became oppressive and Chiang and the anti-Reds were in Taiwan, he moved to Taipei. There was the feel of old battles about him and sometimes when he leaned across a table and his shirt was open she could see the cicatrices twisting in glazed patterns through the chest hair. She pulled on the cap, then shifted it so that it sat at an angle. Joe Mandy laughed and she felt the tension leave her.

"How much?" she asked.

"Nothing."

"I meant for the cap."

"Nothing for the cap. Just pay for the drink."

She gave him a note and he poured some gin, then paused with the neck of the bottle above the glass.

"Enough?"

"A bit more, Joe."

He poured another measure and she saw the doubt in his face. He looked again at the glow from Crooked Pond. She smiled and crushed a lime between her fingers so that the juice ran into the gin. It's the missionary's wife again, she thought; or, more accurately, the picture they have of the wives of English country parsons and tea and seedcake on the lawn. Don't you know what it means to be the wife of a missionary in China? she wanted to ask him. The times of despair and the strain on faith? The squalor and the hardness of life and the incredible total of the dying? She crushed another lime and sipped the drink, then drank half of it. I first drank gin in August of 1937, she could have told him. I remember the date because that was the time of the fall of Shanghai and from the roof of the apartment we could watch the Japanese aircraft dropping bombs on the Chinese trenches that lay beyond the Settlement. It was a view of war in which we had no part and at night the sky bloomed with the flashes that came from the guns of the Japanese warships on the Whangpoo River and, later, was red from the flames of Chapei and Kiangwan. The bombs did not always avoid the Settlement and when Nanking Road was hit and the apartment building collapsed we went to the Cathay Hotel and it was full of journalists and after a week the city water was polluted and therefore dangerous and when all the bottled fruit drinks and the beer and the wine were gone most of the guests, including certain missionaries and their wives, drank spirits and Lewis was content because he had always favored a twelve-year malt and I, Joe, took to drinking gin and enjoyed its flavor and the clean feel it gave to the palate and since that time I have, with moderation, always drunk it. Shanghai in those days had a very fine population of whores. I knew many of them and some were friends and some showed more Christian love than the European ladies of the Settlement and I do not think, Joe, that the whores of Crooked Pond are likely to offend me. She did not tell him these things. Instead she said: "This is my wicked night, Joe. Once a year. Out on the town. Lots of large wicked gins."

"Why not, Mrs. Mackenna?" he said, laughing. "This is the Chinese Hallowe'en."

When the August moon was risen she left the table and began the walk that would lead her into Crooked Pond.

Later in Crooked Pond and sitting in the noise of the Teagarden Bar and the moon now high she felt the long wicker seat yield under weight and, turning, saw that it was Frank Jethro.

"All alone?" he asked.

"Yes."

"Which way did you come?"

She pointed across the square and the market stalls to the twisted alleys that lay behind the flank of the Hospice de L'Etoile Noire.

"Were you scared?"

"No," she said, smiling.

On this night the souls of the dead were released and would wander the lanes in search of food. They were not the souls of the wicked and because there was no fear of them trays of food and bottles of wine had been placed outside the doors of the houses and in the lanes paper lanterns were hung and lighted so that the souls might find their way to the offerings. The lanes were quiet with only the lacewings to crackle against the hot paper of the lanterns but, walking through the pools of light and blackness, she had heard the murmur of Crooked Pond. There had been a typhoon in the Philippines and the skirts of it had swept in an arc from Mindanao across Taiwan and its hot and dying winds had touched her face and there were scents on the winds of curry and frangipani and burning joss sticks.

"It's a bad place," he said.

She nodded. Sandalmakers Road was silent and she could hear the distant sounds of firecrackers, laughter, breaking glass. The road led into Temple Lane. Parties of seamen had come by waterway from the coast and the alleys were filled with them and in the lane four of the seamen were grouped outside the silver doorway of the first of the Hindu temples and the priest was tapping the arch of the doorway and explaining in English the significance of the inscriptions, which were the ten different manifestations of Vishnu. Passing, she felt a hand probe in the division of her buttocks. The man laughed. She had not run or quickened pace and she had followed the curve of the lane, turning then into a narrow alley and stopping in the shadow that was thrown by the lines of overhead washing. She heard the man's feet, watched him appear at the entrance to the alley and stare around him. Then he shrugged, urinated against a wall, returned to the temple. Curiously she had felt no anger at the touch. Sweat was running down her spine, down to where the fingers had stabbed. It seemed she could still feel their pressure. This was the beginning of her monthly cycle and the pains were driving through her pelvic arch. They had always been bad, yet now she did not fear their onset. They were a proof. I am still fertile. I can still have a child. I can walk through the shadows and a man, however crude, can reach out and put his hand in the fork of my body because he has seen me as a woman. She had stood there in the alley, eyes closed and her palms pressed against the pains and the want swelling within her.

"A drink?" Jethro asked.

"Gin."

She watched him move through the throng of people. He was wearing a white shirt and slacks with no indication of his priesthood, not even a gold crucifix to dangle from his throat. Yet he was known to them. A man in a baseball jersey embraced him and now they were gathered around him at the bar and another man said to him with mockery: "I have sinned again, Father," and another said: "I see you have a woman, Father." They began to laugh and a hand ruffled Jethro's hair and when he leaned across the counter to the barman another hand took his wallet from his rear pocket and placed it at his elbow and, then, there was a sudden hiatus in the noise and she heard a Negress in a green bandanna ask: "Are you going to have jig-a-jig, Father?" and Jethro laughing and the noise again and a voice saying: "Who will absolve you, Father?" and Jethro, now, was walking toward her with a bottle of beer, a gin and a saucer of limes. He set down the tray and looked at her cap and said, smiling: "You'll be very popular."

"Popular?"

"With the Jap Army."

She touched the peak as if in salute.

"Does it suit me?"

"It does. But it was better on Lewis."

"It's not the same cap."

"Not the same?"

"No. We each have a Jap cap." She drank some gin. "But Lewis doesn't know."

"Will he be angry?"

"Maybe. He's a collector."

"Of hats?"

"Yes. Of peculiar hats. Do you know what a deerstalker is?"

"No."

"It's a cloth cap with two peaks and is always bought by the tourists in Scotland. Lewis has written to Edinburgh for one."

"It'll look fine in Taiwan."

She drank more gin. She could feel the spirit in her head.

"How many gins have you had, Ellen?"

"Lost count."

"Shall I take you home?"

"No."

She felt the sweat run again. How could he take me home? Home is in Hangchow. She turned on the seat so that she could see from the Teagarden to the corner of Chang Tso-lin Road where the snake-market began. It was lit with colored lamps and there were large gatherings of people around the stalls and shops and restaurants. In one of the shops living snakes hung by their tails and she saw a man in a stained apron reach with a knife and slit the longest of the snakes and the blood shooting in a cascade across his arm and then the flow of it into the tumblers that were set beneath the head. Money passed and two men began to drink from the tumblers and from a small glass that contained the venom. She felt the sickness rise. She had always disliked the cruelty of the Chinese snake-markets; but they were a part of a scene she had learned to accept. She did not believe that the meat, the blood and the poison were prescriptions for a long and healthy life.

"Shall I take you home?" Jethro asked again.

She shook her head. At one of the stalls a man with a pigtail reached into a bag and pulled out a snake and there was a moment in which the shadows of the pigtail and the snake swung in unison on the wall behind him. She saw him bend again and skin the snake alive and the knife explore and prick out the vital organs and the man hold them out for sale.

"Let's walk," she said.

Passing down Chang Tso-lin Road and Jethro's hand against her elbow she smelled the blood and saw from the corner of her eyes the interiors of the shops and bottles of pickled snakes on the shelves, monkeys' brains heaped in their own sectioned skulls. The spasm of nausea came again. A Lascar seaman held out to her one of the little glasses as if in invitation and she saw the irony in his black eyes and the lamps swim behind the milky venom.

"They say it enhances the sexual powers," Jethro said.

"I'll buy some for Lewis."

The words had come without volition, into her mind, onto her tongue. She felt Jethro's fingers move upward from her elbow and knead the flesh above it. She shook them off.

"I need some water," she said.

In the Talifu Bar he brought her Perrier and ice.

"I shouldn't have said that," she said.

"About Lewis?"

"Yes. I shouldn't have said it."

"Why not? I'm used to bedroom secrets."

"You mean as a priest?"

"Yes," he said, laughing. "As a priest."

From the bar she could see the pond that had given the area its name and the ox they had brought in for the ceremonies of the festival. Its horns were tipped with brass and it was in the mud on the fringe of the pond. She watched it move out to the water and the head swing low so that it could drink and nibble at the white lotus blossom.

"Don't play the priest with me," she told him.

"That's what I am, Ellen."

"No. Not when you fondle me."

"Very well," he said, still laughing. "I'm a man out with a woman." He put his hand on her knee. "A frustrated woman."

Beyond the pond was the long boulevard that led to the city and its tall lighted buildings. The bicycle lamps shook like fireflies in the night.

"I suppose that's what I am," she said.

"When did you stop being lovers?"

"It was after Fusan. He was very weak when they released him. He's well enough now. But something has gone. He needs me, but not in that way." She pushed away his hand. "He tries because he wants to please me. But something has gone."

"It'll come back."

"I doubt it."

"It'll come back. In the meantime you could try the snake poison."

"No."

"You could put it in his coffee."

She smiled.

"*You* don't need any snake poison, Frank."

They laughed. Then she said seriously: "We ought not to laugh at him."

"No. He's a very good man. And one day he'll be as lusty as that ox in the pond and surprise you."

She drained her glass.

"Why do I confide in you?" she asked. "I don't trust you and I don't respect you."

"You trust the little bit of priest that's still left in me." He picked up the Perrier bottle. "Some more?"

She nodded and, pouring, she saw the half-healed gash across his forearm and asked: "How did you do it?"

"On the gaff."

"Where did you fish?"

"Deep sea. Right down to Luzon. Just me and my sweetheart."

"You mean the girl at the mission?"

"I mean me and *Justine*." He smiled. "My best sweethearts were always boats. She's an old lady now. And she was never a beauty. But I love her. I'm never happier than when I'm alone with her, alone at sea and not a ship or a neck of land in sight and the engine silent and the pair of us running with the wind. Sometimes I lie on deck at night and watch the mast on the sky and feel that deep vault of water that is cradling us and it seems then that we're sailing straight into God's arms and I know that this is my true church. Nearer to God, you understand?"

"Yes."

"Dear *Justine*." He smiled. "But I was unfaithful to her the other day."

"Unfaithful?"

"In my heart. It was at Nanfangao. I had awakened early and I walked down to the harbor and there, lying offshore, was this poem of a boat. She was a ketch, all white in the sun and so light and graceful on the swell that I felt my throat go dry with desire. I went back to the mission and got my binoculars and walked to the end of the jetty and when I focused them this lovely thing was so close I could stroke her. She was perhaps fifteen meters with a Hong Kong registration and her name was *Cathay Moon*. All that day I waited for her to moor but the swell grew stronger and she remained offshore, moving gently on her hook and showing me her lines. How she tantalized me! Then at sundown she went out with the tide and I watched her until her masts were gone." His voice was soft with yearning. "*Cathay Moon*. One thinks of silver nights on the China Seas."

When they left the Talifu he led her back into the wandering lanes behind the market quarter. The sticks of firework rockets pattered on the roofs. This was the hour before midnight and all the church and temple bells were ringing. "If there were ever any ghosts," Ellen said, "they'll have fled by now." She felt Jethro's hand run across her hip. All the priests, it seemed, had come to Crooked Pond. There were Jesuits and Franciscans and Benedictines, some habits she did not recognize. At the back of the hospice the white robes of three Carmelites glimmered in the shadows. There were also many girls for hire, seamen and tourists arguing a price. She heard one of them say in English: "But what do I get for that?" Jethro took her arm and turned her from the hospice and into Quilt Street.

She had heard of Quilt Street. It was the place of serious prostitution where, it was said, any want or passion or deviant need could be satisfied. It was wide, dimly lit with raised sidewalks and shops on either side and dark alleys that ran between the shops. Some of the windows still exhibited the silks, brocades and quilts that had at one time given the street another kind of fame. The priests were here too and in one of the alleys, where the moon struck, she saw the shadows of platter hats and swinging skirts. Oil lamps and incense-burners glowed within the shops and, passing down the left sidewalk, she could see the women, girls and children that stood or sat behind the glass of the windows like merchandise for sale. One of the women smiled through the glass and oscillated her tongue between Negress lips and another cupped her naked breasts and held them out for offer and another opened her thighs and rubbed her crotch and laughed and children beckoned and behind the shopfronts there were cushioned floors and paper screens and people moving in the sullen lamplight and silhouettes that bucked and heaved on the colored paper. Doors opened and closed so that she caught little wafts of musky scent. In one of the shops an oil lamp threw an aureole of crimson light and there were shapes on the cushions and shadows on the walls above them that writhed or pulsed or beat like wings. "Why have you brought me here?" she asked him. She knew the answer; in the growing ache of her own reawakened flesh. Shame, too, was growing, shame that she should find excitement in the sights and scents of sexual squalor. He led her across the road and they began the return walk down the right side of Quilt Street. His hand slid again across her hip and now the shame was gone and there was only the need and the needs of those that pressed around her and she walked slowly and stared into the shops. Once again the shadows made their jerking friezes. A woman in a sari lifted and held out a girl-child and turned her so that they should see her pale buttocks and girls rouged their nipples and a Chinese monk stood with his back to them and a woman knelt before him with her head inside his robe. They crossed the exit of one of the dividing alleys. A line of hooded figures came from its crevices of darkness and, passing, she saw their haggard faces. "Shansi Friars," Jethro said with distaste. "They live in the mountains and they are drawn to the smell of sin like sharks to blood." The friars mounted the sidewalk and she saw the long candle that was defined by silver thread on the backs of their robes and the five silver nails that were arranged in the form of a Cross on the center. "The Paschal candle," Jethro told her. "A symbol of Christ who is the Light of the World." He pointed. "But see how they defile it."

The friars stopped and a woman with a vermilion face came from one of the shops and beckoned with both hands and the friars followed her inside. They heard the laughter of children from within the shop. "Pigs," Jethro said. "Dirt and flagellation in their mountain caves, vice in the city." He led her from Quilt Street into the alley, through the moonbars to its deepest shadows and stopped her and turned her so that her back was toward a timber wall and pulled her against him and in that moment she felt the gin as strong as fumes inside her head and she closed her eyes and there was only his hardness and the night of the alley and the odor of old priests and the hot and panting typhoon wind and he lifting her and her feet swinging between his legs and she working against him and around her the night and the temple bells and incense and the scent of crushed frangipani the raw earth of the alley floor cascades of snake blood oxen with horns like a lyre and the shine of brass and Filipino whores with golden heels. "Come on," he said urgently. "Come on. Come *on.*" She pushed him away. "I can't," she whispered. "What do you mean you can't? You know you want me." The bells again deep inside her head. "Yes, I want you. But I can't." She pressed her hands inward from her hips to where the cyclic pains were pulsing. "Don't you understand? I can't."

She left him and walked rapidly up Quilt Street and to the hospice. She heard his feet behind her. "Wait," he called out. She did not stop. She skirted the pond and went through the snake-market and down Chang Tso-lin Road.

"We'll go to sea," he said behind her. "Down to Mindanao. We'll sail and we'll fish."

"And make love?"

"Of course."

"What about *Justine?*"

"What about her?"

"She'll be jealous. She'll go and sink herself."

They passed the Teagarden Bar. "Hurry, Father," a man shouted. "She'll get away."

"No," Jethro said. Now he was close behind her. "She won't get away. She's going to sea. With me and *Justine.*"

She stopped and turned to face him.

"Home now?" he asked.

"Yes."

Glass was breaking in Mandy's Bar and she saw two men wrestling on the floor and Joe Mandy bent across them and his hands tugging at their hair. Erich Brandt's shop was in darkness and a warm rain was falling when they reached the house.

"Is Lewis home?" Jethro asked.

"He's on duty."

She saw his eyes gleam.

"No," she said. "You can't come in."

She searched for her key.

"I won't chase you," he said. "Not any more. But eventually you'll come to me."

She opened the door and the house breathed out its urine-smell.

"You could burn incense," he said.

"I prefer horse."

"It's two months now," he said.

"Yes."

"Is Lewis content?"

"Within himself, no. Too much guilt." She saw again the vestments drowning in the river. "And not enough money. But he likes Free China."

"Tell him to be on guard," Jethro said.

"On guard?"

"Against John Chen. He won't give up. Surely you know that?"

She crossed the threshold.

"Someone will come," he said.

"So what could we do? Another Chinese face. A man with a gun. It would be so easy."

"Not guns," he said. "That isn't his style. Chen wants him in the People's Court."

She began to close the door.

"Be on guard," Jethro said. Now his face was framed between the edge and the jamb. "Someone will surely come."

Chapter 10

Lewis Mackenna heard her voice from the edge of Dr. Wei's hillside garden. It came distantly, muted by the trees and shrubs that clothed the slope. This was Tuesday, the first of the three weekly study groups that gathered in the evening when the glare of the sun was gone. He did not recognize the voice of the lecturer and he climbed the path toward it, hearing also the sound of cicadas and the waters of a fountain. The path wound between pots of chrysanthemums and through a grove of yellow prunus and, walking, the voice grew louder. It was low and melodious, so pleasant that he paused once to listen. He emerged from the shade of the prunus and there, below him, was the descending slope of the hill and Dr. Wei's prized ornamental garden. To his right was the house and its vines of wisteria and clematis and the courtyard where the group was seated. There was a half-circle of student nurses, some on rattan chairs and some on the low stone walls of a lotus pool. Sitting apart from the group was Winter, the doctor from California; and below him the small figure of Dr. Wei moved in the rhododendrons.

Lewis went to Winter and sat. The voice flowed. It came from the lips of a young woman who stood facing the group in the space that separated two marble tubs in which goldfish flickered. She held a pointer and its tip glided over the life-size anatomical diagram that leaned, propped, beside her. The diagram was colored and depicted the structures of a male body. Wires and a battery were attached to the frame.

"Stunning, eh?" Winter said.

"Yes. Who is she?"

"Anna Chang."

"A doctor?"

"A student."

"Yes," Dr. Wei said behind them. "One year in the Peking Institute. Acupuncture was her interest. So I asked her to give us a talk."

More of a performance, Lewis thought, than a talk. He watched her slow and graceful gestures and the unhurried movements of the pointer, listened to the cadences of the Peking Chinese that formed and found beauty on her tongue. Each sentence was perfectly constructed and delivered in her grave and tuneful voice as if it were a line from a poem, each sound so clear that it seemed he could see its ideogram imprinted on a page. She reached out and touched some of the buttons that formed patterns on the limbs and torso of the diagram. The buttons glowed with a red light under the pressure of her fingertip. "These are the acupuncture points," Anna Chang said, "and this modern teaching aid illuminates them. But there is nothing modern in the practice of acupuncture. It is one of the oldest of the medical arts and I could show you a bronze of the Sung dynasty that was used for teaching one thousand years ago and in which two hundred holes are drilled. Each hole indicates the point at which a needle was inserted and those ancient holes correspond almost exactly to the buttons on our diagram. So the past endows the present." She took a needle from her pocket and held it up. A tiny packet was attached to the handle. "Our word for this is *chen-chiu*." She pointed at the group. "Can any of the Western girls tell me what that means?"

"It means needle-and-flame," Elizabeth South said.

"Correct. At one time a herb such as mugwort was burned in the packet and allowed to smolder near to the point at which the needle was inserted. That was the traditional way." She smiled. "Today we do not use the herb and an electrical stimulus is passed through the needle."

"She has class," Dr. Winter murmured.

Dr. Wei bent across them. His shirt was open and Lewis saw his starved chest, as cracked as old pigskin.

"She does in fact claim class," Dr. Wei said. "Among her ancestors was a Manchu princess. But then of course they all say that."

Anna Chang turned her face toward the diagram so that they saw her profile. The nose was slightly hooked, the chin proud, the black hair pinned and piled high as if it were a headdress.

"She certainly has the Manchu nose," Lewis said.

"Definitely a princess," Winter smiled.

"There is another important word," Anna Chang said. She pointed with her chin at Elizabeth South. "It is *ching-lo*. Can you translate this word?"

"No, madame."

"I am not madame. I am a student like yourself."

"Yes, Miss Chang."

"In this case the word means a path or paths, paths of communication. These mysterious paths run up the front and back of the body and on either side of it." The pointer moved, following the lines of the buttons. "The acupuncture points are situated on these paths."

Dr. Wei left them and Lewis watched him walk down the slope between beds of Himalayan blue poppies and saxifrage, stop and look admiringly into the branches of a yellow tree peony.

"Soon," Winter said, "he'll retire to his garden." He pointed to the house and then at the slope. "A rich man's house, a rich man's garden."

"How does he do it?"

"Surely you know?"

"No."

"It comes from the foundation. The trustees fix an annual sum that must be spent on the hospital. Dr. Wei has complete control. Any unspent money is his. So he makes economies."

"Such as doctors?"

"Yes," Winter said, laughing. "Such as doctors."

The voice began to flow again and Lewis turned.

"We do not know how acupuncture works," Anna Chang was saying. "But work it does. It is used as an alternative to general anesthesia, even in major surgery. But how do the needles interfere with the messages of pain that are sent to the patient's brain? Some say that it is all related to the nervous system, that the nerve fibers are capable of responding to stimuli from some outside agent. That agent could be chemical or physical or, as with our modern needle, electrical." The tip of the pointer moved to the cranium of the diagrammatic body, then slowly downward. "Certainly this will sometimes be true and sensory impulses received by the nerve endings in the skin will be relayed to the brain." The pointer, now, was hovering above the solar plexus. "Yet it is not the whole truth. It will apply, and then it will not apply. A needle inserted in one of our paths of communication will cause an impulse, yes. But sufficient to defeat excruciating pain? No. So we must search for another explanation." Now she was looking directly at the group. The pointer reached the area of the genitals. "Somewhere in these strange and secret channels lies the answer." The tip of the pointer tapped lightly on the pubic bone and a red light appeared.

Su-ching giggled.

"The old physicians believed," Anna Chang said, "that rivers of energy flowed through the body, vital energy that—"

Su-ching giggled again.

"Have I said something funny?" Anna Chang asked.

Su-ching shook her head. The button continued to glow at the root of the sexual organ.

"It is red for danger," Sweet Hay whispered.

Su-ching put her hand to her mouth and began to cough with laughter through her fingers and Anna Chang stared at her, then turned to the frame. She pressed the button but the light would not extinguish and now

Su-ching's shoulders were heaving and the humor was infectious and the group shook with waves of laughter. Anna Chang did not smile and she stood unmoving until the laughter had died.

"Stand up," she said.

Su-ching stood.

"What is your name?"

"Tan Su-ching."

"How old are you?"

"Seventeen."

The giggles came again and now the group was silent and Anna Chang waited until the giggling stopped.

"Are you composed now?"

"Yes, Miss Chang."

"And all the silliness has gone?"

"Yes."

"How long as a student?"

"Three months."

"Were you laughing at me?"

"No."

"At the button on the diagram?"

Su-ching nodded. Now her eyes were defensive.

"During your training," Anna Chang asked, "did you see the naked male body?"

"Yes."

"Was it funny?"

"No."

"Have you bathed a male patient?"

"Yes."

"Was it funny?"

Su-ching shook her head. Now her eyes were bright with tears.

"Did you laugh when you saw his sexual parts?"

The tears ran.

"Answer."

"No, Miss Chang."

Lewis stood and went to Su-ching and put his arm around her.

"Enough," he said to Anna Chang. Standing close to her he saw her unusual violet eyes. Ai-hua rose from her seat and went to a flower bed and picked a single bloom and came to them and offered it but Anna Chang did not take it and turned away and he watched her walk toward the house, her shadow with its proud chin and proud breasts stamped on the paving in the evening sun. He felt the stirring of something that he had thought was long forgotten.

"Imperious bitch," Winter said.

*   *   *

Only the first of those words was true. She had pride, poise and a natural authority and to some she would seem imperious. But a bitch? Not really a bitch, Lewis thought. Certainly in the two weeks since the lecture at the house she had been a bitch to Su-ching; but it was the particular bitchiness she would reserve for those who were flippant. She herself could not suffer fools, and only fools were flippant. Medicine was serious. To a Manchu of any breeding a good demeanor was important. He had no contact with her during those weeks. He saw her grave face in the wards and corridors of Kodaki's. But he did not speak to her until, one morning, he went to the hospital library for the current issue of the *Lancet*. It was there among the other European journals and, bending to sign for its withdrawal, he saw her head in silhouette against a window. She was seated at one of the bench tables, bent above a textbook and a sheet of paper. He crossed the floor to her and sat at the table but she did not look up or break her utter concentration. He turned the pages of the journal and watched her calm and handsome face and it was not until two male students entered and went chattering to a table in the central aisle that she raised her eyes. She did not greet him and he guessed she would have no patience with such words of convention. He tapped the *Lancet* and said: "Do you read English?"

"Yes."

He reversed the journal and pushed it toward her.

"Read," he told her.

"Read what?"

"Anything. Read it aloud."

She began to read and, listening, he heard the lines on the X-ray diagnosis of gallstones take on a strange dramatic quality. He could also hear the staccato Cantonese of the students and the sound, by contrast, was suddenly ugly and he turned and called out: "Be quiet. This is a library."

The students bowed and spread their hands, then stood. When they had gone he touched the journal and said: "Read some more. This time in your own tongue."

He listened again, she translating slowly and the sounds even fuller and rounder because of the slowness, so clear and perfect in the silence of the library that he stared at the movement of her lips and the curl of her tongue and she sensed that he was watching her and looked up from the page.

"Gallstones," Lewis said, "can be so beautiful."

"So I am told," she said seriously. "Can they really be polished and worn like a jewel?"

He laughed.

"Why laugh, Doctor?"

"Because that wasn't what I meant."

She touched the journal.

"Why the reading?" she asked.

"I'm sure you know."

"The voice?"

"Yes. Beautiful."

"It is the language that is beautiful."

"It still needs speaking."

"I have given many poetry readings."

"Next time we'll have some poetry instead of gallstones."

He felt suddenly absurd. At my age, he thought; to discuss with a young woman the beauty of her voice. It seemed in that moment as deeply personal as the discussion of her breasts. He saw the question in her eyes. Violet eyes, pale skin. Had some European crept into the princess's bed? In those days, if it was as far back as that, a man might be flayed for such a crime.

"I wanted to speak to you," he said.

"About what, Dr. Mackenna?"

"About Su-ching. Don't be so hard on her."

"She's a bad nurse."

"Yes. But very young. Give her time."

"Do the patients have time?"

She returned the journal and bent again across the textbook. He waited but she did not speak and he stood and left the library.

A man was waiting at the reception desk. He was young and a document case was wedged in the armpit of his white linen suit and Lewis saw the receptionist say something to him and he turned when Lewis reached the desk.

"Dr. Mackenna?" the man said.

"Yes."

"My name is Peterhouse."

"How can I help you, Mr. House?"

"Peterhouse. That is my surname. One word."

Lewis saw his eyes go sullen and knew he had made the correction many times before.

"Could we talk?" Peterhouse said.

Lewis pointed and they walked from the building, out into the sun and into the shade of trees.

"I am from the Consulate," Peterhouse said.

He presented a card. The consul's office was located in Tamsui. Lewis felt a sudden fear.

"My children?" he asked. "Has something happened?"

Peterhouse shook his head.

"Not about your children," he said. "Another matter. We'd like you to discuss it at Tamsui."

"Discuss what?"

"Discuss it with my superior."

"Yes, but what?"

"I am merely a messenger, Doctor. It is important. And the appointment is at three this afternoon."

"I shall be on duty."

"No. You are free. Dr. Wei has agreed."

"You have a damn nerve, Mr. House."

"Peterhouse."

Lewis smiled and Peterhouse turned and began the walk to the gate, then stopped and looked back. Lewis saw the anger in his face.

Tamsui was a seaport on the northwestern tip of the island, eighteen kilometers from Taipei. Lewis was early and he stood at the window of the waiting room and Peterhouse sat in hostile silence behind him. There was a view of the fishing village and the Spanish Castle and an area of trees and green hillocks where, distantly, a group of men stood talking. At three o'clock a man in a fawn silk suit entered.

"Mr. Downing," Peterhouse said in introduction. "The consul."

Lewis shook his hand and Downing, releasing it, gestured at the window. "Nice view, eh?"

"Yes, nice."

"They're reconstructing the golf course. Fairways right down to the sea. That'll be nice, won't it?"

"Yes, very nice."

Downing led him into the corridor and along to a half-open door. Peterhouse followed.

"In there, in my office," Downing said, "are two men. From Washington, U.S.A."

Entering he saw them, two figures standing against the brilliance of the window and so dark in silhouette that he could not see the details of their faces.

"Let's all sit down," Downing said. Then to Peterhouse: "Cut along, Peter, and order tea."

The men turned from the window.

"Senator John Nathanson," Downing said. "And Mr. William Maggs."

The men nodded and sat. Both put their briefcases on the desk. Nathanson had a flaccid, ageing face and a corpulent body that filled the chair. Maggs was much younger with hard lips and eyes that roved and missed nothing. He sat erect on the chair, not touching its back.

When Peterhouse returned and all were seated Downing said: "Dr. Mackenna, you don't have to answer questions. But we hope you will."

"Questions?"

"About a crime," Nathanson said. "A very great crime." He took some foolscap sheets from his case and weighted them down with his thick fingers. "You heard my name. Nathanson. Have you heard it before?"

"Yes."

"Where?"

"In the Fusan penal camp."

"Was it Lyndon Nathanson?"

"It was."

"A doctor?"

"Yes."

"He was my son."

A woman entered, bringing tea. When she was gone Downing rose and pulled down one of the window blinds and switched on the ceiling fan.

"You be mother, Peter," he said.

Lewis watched them; Peterhouse filling the pretty bone-china cups and the consul squeezing lemon and Nathanson stirring so nervously that the tea slopped into the saucer and Maggs taking the tea without milk or sugar and grimacing at every sip.

"We are informed," Nathanson said, "that the camp and its inmates were destroyed by fire. Can you confirm that, Doctor?"

"I can."

"Be truthful with me. Could my son have lived?"

"No, Senator. He could not."

"One moment," Maggs said. He too produced some foolscap. "Our informant states that you were the only survivor, that on the orders of John Chen Yuchang, the camp commander, you were taken to a place of safety that was out of sight of the camp." He sipped some tea. It was an ugly voice, quiet and as dry as biscuits. "I am quoting, you understand?" He returned to the page. "It is further stated that you were put into a wooded glade and that you gave your word you would remain there until collected. Is that so?"

"Yes."

"If you did not witness the camp's destruction how can you be certain there were no survivors?"

"Because I left the glade and walked up to the ridge above the camp."

"You, a priest, broke your word?"

"Yes."

Maggs shrugged.

"These days," he said with sarcasm, "what is a man's word of honor?"

"Never mind honor," Nathanson said. "Dr. Mackenna was right. Something terrible was happening. It was his duty to watch, and to bear witness."

Maggs put a finger on the page. "Our informant estimates that there were more than two hundred Americans in the camp. Many had been there since the end of the Second World War. Two hundred servicemen and civilians." He looked up. "That is our government's concern."

"There were also about one hundred and fifty British," Downing said coldly. "That is *our* concern."

He rose and went to the other window and peered out wistfully to where, in the distance, the grass seedheads were rippling in the breeze; as if, Lewis thought, he had formed a mental picture of that first inaugural drive off the tee.

"Is it true about the flamethrowers?" Nathanson asked.

"Yes, Senator."

"How dreadful a sight."

"A caldron."

Downing pulled the blind and sat. The thin bamboo slats threw a diffused brown light. Maggs, already brown of suit and tie and skin, became browner; his wrists brown against the white of his shirt cuffs and his fingers like hard brown bones on the white of the paper. He was ill at ease at the desk and in the office, Lewis thought, somehow caged in this mannered place of files and delicate teacups. But where did he belong?

"Who are you?" he asked.

"Would you like a card?"

The question seemed absurd.

"Yes," he said.

"I have a good collection," Maggs said. "Which one would you like?"

Downing laughed.

"Washington," he said, "is a house of many mansions. But I can vouch for his credentials."

Maggs took from his case a bound document, opened it and riffled through its folios. "This is a deposition and it is sworn by a Lieutenant Pu. Do you recall him?"

"Of course. Is he your informant?"

"Yes. After the burning of the camp he was posted to general army duties. The Korean War began in June of 1950 and as soon as the Chinese troops intervened on the side of the North Koreans the lieutenant found himself in action. He was very severely wounded and taken prisoner. That was at the crossing of the Imjin River. Do you remember?"

"We all remember," Downing said with pride. "The Gloucester Regiment."

"Our chaps did very well," Peterhouse said.

"Yes," Maggs said, "you were defeated."

Downing frowned. They were silent. Somewhere out in the hillocks a voice shouted. Downing cocked an ear.

"Strange," he said. "But that sounded just as if someone shouted Fore."

"Perhaps," Lewis said, "they are checking the acoustics."

Nathanson smiled. Then sadness reclaimed his face and he took from his pocket a photograph in a transparent cover and handed it across the desk. Lewis examined it.

"Do you recognize him?" Nathanson asked.

"I do indeed. But in Fusan he kept his hair cropped short."

"He was a brilliant man."

Lewis returned the photograph.

"The armistice was signed in July of 1953," Maggs said. "Lieutenant Pu was still in hospital in Seoul and was not discharged until twelve months later. He was of course no longer a prisoner of war and was free to return to China. But he elected not to do so. Instead he made an approach to one of the U.S. Army chaplains and said that he was troubled by a matter of conscience and would like to unburden himself. The chaplain listened and advised him to prepare a full written statement. And so it began. The Fusan atrocity was now on paper. The statement went to our envoy at the United Nations. He is a man of discretion and, because the war was over, saw the political overtones and was content to forward the statement to the office of the Secretary of State."

Maggs reached for a water carafe and filled a tumbler. His voice had become drier, as if speech was an effort. He drank, and when the water was gone he said: "This was an atrocity that went far beyond the brutalities of war. We all know bad things happen. But this is different."

"That's right," Nathanson said. "In Chinese hands they wouldn't expect too much. But this." He shook his head. "Twelve hundred men incinerated because disease had struck the camp. It don't bear thinking of."

Maggs bent again across the deposition.

"You will understand," he said to Lewis, "that by itself Lieutenant Pu's statement is not enough. He was an enemy officer, a Red, one of those involved. He is certainly sick in body, possibly sick in mind. Will the world believe him? We need corroboration, Doctor. That's why we're here. To hear your evidence, to obtain your deposition."

"To what end?"

"To establish guilt."

"And then what?"

"Punishment."

Lewis heard the menace in his voice.

"First things first," Nathanson said. "Let's deal with the lieutenant. How would you assess him?"

"A good man."

"Good?"

"Yes. And gentle. He was out of place in the camp, out of place in the army. He should never have gone to war."

"Anything else?"

"He was kind. I remember—"

"Yes?"

"I remember he gave me a handkerchief."

"Why?"

He looked away and did not answer.

"Tears?" Nathanson asked softly.

"Fusan was a place for tears."

Maggs tapped with impatience. "Let's get on, shall we?"

At four o'clock the consul rose.

"We'll meet again," Maggs said. He touched Pu's statement. "I'll deliver you a copy, Dr. Mackenna. Treat as confidential. Read and then return it."

At the door Nathanson shook his hand.

"We have to thank you, Doctor. Later, maybe, we could talk about my boy." He stared at Downing and then at Peterhouse. "You know," he said, "there's something about your names, something that rings a bell."

Lewis smiled.

"Yes, smile," Downing said. "People always smile. Will you explain?"

"They are the names of Cambridge colleges, Senator," Lewis said.

"The university?"

"Yes."

"How extraordinary."

"No," Downing said. "Not extraordinary. Peter was posted here about a month ago. Someone in London was having a joke."

He read Lieutenant Pu's deposition in the little park that lay no more than a minute's walk from the factory. This was the noonday break and there were medical and other staff and dungareed workers from the factory. From the stone seat he could see the willow-plate pattern of the park, pools and pavilions, orange and cherry trees, stone tables where people ate from luncheon boxes or played chess and dominoes and other games. There was a standing group around one of the tables, among them Elizabeth South and Anna Chang. He returned the deposition to its envelope and walked over to the table.

There were two players, between them a large colored map and assortments of playing pieces. The map showed a terrain of roads and railways and mountains, rivers and streams. An umpire sat at the side of the table and there was a base at either end of the map into which a flag was pinned. Anna Chang was carrying a book and Elizabeth South stood frowning at the game.

"I don't understand it," she said.

"It's called *jun qi*," Lewis told her.

"The army game," Anna Chang said.

One of the players slid a piece around a hill and onto the bank of a river, then brought two more pieces from the cover of a forest.

"There are two opposing armies," Lewis explained. "Each army has twenty-five pieces, each of them of a different nature. Troops, guns, bombs, that kind of thing. Some of the pieces like, say, a land mine are placed and can't be moved. The object is to get to the enemy base and take his flag."

The umpire picked up and examined one of the pieces. Elizabeth South shook her head.

"The pieces are secret," Anna Chang said.

"Secret?"

"Yes. The opponent cannot see what is written on the piece. He does not know what has been deployed. This is what makes the game interesting."

Another piece moved and stopped in front of a grain barn. The umpire examined it and said something and the audience clapped.

"That is a point gained," Anna Chang said.

"Why?"

"Because there are soldiers in the barn. And the piece that is facing it is a flamethrower. The soldiers do not have a chance."

Lewis turned away. A flamethrower. He felt the envelope and its document crinkle in his hand. *The tanks came to the road that encircled the camp* (Pu had written) *and they were flamethrowers and they burned the camp and everyone in it.* He could not escape Fusan, it seemed, and he walked down the path and into the shadow of a grove of orange trees. The orange was his favorite tree and he stood there under the glossy dark-green leaves and smelled the ripeness of the growing fruit, stood there until he heard feet on the path and turned and saw that it was Anna Chang. She came toward him and did not speak and they began to walk, through the curve of the path to where there were rhododendrons and hibiscus. A man in blue dungarees approached, walking slowly and eating soybean porridge from a bowl and when he was near to them on the center of the path she moved to allow a passage and for a pace or two her hip kneaded in his own hipbone and pressed and pressed, then left him. He felt the contact run through him like a current, in his loins, his throat, his knees. The path branched. Rhododendrons closed around them. There was a stone bench by a goldfish pool. They sat. The water of the pool was turbid with dead vegetation and in its depths the fishes' eyes gleamed like pearls.

"What is the book?" he asked.

"Verse."

"A reading?"

"If you wish."

She gave him the book.

"Choose," she said.

He leafed through the pages. Some of the poems were a thousand years old. "This one," he said. "A Song of Unending Sorrow." He returned the book, then swiveled on the seat so that he could watch her, enjoy her lips and the emerging sounds.

It was early spring.
They bathed her in the flower-pure pool

> *Which warmed and smoothed the crystal of her skin*
> *And because of her languor a maid was lifting her*
> *When first the Emperor noticed her*
> *And chose her for his bride.*

"It gets sad after this," Anna Chang said.

"Finish it."

He listened. It was an old legend; of the unknown child of the Yang clan whom the emperor had taken to his side, of the war that came to the Forbidden City and the nine-tiered palace, her death under the hooves and chariot wheels of the invading army.

> *The Emperor could not save her*
> *He could only cover his face*
> *And later when he looked the place of blood and tears*
> *Was hidden in a yellow dust*
> *That was blown by a cold wind.*

He watched the flexure of her tongue. It was wet and plum-red, fashioning the lovely sounds so that they touched him and were as sensual as a stroking hand. He felt the beginning of tumescence. He wanted that tongue, against his lips, inside his lips.

> *The Emperor would not turn away*
> *From the soil under which was buried*
> *That memory, that anguish.*
> *Where was her jade-white face?*
> *The pools, the gardens, the palace*
> *All were just as before*
> *The Lake Tai Ye hibiscus and*
> *The Weijang Palace willows*
> *But a petal was like her face*
> *And a willow leaf her eyebrow*
> *And what could he do but cry*
> *Whenever he looked at them?*

She closed the book and raised her eyes from it and saw the tension in him.

"What?" she said softly.

He did not answer.

"Tell me."

He stood and went to the pool.

"Do I disturb you?" she asked.

"Yes."

"It's the same for me."

The words inflamed him. He turned and went to her and, standing, put his arms around her shoulders and bent and put his cheek against the crown of her head and felt her thigh move and rub his leg and smelled her scent and felt the animal warmth of her and whispered into her hair: "You know what will happen, don't you?"

"Yes."

"Do you want that?"

"Yes, yes, yes."

He knew it would happen. There had been the sterile years since he left Fusan, years in which he had gone again and again to Ellen's bed and the taking of her always beyond the weakness of his body. Yet despite those years he knew it would happen; and when, that evening after sundown, he went to the house in Mongolia Avenue he felt that old and half-remembered fever enter him. Most of the houses in the avenue were owned by Kodaki's and each of them had been converted for the use of female students. Number Seven lay at the end of the avenue in the shadow of palms. There were three separate living quarters and Anna Chang shared the house with Elizabeth South and Su-ching. The upper rooms were entered by an outside iron stair and climbing it and standing then on the railed landing under the deep pagoda eaves he could see the cars and pedicabs moving down the boulevard. A glazed door provided window light. It was open and he walked into the living room.

He looked around him. A table lamp shed a mellow light and a door to an inner room was partly open. He could hear the sound of running water. He sat down on an ottoman with scarlet cushions. The room contained the basic teak furniture that was supplied by the hospital. Yet she had brought something of herself to it and there were fringed Sinkiang tent-rugs, some prints of wingless dancing angels, a caldron with wooden legs in which was sitting a Jack-in-the-box. A large lacquered chest was set against the wall and on it were some carved Buddhas and a drink tray, a photograph in a gilt frame. He rose and went to it. A group of nurses, among them Anna Chang, stood in front of a gateway entrance, and a concrete building made a backdrop. Shanghai Hospital Number Six, the board said. He went back to the ottoman and then to the window. The city threw an amber glow. The door opened behind him and he heard the rustle of silk and, turning, he saw her enter.

She came barefoot to the center of the room, bringing with her the scent of lemon soap and tendrils of wet hair spread on the shoulders of her blue kimono. She was carrying a silver hairbrush and a comb. She did not greet him or even smile and she sat on the ottoman, half-turned to face him, and began to brush the dampness from her hair and he watched her and listened to the rasp of the brush and still she did not speak and when she was finished with the brush she put it down and began to plait the hair into braids and, now, her breasts were responding to the upward pulling of her arms and he watched them rise and sink under the silk of the kimono, the fingers deft and the braids lengthening and the silk quivering above the breasts and, then, she coiled the braids high on her head and took a jeweled four-pronged comb from the kimono pocket and pushed it into the coil so that it would not fall and, still not speaking, held out her arms and she pulled him onto the ottoman, onto her, and he closed his eyes and smelled the lemon scent of her and heard her murmuring voice, that voice, that voice, and entered her and strove with her and the fat cushions under the fat of her buttocks and her tongue as sweet as a fruit and how beautiful beautiful beautiful it was to feel again the secret tissues of a woman tight around his hardness and the emptying and she crying out and shuddering like a thing in pain and then the stillness and opening his eyes and the painted face of the Jack-in-the-box staring at him from the bronze lip of the caldron and the braids against his cheek.

Later he found a table at the side of the Teagarden Bar and, drinking beer, watched the people in the square. Anna Chang and Elizabeth South would begin a night duty at eight o'clock and at seven-forty he saw them cross from the hospice to the lane that led to Kodaki's. They walked in step and their gray-white caps and uniform dresses caught the color from the lanterns on the market stalls. He watched the swinging of her hips, those hips that had worked in rhythm underneath him. He felt elation. Is it possible that there, over there, that ripe young girl is carrying my seed inside her? For me, he thought, a small rebirth. For a moment he saw the contours of Ellen's disapproving face. Would she know? Some wives might sense instinctively a thing like that. But there was no guilt, only a growing pride. He had wanted a girl, a particular girl, and she had given freely and his body had not betrayed him and by God he could look Ellen in the eyes and if there was any guilt it would lie in the one who had not aroused him.

He finished his beer. He was about to order another when he saw movement in the shadow that was cast by the hospice wall. The shadow was deep and he could not see if it was a beggar or a whore or a tourist tout. Then the lamp of a bicycle drew an arc of light across the wall and touched the figure and in that fractional second he saw the face of William Maggs. It hung in the darkness. Then it was gone. But he could still feel the intentness of the man's stare. Maggs, uneasy at the desk in the consul's office, had found his place. Maggs was a watcher, a lurker peering out of shadow. But why was he watching? Lewis rose. He decided to walk through the lanes to Mandy's Bar.

Walking he looked back once, but if Maggs was following him that brown and predatory face remained in cover. At the bar he dropped his Japanese Army cap on a vacant sidewalk table and went inside.

"Beer?" Joe Mandy asked.

"Yes."

The bar was different. The familiar pair of Yuan ink-sketches and brass-and-silver temple gongs had been shifted and in their place and occupying the width of the wall were eight oil paintings that had been hung in two lines. They had bamboo frames and each was perhaps three feet by two feet in dimension. He went to them. They were studies of Crooked Pond at night, crudely painted as if the pigment had been applied with a loaded brush or direct with a palette knife.

Joe Mandy brought him his beer.

"You have to stand back from them," he said.

Lewis stepped back a pace. The paintings took perspective. They were vivid and imbued with a strange and primitive force. The first was of the snake-market, a canvas of shops and swinging snakes and writhing shadows and a knife poised for its eviscerating arc and the red of the lanterns making globules of red light in the red of the blood. The second depicted the stalls at the end of Chang Tso-lin Road and monkeys' brains impaled on hanging hooks and men with copper faces selling venom and a seaman drinking from a glass and the venom trickling down his chin and his eyes staring above the rim of the glass at a whore half in shadow and her green silk *cheongsam* split to the thigh and her finger crooked in invitation. The third showed a foreground corner of the Talifu Bar and beyond it the shimmer of the pond and an ox standing black and humped in the shallows and the two points of yellow that was the light touching its brass-tipped horns and there were lotus petals caught like white paper in its jaws and an immense and rampant pizzle hung to the water and pricked its surface and a group of whores were laughing and pointing at the pizzle. The remaining five pictures were scenes of Quilt Street and its alleys; men and women coupling in the shops, shapes against walls, shapes on floors, the face of a child staring from the folds of a blanket, a line of friars coming from the dark of an alley and padding toward a pair of hard-nippled Filipinos and the faces in the cowls gaunt and lusting and the mottles on the skin like the stains of sin, lamplight and a screen and the silhouette of a crouching priest above a knee-spread woman and his crucifix swinging out and down to touch her pouting lips and the shops like caverns and smeared with sulphurous light. He looked again at each of the pictures. There was a feel of decadence in them and he shook his head.

"What do you think?" Joe Mandy asked.

"Unpleasant."

He heard a step behind him.

"You told me to sell a painting," Ellen said.

He turned.

"So I did," she said. "Eight of them."

He saw the challenge in her eyes. She stood there in a *cheongsam*, green and tight like the one in the picture, his Japanese cap slanted on her head. He looked again at the canvases. The child watched from the blanket like an evil cherub. Ellen smiled. It was the smile of a stranger. He saw in that moment the piano in the mission church and she sitting at the keyboard, straight of back in her high-necked cotton dress and her honest face smiling with love. She came to attention like a soldier and saluted.

"Likee cap, sir?" she asked.

"No. And you can damn well take it off."

"Why?"

"Because it's mine. That's why."

Joe Mandy laughed.

"Take it off," Lewis said.

She shook her head, taunting him, then stepped sideways so that he saw the length of the bar and the sidewalk table and his Japanese Army cap sitting in the center. She turned and he watched her walk from the bar and out into the night and her thigh flashing in the silk.

"I reckon you're both in the Nip Army now, Doctor," Joe Mandy said.

Lewis went to the table and sat. Drinking beer he could smell on his hand the scent of Anna Chang's lemon soap. A trellis with a vine of morning glory stood behind his chair and he heard it rustle and, turning, saw the face of William Maggs swing down from the cover of the flowers. The American stood above him and nodded and Nathanson crossed the road through the lines of cyclists and both men sat. Nathanson wiped his face.

"A warm night," he said.

"Yes."

"May we talk with you?"

The anger had not left him.

"It's a free country," he said.

"Yes," Maggs said. "And for you that phrase has a special meaning."

"It has indeed."

"Imprisonment and then four more years in Red China. And now freedom. How does it feel, Doctor?"

"Good."

"An amazing escape."

"We had help."

"Divine?"

He heard the mockery in Maggs' drying voice.

"Perhaps," he said.

"Aren't you sure?"

"Only a fool is sure."

Maggs swallowed, coughed, swallowed again.

"I'll get you a drink," Nathanson said with sympathy.

Maggs stood, went in to the bar.

"He'll take nothing from anyone," Nathanson said. "Not even a drink."

"He took the consul's tea."

Nathanson laughed. Then, seriously: "Maggs has a throat condition."

"A laryngitis?"

"A war wound. Speech hurts him."

"What is he, Senator?"

Nathanson smiled.

"A handyman," he said.

"A handyman?"

"A government handyman."

Maggs returned with a tray and sat. He gave a beer to Lewis, a cognac to Nathanson. Then he poured from a jug of fruit juice and drank. They watched the quiver of the laryngotomy scar. When one-half of the contents of the jug was gone he put down the tumbler.

"Better?" Nathanson asked.

Maggs did not answer. To reply, Lewis thought, was to acknowledge a weakness. Maggs picked up the cap and examined it.

"A Jap cap," he said.

"Yes."

"Why?"

"Should I explain?"

Maggs looked inside the cap.

"My war was in Europe," he said. "A soldier's war. The war is over but I would not wear an enemy cap."

Lewis took the cap from his fingers and set it on his head. Maggs stared at it. Then he refilled the tumbler and drank and Lewis saw the yellow of the juice reflected in his eyes. They seemed suddenly baleful.

"Dr. Mackenna," Nathanson said, "have you read Lieutenant Pu's deposition?"

"I have."

"Is it accurate?"

"Yes. But there is an omission."

"An omission?"

"Yes. About camp records. Pu makes no mention of them. But I can testify that they were removed before the burning. So where are they now?"

"They don't exist," Maggs said. "They were taken to the army base from which the flamethrowers came, and there they were destroyed. The operation itself was never written in the daily orders. So officially it never happened."

"That's right," Nathanson said. "The camp, you might say, has disappeared from history. The site was covered in concrete and then fenced. Today that's all you'd see. A man could go to that lonely place and look down on it and wonder. But he'd never know."

"But we know," Maggs said. "And others know. The camp personnel. The soldiers from the base. And of course John Chen."

"Yes," Nathanson said. "John Chen. That name will not leave my mind. Lieutenant Pu states that he was present at a meeting between Chen and two army officers, that Chen ordered the burning of the camp. That's in his deposition. And at subsequent interrogations Pu was quite emphatic. Chen ordered it. But here, Doctor, we are not quite clear. Did Chen in fact have that power?"

Green flickered in the distant press of people and Ellen's face turned into lamplight. He felt the measureless distance that divided them.

"Doctor?" Maggs said.

"Chen was not of the penal service," Lewis said. "He was a political officer. He had a temporary command of Fusan so that he might question a number of subversives."

"Of which you were one?"

"Only in my heart."

"Not actively?"

"No."

"When did you become a Chiang agent?"

"After Fusan."

"But in Fusan you were on Chen's list?"

"Yes."

"Why?"

"Because I was a friend of Chiang."

Maggs drank again. Lewis watched him. A handyman. Odd jobs for the government. What kind of jobs? The senator had smiled, which gave the word a secret meaning.

"Dr. Mackenna," Nathanson said, "you did not answer my question. Did Chen have the power to give that order?"

Ellen crossed the road. Erich Brandt was at her side.

"Yes," Lewis said. "I believe he had that power."

They were silent. Nathanson shook his head in disbelief. Joe Mandy came and pointed at the table. "Repeato?" Maggs nodded and Mandy went with the tray. Wind stirred the morning glory. Men were laughing in the bar where the paintings were and one of them was touching the bull's pizzle and Lewis heard him say: "They used to flog people with it." More laughter. "You don't say?" The finger ran down the length of the pizzle. "Yes, in the Middle Ages." They were moving back to the bar counter. Another voice said: "They couldn't do that with yours, Tom." A petal fell and Maggs picked it up and crushed it in his fingers.

"But why?" he said. "Why should Chen do such a thing? The camp was isolated. The nearest village was thirty kilometers away. A handful of people. Were they in danger?"

"With airborne spores there is always danger."

"At that distance?"

"It's possible."

"But is it likely?"

"No."

"A small risk?"

"Yes."

"Let me get this clear. For the sake of a few peasant farmers who may not even have been at risk a camp of twelve hundred men was burned to a cinder?"

Lewis watched them. Nathanson wiped his sweating cheeks. There is something missing, he thought, a gap in their understanding.

"I don't think you understand," he said.

"We understand all right."

"I don't think you do."

Joe Mandy returned, set down a tray and left.

"What are you trying to say?" Nathanson asked.

"That Pu's deposition is misleading."

"In what way?"

"He refers to the spread of epidemic anthrax beyond the camp, that this fear was the reason for the burning."

"And isn't that so?"

"Yes. But there's more to it than that. Chen's concern was not with people but with cattle."

"Cattle?"

"The camp was on the fringe of grasslands," Lewis said. "Endless pastures that rose for miles through the hills and up to the mountains. All this land belonged to the cattle. It was a great new undertaking and the State was the farmer. Some said there were a half a million beasts. When the winter cold came the herds were brought down to the warmth of the lowlands. At those times you could hear them from the camp. Anthrax among them would have meant disaster."

Nathanson pressed his palm against his left chest and Lewis heard the little sound when the photograph buckled. Beneath his fingers the dead son smiled in the darkness of the pocket. Outside in the road the crowds parted and Dr. Wei drove through them on his motorcycle and waved in passing and Nathanson stared at the perching figure and waved in response, then returned his hand to his chest.

"Are you telling me," he whispered, "that my son was killed to save a herd of cattle?"

"Yes, Senator."

"Beyond belief."

"But true. I recall the day before it happened. Your son, myself and a bacteriologist named Cao Hai had gone to Chen to report. He asked immediately about the cattle. Were they safe? Could a wind carry the spores to the herds? I told him we should talk of men, men in danger and needing treatment."

"And how did he answer?"

"He pointed to the hills. Out there is an industry, he said. Important to the nation. Exports and meat and hides. So let's talk of that, he said. All of it at risk from this filthy pest-hole. That's what he said."

"I see." Nathanson rose. "I see." He picked up his cognac and went to the edge of the sidewalk. He stood there, slightly raised above the traffic of the road, not drinking, not moving. They waited but he did not return to them. A woman in a sari passed, then stopped behind him. "You want girl?" they heard her say. Nathanson shook his head.

"It's his son he wants," Maggs said.

"Yes."

"He too has power."

"To do what?"

"To move this matter forward. He has the ear of the president."

"And what then?"

"I told you. Punishment."

"Do you expect Chairman Mao to punish him?"

"He might."

"No. With men like Mao and Chen the State comes first."

"At whatever cost?"

"Yes."

"Maybe he got promotion."

"It's possible."

"You mean that?"

"Yes."

Maggs poured more fruit juice. His voice was grating again and he drank slowly, looking out to the flowing movement of the road and the sidewalks. He said into the tumbler: "The State comes first at whatever cost. Those words define Communism, don't they?"

"They do."

"Where I come from, Doctor, we believe in something different."

"That's right," Nathanson said without turning.

"Dr. Mackenna," Maggs said, "why did Chen save you from the fire?"

"For further questions."

"Did he say that?"

"Yes."

"When?"

"On that night. We were standing by his car at the roadside. He touched my forehead and said there were still a few secret things locked inside. We shall talk again, he said."

"And then you were taken home to Hangchow?"

"Yes."

Nathanson turned and sat.

"This is one of the things we don't understand," he said. "Why release you? Why not keep you in custody in some other place?"

"Chen is a very subtle man."

"Granted. One would expect subtlety from a chess grandmaster. But why send you home?"

"At home," Lewis said, "a man could be more vulnerable."

"Could he?"

"Yes. Liberty and a family and a way of life regained. A man would not want to lose those things again."

Maggs nodded.

"Yes," he said. "It would be an intelligent ploy. Did Chen visit you?"

"Yes."

"Frequently?"

"Yes."

"With more questions?"

"Yes."

"Were you under surveillance?"

"Yes."

"Is Chen a cruel man, Doctor?"

"No."

"Violent?"

"No."

"But you were questioned in Fusan."

"Not in that way."

"In what way were you questioned?"

Lewis tapped his head.

"The mind?"

"Yes. He could enter it, search it, scour it out. He knew what you were thinking."

"To do all that," Maggs said, "you would have to drug a man."

"Or deprive him of sleep."

"Is that what he did?"

"Yes. That and chess. Endless games. Night after night. Questions. Wake up. Another game. More questions."

"And answers?"

"Yes. But I could not tell you much of what I said."

"What was Chen after?" Nathanson asked.

"Anything that concerned Chiang. His generals, his forces, his plans, his advisers."

"You mean Americans?"

"Yes. The U.S.A. was the key to the situation in Taiwan, Chen said.

It wanted the Reds out of China and the Generalissimo back in power. He made me write down the names of all the Americans I had met during the six months prior to my arrest."

Lewis saw the hostility in their faces.

"You mean you actually did that?" Maggs said.

"Yes. And so would you with those damn chessmen marching through your brain. And in any case why not? I was a missionary, that and nothing more. Hangchow was full of Americans. Some were friends. But if any of them had a secret role I would not know."

"Maybe not," Maggs said. "But Chen was fishing in a pool. Who knows what he caught?"

Wind moved again through the morning glory. They sat there watching him.

"Dr. Mackenna," Maggs said, "what was your relationship with Chen?"

"Difficult to say."

"Friends?"

"No."

"The lieutenant states that these chess interrogations took place in Chen's quarters at night. Is that so?"

"Yes."

"That you were required to bathe and change before meeting him."

"True."

"Why?"

"I believe Chen had a phobia, a morbid fear of disease."

"Is that a medical judgment?"

"Yes."

"We all loathe disease, Doctor."

"Yes. But this went deeper. There were two major epidemics at Fusan. Typhus. And then the anthrax. I was able to observe him. He was excessively afraid."

"Wouldn't that explain his decision to fire the camp?" Nathanson asked.

"In part. It was a cleansing fire, and I've no doubt it freed him. But the herds were in danger. It was his duty to save them. And he did."

Dr. Wei passed again on the motorcycle.

"Later, after my release," Lewis said, "Chen told me of another fear, a secret fear that was always with him."

"Of what?"

"Of a legacy from his father."

"Why should a man fear a legacy?"

"His father was the warlord General Chen. He had syphilis and it had sent him mad."

"I see."

"I offered to run some tests," Lewis said. "But he declined. He would not need a diagnosis, he said. If the disease was in his brain he would know at once. The chess would tell him."

He stared at the road. He could not see Ellen.

"A complex man," Maggs said.

"Very. His mother was half-French, a madame in a Shanghai singsong house. A strange childhood, was it not? He went to the Jesuit School, but he was never received into the Catholic Church. Chess was his passion, not the Passion of Christ. I believe he was lonely. Certainly he was set apart by intellect. He once told me that he liked me. A very odd cocktail was running in his veins and it may be he was drawn toward me by that pint or two of European blood."

"Yes," Maggs said. "He was drawn toward you. Did he wear his uniform at these meetings in the camp?"

"Never."

"What did he wear?"

"A silk robe, silk trousers."

"Did he give you food and drink?"

"Yes."

"It all sounds pretty friendly to me," Nathanson said.

"Too damn friendly," Maggs said.

"Mr. Maggs," Lewis said, "I don't have to answer your questions. I do so because the consul wishes it. Remember that. Don't be offensive and don't make imputations."

He finished his drink and watched the road. He could not see Ellen.

"Did Chen know your family?" Maggs asked.

"Yes."

"Eat with them?"

"Sometimes."

"And chess?"

"A game or two."

"This is another of the things we don't understand," Nathanson said. "That you should open your door to such a man."

"Knock and it shall be opened. Chen could knock on any door."

"Did he ever discuss Fusan?"

"Never."

"You've been here in Taiwan for several months," Maggs said. "You could have revealed the facts."

"I could have."

"Then why didn't you?"

"What good would it do?"

"What good?" Nathanson said. "For Christ's sake, man, there are people everywhere that don't know the fate of those men." He pressed again on his jacket and the photograph crackled. "Fathers like me."

Lewis stood.

"You should make a list of all the men you knew in the camp," Maggs said.

"Should I?"

"You made a list for Chen."

"Very well. I'll make a list."

He saw Ellen's face glow in the lamplight.

"I have to go," he said.

"One thing more," Nathanson said.

"Another thing you don't understand?"

"Frankly, yes. You work in Kodaki's. Not in a mission, not in a church, but in a hospital. Why is that?"

"I'm a doctor. That's where doctors work."

"But you're more than a doctor. You're an ordained minister. Have you turned from the Church?"

"An impertinent question."

"Yes. But I ask it."

Ellen crossed the road. He went to the sidewalk.

"Do you go to church?" Nathanson said behind him.

"No."

"Why not?" Maggs asked.

He could not see her. Then the green silk shimmered. He stepped down onto the road.

"Why not?"

"Guilt," Lewis said.

Walking and she distant from him and the green lost and then emerging he smiled without humor at the perversive use of that word. Guilt. Let them ascribe it to whatever was brewing in their minds. They could not know of the true enormous guilt. It would not leave him, would never leave him. It sat on him like a weight. He could feel the shape of the tholepin in his hand. Walking down this road in Crooked Pond and the lights of the cycle lamps in his eyes and the heat heavy he could still feel it, feel and hear the awful crunch when it struck the nape of Shameen's neck. *I killed a man at prayer.* There could be no forgiveness. God might forgive me but I could not forgive myself and all absolution was a fake and even if I was absolved and freed of the burden of the first of the dreadful acts there was still the second of them and the ravine and the stream and the gun and its evil thunder in the rock walls and the young man with the good face and the red furrow in his head. Is he dead or alive? Please let him be alive. How could I get that information? Please be alive. The green was near now and she stopped and, turning, saw him and waited.

"Home now?" he said.

"Yes."

They fell in step.

"I saw you," she said. "Were they the two Americans?"

"They were."

"They seemed angry."

"Suspicious."

"Of you?"

A pedicab brushed his arm and he moved against her.

"You smell of lemons," she said.

He smiled. The Jack-in-the-box leered.

"Nice in this heat, lemon," she said.

"Very nice." After all the years of truth, he thought, deceit was a luxury.

Some Tamils passed, stared at them and laughed.

"We look ridiculous in these Jap caps," she said.

"Then take yours off."

"Why should I?"

"Because I got mine first."

"You're still a boy, Lewis."

"The deerstalker is on its way."

"That'll be nice," she said. "Just the thing for Crooked Pond. But you won't be exclusive."

"Why not?"

"Because I saw some in a shop."

"Here? In Taipei?"

She laughed at his dismay.

"Yes," she said, teasing. "I expect I'll buy one."

They walked in silence. Ahead were the lighted windows of Erich Brandt's shop.

"Wait," she said. "I have to buy something."

He watched her cross the road and enter the shop and the crown of her head and the amber beard bent across a drawer. When she returned she was carrying a bottle.

"Poppy oil," she told him.

"Poppy oil?"

"Yes. It's a thinning medium. Better than linseed. The work stays wet longer."

They began to walk.

"You hated the paintings," she said.

"Yes."

"I heard what you said. Unpleasant."

"I preferred your misty lake period."

"More feminine?"

He nodded.

"Willow reflections and little old Chinamen with pigtails?"

"Yes. I like Chinese painting."

"You would," she said with contempt.

"Why paint squalor?"

She did not answer.

"A bit Freudian, though," he said.

"Freudian?"

"Yes. The bull was formidable."

She stopped. He saw the anger in her face.

"Is that your diagnosis?" she asked.

"It is."

"Then why don't you do something about it?"

She left him. Following he watched her rapid steps and the silk flickering in and out of shadow. When he reached the house the door was open and the horse-smell sour on the night air and, entering, he found her waiting in semidarkness.

"What do they want?" she asked.

"The Americans?"

"Yes."

"A sworn deposition about the events in Fusan. And a list of all the men I knew there."

"Will you do it?"

"Yes."

"Is it wise?"

"I have no choice."

"But you do. You can refuse."

He walked past her into the living room and lighted the oil lamp.

"And then what?" she asked.

"An investigation. Then a government report."

"Which will name John Chen?"

"Of course."

"It might harm us. Have you thought of that?"

"Yes."

"Bring Chen down on us."

"It might."

"Don't do it, Lewis."

"I have to."

Lacewings circled the lamp and he saw their shadows move down the walls and on her face. She turned and went out into the street and he heard the tap of her feet and listened until the sound was gone.

Chapter 11

Lewis Mackenna watched Dr. Wei's finger brush against the boy's cleft lip. There were students in the theater and Dr. Wei said to one of them, a Japanese named Kiyokawa: "Tell us about the embryology." He ran a loving hand across the boy's grotesque face. "Here is an example of one of nature's errors. What do you understand by the word mesenchyme?"

"It is tissue, Doctor."

"Yes. But what kind of tissue?"

"Fetal."

"And?"

"It is the undifferentiated tissue of our early months."

"Which months?"

"The first three months of pregnancy."

"Is it stationary?"

"No. It is changing."

"And its destiny?"

"To form us."

"Yes," Dr. Wei said. "To form us in a multitude of perfect shapes. Why do I have to drag this out of you? You obviously know it. Be accurate. And answer fully. That is how we teach here. Question and answer."

"Yes, Doctor."

Dr. Wei drew a line laterally across the deformed lip. "With luck," he said to Anna Chang, "it will one day be as red and shapely as your own Cupid's bow." He turned his scalpel so that the light made stars on the blade. Then he bent across the anesthetized face. "The mesenchyme," he told them, "is obeying a genetic code. If we could observe this miracle we would see its ever-changing movement as it sculpts itself into our human structures. But in the case of this poor child the code is defective. Why?"

"Congenital," Kiyokawa said.

"Yes. The mother has a similar deformity."

"Then how can the code be defective?" Anna Chang asked.

"How?"

"Yes, how? The code is being entirely faithful to the parent."

Dr. Wei looked up. Lewis saw a spark of anger in his eyes. Then he shrugged and turned again to the boy. "Let us say," he said coldly, "that at one time in the family history the code was flawed. Do those words satisfy you, Nurse Chang?"

"Yes."

Dr. Wei bent again.

"The mesenchyme," he said, "has failed to join somewhere at the center line of the face. So we have a fissure, a cleft lip and a cleft palate. Once again the unborn suffer."

Dr. Wei did not speak for thirty minutes. They watched his infinite patience, his small fingers working on the final sutures.

"This is the important muscle," Dr. Wei said. "It is in two halves. Can you tell me its name, Nurse Chang?"

"Orbicularis oris."

"Good. And when you use this muscle what are you doing?"

"Sipping."

"And?"

"Pouting."

"And?"

Anna Chang hesitated.

"Sucking," she said.

"And what else?"

"Kissing."

Now they were laughing.

"I am told, " Lewis said gravely, "that pouting and kissing can be simultaneous."

"Thank you, Dr. Mackenna," Dr. Wei said. "But I am too old to remember."

When the last of the sutures was tied and the left distorted nostril had risen so that it was restored to harmony with the right Dr. Wei closed the central defect. Lewis followed him from the theater.

"That was awfully good," he said.

"Thank you, Lewis."

Dr. Wei removed his gown.

"Are you happy here?" he asked.

"Yes. But I need more money."

"Don't we all?" Dr. Wei said sadly.

In the common room Anna Chang poured him tea.

"You upset Dr. Wei," he told her.

"Was I right?"

"I'm no embryologist," he said, smiling. "Just a clumsy old bush surgeon."

"But was I right?"

"You were wrong to argue."

He saw her eyes go sullen.

"But you were very good on the questions," he said.

Dr. Winter passed and touched her shoulder.

"My princess," he said softly.

"I wish he wouldn't call me that," Anna Chang said.

"Isn't it true?"

"Not of me. But there was once a lady with some noble blood."

"Who?"

"My great-grandmother."

He poured more tea.

"I have her ceremonial clothes. I'll show you, Lewis."

"When?"

"I'm still on nights. But soon."

"Tomorrow?"

"Yes."

"A poetry reading?"

She smiled.

"It's all of two days since I had a poetry reading," he said. "Poetry can be very exhausting."

"Yes, very."

"And I ought to check your orbicularis oris."

"The sipping and the pouting?"

"And the rest."

She laughed.

"Whatever you want," she said.

She stood.

"I have to go now."

He watched her leave and felt again the pressure in his loins. Ellen's voice spoke distantly within him. Why don't you do something about it? But I don't want you, he said to her. Not in that way. I want this creature with the swinging hips and the lemon scent and the animal heat. I don't love her and I doubt if I even like her. But I am sick with the lust for her. That body. That voice. Whatever you want. That voice and those words. His mouth had dried and he drank the tea and stood.

His turn of duty was finished at noon and he would not report again until eight in the evening. The house bills were accumulating and four rental payments were overdue. There was nothing of value left except the sheaf of Imperial Chinese Bonds and later in the afternoon he took them to Erich Brandt.

"I will offer for the two Gold Loans," the Austrian said. "But the price will not be high."

"But they're rare."

"On the mainland, yes. But not here. So much was brought over at the time of the revolution, you understand."

Lewis picked up the bonds.

"There is a reputable dealer in Hsuchow Road," Brandt said gently. "He'll confirm what I say."

Lewis went to the door. Sun glared outside. Then he returned to the counter.

"Give me the market value," he said.

After Brandt had made the payment he walked through Crooked Pond and settled the house accounts. Then he discharged the rent and paid a quarter in advance; and after that he went to the house. It was empty and he sat in the garden in the shade of the plums and finished the deposition. He read it and added a final sentence. *John Chen Yuchang would never have released me if he had known that I witnessed the burning.* Then he examined again the list of names of those he had known in Fusan. There were three folios. Many were friends. A few he had loved. Faces formed, peeling in heat as if the folios were afire. He could recall no other name and he put the documents into his briefcase. Later, he decided, he would take them to the consul at Tamsui (where they could be notarized) together with the copy of Lieutenant Pu's deposition.

It was seven in the evening when he left the house. He had resolved to make an offer for General MacArthur's jeep and, the sun gone behind the mountains and the city thick with heat, he walked to the plaza and from there to the dealer's shop. The jeep was in the compound and within fifteen minutes the price was agreed and the documents completed. Then he drove to Kodaki's.

At ten minutes after midnight Su-ching came to him and said: "Will you come, please?"

He saw the distress in her eyes.

"My father," she said.

The man on the bed in the medical inspection room was in his middle years, gaunt of face with a fine high forehead and mustache whiskers that fell sparse and straight down the corners of his mouth. Anna Chang was bent across him and, turning, she said accusingly: "It's very irregular, Su-ching."

"He is my father."

"You know the rule. No one comes here unless he's referred to us by a doctor."

"Except in an emergency."

"Is it an emergency?"

"I thought so."

"*You* thought so?"

Lewis heard the contempt in her voice. Su-ching turned to him and said miserably: "I was afraid. So I brought him here." She was wearing a colored dress on which a coral necklace hung. "Afraid," she said again.

"Tell me what happened."

"He collapsed."

"Were you with him?"

"Yes."

Lewis waited.

"Be precise," he said.

"A blackout," she said. "It has happened before. There are chest pains. Things go gray. Then he collapses."

"How many times has this happened?"

"Four," the man on the bed said.

Lewis went to him and Anna Chang unbuttoned his shirt and trouser-band.

"He is Tan Haifeng," Su-ching said.

"How do you feel?" Lewis asked.

Tan smiled and the whiskers quivered like thin black wires.

"Weak," he said.

The pulse was slow but not thready. He was very thin, the bones of the chin and cheeks sharp under the light. Lewis ran his fingers down the ribcage.

"Have you eaten today?" he asked.

"A little."

"Do you eat every day?"

"Yes."

"He cannot eat large meals," Su-ching said.

"Why not?"

"He has a small stomach."

A scar made a white line on the abdomen, running down to the right of the navel. Lewis touched it.

"What is this?" he asked.

"An operation."

"Yes. I gathered that. Describe it."

Footsteps rapped in the corridor. Sister Chu entered.

"Hurry," she said.

Lewis turned.

"The boy Chih," she said.

"Chih?"

Sister Chu touched her mouth.

"The cleft," she said. "He is hemorrhaging."

Lewis followed her.

"Where is he?" he asked.

"In the theater. Dr. Winter has him."

The boy was on his side on the table when Lewis entered. Winter, the anesthetist, had placed a pad against the palate and his index finger was in the mouth and pressed up and into the pad. Blood had pulsed from the pad and down the boy's throat and chest and was streaked on Winter's wrist. Lewis smiled down at the boy and when he was anesthetized and the tube was in his airway he nodded and they turned him on his back and padded the throat so that there would be no aspiration of the blood. When the mouth-gag was in place and opened Lewis bent and eased the gauze from the roof. Blood bubbled, then pulsed. Now he could see the tear in the artery. He worked for ten minutes, using a single suture and crossing the thread against the center of the incision. When it was finished he bent again and watched the site.

"Dry now?" Winter asked.

Lewis watched for half a minute, then straightened.

"Yes, dry," he said.

After he had removed his gown he walked back down the corridor. He could hear their angry voices.

"But what do you mean by a small stomach?" Anna Chang was saying. "Do you mean reduced?"

"Yes," Su-ching said.

"Reduced by surgery?"

"Yes."

"Then why not say so? Medical language must be exact."

Lewis entered.

"Be quiet," he said. "Both of you."

He went to Tan Haifeng and sat on the bed. He stroked the scar.

"Where was it done?" he asked.

"Nanking."

"The big hospital?"

"Yes."

"I know it well. How long ago?"

"Five years."

"Who was the surgeon?"

"Dr. Kao."

"A very good man."

"Yes."

"Do you have any papers? Any medical records?"

"No."

"May I go now?" Anna Chang asked.

"Yes, Anna."

He watched her walk into the corridor, buttocks moving, her long and sinuous stride. *Tomorrow. It will be tomorrow. But it's past midnight. It is already tomorrow. It will be today.* He heard her speak, a door close.

"Now, Su-ching," he said. "Tell me about your father."

"It was an ulcer."

"What kind?"

"Gastric."

"And Dr. Kao removed some stomach?"

"Yes."

"How much is left?"

"One-third," Tan said.

"Is that all?"

"Yes. One-third."

"Not very much."

"No," Tan said, smiling. He had warm wise eyes. "So very small meals."
Lewis palpated the upper and lower abdomen.

"Where do you get the pains?" he asked.

"In the chest."

"Not lower?"

"No."

"Are you ever sick?"

"No."

"Indigestion?"

"No."

"These attacks. When do they occur?"

Tan shrugged.

"Any time?"

"Yes. Any time."

"Not after exertion?"

"No."

"And the pains? Do they coincide with the attacks?"

"Yes."

"Before?"

"Yes," Su-ching said. "At those times a deep breath is painful."

"Has he been well since the operation?"

"Yes. Until now."

Lewis listened to his heart and lungs.

"We'll keep him in," he said. "Tomorrow there'll be tests, X rays."
He stood.

"Tell me," he said to Tan, "did Dr. Kao describe this ulcer?"

"Yes. He said it had been there a long time."

"Chronic?"

"That was the word."

"Do you remember any other words?"

"No."

"Did he mention the biopsy?"

"The biopsy?"

"The laboratory tests on the excised tissue."

"No."

"Are you a nervous man, Mr. Tan?"

"Yes."

"Do anxieties affect your stomach?"

Tan nodded.

"Has it always been so?"

"Yes."

Tan closed his eyes.

"Tired?"

"Yes, very."

"We'll leave you now. One last question. In the years before the operation were you under stress?"

"Oh, yes."

"Continuing stress?"

Tan opened his eyes.

"Yes," he said. "Years of it." Sleep was thickening his voice. He closed his eyes again. "Experiences. Such experiences."

When Lewis climbed the iron stair of the house in Mongolia Avenue darkness lay on the city and the lantern was alight at the foot of the stair and the trunks of the palms were black with rain. He entered the apartment. The living room was empty but he could hear Anna Chang moving in the bedroom.

"Is that you, Lewis?"

"Yes."

"Are you ready for poetry?"

"I am."

He went to the drink tray and poured a whiskey, sat down on the ottoman. The Jack-in-the-box grinned at him from the caldron; waiting, Lewis thought, for another performance on the cushions. He rose and turned its stuffed body so that the clown's face stared at the wall. Then, smiling at the absurdity of it, he sat again and drank some whiskey and listened to the sounds in the bedroom. Garments swished and rustled. Studs clicked. He finished the whiskey and still the sounds of opening drawers and silks and linen and patting hands filled her room. He stood. These were not the sounds of a woman undressing.

"What are you doing?" he asked.

"Dressing."

"Dressing?"

He heard her laugh.

"I am turning into a princess," she said. "The clothes. Remember? I told you I would show you."

He poured more whiskey, went out onto the railed landing and watched the traffic on the boulevard and the smears of light that moved through the rain.

"I'd rather have a poem," he said.

"Be patient."

He returned to the ottoman. He could hear only the faint tap that came from jars or bottles touching on some glass or china surface.

"Now what are you doing?" he asked.

"Painting my face."

"Like a Manchu?"

"Yes. The ladies of the court used a very heavy paint."

He waited for a time. Then he heard her cross the floor.

"I can't get her shoes on," she said. "In those days the feet were very small."

She appeared, standing in silhouette against the bedroom light. Then she moved into the room, gliding with tiny hobbled steps as if the feet belonged to the great lady of those distant times. She turned at the angle of the wall and, not approaching him, went to the center and stopped. He could not recognize her. Her face had changed. She was as vivid as a peacock. She stood there in the garments of a vanished feudal power, then turned toward the lamp and held out her hands into the fall of light, moving and fluttering them as if in mime. He watched. Light seemed to flow like liquid through and round her fingers, forming shapes. There was an illusion that she stood upon a stage, that figures came to her and went. The hands drooped and were still. There was the feel of sadness, perhaps despair. She lowered her arms and looked at him. "Beautiful," he said. "Beautiful." He stood and went to her, touched the headdress and its patterns of blue and scarlet, traced with his fingertips the intricacies of pearls and jewels that made an arch on a deep black fringe of hair. Yellow tassels framed her face. He could see on her flesh the thickness of the colored pastes. Her cheeks were as red as a peony. A pale pink paste made a bar down her nose and her eyes were lined with black mascara so that they were sharply pointed like those of a lynx. He ran his fingers down the folds of her brocaded gown, down the embroideries of pearls and flowers, down her arms to the big horseshoe cuffs, up again to the jeweled brooch that secured the gown, touching, then, her heavy earrings and the wax campanulas that were pinned to the tassels. She watched him. In the mask of paint she was as crude and sensuous as a whore. He felt the swelling of his erectile tissues and he pulled her against him, pulled at the brooch and the folded silks. "Careful," she said. "Be careful. You must not tear them." She led him to the ottoman and pushed him down onto the cushions. She unpinned the brooch and dropped it on the floor and then, taunting him, withdrew and watched his desperate need and he jerked her down across him and parted the gown and the tangerine undergown and pulled at the silken strings and the linen bodice and the fragile silk that was a barrier to her flesh and began to tear at the rows of little silver hooks. "Careful," she whispered again. Her own fingers worked on the hooks and when she was freed he buried his face in the darkness of the garments and against her breasts and entered her and the old linen was as warm and crackling as a bird's nest and scented with age and as stiff as parchment at the seams and there was the scent of lemon and the colored pastes slid against his face and left their taste upon his lips and when it was finished he felt the ebb of strength and shut his eyes and slept.

It was a brief and shallow sleep and when he awakened the weight of her had gone and he could hear the sound of splashing water in the bedroom. He sat up and stared at the calico neck of the Jack-in-the-box. He was aware of emptiness, of a deep unsatisfaction. Without love to exalt it the sexual act was nothing. In his preachings he had always referred to it as the act of love. Now he was a man delivered of a fever, no more than that. But the fever would return.

"Are you awake, Lewis?"

"Yes."

"Your heart was beating very fast."

"Was it?"

"Yes. It frightened me. You could give yourself a stroke."

"Yes."

"Or worse."

He heard a spray hiss.

"Does that ever happen?" she asked.

"I'm sure it does."

"It would be embarrassing. What would I do with you?"

"I don't know."

"What would I tell them?"

"That you were giving me a poetry reading."

"Some poem."

"I shall frighten you again," he said.

"When?"

"Soon."

"Yes, soon."

He stood.

"I have to go now, Anna."

"Goodnight, Lewis."

Heavy rain lashed the iron stair. Descending he saw a figure in a yellow oilskin walk from the ground floor of the building and stop at the foot in the light that was shed by the lantern. It was Su-ching. She stared at him, then up at the door that led to Anna Chang's apartment. Her black hair was stuck with rain to her cheeks and she put her hand to the strands and brushed them aside and stared again at the door under the eaves and shook her head and her eyes had the stricken look of a hurt child. She clutched his arm, then turned and walked rapidly in the direction of the hospital. "Su-ching," he called out. She did not stop and he watched her until the gleam of the oilskin was gone behind the rods of rain and into darkness.

He climbed the stair and as he reached the landing the glazed door opened and Anna Chang came out into the cover of the eaves.

"Did you see?" he asked.

"Yes. Who was it?"

"Su-ching. She was upset."

"She would be."

"Why?"

She smiled and did not answer and he stood there with the rain driving at his back.

"Why?" he said again.

"There's a Western phrase for it. She has a crush."

"On me?"

"Didn't you know?"

"No."

"It's true, Lewis."

"She's awfully young."

"That's when it's painful."

"It'll be painful for us if the hospital finds out."

"Yes."

"They have a rule about doctors and nurses."

"I know."

"Will she talk?"

"She might."

"Yes, she might. You don't like each other. She might easily talk."

"Then we shouldn't meet here."

"No. Not for a time."

"I need some air, Lewis. The city is so hot. We could go to the coast."

"That's easy. I have some business there."

"Where?"

"Tamsui. It's a port."

"A port," she said, nodding.

"Yes. I have to see the consul."

"When?"

"To be arranged."

"Then arrange it."

It was arranged; and three days later at ten in the morning they saw below them the port and the mists of the sea horizon. There were produce trucks on the road, strings of cyclists with clutches of bananas tied across their backs. Anna Chang sat beside him in a red shirt and blue trousers, eyes closed and her hair lifting in the wind.

"Why the consul?" she asked.

"A passport matter."

After the documents had been copied and notarized Peterhouse took him to the door and said: "The senator is back in Washington. There are tactics to discuss, you understand? Perhaps a search for further witnesses. But at this stage there will be no publicity. The matter is secret. Please remember that."

"And Maggs?"

"Still here."

He rejoined Anna Chang and, leaving the jeep, they began the walk to the port. He felt her fingers slide into his hand. He put his arm around her. It was good to walk like this again with a young and vibrant girl, the steps synchronized and the hips touching and the crown of her head against his neck. He had forgotten how good it was. There were many ships and small boats in the port, crowded wharves and jetties, working junks with ragged lugsails. Ahead was the fishermen's village and the Spanish Castle and, inland of the village, sand dunes and bleached white trees. They stood for a time amidst the huts and watched the sampans and men hauling at the seines. Seaward they could see the boats coming in with the first of the catches.

"Where now?" he said.

She turned him toward the dunes. Behind the strange skeletal grove the dunes were high with thick tussocks of grass. It was a solitary place and she lay down and held out her arms and he took her immediately. Then he lay on his back beside her and, not speaking, they stared at the sky and the moving cumulus. Later she turned and knelt across him and he took her again and afterward they lay in the sour and insect-humming sand until the sun grew hot.

"Let's find some shade," she said.

There were tourist shops by the fish market, a bar with outside tables that were set under a palm-leaf thatch. She led him to a table that faced the longest of the jetties and they sat there and drank Taipei Golden Beer and watched the boats landing fish and the motorized sampans moving through the wavering seagrass.

"How ill is Su-ching's father?" she asked.

"Can't say."

"Are the tests complete?"

"Not yet."

"Is it serious?"

"It could be. A chronic gastric ulcer is potentially malignant. Perhaps it was malignant when it was removed and Dr. Kao chose not to tell him. Or perhaps not. Who can say? I have no medical records."

"A nice man," she said.

"Very."

"A scholar. Did you know?"

"No."

"It was in Peking. A long time ago."

Most of the fish barrows had gone from the jetty and he could look down its long perspective to the lip. Beyond it, offshore and moored to a buoy, was the profile of a large junk. Its silhouette was black in the sunpath and men were rigging the lugsail.

"Tan Haifeng spoke of experiences," he said.

"Experiences?"

"Yes. I asked him if he had ever suffered stress. Years of it, he answered. Such experiences. That was all he said. Do you know what he meant?"

"I think so. He was one of those who brought the imperial treasures to the safety of Taiwan. Su-ching told us about it. Some of those men wandered through China for sixteen years, taking the treasures from one place to another. The country was torn apart by war, first the Japanese, then the Communists." She smiled with a kind of pride. "The best of it is here in Free China, safe forever from those dirty Reds."

"Quite a story."

"Yes."

She stood.

"Let's walk, shall we?"

He shook his head and stretched his legs.

"No. I am very lazy," he said.

"You mean tired." Then, laughing: "Twice is too much."

"Perhaps."

"But the heart was not so fast."

She held out a hand.

"Come," she said.

He rose and she led him from the shade and into the sun and across the road to the jetty and onto its wooden planks, through and around the debris of blood and fish-heads.

"A bit messy," he said.

She put an arm around him.

"Just down to the end," she said. "We can spit in the sea for luck."

At the end of the jetty he kissed her and said: "Got plenty of spit?"

"Enough."

"You first."

He watched the little bead arc down into the water.

"A Manchu lady shouldn't spit," he said.

"It wasn't very good."

"Try again."

She tried.

"Not much better," he said.

"Your turn."

He gathered the saliva and spat high into the air and in that second in which the globule fell he saw behind it the details of the junk. The lugsail was set and she was free now of the buoy and turning slowly and he could see the massive bow sweep that was made from a tree, the stern tiller and its redwood dragon jaws, the two tiers of mullioned windows, the cypress turret of the hull. It was the *Shantung*.

"Did you wish?" she asked.

The junk was perhaps one hundred meters from the jetty. He felt the rage rise and he held out his hand as if he might detain the moving junk and there was a tremor in the fingers and he watched her grow smaller and saw the diamonds that the sun made on the engraved glass and the place at the flank of the junkmaster's cabin where he had killed Shameen and the space on the deck where the two Long Jing tea chests had stood on that moonlit night. The smell of the fish blood entered him and touched his stomach and commingled with the rage and became a nausea and the sea was heaving and he turned from it and looked into Anna Chang's anxious face. Then, turning seaward again, he saw the familiar figure of the junkmaster in the bows and heard his distant voice.

"What is it?" she asked.

"I'll tell you."

Seated once more under the thatch he told her of the escape from Hangchow, reliving the details of the flight and Chen's pursuit and she listening intently and her eyes gone soft and sympathetic. He paused when the tholepin was raised above Shameen's neck and was silent until he felt her fingers press around his arm; paused again when he leveled the pistol at the policeman in the ravine. "Shameen was praying," he said, "and when I killed him I also killed my priesthood. That night I threw my vestments into the river. He lived by the sword and there was some inevitability in his death and perhaps, if he had not been praying, there might in time be forgiveness. But with the policeman it was even worse. He was so young, you see. Like a boy. I keep seeing him standing in the stream with his trousers rolled up. His gentle face is always with me. Is he alive? I keep asking. If only he were alive there might be some hope." He felt her fingers press again. "If only," he said.

The junk, now, was following the line of the coast.

"The antiques could be on board," he said.

"It was months ago," she said. "He must have sold them."

"I'm not so sure. But let's consider. As soon as he opened the chests and looked inside he'd have known there was a fortune in his hands. But what then? How would he sell? And where? Not in Red China, that's for certain. It would be too dangerous. He's in the business of ferrying fugitives and they'd chop him if they caught him. And that means he'd have to find a buyer elsewhere."

"Like Hong Kong?"

"Yes. Or Macao. There'd be a market in both those places. But to get

there he'd have to sail two hundred miles of very perilous water. It's an escape route in itself, heavily patrolled."

"He could have sold them here."

"Yes. There are dealers in Taipei. But the best of them would inquire about the provenance."

"Provenance?"

"A new word for you," he said, smiling. "It means source, place of origin."

"But there is always someone," she said. "The Chinese will buy or sell anything."

"Yes. But at a price. That's the point, isn't it? Would he get his price? My guess is that if he couldn't get it he'd hold onto the goods."

She shook her head.

"It's possible," he said stubbornly. "They could be on the junk."

He stared through the masts and rigging to the open sea. The lugsail of the junk was no more than a point of brown in the mists.

"I wonder where she's going," he said.

"I'll find out."

He watched her red shirt move along the quays, through the press of barrows and blade-sharp walnut backs and turbans and coolie hats, a word here and a word there, a talk with a woman selling dishes of meat and rice, the shirt gone and reappearing red on the red-wet timbers of the jetty and seabirds swooping on the blood and she talking now to a man seated on a bollard.

She returned.

"Any luck?"

"Yes. The junk first came to Tamsui about one month ago. The master was given a trading permit and now, they tell me, the boat works the rivers and most of the northern ports. She's off now to Chilung and down to Suao. There's a mixed cargo of cotton cloth, figs, melons, rice."

"When is she due back?"

"In five or six days. But it cannot be exact. She will go wherever there is trade."

"You did well, Anna."

"Then buy me another drink."

He bought the drink and, standing, looked seaward.

"Trade," he said. "Why trade?"

"Why not? She's a working junk."

"But a rich man wouldn't work."

"Some would."

"Yes. But not his kind. If he'd sold the collection for only a third of its value he'd be rich. He wouldn't be tramping around for cargoes." He could not see the lugsail, only mist. "Those tea chests are on board," he said. "I can feel it. I tell you they're on board."

"You want to believe that, don't you?"

"Yes. I want to believe it."

The mist parted and the sail rode for a second through the gray. Then it was gone.

"Damn pirate," he said with anger.

Tan Haifeng awoke.

"What time is it?" he asked.

"Two hours after noon," Lewis told him.

"I had a good sleep."

"Yes."

"I heard a man crying. Or was it a dream?"

"No. No dream. A mountaineer was brought in from central Taiwan."

"A fall?"

"No. He'd been stung by tigerhead bees."

"And how is he?"

"I'm afraid we lost him."

Tan's gentle eyes clouded with sadness.

"How did the test go?" he asked.

"It didn't. I couldn't get the light down into your stomach. You have a very narrow throat."

"So I had an anesthetic for nothing?"

"Yes."

Tan smiled.

"No matter," he said. "The sleep was nice."

Lewis opened a file.

"Most of the tests are done," he said. He held up a chest X-ray to the light. "There are some old scars on your lungs. Did you know you'd had the tubercle?"

"No. Is this serious?"

"Not now. All is healed." He put down the plate and spread some reports on the bed. "The blood tests were satisfactory and well within normal limits."

"Good."

"You have a heart murmur. But nothing alarming."

"Good."

"And the rectal examination was also satisfactory." He returned the plate and the reports to the file. "I have you booked for a barium enema tomorrow."

"Painful?"

"Embarrassing. It's an X-ray examination of the bowel. The next day there'll be a barium meal for the purpose of examining your stomach."

"Is that also embarrassing?"

"No. But it's costive. I'll tell the Sister to give you a laxative."

"Dr. Mackenna."

"Yes?"

"This embarrassment. I would not like my daughter to be involved."

"Of course not."

"Nor Miss Chang."

"Miss Chang is a nurse, Mr. Tan."

"She is young and beautiful."

Lewis smiled.

"We'll find you someone old and hideous," he said.

Sister Chu entered. She stood for a moment in a lance of sunlight so that they saw her puckered face and heavy limbs. Then she came to the bed and proffered a surgical requisition and Lewis signed it and returned it and said: "Sister Chu."

"Yes, Doctor?"

"Mr. Tan is down for a barium enema. Will you attend him, please?"

"Of course."

She left and closed the door and Lewis laughed and Tan lay back on the pillow and the whiskers shook with merriment. He brushed his brimming eyes, then sat up.

"We are being unkind, Dr. Mackenna."

"Yes."

"She is not really old."

"No."

"And certainly not hideous."

"Of course not."

"But eminently suitable for the barium enema."

They laughed again and Lewis picked up the file and went to the window. Below him in the gardens sun was striking through the oleanders. "They tell me you're a scholar," he said.

"At one time."

"What is your subject?"

"Books and manuscripts."

"Of the past?"

"Yes. Of the old dynasties."

"Where did you work?"

"At first in Peking. I went directly from university to the Imperial Library. Eighteen years of age. Hungry for knowledge." Tan relaxed again on the pillow. "A long time ago."

"Yes."

"But not much to show."

"You helped to make history, Mr. Tan."

"Did I?"

"You were one of those who brought out the ancient treasures, were you not?"

"Yes. But that is to preserve history, not to make it."

"You did both. You should be proud. Did you keep a diary?"

"No."

"Or write an account?"

"No."

"A pity. It was a great adventure."

Lewis turned from the window.

"You must tell me about it," he said. "I'd like that."

"One day perhaps."

Lewis heard the weakness in his voice.

"Tired?" he asked.

"Yes."

"You're not very strong, you know."

"I know that."

"Sleep now." He went to the door. "Dream of Sister Chu."

Next day in midmorning Lewis drove again to Tamsui. Five or six days or even longer, Anna Chang had said. But such estimates, he knew, could not be trusted. The junk might return at any time. The tea chests, now, were seldom absent from his mind. He saw them on the mountain faces, on the road, in the mists of heat that lay above the port.

The wharves were quiet, with only a few fishing boats and a Hong Kong steamer anchored in the roads. He walked the length of the harbor until he reached the sand dunes (time, he thought, for another poetry reading), then turned back along the waterfront strip of shops and bars. Peterhouse was seated under a date palm with his long nose quivering in the steam of a coffee cup. He pointed to a chair and Lewis sat.

"I'll get a cup," Peterhouse said.

He went inside to the bar and, returning, poured from the jug and breathed again of the coffee fragrance.

"Favorite place," he said.

"Every day?"

"Yes. Unless we're busy. Which isn't often. There's not enough work, you see, for a consul and his staff."

"It'll be better when the golf course is ready."

"I don't play. But Downing can't wait." He pointed toward the Spanish Castle. "He's out there now. He objected to the plans. Apparently the course will be too easy."

Lewis smiled.

"You can smile. But there's a social side to our work. Downing says a difficult course will attract a better class of player."

"Obviously you don't want the coolies on it."

"By class I meant skill."

"I see."

"Why are you here, Doctor?"

"To watch for a boat."

"What boat?"

"A junk. The *Shantung*."

Peterhouse nodded.

"I know her," he said. "She's very fine. Why do you want her?"

"I'll tell you."

When he had finished the story Peterhouse poured the last of the coffee and said: "This is how I see it. If the junkmaster has sold the collection you have no case. Mrs. Mackenna would support your charge of theft. But that might not be enough. The master could claim that he delivered you and your family and your possessions safely that night on the river shore. He too would find support among the members of his crew. Agreed?"

"Yes."

"It follows that you'd have to catch him in possession. Even then he'd claim that the collection was his personal property. On the other hand if you had provided the police with an inventory of the pieces in the tea chests that would, I'm sure, be prima facie evidence of theft. I have a law degree, Doctor, but I don't know much about the Taiwanese criminal law and I'm not at all sure that the police would board and search the junk unless they were reasonably confident that the collection was aboard. You'd be in a better position if you could persuade them of that."

Peterhouse looked at his watch and stood.

"Why not forget it?" he asked. "The junkmaster helped to get you out. He risked his neck. You're safe now. Isn't that enough?"

"He took my property. Property is important."

Peterhouse put on his sunglasses. .

"I'll keep an eye open," he said. "If I see the junk I'll let you know."

He turned away, then stopped.

"By the way," he said, "we've heard from Washington. Senator Nathanson has formed a committee of influential men. And he's found another witness."

"Who?"

"A Dr. Cao Hai."

"I remember. He led the anthrax team in Fusan."

"That's the man. He's working now in Manila. He saw what happened and they have his affidavit. So that makes three. A Chinese officer, an eminent bacteriologist, a missionary. I call that good testimony. The world will have to listen."

"Will the world care?"

The world would not care. Twelve hundred men. A small number among the ever-marching legions of the dying. He could remember when the Japanese had sacked Nanking just before the Christmas of 1937 and his

escape with the Chinese troops across the Yangtze to the northern bank
and the bodies, many more than twelve hundred, that were piled at the
Hsiakuan Gate; and the following year when the Japanese were in occupation of Shanghai and there were surely more than twelve hundred heads
in the bamboo baskets that were hanging from the lampposts; and the time
when the Chinese had captured the whole of a bandit army and had be-
headed them on a Chekiang beach and, removing the bodies, had left the
heads so that from a distance it was as if a line of coconuts was awash in
the lapping tide. Without doubt there were more than twelve hundred
bandits in that particular army. The world would not care. Twelve hundred.
What was twelve hundred? Most days of the year men would read in their
daily papers of the famines and the wars and the epidemics and the typhoons and would turn, unmoved by the huge addition, to the sports page.
Indifference was another face of evil. Twelve hundred in a Chinese camp.
The world would not care, but the politicians might.

There was heavy rain that evening and after nightfall and walking the
wards at Kodaki's he could still hear its beat against the windows. Dr. Wei
and Anna Chang were standing by the single bed in Room Six and they
turned when he entered and the doctor gestured at the patient, a girl of
nine, and murmured: "I'm sure she'll do well." He touched her bandaged
face. "There'll be a brief regression, perhaps some bedwetting. And she
has some pain. But that's worth enduring, isn't it? A small price for a
better future." He put the medical chart into Lewis' hands and said with
irony: "I'll leave you now with Nurse Chang."

They watched him go.

"He knows," Anna Chang said.

"Yes."

"Who could have told him?"

He shrugged.

"Perhaps Su-ching," she said.

"I doubt it."

"Yes. Su-ching might do that."

He studied the chart. The child, a daughter of one of the rich Eurasian
families, was a case of mongolism, so pronounced that the father had come
to Dr. Wei with a plea (and the offer of a very large sum) for the new
cosmetic surgery. Dr. Wei had found the subject as interesting as the offer
and had agreed. There was a photograph in the file that exhibited the
slanted eyes and flattened features and perpetually open mouth that was
characteristic of Down's syndrome children. There was also a condition of
macroglossia, an outsize tongue that filled the mouth. Dr. Wei had corrected the receding chin, removed the skin that was folded thickly above
the eyes, sewn the ears back so that they would lie closely against the head,
constructed a new bridge to the nose and, finally, had trimmed the tongue
to a normal shape. Now there was nothing visible except the nostrils and

the two wincing eyes that stared from the white of the bandages and Anna Chang bent and looked into them and said with concern: "I don't agree with it."

"Why not?"

"Such pain."

"We can control that."

"Yes. But should we subject a child to all this? Does she understand?"

"She'll understand when she grows older. She won't dribble or make a mess of eating. She'll learn to speak well and her lips will meet. People won't stare because she looks subnormal. She'll develop intellectually. One day, if all goes well, a pretty girl will walk into Kodaki's and thank Dr. Wei for all he gave her."

They went into the corridor.

"I drove to Tamsui today," he said.

She walked into the long linen compartment that joined the two adjacent wards and he stood at the entrance and watched her take sheets and pillowcases from the shelves.

"Any news of the junk?" she asked.

"No."

"Did you make inquiries?"

"No. But I met a man from the Consulate. He'll watch out for her."

She came out into the corridor with the linen piled on her arms.

"This man," she said. "Does he go down to the harbor every day?"

"Most days."

"When?"

"Elevenses."

"Elevenses?"

"An English ritual," he said, smiling. "Coffee in the morning."

"At eleven o'clock?"

"Or ten."

He saw her confusion and laughed.

"Elevenses is any time," he said. He looked at his watch. "Must go. Will you watch the little girl?"

"I will."

He turned to go.

"Lewis," she said.

"Yes?"

"Does your friend go to the harbor after dark?"

"I doubt it."

"What if the junk comes in at night?"

"Let's hope she'll stay until morning."

"And what would you do?"

"Police."

"Police," she repeated.

"Yes. If I could take a policeman aboard and search her and the collection was there I'd have a good case."

Later he went to Tan Haifeng's room, sat by the bed and spread on it some X-ray pictures and papers from his file. Tan was sitting upright and a writing pad was turned into the light from the bed lamp.

"How are you?" Lewis asked.

"Recovered."

"Recovered?"

"Yes." Tan tapped his thighs. "Did they not tell you?"

"No."

"It was yesterday. After the anesthetic. I could hardly walk. I spent an hour in the hospital gardens. Walking round and round. Only then did my legs begin to function. Is this usual, Doctor?"

"No."

"Do you know what happened?"

"I do," Lewis said coldly. "Dr. Winter is one of those anesthetists who like to use a muscle relaxant."

"Don't you approve?"

"No."

"May one ask why?"

"Put it this way. By using a significant amount of that particular bromide I could stop your breathing."

"Really?"

"Yes. But I have never known it happen."

Tan smiled faintly.

"I think I am breathing," he said.

"Good. Are you writing letters?"

"One. For my sister Lailan."

"Is she in Taiwan?"

"No, I am sad to say. She is still on the mainland. The Reds will not permit her to join me. The letter, of course, will go via Hong Kong."

Tan slid the pad across the covers.

"These are headings," he said.

"Headings?"

"About the great adventure. Remember? The ancient treasures. I might try to write it down."

"You must do so."

"Perhaps. But such an article would never be published. Not here. The authorities are very sensitive about the matter."

"History deserves a record, Mr. Tan. Memory cannot be trusted."

"No."

"And you won't be here forever."

"True."

"Where are the treasures now?"

"In a village named Peiku. They are stored in the mountain caves and there is a company of soldiers to guard them. One day they will build a national museum in Taipei and people will come to marvel at the greatest collection of Chinese artworks in the world. They are safe. But they belong in Peking, Dr. Mackenna. And in the course of time they must return."

Sister Chu came to the door, nodded, walked away.

"It was a very discreet barium enema," Tan said. "Did you get a good picture?"

Lewis held up the X-ray plate to the light.

"You have some *diverticuli,*" he said. "Do you know what that is?"

"Worms?"

"No." He ran his finger down the colon and tapped the little pouches. "It is a disease of civilization. Sometimes due to a lack of fiber in the diet. I probably have them too."

"Dangerous?"

"No. They are for the moment simple."

"Have you made a diagnosis?"

"Not yet. But there is still the barium meal."

"Tomorrow, is it not?"

"Yes."

But the radiography screen was defective and would need two days for repair and in the morning Tan Haifeng sat in the day room at a table with a pack of hospital graph paper spread beneath his pen, his thin back hunched and his shoulderbones thrust up sharp against the red chrysanthemums of his bathrobe.

At noon Lewis went to him.

"How is it going?" he asked.

"Finish."

"Already?"

"I mean that I cannot continue."

"Why not?"

"There is no point in writing an article if it will not be printed."

"It could be printed. In other countries. We could do translations."

"Yes. And eventually it would be read by the Maoists. It might put Lailan in danger."

"Why?"

"Because she is the sister of a man who helped to steal the imperial treasures. She was questioned at the time. Then they left her alone. Let us leave it like that." He made a neat sheaf of the graph paper and pushed it across the table. "No article," he said firmly. "It would only revive their interest." He turned on the chair so that Lewis looked down into his eyes. "Surely you see that?"

"Of course."

Tan picked up the one completed page.

"I have written many technical papers in my time," he said, "but now I have no patience with the act of writing."

"May I see?"

Tan gave him the page. The characters were drawn in a fine patrician hand.

I was eighteen when I went to the Imperial Library. This was where I would work and learn. It was the greatest library in all the Eastern world and was located in what was known then as the Forbidden City. For me it became the fount of knowledge. Nearly eleven hundred years had passed since the printing of the first book. That book was there, and every book that had been printed by the emperors in the centuries that followed. There was so much to learn; the care and preservation of paper and silk and vellum and the beautiful ancient bindings. There were also the manuscripts and calligraphies that predated them, documents and Imperial mandates, palace records and the annals of the dynasties, Tibetan canon and Buddhist sutras. How happy I was! There is a human heartbeat in every nation's history and if one paused and listened in that magic place of books and archives one could hear its living pulse.

Lewis returned the page.

"It reads well," he said.

"Thank you."

"Won't you reconsider?"

Tan crumpled the page.

"A pity," Lewis said.

Chapter 12

But the story could still be told, and he heard it that night from the lips of Tan Haifeng. There had been an explosion in the coal mine at Haishan Yikeng, which lay sixteen miles southwest of Taipei; and because he was on call for emergencies he was summoned to Kodaki's at seven in the evening. There were many casualties and he worked in the theater until midnight.

"Go home now," Dr. Wei said.

But he did not go home. Home was Ellen and the barrier that stood between them and the bed he did not wish to share. After he had washed and changed he went to Tan's room and softly opened the door. Tan was reading.

"Not asleep?" he said.

"I do not read in my sleep, Doctor."

Lewis smiled.

"Would you like some tea?"

"Please."

Sipping tea and perched on a mound of pillows and as alert as a sparrow Tan looked back again into those distant valleys of youth and time. The Purple Forbidden City lay at the center of Peking and the Imperial Library was contained within the Pavilions of Learning. He had gone there in 1925. The last in the line of the Ching emperors had been banished in the previous year and, now, the people were free to cross the moat and wander through the squares and courtyards and visit the throne halls and the palaces and gaze at their incredible heritage. The library, of course, was merely a part of a greater treasure, works of art that seemed to fill the entire inner city. To walk those halls and temples and palace apartments was to feel the mouth go dry with wonder. He had gone into residence in the old Tatar city where once had lived the courtiers and administrators of the imperial households. They were elegant houses of one story and built around a central courtyard and the house to which he had been assigned was shared with three other students, one of them a girl. There was a garden with a lotus pond, a moon door and a ginkgo tree; and it was under its leaves, lemon in the autumn month, that he had met the girl. Her subject was porcelains, jades and ceramics, and her name was Sian. From the beginning they had been kindred spirits; united, as you would expect, through their work and a love of the things of beauty with which their lives were interwoven. There was also, of course, Tan said with a smile, a less ascetic kind of love. But the authorities did not approve of marriage among those who were not yet expert. Five years of study were to pass before he asked her if he could make the customary formal approach to the assembled members of her family. She had agreed and they had embraced. They were standing, Tan recalled, in the courtyard of the observatory and there was a sheen of rain on her cheeks and behind her he could see the shapes of the armillary sphere and the astrolabe that Kublai Khan had brought from Persia. They were the finest bronzes in the world. "Is it not incredible," Tan asked, spreading his hands in disbelief, "that they should be allowed to stand exposed in the open for six hundred years?"

"Incredible," Lewis said.

They had married and there was no more than a year of tranquil living. In 1931 the Japanese invaded Manchuria. There had been earlier wars, a kind of endemic state of continuous fighting. But this was different. Northern China was at risk and soon the invaders would stream across the Great Wall. Now they were massed only two hundred and fifty kilometers from Peking. At one of the councils of war Chiang Kai-shek and the Kuomintang government resolved that the treasures could not be left in the path of the barbarians and their destructive lust. They would be moved south to a place of safety. They had already been catalogued (this alone had been a two-year task) and within the covers of those leather volumes was a truly wondrous inventory, millions of items accumulated down the centuries by the emperors. But only the best and rarest could be moved. A committee of university professors and antiquarians made their selection. And now, as the fires of war drew nearer, began the labor of crating them for what was to be a journey of unendurable length. But the packing was itself a long and arduous task. Every object, most of them fragile, must be protected. Another year had passed before the task was finished. There were nearly twenty thousand cases. Tan repeated it. Twenty thousand. Each case was of a uniform dimension. "How can one describe it?" he asked. He made with his hands the shape of a rectangle. "Can you imagine a tea chest?"

"I can indeed," Lewis said drily.

"Then double it and you have the size of a case." Tan poured more tea and drank. This, he said, was in the spring of 1933. The cases were loaded onto trucks and on the night of departure an order of curfew was imposed on the city. Troops lined the dark and silent streets and the trucks passed between them and when they reached the railway depot there were two long waiting trains. This represented one-half of the convoy; and the second would, for considerations of security, follow after a period of seven days. The cars were sealed. The destination was Nanking and aboard the convoy were the professors and other experts and the armed guards whose charge was to protect the treasures.

The journey to Nanking took two days. An area of the freight yard was cordoned by troops and no person was permitted to leave. The second convoy arrived and the four trains and their passengers and cargoes remained there for a month. It was a time of frustration and he could remember walking the yard in the bitter river wind, his arm around Sian and across the Yangtze the unreachable city and its nighttime glow of yellow light. During that month the senior professors made numerous visits to Government House. But the answer never varied. There was no space. How could the city store or exhibit so vast a collection? An extension would be built on the Confucius Temple but this would take years and in the meantime the Generalissimo had directed that the cases be shipped to Shanghai.

The trains were unloaded and steamboats took the treasures down the Yangtze. They were stored in warehouses behind the Bund with a company of troops to guard them. He and Sian were allotted rooms above a teahouse near to the Settlement, and there began a long period of further frustration. Civil war had spread like a pestilence and the Communist armies, at grips with Chiang's forces since 1934, were marching down from Kiangsi. The years passed. Most of the time was spent in the care of the books and manuscripts. They could not remain undisturbed in the cases and it was essential to check them against dampness and the ravages of termites. There was a continuous process in which the books were spread on trestle tables and the pages opened so that they might feel the flow of air.

In the final days of 1936 they learned that the Temple extension was complete, that they would return to Nanking. Transportation was slow. There were delays. Spring came, then summer; and still the warehouse that contained his cases had not been cleared. They were about to leave when the Japanese war, static for a time, erupted again and on the day of the double-seventh (the seventh of July, 1937) the Nippon flag was raised above the old walled town of Wanping, only twenty-five kilometers from Peking. Within six weeks the city had fallen. This was the day, Tan said, when Sian had shown the first signs of strain. She was a gentle creature, now swollen with child, and he had found her that night in the darkness of the bedroom on a chair placed in the center and she was staring into the shadows and he had held her and she had talked in a yearning voice of the little house in the Tatar quarter and the moon door and the ginkgo whose leaves would soon display the first lemon tint. It was four years since they had seen it. But Peking had gone. Tientsin followed. Soon the battle reached Shanghai. From the teahouse they could hear the Chinese batteries and the Japanese bombers diving down the sky.

"Yes," Lewis said. "I was there."

Tan smiled. The British and other foreigners were safe in their Concessions. Nothing much had changed. There were still the races, tiffin under the sunshades, a splendid view of the fighting from the dining room at the top of the Park Hotel. Two months were to pass before the Japanese poured through the Chinese lines, but by that time they and the remainder of the cases had returned to Nanking. But the city, the seat of government, was under immediate Japanese threat. These were desperate times and Chiang Kai-shek moved the government west to Chungking, a distance of thirteen hundred kilometers. The treasures, most of them still in their cases, would be transported inland.

So, Tan said, there was to be no haven, no place where they might make a home and raise the child and find some peace in the family and the academic life. It had become obvious that the collection as a whole was too huge to be handled and it was decided that it would be divided into three sections and that the cases would be embarked on three separate routes. Each convoy was assigned a team of palace scholars and a guard of soldiers. The first of the three sections would go to Changsha, a journey of five hundred kilometers, there to be placed in the care of Hunan University. The second would be shipped down the Yangtze to Chungking. And the third, a convoy of seven thousand cases, would be entrained on the Nanking-Paochi line. Paochi was the end of the track but the cases would not necessarily travel the whole of those twelve hundred kilometers. A repository for them might be found at any one of the towns en route. Instructions would be received. All depended on the tides of war.

Those tides were already nearing the city wall of Nanking. The third convoy left only a few days before the Japanese entered. The train contained, among other antiquities, the Imperial Library, and as it steamed westward the news reached them of the atrocity that history would condemn. The Japanese troops ran wild in an orgy of killing and burning and when the lust had spent itself the smoke from the ravaged city made a haze across the Purple Mountain and the kites ate from the bodies of a multitude of dead. The stories would not leave their minds and Sian sat throughout the days with her arms folded across her distended shape as if she would protect the unborn child.

At Suchow the train stopped for fuel and water. Within minutes they heard the sound of aircraft. Whistles were blowing. The first bomb fell and he could remember Sian's cry of terror and the splinters of glass from the carriage windows that glittered in her hair. The train began to move and he stood above and against her so that he might shield her and when the train was curving through the outskirts of the town he could see the burning station and the Japanese bombers coming out of the smoke and toward the tail of the train. More bombs fell, excavating pits around the track. It was not until the folds of the land closed around the train that the aircraft left.

The following day, Tan said, they reached Chengchou. When the locomotive was replenished he went to the stationmaster's office. But there were no messages, no instructions; only an army commander who told him that there was an emergency and that sixty out of the one hundred soldiers must be returned to field duties. The entire station at Suchow, he added, had been destroyed. The soldiers were disembarked, began the march to the waiting trucks. In that moment a wave of bombers came low across the yards and once again they felt the detonations, saw the balls of flame and the rains of debris; once again they were pursued, strafed and bombed until the aircraft, their bays empty, flew away into the early mists.

Three days later, the land rising and the wind bringing with it the cold of the western ranges, the train stopped at Tungkwan. They were there for two hours. When the last box of provisions had been loaded and the train moved from the station the palace officials and the soldiers were smiling and clucking with relief. There had been no attack. But then, outside Tungkwan, the bombers came again and the train shuddered from the impacts. There were three separate bombing runs. But the track survived and they were not derailed. Sian, now, lay silent and shivering in her blanket.

That evening in the town of Siking one of Chiang's senior political officers was awaiting them in the station. He wore the astrakhan greatcoat and knee-high boots that had become a uniform exclusive to his rank. There is a situation, he told them, that is causing the government concern. Hunan University had been bombed and leveled to the ground. No other building in Changsha had been bombarded and it was plain that the objective of the attack was not the university itself but the treasures that were stored there. But they had been stored in the basement and were safe, he reassured them. He was a nervous man and he had begun to button and unbutton the coat. The second of the convoys had also been attacked. Its nine thousand cases had been hidden in a district of Chungking, but three weeks later a squadron of bombers dropped their loads systematically on the very street where the warehouses stood. Once again there was a miraculous escape and the cases were taken from Chungking to a locality whose name he could not in the circumstances disclose. He had turned, then, and pointed at the locomotive. Your own train, he said, has been bombed; at Suchow, at Chengchou, at Tungkwan. He gestured at the sky. Without doubt only darkness is now protecting you. Government, he said, is satisfied that spies are informing the Japanese of the exact position of the treasure trains. Communist spies. Such men could be anywhere. In the stations and the goods yards, in high places, even on the trains that are carrying the cases. And why, he asked, has the enemy set out to destroy our treasures?

They are not, after all, the materials of war. They have become a symbol, that is why. A symbol of the Chinese will to resist. To the Japanese those twenty thousand cases contain the spirit of a nation.

But the darkness, Tan said, only partially protected them. There were four other trains in the station and in the sidings and when the aircraft came they made patterns of carpet bombing and when they were gone three of the five trains were blazing and the track ahead was twisted and impassable. A day would be needed for its repair but it would be too dangerous to remain in the station after sunrise. The locomotive reversed and pushed the train back to Tungkwan and then on through the daylight hours toward Chengchou. It was this reversal, this retreat from a destination that might have provided safety and some respite from the wandering that plunged Sian into a deeper and more fearful silence.

An arrangement must now be made for the birth of the child. That event was perhaps four months distant. Chungking was the obvious place. There were good medical services and his sister lived there. Lailan was ten years his senior, now a distinguished botanist who had roamed the world and had given it many rare or unknown specimens, mainly of Himalayan flora. As brother and sister, Tan said softly, they were exceptionally close and in his childhood years it was she, not their mother, who had been his protector. Now, he knew, she would give her warmth and lovingkindness to Sian and the baby.

In Chengchou there was a telegraph message informing them that the track at Siking was now repaired. The train was there for twenty minutes and during that time he wrote a letter to Lailan and begged the station-master to undertake its reliable delivery. The train moved out. Paochi lay ahead.

Tan fell silent.

"You should sleep now," Lewis said.

"No."

"Try."

"I have paused," Tan said, "because I have to tell you of Sian's death. After all these years it is still painful to recall."

Lewis rose.

"I have a round to make," he said. "But I'll be back."

He spent an hour with the night Sister, at her desk and in the wards. Then he drank tea in the staff room; and then he went to the terminal patient in Room Fourteen. Sister Chu was there and he watched her moistening the old man's lips.

"In pain?" he asked.

"Yes. Very bad."

He wrote a drug prescription, increasing the dose of Diamorphine, gave it to her.

"A large dose, Doctor," she said.

"Yes."

"It may kill him."

"Probably."

He went out into the corridor. There was a time when the priest and the doctor would have been in conflict. But no longer. He did not believe in the value of life on any terms. He walked to one of the balconies and stood there breathing deeply and watched the white flowers in the gardens turn pale when the moon emerged from the traveling clouds. Perhaps Tan Haifeng was now asleep? But when he returned the light was burning and Tan put down the newspaper and said: "Where were we?"

"On the way to Paochi."

Paochi was hardly more than a village. But there were many temples, and processions of army trucks took the cases from the terminus and stacked them in the six largest and guards of soldiers raised their tents outside the temple doors. Quarters in the village were requisitioned for the palace staff and the officers. Perhaps, now, there would be a time of peace. But within the month the Japanese marched nearer. Paochi was in danger. The orders came. The treasures must be taken south to Hanchung. There were choughs in the sky when the orders were read and, watching them, he had reflected that one of these red-legged mountain birds could fly easily the eighty kilometers to the town. But that was a straight line drawn on the map. It concealed realities; the awful nature of the terrain, the landslips and the sliding screes, the primitive road, and above all the Tiensha Pass.

The pass was more than three thousand meters high. That evening there was a meeting in the stationmaster's office. All the staff attended and the superior, Professor Chiao, addressed them. He was an expert in the field of Sung and Yuan paintings and nearly five hundred of them were stored in the cases. Ahead, he told them, was a difficult and dangerous journey. He had discussed the question of transport with the senior army officer and it transpired that no more than fifty military and civilian trucks were available. He was not celebrated as a mathematician, he said in his wry and self-deprecating way, in fact barely numerate, but he had made a calculation by reference to the seven thousand cases, the number of trucks and their average capacity; and it appeared that perhaps two hundred separate loads would have to cross the pass. No time could be lost and at first light the trucks would go to the temples. After the meeting, Tan said, he had watched the professor walk from the station and down the track to where it ended and he had followed him and they had stared out across the buffers to the awesome shape of the mountain. Sian, he told Chiao, was unwell, depressed and a prey to high temperatures. She should go at once to Chungking, to the care of his sister and the hospital; and he requested the use in the morning of one of the trucks.

Chiao refused. Not a truck could be spared. Anything could happen;

bombing, bad weather, accident, mechanical failure. The trucks must negotiate the pass, unload the cases at the foot of the mountain, return for further loads. And this would continue until the temples were emptied. Only the artworks had importance. People did not matter.

The phrase simmered in his mind. People did not matter. The professor was a kindly man and had expressed what was for him a concept of his duty. Perhaps he had never loved a woman. At sunrise the operation began and the arithmetic immediately went wrong. The fifty trucks had shrunk to forty-three; and in the first week seven of those failed and were unserviceable. Some of the smaller trucks could accommodate no more than fifteen or sixteen cases. The Tiensha Pass. That place would forever haunt him. The mist fell about them in wet gray shawls. Sometimes a truck would plunge from the road and break on the scree and they would have to retrieve the cases from those perilous slopes. There were absurd encounters in which ascending and descending trucks met and were locked in unmoving columns on the narrow bends. Six weeks passed before the last of the cases crossed the mountain, and in that time the two hundred projected loads had almost doubled. Sian lay on a mattress in her room in Paochi and listened to the Japanese guns. They were near and at night she could see their flashes reflected on the sky. She had become a frail little creature, Tan said, so withdrawn that when he returned at nightfall from the pass she did not speak or turn her head. He did not tell her that Hanchung had been bombed and could not now provide a sanctuary for the treasures and that, by government order, they must be driven farther south to Chengtu.

The cases, now, were stacked at the end of the pass in the cover of trees and gullies. The professor's calculations were again compromised when the civilian trucks refused the coming journey. Paochi would surely fall and there was money to be earned from those who could afford evacuation. When the first convoy was loaded it consisted of only twenty-two army trucks. Chiao and the other professors declined another essay in arithmetic. The initial loading had made little impression on the piles and pyramids that were the seven thousand cases. How long would the journey take? Would there be sufficient food, fuel and money? Were engine parts obtainable? Could trucks be replaced? The logistics were beyond the academic mind. Plainly it was a matter for the captain of engineers. He was a man of obvious ability and he had warned them of the difficulties of the route. But the first priority was to remove all of the cases from this area of the Tiensha and to haul them with maximum effort, day and night. Otherwise the Japanese might cross the pass, there to find, conveniently stacked, an unexpected gift. At sunrise the convoy left. Snow clouds concealed the peak of Ta Pai Shan. The first flakes were falling.

Fenghsien lay eighty kilometers to the south. Sian sat in the leading truck. But the dirt road was slow and potholed and the town was not reached until dusk. Space was requisitioned for the soldiers and the staff and Sian was given a room in the market square. The captain was too wise to make predictions but he had thought it reasonable to hope that with each convoy carrying four hundred cases and achieving two return journeys in every twenty-four hours the whole of the treasures would be safe in Fenghsien within eight or nine days. But savage weather followed those first snowflakes, the worst for many years. There were hazards of ice and landslides. The cold was intense and the snowfall so heavy and unrelenting that the convoys were marooned in deserts of whiteness. Ten weeks had passed when the last truck in the last convoy unloaded in the square.

Sian was becoming weaker. From the beginning, Tan said, it had seemed to him that her fragile body with its hips that were as narrow as those of a slender boy was ill-constructed for the mysterious processes of birth. There was a small Quaker mission in the town and when the American doctor made his weekly visit he had asked him to examine her. The pregnancy, the doctor thought, was more advanced than she believed. She needed care and there was some evidence of a slight toxemia. There were no adequate facilities in Fenghsien. Chengtu would be the nearest place or, better still, Chungking.

That night he made another approach to Chiao. The professor and the captain were sitting in a hut in front of a brazier of flaring coals. They were bent across a map. He explained Sian's condition and begged for the use of a truck. Neither of them looked up and he watched their index fingers moving on the contours of the map. He repeated the request, but Chiao shook his head, stood and put on his huge fur hat and went to the door. The situation was serious, he said, and he would not detach a single truck from the convoy. He left and the captain rolled the map and slid it into its cylinder and then stared up at him. There are ways, he said. Liupa is our next destination. It is forty kilometers south and there is a military airstrip. Twice weekly a small airplane carries mail to Chungking. Sometimes a passenger can be taken. But it is forbidden to do so and a pilot would risk a heavy punishment. Therefore it is expensive. Cupidity gleamed in his eyes. Very expensive.

In the morning the convoy left Fenghsien. As always there would be a succession of trips until all the cases were in Liupa. He was now desperate, Tan said. He had made inquiries but there was no transport for hire in Fenghsien. Ahead was the terrible ice-bound terrain and the driving snow. The journey took two weeks. There had been mechanical breakdowns but because the treasures traveled under the president's seal the army base was bound to accept the trucks for repair and service. Another week passed. Sian lay in his arms at night with her hot little body shivering against him. There was a dream in which she had seen clouds of fireflies hanging like rubies in the darkness and, listening to her, he had remembered the old superstition that fireflies were the wandering souls of stillborn babies. He had put his hand on her stretched skin, feeling for that unseen life.

Su-ching entered. Lewis watched her place a carafe of water on the bedside table. Had she been listening at the door?

"Did you hear?" he asked.

"Some of it."

"Stay with us."

She arranged Tan's pillows and sat.

He had learned, Tan said, that the route to Chengtu ran through a land of wilderness and rivers and would be the worst they had yet experienced. Months might pass before the operation was complete. Sometimes he saw the mail plane leave the strip and watched with longing until it was gone from sight. He spoke again to the captain, but he had very little money and could not meet the sum demanded. The anxiety was enough to make him physically sick. One day the captain pointed at the long line of stacked cases that ran between the soldiers' tents and asked him why he could not find some small item with which to make the payment. Because, he answered, they have been entrusted to me. The captain shrugged. And so has your wife, he said. He had dismissed the suggestion. He was not a thief. But the words were there and would not leave him. One small item. Your wife. One small item. The conflict raged within him. That night there was a full moon and the skies were free of cloud and the Japanese bombers came down the Tiensha Pass to Liupa and attacked with great precision and when they were gone the snow was red and melting in the fires and the cases were scattered among the burning tents. The soldiers and the palace team worked throughout the night. Many hundreds of cases were broken and their contents spilled. He could remember one of the professors kneeling in the snow and weeping above the fragments of plates and vessels and ceramics. When the sun rose he had stood among a litter of straw and smoldering wood, rubbing snow onto his scorched hands. A point of color glowed in the slush and when he bent to it he saw that it was the edge of a rosette decoration. Was it a vase? He moved it gently. It was a fifteenth-century moon flask of the Ming period. He picked it up. One small item. He put the flask inside his coat and walked away.

Three days later he watched the mail plane rise from the strip; and although she could not see him he waved until the tiny speck was gone. Soon she would be in Chungking. Some of the anxiety had lifted with the plane. Now there was only loneliness. Three weeks were spent in the repair or replacement of the damaged cases, in repacking, in deleting from the inventories those items that had been destroyed. Beauty, he had thought with pain, transformed into a pile of shards.

The land ahead was a pattern of rivers. The season was turning and when the snow and ice were gone the rivers and their branches filled from the melting of the high snows and overflowed and joined. Sometimes it seemed that there was nothing but water; water smoking in the dawn, water gleaming as far as the horizons, water spread before the trucks in lakes and marshes. Four hundred and fifty kilometers was the distance to Chengtu. Not a great distance when measured on the map, Tan said, but the road was broken by the winter cold, at times submerged. There were rivers to ford, bridges to repair, trucks to be winched from the grip of mud. He had lost all sense of the passage of time, never registering its progression because, like that, it was easier to endure. The road crossed the Kialing River, ran down into the town of Kwangyuan. A telegraph was waiting. It was from his sister Lailan and it told him that Sian had died in childbirth but that the baby, a girl, was well.

Tan paused and looked down at the coverlet and Su-ching reached out and took his hand. In the silence they heard the distant siren of an ambulance. Sister Chu entered and beckoned and Su-ching rose and kissed Tan's cheek and followed the Sister into the corridor. They listened to the sound of their shoes and Sister Chu's reprimanding voice.

Tan looked up. Fourteen months passed, he said with disbelief, before they reached Chengtu. During that time of struggle war raked the land from the wheatfields of the north to the ricefields of the south. The Japanese took Taiyuan and advanced through Shansi. There were landings in southern waters. Canton fell. And still the treasures journeyed across the endless routes; twenty thousand cases of incalculable wealth that must forever flee, it seemed, before the invader's tanks. They had hoped that Chengtu would afford a refuge for their own caravan of seven thousand cases. But it was not to be. The city was the capital of Szechuan. There were tea-packing plants and markets for the other produce of that fertile region. But there were no buildings large enough or strong enough to house the treasures. Chiao and his council of professors decided that rest was essential, perhaps four weeks; and that throughout that period they would make excursions from Chengtu in search of a sanctuary.

He alone had found that sanctuary, Tan said. He had studied the map and a name appeared under his fingertip that evoked an immediate response. It was Omei Shan, a mountain of some three thousand meters, and it was in this region that Lailan had camped and trekked and made important voyages of discovery. She had loved the place, returning again and again, and in that moment he recalled her voice, gone soft with a kind of desire, describing how the monsoons came from the northeast across India and saturated the hills with warm rain and made them so fertile that there, in the valleys and on the hillsides, was a kingdom of flowers and shrubs and trees. Omei Shan lay 160 kilometers from Chengtu and that morning he took a truck and drove in its direction; not because there were reasons that might favor the district of Omei but because it was a link with a loved one and through her the child he had not seen.

Omei Shan was a sacred mountain and, climbing on foot to the highest of its shrines, he had felt its peace enfold him. There were many temples set in the enclosing hills, and everywhere the greenness and the drifts of color. Standing there he felt Lailan's presence. It was from here that she had brought back new species of rhododendrons, gentians and other alpines; and down there in the distant town of Omei would be the place where she had lived and worked at the propagation of seeds, roots and cuttings. He climbed higher. There were old gardens with broken columns and the ruins of marble fountains, a pair of stone lions where a monk and a novice were standing. The monk had greeted him (another pilgrim?) and talked to him for a time, then led him even higher to the lip of a precipice that was said to be the deepest in the world. He had looked down, reeling with vertigo. Sometimes, the monk said, one could see in the depths a strange and mystical light and a rainbow curved around it and this phenomenon was known as the Glory of the Buddha. Here on the mountain and in the surrounding hills, he continued, there were hundreds of monasteries and temples but the sight was so rare that only three old priests had seen it. He had paused with curiosity in his fading eyes and, Tan said, he had told him then of the works of art, the nation's heart and heritage, that lay crated in Chengtu and asked with humility if amongst all the monasteries and temples they could find a haven.

Within a month the cases had been brought to the mountain. A high proportion of the treasures were Buddhist in origin and many thousands of them had come from the lamaseries of Mongolia and Tibet; and it was perhaps for this reason that there had been so devout a response. Motor transport could negotiate no more than one-quarter of the mountain's height, and when the cases had been offloaded priests and novices and superiors came in their hundreds from all the holy buildings in the valleys and the hills and down from the crest. They would carry the treasures with no help from the soldiers, they insisted. For one month they labored day and night. It was a most wondrous sight, Tan said. During the daylight hours processions of men could be seen, crossing like insects on the grain of the mountain and vanishing into mist; and after darkness a rope of moving light hung on the slopes where the oil lanterns and the cases moved ever higher.

The monastery was built near to the summit on a rock outcrop. It was ancient with stone walls and vast halls and it was there and in four temples that the cases were stored. One of the temples stood in the shadow of an overhang and received the whole of the Imperial Library. This was of course his special charge and he was to live and work there for years to come. Tranquility dwelt on Mount Omei; but too late, it seemed, to heal his acidulated stomach. The pains always returned, usually at night, and sometimes he left the temple and walked up the path through darkness. The outer door to the monastery was always open and inside was a lighted chamber on whose walls were paintings from the Courts of Hell, depicting the punishments reserved for sinners. The Five Commands of the Buddha were inscribed on the lintel above the door and when the moonlight touched the second of them, which was *Thou shalt not steal,* he could never escape a sudden twist of guilt. Guilt was a part of the tension and somewhere in the lining of his stomach, he imagined, was a lesion in the shape of a moon flask. He had tried to justify the act. It was an act of love. It had sent her to Chungking and if it had not saved her then perhaps it had saved the child. And in any event the flask could easily have been destroyed in the bombing and would have been just as irrecoverably lost. But it was theft. He knew that. He had betrayed a trust.

A team of four men was assigned to the care of the library. It was led by a professor named Hsiao Ke. He was an acknowledged expert in the field of preservation and his first priority was to test the aeration, the temperature and the moisture content of all the halls, rooms and galleries in the temple. He was not unpleased. But when the immense collection was removed from the cases it was found that some of it had suffered damage. Much of the damage was recent and had arisen from conditions of dampness or from actual immersion on the river crossings. But this, Hsiao Ke explained, was not the only problem. He had come to Peking from the Academy of Fine Arts in Yenan and with his long black fringes and a heavy head that he swung from side to side during his addresses he had the appearance of a Mongol pony. He had held up for their inspection one of the volumes of the Ming Public Record. It was far too thick for its binding and the tightness had caused cracking to the pages. It had last been rebound in the sixteenth century, but the parchment and the leathers used were of inferior quality. The book would not close properly and the years in the cases, in which volume had been piled on volume, had accelerated the cracking. In his opinion there might be a thousand of them in need of urgent treatment and it was his decision that they must be divided and then rebound. A momentous task, he told them, for the years that stretch ahead.

The years on Mount Omei did in fact stretch ahead, Tan said. In May of 1939 there were a series of savage air raids on Chungking. The Japanese were based in Hangchow and the bombers were able to follow the moonlit waters of the Yangtze to where it joined the Kialing, there to drop their loads on the blacked-out capital. The raids continued throughout June and because he was desperate with anxiety he wrote to Lailan and implored her to leave Chungking and come with the child, Su-ching, to Omei. Needless to say, Tan said with a smile, she needed no persuasion to return to that region, which, she had once told him, she regarded as her own flowering wilderness. But there was the university contract to complete and it was not until September that she and the child arrived in Omei town; and it was on that tearful day when he had first held the child in his arms that the Second World War began in Europe.

But that distant war did not touch them for a time. The Communists continued to prey from bases in northern China. Sometimes there were fragile alliances with Chiang's armies against the common foe, the Japanese. But they never lasted; and already, as events in Europe were to prove, the Reds were planning far beyond the heat of war for future power and future conquests. In 1941 Hong Kong fell to the Japanese, and toward the end of that year the U.S.A. entered the struggle.

But in Omei there were only the winds of peace. These were the happiest years of his life. There was an intense pleasure, almost sensuous, in the work; the use of his hands and the feel of the ancient folios and the bindings that centuries had turned as dark and hard as the husks of coffee beans, the cutting of the fine new vellums that came from the skins of calves, and always the smell of age and fragrant Burmese gums. Each week he set aside a day for exercise and air and he would descend the mountain and (with the child in a wicker cradle fixed upon his back) wander with Lailan in those enchanted valleys. For her they were expeditions and he had shared in her enthusiasms. See that *amherstia*, the one with the scarlet flowers; and that yellow tree peony, more of a bush than a tree, that has traveled from Tibet; and that *davidia* with the huge white bracts that was discovered by Père Armand David; and over there the elegant *sorbus* that Père Delavay found in Yunnan. Why, she had asked him seriously, have so many priests become great botanists? Why not? he had answered. It is all the work of the Creator and perhaps, for some of them, the face of humankind has become too ugly. There were many such discussions as the child grew and crawled and, balanced between them, took her first uncertain steps. Sometimes they drove a truck to the east of the mountain where there were outcrops and the ruins of a temple. It had a gilded parasol, which signified that once in the past it had housed the relics of a saint, and it was in the crevices behind the temple that Lailan had discovered a plant that was to become the most beautiful of the Asiatic gentians.

But he too had made a discovery. From the window of his workroom on Mount Omei he could look across the wooded slopes to the hills and it was his habit to stand at the aperture in the early light and enjoy a moment or two of idleness before going to his bench. On those mornings when there was no mist it was possible to see the abandoned temple, tiny at that distance, and two of its high brown flanks. He could remember clearly that particular morning and the way in which the sun touched the parasol and made a bulb of yellow in the green. High on the flanks were the two pairs of painted eyes that, as with all such decoration, denoted the all-seeing power of the godhead; and beneath the eyes were the noses that had been painted in the shape of a question mark. None of the monks could tell him why a nose should be stylized in that fashion and he had stood there searching, as he had searched so often, for some significance. He turned.

The sun was still low and a shaft struck directly through the window and onto the shelves on the opposite wall of the workroom. The volumes on the shelves were all examples of the malpractice of the centuries and were awaiting division. In one of them there was an accumulation of gum from previous rebindings that had, he estimated, increased the spine width by at least seven centimeters. He decided that it deserved priority and he walked toward it. He stopped. It was lying flat and there was a lateral view of the edges of the folios and where the sun irradiated them he could see a difference in the coloration of the text-block, a darker band that was seen against a paler ground. It was a slender band, no wider than a finger. Was it an insertion? He took the volume to the bench, sat and opened it. The code on the undercover revealed that it had been rebound in the tenth, thirteenth and sixteenth centuries. He began to turn the folios with the ivory spatula that was always used so that there should be no contact with the fingers.

The volume contained a collection of Buddhist Canon. There were three separate texts, known as *Tripitaka*. These were the sources of all knowledge of Gotama the Buddha and his teachings. The band occupied the space between the texts of the *Vinaya-Pitaka* and the *Sutta-Pitaka,* and was clearly an insertion. There were fifteen folios, rippled by the passage of time and written, he thought, on sheepskin parchment. Now his curiosity was aroused. Inside every scholar lurked a detective. A minute spider scuttled down the parchment and because he was bound by his creed to preserve it he brushed it onto his palm, took it to the window and released it. Then he returned to the bench and began a re-examination of the volume. The ivory blade moved slowly, parting and lifting the folios; through the *Vinaya* and the rules that governed the life, behavior and duties of monks and nuns; through the *Sutta* and its sayings and special rubrics and the Word of the Buddha; and then through the *Abhidhamma* and its seven books of Metaphysics. The texts were written in the language of Pali.

He turned to the insertion. There were heavy encrustations of gum at the base of the fifteen folios. He took a scalpel and, using a magnifying glass, cut through the gum (gone crystalline with age) and then deeper into the spine until the folios were freed. Then he arranged them in three rows on the bench and leaned, glass in hand, across them. The calligraphy was indistinct, some of it obliterated by stains. At first sight the language was unfamiliar. Pali, it was thought, was an artificial language devised by scholars in an age when the art of writing was hardly in existence and had not appeared until hundreds of years after the Buddha's death. Yet here beneath the glass were the forms and characters of a primitive but recognizable Pali. He felt the stirring of excitement. He passed the glass rapidly over the folios. A phrase isolated itself. *He asked me to feed Kanthaka.* He read it again. That name. Kanthaka. The snow-white horse that was the Buddha's favorite. On the sixth folio he found another name: Isipatana. It was here in Benares that Gotama had preached the famous sermon, had begun his ministry with the doctrine of the Sacred Truth of Suffering. The words were there on the seventh folio, also the four truths that were the essence of all the Buddha's preaching. But who was the one who had fed the horse and had written this account? He found the answer on the last three folios. It was a description of the Buddha's death. He was eighty years of age and he had journeyed north with his disciples so that, already frail and ill, he might die near to the Himalaya. *At Kusinara* (the narrative continued) *the Master said to me: Ananda, place my blanket under the two sala trees with my head to the mountain snows. And the brethren of the Order were assembled and the sala flowers were falling from the trees upon his face and he held my hand and said: Ananda, hold fast to the Truth as your lamp. These were the last words of the Exalted One and he passed into Parinirvana.* The fifteenth folio concluded with the funeral rites and the burning of the body.

Now, Tan said, he could feel the clutch of an unbearable emotion. He put down the glass and walked from the workroom and through the temple and out onto the path and up the mountain to the precipice. He stood at its edge and looked down into its awful depths and began to weep, at first silently and then with abandon so that the sounds of his grief echoed in the rock buttresses and were lost in mist; tears for Ananda and the closeness of the Buddha and that voice that had spoken across the centuries; tears that he had been unable to shed at the time of Sian's death. All of it was linked and he stood there swaying on the edge until the grief was spent.

Tan brushed a knuckle across his eyes.

"Ananda," he said, "was the closest of his disciples. Do you understand, Dr. Mackenna? As close as Matthew was to your own Lord Jesus. How would you feel if you found an account in Matthew's hand of those final moments on the cross?"

"I too would weep."

He returned to the temple. He was an expert and he would behave like an expert and, now, he would approach the folios in a proper mood of skepticism. Throughout the ages scholars and archaeologists and those whose subject was rooted in the past had perpetrated frauds. But mostly the object would be money or to enlarge a reputation. Yet these writings of Ananda had never been proclaimed. There were four hundred million Buddhists in the world and for them the folios would be the most hallowed of all the relics. What a shrine they would have built! He bent again across the parchments. Could they be an academic joke? He shook his head. What profit could there be in a smile from the vaults of death?

He spent the rest of the day in making a transcription from the ancient Pali. The folios were not consecutive. There were gaps in the narrative and it became obvious that Ananda's words were only a fragment in a longer story. Time had destroyed so much. When the transcription was finished he read it slowly. It had the feel of truth. In those days the art of writing had existed but very few had practiced it. The Buddha, like Jesus, had taught the people through the spoken word, addressing them in the dialects of Kosalan and Magadhan. If he had written down the text of a sermon, which was unlikely, it had not survived. But Ananda, who was a Sakya prince and therefore a literate man, might well have decided to make a record. The excitement grew again. The text convinced him; but the parchment must be examined.

Twenty-four centuries had passed since the death of Gotama Buddha. He had seen parchments as old as that, but with most of them time and fading inks had reduced the script to an indecipherable mass. Everything depended on humidity, on degrees of light and darkness. Here on Mount Omei he had nothing but a high-power microscope to aid him; yet even in Peking there had been no techniques that would accurately date a parchment. There were only areas of time, several centuries that lay above and below a line. Somewhere in that band a parchment might have its origin. But that was often as near as one could get. In such cases a comparison might be made with parchments whose authenticity was proved and, then, the fakes and the wrong attributions were easily recognized. But within the band? That was difficult. He decided to examine microscopically the inserted folios side by side with the texts that had enclosed them.

To this end he took the scalpel and cut slivers from each of the fifteen folios, and similar slivers from the texts. The evening sun was low and rain was falling when the work was finished. His eyes were blurred with the effort of peering through the lenses at textures and stainings and ink penetrations. But without doubt the folios were some centuries older than the other parchments. A tremor had entered his fingers and the tears were near again. He left the temple and walked up the path to the precipice and stood there with the rain on his face. An old professor had once told him that there was something in every man more valuable than knowledge: and that was instinct. Do not bury it, he had said. Follow it and believe it. He heard the voice quite clearly. I believe it. I believe what it is telling me. Standing there on Omei Shan, that point in sacred space, he felt the silence of it, so deep that it was like a presence at his elbow, saw below him in the mist a light no bigger than a candle flame and the light grow until the void was filled with a luminous pink that became ever more brilliant and the rainbow making an arc across the globe of pink and the color of it all reflected on his hands and on the rock walls. Then it was gone and there was only mist. He turned. He had seen the Glory of the Buddha. It had shone for him. It was as if the light had touched and sanctified Ananda's script.

His immediate reaction, Tan said, was to run to the monastery and bring to the monks the news of the great discovery. He could imagine their joy, their wonder. Soon the valleys would ring with bells, and then beyond the valleys to other temples in other lands. The pilgrims would come in endless procession and Omei Shan, already one of China's sacred mountains, would become the most famous shrine of all. But he did not run with the tidings. Instead he returned to the workroom and stood at the window and watched the rain clouds unfurl across the hills. He was one of the custodians of the Imperial Library and, although an expert in his own right and a man of some repute, he was not a professor and was junior to men like Hsiao Ke. It was his duty to report the discovery to Hsiao. He left the window and sat at the bench and stared at the folios. And it was then, Tan confessed, that the first of the ignoble thoughts began to stir within him. Hsiao was an arrogant and ambitious man. He had the ultimate responsibility for the collection and the teams at work on it. Inevitably he would claim the credit. His name would emerge from the academic shadows. There would be honors, lectures, published papers. What would Hsiao call the manuscript? The Ananda Folios? The Ananda Fragment? The latter had the better ring.

In the morning he went to the refectory and ate his fruit and drank his tea. Hsiao entered and sat across from him. This was the moment when he should have confided the amazing news. Indeed the words leaped to his tongue. But he did not speak and the moment passed; and when Hsiao stood and walked away, strutting with conceit, he felt a sudden satisfaction. It was his secret. He would keep it for a time.

He worked for five days on Ananda's script, using the original binding and reducing the spine width so that it would fit the fifteen folios. Then he rebound the texts of the *Tripitaka* and placed both volumes, the slender and the thick, on the shelf. He decided to check the catalogue but, as he expected, there was no reference to the insertion or even to parchments of unproven source. Who had made the insertion? And when? He sat smiling at the volume. There was a delicious pleasure in his secret knowledge. He felt an affinity with that man who, centuries ago, had preferred a secret to a revelation. He understood him.

There would be many secret smiles in the years ahead. The world war ended and with the defeat of the Japanese in September of 1945 and the American forces gone from China the Ananda Fragment (as he liked to call it) still sat anonymously among the hundreds of rebound volumes that had grown to fill the shelves. Omei was still a place of peace; but beyond it the civil war had flared again. The Nationalist forces of Chiang Kai-shek could not hope to resist the Communists without the American combat troops. In March of 1947 Chiang suffered a major defeat at Yenan, and it was at that time that the first tentative plan was made for a withdrawal from the mainland to Taiwan. This would involve the transfer of the best units of the armed forces, the officer corps, the gold reserves and, of course, the treasures. The tranquil years on Omei Shan were over. Now began the task of returning the Imperial Library to the cases. Elsewhere in that land of turmoil where the old regime was dying other teams in other havens were recrating for the journey. When the work was done and the order came some twenty thousand cases would move down the Yangtze and through Shanghai and across the Formosa Strait.

Lailan and Su-ching returned to Chungking. What kind of future would they have? Lailan was no longer young. These were times of danger and uncertain future. The separation was cruel; and perhaps it was his fear for them and his loneliness that brought again the familiar tension so that once more he left his bed and walked in darkness up the path to the monastery and felt the pain gnaw within his stomach.

A year passed. The alpine flowers of the early months were coloring the slopes when the cases were brought down the mountain to Omei town. During that year there had been, on the order of the government, a process of evaluation and the works of art had been graded so that in the event of an emergency the rarest and the finest could be saved. The cases containing them (about one-quarter of the total) each bore a mark of recognition, which was a stenciled red peacock. There was a heavy mist when the column of motor transport and its cargo, soldiers and palace staff began the move across country to Ipin and the big river. He looked back once and the monastery on the mountain gleamed momentarily where the mist had parted and then was gone.

A flotilla of small boats carried the cases down the Yangtze to Nanking. Sometimes from the breast of the river they could see the gunflash that came from the artillery in the hills. The war was near and when the river began to broaden naval ships came to act as escort. In Nanking the cases were stored in the Confucius Temple and its new extension. The city, now, was in the grip of the winter cold. It was a time of waiting. Victory for the Reds was certain and already Suchow, only three hundred kilometers north of Nanking, had fallen. Three months later the People's Liberation Army entered Tientsin and then, within weeks, Peking. Nearly sixteen years had passed, Tan said, since that night when he and Sian and the treasures had left the capital. Sixteen years. How unbelievable that was. But now there were choices to be made.

Spring came. Chiang Kai-shek had resigned the office of president and was now in Chungking. But the Kuomintang was still in power and Chiang's puppet, the vice-president Li Tsung-jen, remained locked in negotiation with the Communists. From Chungking the Generalissimo was implementing the plans for the transfer of military strength and the nation's wealth. Already a half a million men had crossed the Strait to the island of Taiwan, taking with them all the arsenals of war and every ounce of gold and silver bullion that had lain in the vaults of the Central Bank. The great exodus would continue until Taiwan became a fortress. We will return; this was the new battle hymn, and Mao and Chou En-lai would themselves be driven to the sea.

At the beginning of April 1949 Hsiao Ke called a meeting of the palace staff. Thirty-three scholars assembled in a room in the temple. Hsiao held no overall authority, except in matters of the Imperial Library; yet they had obeyed without question and when he entered and stood there staring at them with his arrogant chin thrust out they saw that authority now in fact clothed him like a new garment. He was accompanied by a little man in a worn gray suit and he too stared in that imperious way and his finger went to the small red star that was fixed on his lapel. They sat and the room was silent and Hsiao took a similar red star from his pocket and pinned it on his suit. Yes, he told them, this is the sign of my belief and my allegiance and my companion is or soon will be the chief political commissar for this district. Every man in this room must take one of two paths. He may remain in China and work for the reborn nation and the new People's Republic; or he may follow Chiang and the Kuomintang to Taiwan. He had turned then to the man at his side and the commissar stood. You, he said to them, were the guardians of our treasures. You saved them from the Japanese. Here and now you are men of distinguished service and will be honored as such. The nation's gold has already been shipped and soon the treasures too will have left these shores. He paused and his face became cold and dangerous. Theft on such a scale amounts to treason. He pointed a finger at them. I have the name of every one of you. And I tell you this. Follow the treasures to Taiwan and you become your country's enemies. You become accomplices. So the choice is clear. Stay here and help us rebuild. Go and be listed as traitors. He drew a finger across his throat. And for that the punishment is death.

The commissar sat. The room was silent. The stomach pains, Tan said, had begun to throb. This threat, he thought with a growing outrage, was the reward for the sixteen lost years, the ulcers, the bereavement. He stood. At the Imperial Library, he said, he had lived close to the pages of the nation's history. It was a feudal past and he had smelled on those pages the cruelty, the starvation and the poverty. The emperors had absolute power. Many were tyrants. But some gave law and ceremony and exquisite art. The scholars, now, were looking down at their hands, listening to his reckless tongue. But what will you give? he asked the commissar. You claim you will feed and clothe the peasants, give them title to the land they plough, banish the old oppressions. But will you? He shook his head. They will own no land. The State will be their landlord. They will exchange one oppressor for another, palaces for prison camps. You, he said with contempt, have shown us the face of the new China.

He sat and the commissar stood and stared at him. He felt in that moment, as from a heat, the man's smoldering Marxist mind. Hsiao whispered something and the commissar put a hand in his pocket and produced a square of folded fabric. He unfolded it and they saw that it was a miniature flag. The commissar stroked it. This, he told them, was the first five-star flag of the People's Republic of China. Hsiao stood and bowed his head. Now scholars were rising from their seats like men hearing the notes of a national anthem. Eight remained in their chairs. The commissar handed the flag to Hsiao and made a gesture at the table and the flag began to pass from man to man and each man, other than the eight, touched it to show acceptance. When the flag reached him, Tan said, he stood, threw it on the floor and left the room.

Now he was in danger. Soon the Communists must take formal power. Four naval ships had been allotted for the transfer to Taiwan of the remaining army units and the treasures. But there was no room on the ships for the twenty thousand cases, not even for all of the cases that bore the stencil of the red peacock. Twelve hundred cases had been filled with the best of the antiquities from Nanking's museums and libraries and these were loaded for the voyage together with three thousand from the Temple. Only three thousand, Tan said sadly, out of the original twenty thousand that they had brought out of Peking. But soon he and the eight scholars would sail to freedom. Or so he had planned.

Never make plans, Tan said. Speech had tired him and he drank some water and sank deeper into his pillows. He could remember pain, a hemorrhage, an awakening, the face of a nurse and, later, the smiling lips of Dr. Kao. We will talk in the morning. The next afternoon Dr. Kao sat on his bed and told him he had suffered a partial gastrectomy, that he was fortunate and that if the ulcers had been more generally distributed he would have lost the whole of his stomach. That would have been disabling but there was still sufficient to accommodate a modest meal. But not yet. There would be a week without food or water.

During that week of initial recovery he and the doctor formed a mutual affection. Kao was a man with the heart (if not the knowledge) of an antiquarian. They talked often of the treasures, of the fate of the seventeen thousand cases that must remain in Nanking. He had heard, Kao said, that they would be returned to Peking. In the second week he had carried his drainage bottle to the window. It was evening and he watched the last four ships of Chiang's fleet move out on the river. He should have been on one of those ships and because of his weakened state he wept like an abandoned child. He stood at the window until the ships were distant. Turning he heard in the corridor the voices of the commissar and Dr. Kao. The commissar's voice seemed sharp with menace. Kao entered and came to the window. He wants you, Kao told him, and he will take you as soon as the city falls and power is vested in him. But he was not without influence and arrangements would be made.

In the following week the tubes and the stitches were removed and on the twenty-third day of April Dr. Kao told him that he must dress and go immediately to the rear of the building where a rickshaw would be waiting. Documents would be prepared and signed that would explain his absence. He remembered the date clearly because this was the day when the Communists entered Nanking. Traveling in the rickshaw through the city toward the docks he saw the Red soldiers standing in a line on the roof of the presidential palace. Two hours later he was in the stern quarters of a German freighter. Downriver was Chungking.

Tan slept.

"He talks too much," Su-ching said.

"Is he lonely?"

"Yes."

Lewis switched off the lamp. She came to his side and he felt her hand slide against his palm and press. Anna Chang's voice sounded in his mind. There's a Western phrase for it. She has a crush.

"He was on the boat to Chungking," he said.

"The boat?"

"When he fell asleep. The escape from Nanking."

"That was five years ago."

He disengaged his hand.

"How long in Chungking?" he asked.

"A few weeks."

"The three of you?"

"Yes. We were together again. But it could not last. It was too dangerous. There is no worse crime than to oppose them."

"Another escape?"

"Yes."

"To Taiwan?"

"No. That was much later."

"Where, then?"

"Portuguese Macao."

"Why Macao?"

"It was arranged with the German boat. After Chungking she was due to return upriver to Shanghai and then to trade on the eastern coast. That would take a month and bring her down to Canton. And from there she would sail to Macao. When the time came we took the train from Chungking to Canton. Soon we were in Macao."

"We?"

"Me and my father. Aunt Lailan could not go. She had her university work, plans for another expedition. One day she would join us. But it was not to be. The Reds closed the ports and the frontiers. It became a prison. Nobody could get out."

"Is she still in Chungking?"

"No. She works in Amoy. But we want her here, Doctor. It is our dearest wish. And hers too."

In the doorway she turned to him.

"Is he very ill?"

"Can't say yet. There is still the stomach X-ray."

*   *   *

In the evening of the following day Lewis Mackenna went to Tan's room, sat by the bed and placed on the covers a report and an X-ray plate. Tan stared down at it with anxiety.

"Bad news?" he asked.

"No."

Lewis picked up the plate and traced its detail with his finger.

"I can find nothing nasty," he said.

"Good."

"But the barium, you understand, is not infallible. It may not reveal the smaller lesions."

He held the plate to the light. What did the pains signify? Indirect signs? Somewhere, perhaps, were the small mucous erosions and tiny slitlike ulcers that would not hold sufficient barium to make a visible projection.

"What do you suspect?" Tan asked.

"Nothing."

"And the pains?"

"I don't know. Pain is a warning. But is is also one of the mysteries. It can be a referral."

"A referral?"

"Yes. It originates in one place but is referred to another."

"Confusing."

"Yes."

"And the blackouts?"

"I have written down a diagnosis," Lewis said.

He reversed the report and Tan bent across it.

"Hypoglycemia," he read aloud.

"Do you know what that is?" Lewis asked.

"To do with the blood?"

"Yes. A sudden loss of sugar content."

"There is a question mark against it."

"Because I can't be certain. To be certain I would need to take a blood test at the precise time of the attack. So there is no clinical proof. But it all suggests hypoglycemia."

"Is there a cure?"

"A treatment. A daily dose of glucose."

"Is that all?"

"Yes."

Tan returned the report.

"I am relieved," he said.

Lewis stood.

"Go home, Mr. Tan," he said. "And see me in a week."

Later he walked with him through the gardens. Tan stopped and held out a hand.

"I am grateful, Dr. Mackenna."

"Next week, then."

Tan picked up his case.

"Such a pleasure to know you," he said. Then, shyly: "We do get on so very well, don't we?"

"We do, Mr. Tan."

Lewis watched his frail figure move through the shadows of the oleanders and out through the gateway. A hand waved. Then he was gone.

PART THREE

Return

Chapter 13

The deerstalker arrived from Edinburgh on the day of his appointment with Tan Haifeng. He wore it on the route to Kodaki's Hospital. There was always a fine variety of headgear on the streets of Taipei and, among the turbans and fezzes, the birettas and cowls, the coolie straws and the seamen's caps, a tweed hat with a brim back and front did not attract attention.

Tan was awaiting him. He had kept well, he reported, and there had been no further attacks. He had sprinkled the glucose on a morning dish of bran, thereby achieving in one operation an intake of sugar and a high-fiber diet.

"That was intelligent," Lewis said.

Tan bowed.

"See me in a month, Mr. Tan."

But Tan did not rise.

"Is there something else?"

"Yes, Dr. Mackenna. But not here, please. It is private."

"At noon," Lewis said. "In the gardens."

At fifteen minutes after twelve Tan came down the path toward the hibiscus hedge and sat beside him. He seemed embarrassed and he stared across his locked fingers at the flank of the hospital.

"Tell me," Lewis said kindly.

"It is about my sister."

"Lailan?"

"Yes. We want her here with us. I think Su-ching has told you that."

"Yes."

"She was a mother to Su-ching, a beloved sister to me."

"I know."

"We should be together. The three of us."

"Has she applied to leave?"

"Again and again. But always they refuse. In their eyes she is the sister of a thief and a traitor. They will keep her there forever."

"I am truly sorry."

"There is an infrequent letter. Routed through Hong Kong or brought on a foreign ship. But that is all. She is growing older. And she has arthritis in her hands."

"But she works?"

"Yes. At Amoy University. A professorship. She is the very best in her field, you understand?" Tan smiled. "She tells me in a recent letter that they have in the grounds a famous roller."

"A roller?"

"Yes. It was once used by the English to roll the green for their game of cricket."

Lewis laughed.

"Dr. Mackenna," Tan said seriously, "I have to get her here."

"But how?"

Tan looked away again.

"Forgive me," he said, "but I have to ask."

"Then ask."

"Your personal story is well known, Doctor. You were a missionary, and you and your family escaped from the mainland."

Lewis nodded.

"I hesitate to probe," Tan said. "These affairs are by their nature secret. I know that." His fingers, locked again, began to work. "But perhaps you can help."

"I doubt it."

"You yourself received some help."

"Yes."

"Then help Lailan."

Lewis shook his head.

"You must have come by sea."

"Must I?"

"Of course."

"I wish you would stop wriggling, Mr. Tan."

"It's because I'm nervous. I hate to raise these matters."

"Then don't."

"There is no one else to ask."

"I cannot answer."

"Some person, some organization," Tan said desperately. "A little information."

"No."

"Please."

"I cannot answer." Lewis stood. "How could I? You might be a Red agent, Mr. Tan."

Tan pulled at his mustache, began to twist the whiskers into a single strand.

"Well, yes," he said, "I suppose I could be." He laughed at the absurdity of it. "I should not have disturbed your quiet hour."

"It is nothing."

"I will go now." He rose. A stalk of fallen tree-blossom lay on the path and he bent and picked it up and placed it in the foliage of the hedge so that it should still display its beauty. "I will go." Then, earnestly: "If, perchance, you should meet some party on this island, some party with the power to help, I beg you to mention my name." He walked away, then stopped and smiled.

"If only in a whisper," he said.

He had no intention of mentioning Tan's name, not even in a whisper. But three days later he saw in the inner shadows of Mandy's Bar a man in an unbuttoned white shirt with a gold crucifix hanging from a chain into a thicket of black chest hair. He went to the table and sat and Jethro ordered beer and when Joe Mandy had brought the tray they drank and he could see behind Jethro's profile the wall and the eight oil paintings that had come from Ellen's brush.

"How are you, Frank?" he asked.

"Fine."

"And your sweetheart?"

"You mean *Justine?*"

"Of course."

"She's getting old. The *teredo* is eating at her timbers. The engine is terminal. And the sailcloth is rotting."

"Seaworthy?"

"Just."

Lewis removed the deerstalker.

"A nice hat," Jethro said.

"Do you know what it is?"

"A deerstalker. A cloth cap with two peaks that is bought by the tourists in Scotland."

"How did you know?"

"Ellen told me."

"When?"

Jethro smiled and his eyes went briefly to the paintings; as if, Lewis thought, their sensuality was linked in some way to the question.

"Why did you ask about the boat?" Jethro said.

"I have a patient. His sister lives in Amoy. They are very close and he wants her here."

"Is she in danger?"

"No."

"So it would not be a rescue?"

"Not in that sense."

Jethro swirled the beer within his glass, stared down into the bubbles. "Lewis," he said seriously, "I hope you did not give him my name."

"Of course not."

"Did he approach you?"

"Yes."

"Why?"

"He'd heard of my escape. But that's not suspicious. Many people know."

"What is his name?"

"Tan Haifeng."

"Does he have money?"

"I doubt it."

"Then he has no chance. It is now a highly dangerous trade. So big risk, big money." Jethro shook his head. "I myself would not take that risk, Lewis. This is a nice island. I have the boat and the sea and a bishop who forgives me my indiscretions. I have freedom. And certainly I would not risk my neck so that a brother might be joined with his sister." He stood. "Tell your patient there are men on this island who will make the crossing. But it will cost him a lot of money."

"A lot of money," Su-ching repeated.

"Yes."

"But my father is poor."

"And your aunt?"

"Aunt Lailan has her work. But that is all. There are no big salaries on the mainland, Doctor."

"I know that."

He saw the tears spring to her eyes.

"I am sorry, Su-ching," he said. "Please tell your father."

That evening he went to the house in Mongolia Avenue for a poetry reading. It was a short poem with a final stanza of great passion. Usually there would be an interlude for tea or whiskey and then a second poem that was read more slowly. But on this occasion Anna Chang must report at Kodaki's for an eight o'clock duty and there was insufficient time for the slower reading or even for the whiskey. "Walk with me," she said. He went with her to the hospital entrance and then returned through the alleys of Crooked Pond and emerged where the flank wall of the hospice led onto the square. He had not eaten since noon and he crossed to the Teagarden Bar and sat at a sidewalk table and ordered a plate of yellow croaker fish. When he had finished he drank coffee and an Armagnac and watched the people and the traffic. A figure was standing in the shadow beyond the light of the hospice lamp. Was it William Maggs? The figure

moved forward and he saw that it was Tan Haifeng. Tan crossed and came
to the table and stood above him.

"Once again," he said, "I disturb your quiet hour."

"Yes, you do."

"I am very sorry."

"Are you ill, Mr. Tan?"

"No."

"Then we have nothing to discuss."

Tan did not move.

"Nothing," Lewis repeated.

"Su-ching gave me your message," Tan said. "But we have very little
money."

"A pity."

"But there is an asset."

"An asset?"

"Yes. A valuable asset."

"Then sell it."

"I cannot do that."

"Why not?"

"Because it is not in my possession. It is in mainland China."

"That is your problem, not mine."

"May I sit, Doctor?"

"If you have to."

Tan sat.

"I am very sorry," he said again.

"Would you like an Armagnac?"

"No."

Tan produced an envelope from his pocket.

"A letter," he said. "From Lailan."

"Is she well?"

"The arthritis is bad."

"And will remain so."

"Yes. Her fingers are as knobbled as an old oak."

Tan took the letter from the envelope and pushed it across the table.

"I have no wish to read a private letter," Lewis said.

"The final words. Please read them."

Lewis turned to the last of the four pages, held it into the lamplight.
The characters revealed an artistry that could come only from Lailan's
generation. He read the concluding words. *The old tortoise is safe and in
good condition.* He returned the letter.

"I am so pleased about the animal," he said.

"It is a code."

"A code?"

"A secret code."

"Most codes are. Isn't there a tortoise?"

"No. But if it existed its name would be Ananda."

"Like the Buddha's white horse?"

"That was Kanthaka."

"Yes, of course. I remember. What does the code mean, Mr. Tan?"

Tan looked down at his hands.

"I feel ashamed," he said.

"Why?"

"I am guilty of deceit. We have a good relationship, Dr. Mackenna. I respect you. Yet I have deceived you. I told you the story of the antiquities. And every word was true. But I omitted something."

"Something you did?"

"Yes. Do you recall that point in the story when the Japanese bombed Liupa and I stole the Ming moon flask?"

"I do."

"That was the first act of theft. I regret to say there was a second." Now his feet were shuffling nervously beneath the table. "Do you recall also when I threw the Communist flag to the floor?"

"Yes."

"I left the room. I actually wept with anger. After all my years of service I was now an outcast, a man marked for punishment. I had chosen freedom in Taiwan but I could not read the future. I had a moral right to protect myself and my child, to make provision. In the morning I went back to the Confucius Temple and into the extension halls where the cases awaited shipment. I was of course well known to the guards. This was like any other working day and some of the scholars and a group of naval officers were checking manifests. Many of the cases were not yet sealed and indeed the final selection was still not complete. My numbered inventories revealed that case 357 was located in the annex to the rear exhibition hall. I walked through to the annex. The case was accessible and I lifted the lid and took out the Ananda Fragment and put it among the documents inside my pigskin bag. At the entrance I stopped and exchanged a few pleasantries with the guards. Then I left." Distress touched his eyes. "When a man is trusted how easy it is to steal." He was silent for a time. "An hour later I collapsed in the street and was taken to the hospital. And when I emerged from the anesthetic I found they had put the bag together with my clothes inside the closet." Tan smiled. "During my time of recovery I often stared from my bed at that closet door and reflected that behind it was the world's most valuable manuscript. It became a private joke. Later in Chungking I delivered it into Lailan's keeping. And to this day it is with her in Amoy. It has become a tortoise and that is how she refers to it when she writes to reassure me."

Tan licked his lips.

"Speech exhausts me," he said.

"Some tea?"

"Please."

Lewis ordered; and when the tray was brought and the tea poured Tan held the cup in both hands and sipped and kept the cup at his mouth so that the long whiskers hung down across his fingers.

"Are you shocked?" he asked.

"No."

"Not even as a minister?"

"I am not a minister. And I am never shocked by human nature."

"It was theft."

"You could always return it."

"I have thought of that. Many times. It would ease my conscience. But there are always the sixteen wasted years. Health and career both gone. Someone should pay."

"What is it worth?"

Tan shrugged.

"Have you no idea?"

"No."

"A million American dollars?"

"Who can say?" Tan said. "It is a unique object. There is no precedent."

"There is also no provenance."

"True. But that is an advantage. Its existence was never recorded. It has no history of ownership. My right could not be challenged."

"And if it were?"

"I would say that I discovered it in a bookshop."

Lewis smiled.

"You are becoming a scoundrel, Mr. Tan."

Tan laughed and some of the whiskers fell inside the cup. He pressed out the globules of tea between thumb and forefinger, then smoothed the whiskers down his jowls.

"Its value," he said seriously, "will be whatever the market offers."

"It would have to be an international market."

"Yes."

"Or a very rich collector."

"Yes."

"Auction would test the market. New York or London or Hong Kong."

"First things first," Tan said. "I have to get Lailan and the manuscript out of Red China. But how? That is my awful problem. How?"

"How would he make payment?" Jethro asked. "That's the question." He stood outlined against the vestry window. Behind him and above the harbor Lewis could see the swiftwing flights of seabirds. Jethro removed his cassock and hung it from a peg. "He can't sell the manuscript on the mainland. And if he could make a secret sale he couldn't get the money out. As I told you there are men here who will make the crossing. And there are men on Quemoy and the offshore islands who are prepared to take that chance. But always for big money and always for a substantial payment in advance. I never took money for getting people out, Lewis. And I'm proud of that. But these other men are different, not much better than pirates. You cannot go to that kind of man and ask him to speculate. Because that's what it is, isn't it? Speculation. He would have to bring out the woman and the manuscript. He would not touch money until it was sold. He would have to trust your Mr. Tan. He would have to believe that the manuscript was genuine and would fetch this incredible price." He pulled on a fisherman's jersey. "Where would you find such a man?"

"Here."

"Here?"

"Yes, Frank. You."

"I told you. I would not accept the risk."

"You could meet Tan and strike a bargain."

"No."

Jethro moved to the door.

"Would you like to come fishing, Lewis?"

"No. I am on duty at four."

Lewis stood.

"Do you trust this Tan?" Jethro asked.

"I do."

"Why?"

"Why trust any man? It is instinct. I like him. He came to me as a patient. His daughter is a nurse at the hospital. Yes, I trust him."

Jethro went to his desk.

"Will you reconsider?" Lewis asked.

"No."

"It would buy a refit for *Justine.*"

Jethro wrote on a slip of paper and gave it to him.

"Go to this man at this address," he said. "He might help. But I doubt it."

The address was in Chilung, which was the seaport to Taipei. It was a tourist agency and from the window Lewis could see the distant statue of Kuan Yin, Goddess of Mercy, that was built on the hill that stood above the harbor. Rain began and the statue blurred.

"This city," Wauters said, "is one of the wettest in the world." He was a Belgian with a malarial face and fingers that were ridged with thick white callus. He listened to the drumming on the panes. Then: "I must ask you to be discreet, Doctor. Avoid names. I have heard from a certain party who, like Saint Peter, is a fisherman. He has told me of your business. But perhaps you should tell me again."

Lewis told him; and when he had finished the rainstorm had passed and the goddess on the hilltop and her black marble pedestal were glistening in sun.

"I am merely an intermediary," Wauters said. "I do not own boats. I receive a commission and those who make these voyages accept my judgment in each situation and if I am satisfied I make an arrangement. In this case I regret I am unable to do that. You must understand that the crossings have become more difficult, more dangerous. The Americans are continually overflying the mainland, dropping agents, bringing them back, making aerial film. All this is common knowledge. American money and all the weapons of war are flooding into Taiwan in support of an invasion that I, personally, believe will never happen." He was a man who liked to talk with his hands and they had begun to gesticulate against a backdrop of tour posters, the ugly fingers rising and diving across the colors of the Coral Lake, the Sea of Clouds at Alishan, the Yehliu Rocks, Sunrise at Pilu and Snow on Mount Hohuan. "The eastern coast is in a state of siege and only the rich can afford escape. Perhaps your friend is rich. But his riches are in Amoy, not here. Sometimes, in special cases, we will assist a party who will carry jewelry. Each of the boat captains can recognize a genuine stone and with such arrangements the jewelry can be sold in Taiwan and our fee recovered from the proceeds." The fingers spread across the peak of the Jade Mountain. "But emeralds and diamonds in the hand are a different proposition to a manuscript. Very different. Who can estimate its worth? Who can say it is not a fake?" Wauters shook his head. "I have to decline."

He stood and went with Lewis to the door and out onto the sidewalk. The outline of the goddess was sharp on a sullen sky.

"It's going to rain again," Wauters said. He held out his calluses into the first of the drops. "I respect you, Doctor. So let me give you a warning. The penalties on the mainland for assisting the escape of fugitives are very severe. The shores are alive with soldiers. There are patrol boats on the seas. The crews of our own small craft are in considerable danger. They have to protect themselves and it is sometimes necessary to use certain measures."

"Measures?"

"Drastic measures."

The downpour came and they moved back into the protection of the eaves.

"There is a rule," Wauters said. "It is inflexible. It applies if capture seems certain. The fugitive is the evidence of crime. Therefore the evidence will not be found."

Lewis saw the distress in his eyes.

"What are you saying?" he asked.

"I know it's terrible," Wauters said unhappily. "It is something that is never discussed. But that is what happens."

"You mean overboard?"

"Yes."

"Surely not?"

"That is the rule. We make this clear to the party before the contract is agreed. Most accept. Some do not."

Wauters returned to his desk, picked up a tour leaflet and wrote on its margin.

"As I told you," he said, "I must decline. But I have written down the particulars of two boat owners. One is based on Penghu Island. The other is at Kaohsiung. Who knows? You might be lucky."

"The same rule?"

"Yes. The same harsh rule."

Wauters pointed at the leaflet.

"In fact," he said, "there's a nice tour to Penghu. I could arrange it for you."

"I might get thrown overboard."

Wauters laughed and took him to the door. The rain was easing.

"What is your interest in this, Doctor?"

"My interest?"

"Yes. You are going to a lot of trouble."

"No trouble."

"All for a patient's sister?"

Driving north to Yehliu Park, through Chinsan (which was the Golden Mountain) and then toward Tamsui the questions occupied his mind. What is your interest? And then the faint accent of cynicism. All for a patient's sister? They required an answer. The tea chests, as usual, were clearly visible. He was on the road to Tamsui, drawn there because the junk *Shantung* might be moored at the jetty. But now another object had joined the lost collection. He could see its shape juxtaposed to the two Long Jing chests, hear the crackle of its fifteen sheepskin parchments.

At the port he walked past the fish market and parallel to the wharves and on to the village, then returned. There were three working junks among the sampans and tourist boats, but no *Shantung*. He went to the bar that was opposite to the longest of the jetties and sat under the palm thatch and ordered a Golden Beer and when he had drunk it he crossed the road and walked to the end of the jetty and stared out through the heat shimmers to the horizon. The Ananda Fragment. It lay secreted in a flat or a house in Amoy in the custody of an elderly woman and it was the rarest manuscript (or tortoise) in the world and if and when Lailan died there would be no next of kin to collect her possessions and all of them, including the manuscript, would pass into the grasp of the State receiver. The very thought of it offended.

Tan shook his head in rejection. "Dr. Mackenna," he said, "I would not consider it. Throw her overboard? I can hardly believe it." He began to pace and turn in the confines of the tiny room, navigating paths between the screens of painted paper and the cushions that were arranged in patterns on the floor. The bedroom door was open and Lewis could see a low pallet bed with a spring that sagged and almost touched the boards. "How could I place her in such danger? I would rather forget the matter. Better to leave her where she is. At least she is safe. She has her work and she has a roof." Anger vibrated in his voice. "What kind of men are these?"

"Hard men."

Tan poured tea and gave him a cup. Then he sat on the cushions and stared up like a small wizened idol. He folded his hands on his chest and began to rock.

"Be calm," Lewis said. "These men would not believe in the value of the manuscript. So it will not arise."

"No."

Lewis sipped the tea and looked around him.

"I regret the poverty of my home," Tan said. "I have some translation work. But it is not well paid. Perhaps when the new museum is built they will give me an appointment."

"I'm sure they will."

"They owe me that."

"They do indeed."

Lewis rose and went to the window. The two-story houses leaned across a narrow alley and were joined by overhead lines of washing. He could see through the opposite window into a decaying room with a brick bed. A cart containing drums of night soil moved down the alley and human waves pressed around it, going with the dripping cart like mourners with a hearse.

"You deserve a better place, Mr. Tan," he said.

"One day."

"There won't be a one day unless you get that manuscript."

"Then so be it."

"Lailan is growing old."

"I know that."

"She may die. Have you thought of that?"

"Of course. And I want her here. Now. Isn't that what we're talking about?"

"Yes. But if she dies on the mainland the State will take her assets. Isn't that so?"

"Yes."

"Including the manuscript."

Tan was silent. Lewis turned from the window.

"An awful thought," Tan said.

"Yes, awful."

"I will not place her in danger, Doctor."

"Of course not."

"Then there is nothing I can do. Your friend refused."

"He's not my friend."

"He got you out, did he not?"

"Yes."

"Did you pay him?"

"No."

"I call that friendly. Can he be trusted?"

Lewis smiled.

"Not with a woman," he said.

"Would he throw one into the sea?"

"Not if she were young and beautiful."

Tan laughed. The whiskers sprang like wire.

"We are joking," he said. "And in any event Lailan is neither young nor beautiful. So would he defend her?"

"I cannot say."

"Would he steal a priceless script?"

"I cannot say. I doubt it."

"But he has this weakness?"

"Yes."

Tan closed his eyes and began to rock again.

"I am trying to assess his character," he said. "If I could meet him?"

"He wouldn't agree."

"He might."

Tan rose from the cushions and took the teacups to a basin and poured water from a ewer.

"He has this weakness," he said without turning. "Would he steal another man's wife?"

"If he wanted her."

"A man who could steal a wife could steal a valuable."

"I don't think that follows, Mr. Tan."

"Perhaps not."

"And it doesn't arise. He will not make the trip."

Tan turned from the basin, began to rub with a rag at the cups.

"Does he work?"

"Yes."

"As a boatman?"

"No."

"What as?"

"I can't disclose that."

"Honorable work?"

"Some think so."

"Why do you smile, Doctor?"

Lewis did not answer. Tan hung the cups on wall hooks. Plaster fell. He returned to the cushions.

"Let me give you my thoughts," he said. "I will not risk Lailan with any of these crews. I told you that. But I want her here and I want that manuscript. This man with the boat is not your friend and you cannot guarantee him. But he brought you and your family out of China. That took courage. He did this without payment. Evidently he is a man of quality. I believe I would entrust him with my sister and the script. He says he will no longer take these risks." Tan shrugged. "That is what he says. But a man who can be tempted by women can be tempted by wealth."

"What is wealth, Mr. Tan?"

"A share in the proceeds."

"Such as?"

"One-half."

"One-third?" Jethro repeated.

"Yes," Lewis said. "One-third for you. One-third for Tan. And one-third for me."

"Why you?"

"A matter of risk."

"Risk? As a go-between?"

"As a hand."

"You mean on board?"

"Yes."

"I work alone, Lewis."

"Not this time. Tan wants someone he can trust. He doesn't know you. But he does know me."

"You'd actually go back?"

"For one-third, yes."

"But a third of what? That's the question."

Jethro stood. He was wearing dungarees.

"I have some painting to finish," he said.

"The boat?"

"Yes. Walk down with me."

Walking through the shadow of the spire and out into sun Jethro pointed up at it.

"Dutch," he said. "The oldest Christian churches on the island are Dutch."

They crossed the road to the quay. Boys were fishing from the break-water. Jethro stopped.

"The answer is no," he said.

"Think on it."

A pair of herons rose from the canal, circled the port buildings, landed again.

"I have a maggot wriggling in my mind," Jethro said. "I felt it move. Its name is Chen."

They began to walk.

"You tell me that you trust Tan Haifeng," Jethro said. "And your instinct may well be true. He came to your hospital. You treated him. You listened to his story. But what is the result? You have come to me with a plan that will take you back to China. Isn't that what John Chen wants?" He led Lewis onto the jetty. "Chen is a man of power. He could send an assassin with a gun. He could have you kidnaped. But these are acts of violence. And violence is not Chen's way. Violence for him would be defeat. Victory would be Lewis Mackenna in the People's Court." He pointed to the paint tins on the motor-sailer's deck. "Dear *Justine,*" he said with affection. "A little cosmetic to cover the scars of age." He climbed aboard. "We could do a trip together, Lewis. Fish, talk, enjoy the sea." He leveled a finger at the horizon. "There are no traps out there. Only freedom." The finger made a slow arc across the seascape. "We could go south to Mindanao."

The finger stopped.

Beyond its tip a yacht, turning in a sleeve of mist, had put her helm down to tack toward the jetty. She was as white and graceful as a gull.

"She's back," Jethro said softly.

The yacht grew larger.

"Her name is *Cathay Moon,*" Jethro said.

"Beautiful."

"Yes, beautiful."

The yacht, rigged with a single sail on her mainmast, tacked again.

"A ketch," Jethro said. "I saw her once before. And I never forgot her."

The yacht, now, was near the jetty.

"Watch her," Jethro said with admiration. "You see how gentle she is? How she comes in with only the mainsail set?"

"Is that important?"

"Yes. It means she'll maneuver just as easily when she's rigged out with the headsails and the mizzen. And that's vital if you're sailing single-handed."

They walked the length of the jetty and when the yacht touched timber Jethro caught the thrown mooring rope and made her fast. They could see two men; a turbaned helmsman whose flesh was as grained and brown as the teak of the deck, a man standing aft in a pool of shadow. He was a Chinese and he wore an azure linen suit and a peaked cap with a gold-embroidered badge and he came smiling out of shadow and removed the cap so that they saw his cropped scalp and the birthmark that ran in a mottled pattern from the faint hairline and down the right temple. He opened an umbrella of varnished paper, twirled it and bowed.

"Are you the owner?" Jethro asked.

"I am."

"I envy you."

The man bowed again.

"I am Mr. Choy," he said. "Kenneth Choy." He stared down the jetty at *Justine*. "What is that?"

"A conversion," Jethro said.

"Yours?"

"Yes."

Mr. Choy sighed with sympathy. He turned and looked across the water at the point of land where the spire climbed on the sky.

"That too is mine," Jethro said.

"The church?"

"Yes. I am Father Frank Jethro."

Mr. Choy bowed.

"And this is Dr. Mackenna."

"A medical doctor?"

"Yes."

Mr. Choy closed the umbrella.

"Come aboard," he said. "But first remove your boots."

Padding behind Mr. Choy's corpulent but agile body they moved from stem to stern and back again. He was a Hong Kong Chinese, he told them, with a flourishing business in that exciting city. He had built tall properties and he was one of those who had left his mark on the changing skyline. *Cathay Moon* was his toy. Pride warmed his voice. He described everything, pointing or tapping with the ferrule of the umbrella; from the forward cabin with its single bunk and let-down bed to the self-steering gear in the bow. He showed them the navigator's chart table and the radio telephone, the cockpit and its instruments and engine controls and steering, the engine and generator. A Lascar was mixing food in the galley and a Thai girl was eating figs and cream in the saloon. She was as sensuous as a cat and a trickle of cream ran from her lips and down her jaw. The saloon was very fine. There were two berths and six seats and the walls and door were patterned with oak and tulip wood and there were silver filigree dishes on the folding table. "You are eating too many figs," Mr. Choy said with anger. The girl shrugged and took a stalk of purple grapes from the fruit dish and began to nibble. Mr. Choy led them from the saloon to the deck. "My daughter," he said untruthfully. "She has a craving for figs." He opened the umbrella and spun it behind his head in ellipses of varnished color.

In the stern Mr. Choy recounted the yacht's brief history; from the designs to the birth pangs, the trials, the delivery. "At first," he said, "nothing was right. When we launched her we saw at once she was a rocker."

"A rocker?" Lewis asked.

"It means," Jethro said, "that she might heel over."

"That's right," Mr. Choy said. "And that's what happened. You could see the hull was too high in the water. She'd rock in the slightest breeze of wind. On the day of the first trial she got caught in a very moderate wind and heeled over so bad that her masts were level with the water. It gave me a fright, I can tell you. But that weren't the only thing. She was as full of vices as an alley cat. She was undercanvased. The mainmast was too heavy. There were leaks. She wouldn't always answer the helm. Sometimes she got out of control. And when the engine was fitted the propeller hardly touched the water. How can shipwrights do these things? But all came well. We pumped two thousand pounds of lead into her keel. We drew a new sail plan. We gave her a new mainmast. We sealed her. We moved the engine and got her screw down where it should be. And came the day when she skimmed the sea like a ballerina. Yes, a ballerina. I swear she danced that day, danced because we had made her perfect." Mr. Choy smiled at the memory of it, began to twirl the umbrella so that rainbow whorls darted on his azure chest. "And here she is. A thing of beauty. Sixteen meters. Nine tons displacement. A hull with no less than seven mahogany skins. Stainless steel rigging. The very best that money can buy."

"I envy you," Jethro said again.

"Isn't envy a sin, Father?"

At noon the Lascar and the Thai girl went ashore. They watched the quiver of her buttocks.

"I'm sorry I told a lie, Father," Mr. Choy said.

"Perhaps the figs are your punishment."

Mr. Choy laughed.

"Would you like a trip?" he asked.

In the open sea and the jib and the mainsail set Jethro took the helm. Lewis watched him. He sat silent in the cockpit, lips parted with the pleasure and at one with the motion of the boat and the sea and with a peace on his face that he had not seen before. The wind was warm and when it strengthened the staysail and the mizzen were added and *Cathay Moon* ran and lifted and there was a feeling of joy in her and no one spoke and there was only the sound of the wind and the booming where the waves struck at the bows and the seabirds poised above the wake. Then when the wind became aggressive and the area of sail was too much they dropped the staysail genoa and the ketch began to glide, seeming to reach into distance for the edge of the sea. They sailed like this, still not speaking, scudding straight and fast before the wind and *Cathay Moon* alive beneath their feet and always the line of the horizon breaking in the spray. The sun was dipping when the ketch turned and moved back into the shelter of the lee shore and later, when she was moored, Jethro rose and went to the bow and stood there unmoving with his face to the sea.

"Let's stretch our legs," Mr. Choy said.

Walking down the jetty and Jethro still silent and not looking at *Justine* they saw the Thai girl approach. She was carrying a green paper bag.

"Guess what she's bought," Mr. Choy said bitterly.

The girl passed them and, as if in response, took a fig from the bag and buried her sharp white teeth in its flesh.

Mr. Choy led them to a table at a harbor bar.

"Did you enjoy your trip, Dr. Mackenna?" he asked.

"Very much."

"What do you think of the boat?"

"A lovely thing."

Drinking beer and watching the sea turn flat and green they sat without talking. Mr. Choy removed his cap and showed his birthmark. It was like the droppings from a bird. "Yes," he said. "A lovely thing. Sadly it is our last voyage."

Jethro turned.

"The last?"

"Yes, Father. We go from here to the Philippines. Then to Hainan. Then home to Hong Kong. There she'll be sold."

"You said she was perfect."

"And so she is."

"Then how can you bring yourself to sell her?"

"It won't be easy. But I've made the decision. You see, Father, she's an ocean racer. She's built to circle the world singlehanded. Another kind of man would do that. He'd set off, totally alone, and time would be meaningless and somewhere on the seas he might even find his god. I use those words because I watched you at the wheel and I know it would be like that for you. Isn't that so?"

"Yes. It would be like that for me."

"The truth is," Mr. Choy said, "I need something different. I am no longer young. Sail can be very hard work. I am a successful man with many friends, business colleagues, potential customers. I plan to buy a much larger craft. She will be a motor yacht and there will be accommodation for at least ten guests. She will cost a great deal of money." He stood and looked at the sun. "I have to leave now."

They returned to the jetty. The Lascar followed, trundling a handcart filled with produce. Mr. Choy paused by *Justine*.

"Is she very old?" he asked.

"Yes."

"Poor old girl."

At the ketch Mr. Choy held out a hand.

"Such a pleasure," he said.

"How much will she sell for?" Jethro asked.

Mr. Choy smiled.

"That sounded wistful, Father."

"How much?"

"I cannot say. I may sell privately. Or put her on the market. Or put her up for auction."

"You must have some idea."

"Yes."

"Won't you tell me?"

"No. She's beyond your reach. A rich man's toy." Mr. Choy stared again at the sky. "I have to sail into the sunset, as they say. So goodbye."

"When will you sell?"

"I told you. After the voyage."

"Three months?"

"Two."

"Will you give me an address?"

"There is no point."

"Please."

Mr. Choy shrugged.

"Very well," he said. "For what it's worth." He took a card from his pocket and put it in Jethro's hand. "You can find me at Queens Road Central, Hong Kong." He pointed at the spire, now flushed with pink. "Are you going to steal the church silver, Father?"

"No."

"You could sell the church itself and you still wouldn't have enough for *Cathay Moon*."

Lewis smiled.

"His Bishop wouldn't like that," he said.

Mr. Choy turned from them.

"Are we agreed?" Jethro asked him.

"On what?"

"On two months. Two months in which to make an offer."

"Very well."

"A firm agreement?"

"Yes, firm."

When the ketch was gone and the sails no more than a flicker on the evening sea Jethro turned his face from her and said: "Yes, Lewis, I'd take the risk to get that boat. A prison cell. A script that has no value. Those are the risks. I accept them. But I'll not walk blindly into a trap. So we have to be wary, don't we? We have to check, here and on the mainland. It'll take time, and it won't be easy. And even then the right answers might be suspect. If Chen's involved that chessboard brain of his will anticipate our moves. But I want that boat. So let's make a plan of inquiry."

They began the walk from the jetty.

"Where are the treasures now?" Jethro asked.

"At Peiku."

"Where is that?"

"Near Taichung."

"Then start there."

Peiku lay in the shadow of mountains. In the village there were more soldiers than people. Below it where the land dropped into distance were the roofs of the market town of Taichung. Above it on the rock slopes were the caves, timber buildings, many more soldiers, an army command post. There was also an administration hut and within it a desk for the keeper of antiquities.

"American?" Yang Pufang asked.

"British."

"We received your letter of introduction, Doctor. You are of course welcome."

"Thank you."

"But we are not a museum, you understand?" Yang smiled. "More like a fortress."

"I noticed."

"The collection was in Taichung. In warehouses. It was feared that the Communists might bomb them. So we moved the collection up here." Yang stood. "But I never believed that. After all, they want the antiquities back in Peking. They would not destroy them."

"No."

"Shall we walk?"

Walking up the path and into the shadow of the overhangs Yang pointed to the mouths of caves.

"We have arranged a few exhibits," he said. "A small proportion of the whole. But no proper lighting or presentation. We allow selected visits. University groups, scholars, foreign guests. What made you come?"

"Curiosity."

"A good answer." Yang pointed again. "In that mountainside is stored the world's finest collection of Oriental art."

The major cave was as high and wide as a cathedral. The walls were lined with cases and there was a central aisle around which were set patterns of long and circular tables. Works of art were displayed on each of the tables. Above them and stretched across the width of the cave were areas of green netting, fixed so that there would be protection against falls from the roof. A few bats had been caught in the mesh. Electric bulbs threw washes of light and Lewis could hear the sound of a generator. Yang led him around the tables, murmuring with pride amidst the jade and porcelain, the lacquers and enamels. Interconnecting tunnels had been bored and Yang took him into other caves where the bronzes and paintings were kept, then out into sunlight and back again into a system of tunnels and through to four smaller caves. "This side of the mountain is as dry as an old bone," Yang told him. "That's why we chose it." Lewis followed him. Sometimes the generator throbbed like a heart in the dark of unlighted tunnels. The fourth cave contained selections from rare books, calligraphies and Imperial archives. Men were working at benches. Lewis bent across a Ching execution warrant.

"I once knew a man," he said, "who had worked at the Imperial Library in Peking."

"Yes?"

"His name is Tan Haifeng."

Yang smiled.

"Before my time," he said.

"He was one of those who saved the treasures."

"Then we owe him a debt."

"Do you recognize that name?"

"No. But jade is my subject and I have worked only in the Academy in Yenan."

"Perhaps there is someone here who knew him."

"Perhaps."

"Will you inquire, please?"

"If you wish."

They returned to the administration hut.

"Sit down, Dr. Mackenna."

Lewis sat at the desk. Yang went to the door.

"Tan Haifeng, you say?"

"Yes."

When he had gone Lewis rose and went to the window. Above the crowns of palms there was a view of Taichung harbor. He stood there until boots rang on the path and the door opened. But it was not Yang Pufang. It was an officer in the uniform of the Taiwanese Army. He carried a sheaf of papers.

"I am Colonel Wu," he said. "Let us sit."

At the desk Wu bent to the papers. He was a deliberate man with an intent face and he ran his finger very slowly down the typewritten lines, not speaking until the finger reached the end of the final sheet. Then he looked up and the finger traced the bristles of his vain mustache.

"Security is my business," he said.

"Security?"

"Yes."

"Is there a problem?"

"In Peiku there is always a problem. We have greater riches here than in all the banks and the national reserves."

"It seems well guarded."

"It is."

Wu stared again at the papers.

"Did you enjoy your visit, Doctor?"

"Very much."

"You saw only a fraction. Most of the collection is still in cases."

"What I saw was remarkable."

"You inquired about Tan Haifeng."

"Yes."

"A friend?"

"A patient."

"When was this?"

"Some years ago."

"When? Be precise."

Lewis reflected.

" 'Forty-seven, I think." Lies, he thought with shame, came ever easier. "Yes, '47."

"He consulted you?"

"Yes."

"Where?"

"Omei."

"In Szechuan?"

"Yes."

"Were you in practice in Omei?"

"No. The mission doctor was sick. I went there to relieve him."

"What was wrong with Tan?"

"That is a matter of professional confidence."

"And this is a matter of security. Now answer."

"I suspected stomach ulcer."

Boots were marching on the road outside. Colonel Wu rose and went to the door and watched the passing squad. Sun struck his cap and made a mirror of its polished peak.

"Were you ever a soldier?" he asked without turning.

"No."

"I have a great responsibility. To the Communists we are thieves. We stole the best of Chinese history. It outrages them. Would you believe that Communists could value the ancient past?"

"I would not."

"Yet they do. They yearn to recover the collection. And I have bad dreams about it. Absurd but bad." He pointed. "Down there is the sea. Night, a Red warship, assault troops. That is my bad dream. But, as I say, absurd. Such an operation would need time."

"Yes," Lewis said. "Four thousand cases. It would take a week."

Wu returned to the desk.

"How long were you in Omei?"

"One month."

"How many times did Tan consult you?"

"Three. Perhaps four."

"And he talked to you about the treasures?"

"Yes. It was no secret. People knew they were on the mountain."

"But you did not regard him as a friend?"

"Friendship is rare, Colonel."

"Yet you came here to inquire about him."

"I came here to see the treasures. And then I inquired about a man I liked. I thought it possible he had come to Taiwan with the final shipments."

Wu shook his head.

"He chose to stay in China," he said. "With the other Communists."

"Was he a Communist?"

"I told you. He chose to stay."

"Does that make him a Communist?"

"We think so."

Colonel Wu made a note. He sat in silence. A mosquito whirred. Then: "Where did you get that figure, Dr. Mackenna?"

"Figure?"

"The four thousand cases. How do you know that?"

"It is common knowledge."

"No. It is not common knowledge. Nothing has ever been published about the treasures and the removal from Peking. And certainly nothing about the transfer from the mainland to Taiwan Free China. This is strict government policy. Yet you have a figure. Where did you get it?"

"I don't remember."

"Try."

"Perhaps it came from Tan Haifeng."

"In '47?"

"Yes."

"How could he have known at that date the eventual number of cases? They were not shipped until two years later."

"Then it could not have come from Tan."

"Where did you get that figure?"

"I really don't remember," Lewis said. "You say the figure is secret. But people work here. There are many soldiers. Men talk."

"Have you met Tan recently?"

"No."

"Have you met him since '47?"

"No."

"Do you know where he is now?"

"No."

Lewis looked away. He could not meet Wu's eye.

"You seem disconcerted, Doctor."

"Puzzled."

"About my interest in Tan?"

"Yes."

"Let me explain." Wu shaped the papers into a square, then clipped them. "For sixteen years those twenty thousand cases were in transit. For the teams of men in charge it was a time of hardship and personal trial. It is always claimed as a matter of national pride that they were patriots of such honesty and dedication that, apart from losses due to bombing, water damage and transport accidents, the collection survived intact."

"And isn't that true?"

"No. There were very significant losses due to theft. This is not suspicion but proven fact. Most of the scholars, certainly those who crossed with the treasures to Taiwan, were men of integrity. But a minority was tempted. It probably began with an occasional piece. A justification perhaps for careers gone and the best years lost. But it grew in scale. It became organized. When the cases were opened in Taiwan we checked the contents with the inventories and discovered the deficiencies. I am informed that Peking found similar deficiencies in the sixteen thousand cases that had remained on the mainland although, like us, they will never publicly reveal it. Years have been spent in investigation. And throughout those years the stolen pieces have continued to surface in the art markets of the world. Tan Haifeng disappeared on the day the Communists marched into Nanking." He shook his head in disgust. "Human nature never changes."

"Are you sure that Tan was involved?"

Colonel Wu stood.

"Put it this way," he said. "I am anxious to question him."

"And so am I," Jethro said. "I am becoming nervous."

"I don't see why."

Across from Mandy's Bar firecrackers were exploding in the darkness.

"Another damn festival," Lewis said.

A rocket rose.

"According to Tan," Jethro said, "he was anti-Red and had chosen to leave Nanking with the treasure ships and the eight other scholars."

"Yes."

"But Colonel Wu thinks otherwise."

"Only because Tan stayed behind. Wu doesn't know that he collapsed and was admitted to the hospital."

"Do you know that, Lewis?"

"I know he had abdominal surgery."

"Which could have been anywhere, any time?"

"Yes."

"Do you have his medical records?"

"No. They are in Nanking."

"Did Tan name the surgeon?"

"Dr. Kao."

"Do you recognize that name?"

"I do. He's first class. And I knew him."

"Good." Jethro wrote down the name. "I still have contacts. And I'll check in Nanking. Now about the girl Su-ching. How long has she been at Kodaki's?"

"About four months."

"After five years in Macao?"

"Yes."

"Did Tan work in Macao?"

"I don't know."

"He must have worked."

"Not if he had a share in the art thefts."

"But you don't believe that, Lewis."

"No. I don't see him as a thief."

"He stole the manuscript."

Dr. Wei passed on his motorcycle.

"One thing disturbs me," Jethro said. "Tan and the girl appeared here soon after your escape."

Lewis shook his head.

"I'm not disturbed," he said. "They are both nice people. Su-ching is hardly more than a child and behaves like one. Tan is not very well and lives in poor conditions. I can't believe that they're figures in a complex plot. And Colonel Wu has confirmed that Tan was one of the scholars. So far so good, say I."

Jethro watched the road. It was filling for the festival. A column of children came, each with a paper lantern.

"I'll also check Lailan," he said. "A botanist, you say?"

"Yes. Of reputation."

Then her name will be on record."

Star shells cascaded on the sky.

"What next for you, Lewis?"

"Ancient manuscripts. A talk with an expert."

Jethro pointed. A man stood tall in the moving crowd. His beard shone like straw when the lantern light struck it.

"Erich Brandt might help," Jethro said.

Erich Brandt listened.

"How old is this manuscript?" he asked.

"Twenty-four centuries."

Brandt smiled.

"Before my time," he said. "I have a slight knowledge of medieval script. But not of so early a period. In fact I have never seen a script of such enormous age."

Someone moved in the room behind the shop.

"Chinese?" Brandt asked.

"Indian."

"And you want it authenticated?"

"Not exactly," Lewis said. "It's not in this country, you see."

"Where is it?"

"I can't say. It's all very confidential."

Brandt smiled again.

"It always is," he said skeptically. "It is of course a fake."

"Why?"

"Because it's rare. If it's genuine then you, Lewis, could not afford to buy it."

"True. But I am able to acquire it."

"Acquire?"

"Yes."

"What does that mean?"

"I cannot say."

"Is it stolen?"

Lewis did not answer.

"Is it?"

"Yes."

"Then forget it, Lewis. This government is very sensitive about stolen antiquities. There's a good reason for that. The police are always here, examining stocks, asking questions. I have to be very careful. So forget it."

"I cannot."

"I assume you'd sell?"

"Yes."

"All that risk for a bit of money?"

"It's not entirely for money, Erich."

"Then why?"

"It replaces something."

A garment rustled in the inner room.

"An enigmatic answer," Brandt said.

"It's the only one you'll get."

Brandt laughed.

"One day," he said, "you must explain." Then, politely: "If there is anything I can do?"

"I need a talk with an expert."

Brandt searched a drawer, produced a printed card. Lewis took it. It read: *SEAMEN'S BAR. In bounds. The best place for drink our girl will offer you a pleasant time on shore. Chi Hsien San Road. Kaohsiung. Taiwan.* A name, Shivadhar Mitra, was scrawled across it in violet ink.

"Shiva Mitra lives above the bar," Brandt said. "One-time professor at Bombay University. Old, not very clean. But he's the man you want. Of course, you'll have to give him a few bank notes."

"Of course."

Brandt followed him outside.

"Be careful, Lewis."

He began to walk.

"I can sell you a genuine tooth of the Buddha," Brandt said, laughing.

Lewis waved, without turning. From the roadway he heard Ellen's voice speak within the shop. "I can't find the cadmium yellow." He stopped, then continued. The shop door closed.

"How can I express an opinion?" Dr. Mitra asked. "You have nothing to show me."

He reached for the basket of nectarines and the cane chair groaned under the shifting of his great weight. He offered the fruit and Lewis shook his head. He could not eat in Mitra's filthy room. The walls were speckled with the bodies of crushed mosquitoes. A dish of congealed rice was on the table and flies made a crust on a mound of chutney. The floor was unswept. There were prints of river scenes on one of the walls. Arab dhows sailed behind films of dust.

"When I have the manuscript," Lewis said, "I will ask for your opinion. At this stage I thought it prudent to discuss the matter with a man of special knowledge."

"There will be a fee."

"Of course."

Dr. Mitra bit into a nectarine. He was wearing batik shorts and a cotton undervest. The juice from past nectarines had made yellow scarabs on its front.

"What period is this script?" he asked.

"The time of the Buddha."

"The Buddha lived for eighty years. Be more precise."

"It describes his death."

Dr. Mitra scratched in his armpit.

"That was in 483 B.C.," he said.

"Yes."

Lewis waited, but Dr. Mitra did not smile.

"It is a fragment of fifteen pages," Lewis said.

"And who is the author?"

"A disciple."

"Which disciple?"

"Ananda."

Music began in the bar below. The drumbeat filled the room.

"Sometimes," Dr. Mitra said tiredly, "that noise goes on all night."

"You should move."

"At my age I could not make the effort."

Dr. Mitra's foot began, illogically, to tap in rhythm with the drum.

"I want to believe in the manuscript," Lewis said. "But there are two questions in my mind. Could a parchment survive after twenty-four centuries? And if that is possible could Ananda have inscribed it?"

Dr. Mitra took another nectarine, flicked a little dust from off its skin.

"Are you sure you won't have one?"

"Quite sure."

"Mankind," Dr. Mitra said, "has written for five or six thousand years. Not handwriting as you would understand it. Primitive and crude. But nevertheless a message, sometimes a narrative. The first rudiments of an alphabet, sets of letters that would be the bones of language, were already developing two thousand or fifteen hundred years B.C. Script of a kind appeared on bronze or stone or other hard surfaces. But the first primitive paper was papyrus." He had begun to speak didactically, as if some half-forgotten lecture had been dredged up from the distant past. The earnest faces of students seemed to float for a moment in the room. "Written records date back to the Egypt of three thousand years B.C., even earlier than that in Mesopotamia. And many papyrus records still survive. There have been recent discoveries in the Palestine of the Old Testament, scrolls of leather and papyrus found in caves on the shores of what was known then as the Salt Sea or Sea of the Plain but known today as the Dead Sea. The sites are still yielding documents and the earliest group has been dated with authority to the fourth century B.C. or, to put it in another way, less than a hundred years later than the script we are discussing. Does that answer one of your questions, Dr. Mackenna?"

"It does."

"Survival," Dr. Mitra said, "is a matter of conditions. In a hot dry climate a parchment would dry out and then remain in a state of magnificent preservation." He wiped juice from his lips and fingers. "Did you read in your newspaper about the sedge?"

"Sedge?"

"The water reed from which they made papyrus. It has begun to die on the banks of the Nile."

"Tragic."

"Yes, isn't it? The forgers will find it difficult to prepare an ancient script." Dr. Mitra smiled at his own joke. "Ananda," he said, "was one of three Sakya princes to enter the Order. They were cousins of Gotama Buddha. But Ananda was his favorite and became the most loved of all the disciples. Ananda was at his side on the last long walk that would take him, sick and dying, across the Ganges to Kusinara where he could lie in his final hour and see the high snows. Ananda knelt beside him and watched him pass through the various trances into the state of *Parinirvana* or, as you would call it, death. We know this from the accounts that were written later, some of them centuries later, after the event. And therein lies your problem."

The music swelled. Dr. Mitra rose and went to the door and opened it and shouted down the stairs. "You pay your rent," a voice said, "and we turn it off." Dr. Mitra shuffled back toward his chair and when his left face passed through the window sunlight Lewis saw that at one time it had been wrenched by stroke.

"Tell me," Dr. Mitra said, "where do we draw our knowledge of the Buddha?"

"From the *Pitakas*."

"And what are they?"

"Three texts."

"How do you know this?"

"The owner of the script told me."

"And what is the language of the script?"

"Pali."

Dr. Mitra nodded.

"Are you a Christian?" he asked.

"Yes."

"The New Testament is your source. For Islam it is the Koran. And for the Buddhists it is the *Tripitakas*. But you must understand they began by being oral. The Buddha preached. Nothing was written. He addressed the listeners in their own vernaculars. His teachings were memorized and sown like seed throughout the land. This was the oral tradition. And it was not until some centuries after the Buddha's death that the great sermons were plucked from the collective memory and translated into writing." Dr. Mitra smiled. "Or so it is said."

"Don't you believe that?"

"I do not. Some experts claim that the scholars of those days invented the Pali so that the teachings could be recorded. But I do not accept that a language could ever have so artificial an origin. Language evolves. It is a living thing. It becomes complex and men perfect it. Who can say when those first characters were transmuted from the spoken word?" Dr. Mitra leaned back in the chair, closed his eyes and locked his hands on his paunch like a man prepared for sleep. "Is the owner an expert?"

"Yes."

"How did he describe the characters?"

"As a primitive but recognizable Pali."

"Will you tell me his name?"

"I cannot reveal that."

"Then tell me his background."

"The Imperial Library of Peking."

"Impeccable."

"Yes."

"Perhaps I could talk to him?"

"That would not be possible."

"I could form a better judgment."

"He is not in Taiwan."

"Where is he?"

"In Macao."

"Did he flee from China?"

"Yes."

"Was the manuscript stolen?"

"Discovered."

Dr. Mitra smiled.

"It could be a forgery," he said. "The odds are in favor of that. Throughout time artworks and artifacts and rarities have spawned their fakes. Copies circulate the world. Gaps in knowledge are mysteriously filled. Proofs appear where none existed. From the skull of the missing link to the shroud that wrapped the crucified Christ. Not all of this is the work of rogues. There are guilty men among the academics. I sometimes think there is a perversity in the minds of certain scholars. A little joke on posterity. What could be more droll?" Dr. Mitra settled deeper in his chair. His eyes were still closed. Sleep was near. "I am denied an examination of this script," he said. "Therefore I cannot advise on authenticity. If I could feel it in these hands of mine I think I would know. Is the parchment sheep or goat?"

"Sheep."

"Yes, sheep. But when did it lose its skin? That is the vital question. There is no way in which we can assess the exact age of such a parchment. A powerful microscope assists us and we can see more clearly its texture and the changes wrought by time. We can compare it with other manuscripts whose origins are known. All this helps. But still we cannot place it accurately in its century. Certainly we can tell you if it is a modern or medieval forgery. But not much more. The scientists claim that a new technique will soon evolve that will explore the structure of a parchment and reveal its age in the same way that a felled tree can be dated by its rings. But, I fear, not yet." Dr. Mitra was silent for a time. His breathing became stertorous. Then: "Dr. Mackenna, I am quite clear that Ananda could have written this account. And if you are convinced of the bona fides of the owner of the script then you might at this stage accept his claims. After all, if he was a scholar at the Imperial Library then he is exactly the kind of specialist to whom one would go for an opinion." The voice blurred. "But be cautious. Pass no money. Be cautious. Be cautious."

Dr. Mitra slept.

Lewis stood, took some notes from his pocket and placed them on the table. Was it too much? He retrieved two of the notes and went to the door. He looked back at Dr. Mitra's sleeping face and the money at his elbow. He felt a moment of shame. Lies. Parsimony. There was no end to the guilt. He returned to the table and added six more notes. Then he left.

Walking from the dockside and away from the sea wind and the smell of the petrochemical factories he was aware of a growing elation. There had been no derision in Dr. Mitra's eyes. He had listened with gravity and he had not dismissed as improbable the existence of the Ananda Fragment. He hired a bicycle rickshaw that would take him to the center of the city and the curve of the Love River and when he saw the water of the Cheng Ching Lake he paid off the rickshaw man and went to one of the restaurants that faced the zigzag bridge. Later, when he had eaten, he returned to Chi Hsien San Road. He looked across from the jeep to the Seamen's Bar. Music no longer blared. Perhaps Dr. Mitra had paid his rent.

Chapter 14

From the wicker seat outside the Teagarden Bar they could see across the square to the hospice and the darkness of the alleys. Young men on motorcycles, some of them with girls sitting sidesaddle on the pillions, were puttering around the square. Jethro sat in silence, poured a second cognac. Then he pointed at the flank wall of the hospice.

"Is that him?"

"Yes," Lewis said.

Tan Haifeng came from shadow and out onto the roadway, waited for a gap in the ring of motorcycles, crossed the square to the table.

"This is Father Jethro," Lewis told him.

Tan offered his hand. Jethro ignored it.

"Sit," he said.

Tan sat.

"Do you know who I am?" Jethro asked.

"I can guess."

"Tell me."

"The man with the boat."

"Yes. In talking to you I am breaking a rule. But there's no secret now. I am known to your people."

"My people?"

"The ones on the mainland."

Lewis saw the perplexity in Tan's eyes.

"The ones with the pretty red flags," Jethro said. "For three weeks I have made inquiries."

"About me?"

"Yes. Wouldn't you expect that?"

"I suppose so."

"Tan Lailan is, as you claim, a botanist. She has worked at Chungking University and is now at Amoy."

Tan nodded.

"But is she your sister?"

"Of course she is my sister."

Tan began to tug nervously at his whiskers.

"Why do you doubt it?" he asked.

"I'll tell you. My other inquiry was at the Nanking Central Hospital. You claim that you entered as a patient in April of 1949 and that you underwent an operation and that the surgeon was a Dr. Kao."

"Yes."

"And that because the Communists were about to arrest you Dr. Kao arranged your escape."

"That is so."

"And that you were put on a ship to Chungking."

"Yes. Dr. Kao will confirm."

"No. Dr. Kao will not confirm. He left Nanking in '51. He cannot be traced."

"It is the truth."

One of the motorcycles fell. Now, laughing, they were circling it. The pillion girl rose, began to brush her skirt.

"However," Jethro said, "we were able to see your medical file. It contains an interesting document. Shall I tell you what it is?"

Tan waited.

"It is your death certificate."

"Death?" Tan whispered.

"Yes."

The motorcycles went into the hospice alley. The sound of the engines made cannonades within the narrow walls, then faded.

"But I am here," Tan said absurdly.

"Yes. We can see you. But who are you?"

"I am Tan Haifeng."

"Did Chen send you?"

"Chen?"

"Mr. Tan," Lewis said, "what did Dr. Kao say to you that day?"

"I told you."

"Tell us again."

"He told me to leave immediately, that documents would be prepared that would explain my absence."

"Was that all?"

"Yes."

"What did you take that to mean?"

Tan shrugged.

"A discharge," he said. "Perhaps a transfer to another hospital. Something like that."

"Like death?"

"He did not say that. But obviously this is what he did."

"It isn't obvious to me," Jethro said.

He stood.

"Mr. Tan," he said. "If that is your name. It may be that you are telling the truth. But the fact is that the hospital recorded the death of one Tan Haifeng. I can't ignore that." Then: "I'm sorry, Lewis. But it's off."

He turned and walked away. Lewis followed.

"Frank," he said.

Jethro stopped.

"Lewis," he said tiredly, "my head is going round and round with it. God knows I want that ketch. She sails through my dreams. But the risk is now too great. I have the sea outside my window. I have *Justine*. I shall have to be content."

"But you won't be."

"I must try."

"Remember what you said."

"About what?"

"About Chen. You said his brain would anticipate our every move."

"So?"

"So he'd never have left that death certificate in the file."

"Goodnight, Lewis."

Lewis watched him go. Then he returned to the table. He did not sit. Tan looked up.

"Do you believe me?" he asked.

"I want to, Mr. Tan."

"You know me. You know Su-ching. We are not your enemies."

Lewis put some money on the drink tray.

"I have told the truth, Dr. Mackenna."

He turned and walked from the bar and down one side of the square. When he reached the road junction he looked back. Tan had not moved.

Lewis crossed to the basin and washed his hands. Morning sun made shafts across the room.

"You can put your trousers on," he said.

He heard Dr. Winter climb down from the bench.

"You have some very fine hemorrhoids," Lewis said. "The best of the new season's crop."

"I don't find it funny."

Lewis dried his hands.

"An operation?" Winter asked.

"An injection."

"What kind?"

"Gall-nut."

"Gall-nut?"

"Yes. A chemical extract."

"Not another quaint old Chinese remedy?"

"Yes. And known for two thousand years. It will harden and wither them. And then they will disappear."

Doubt touched Winter's eyes.

"Are you sure?" he said.

"I'll cut you if you wish."

Winter put on his shoes.

"Well?" Lewis asked.

"I'll take the quaint old Chinese remedy."

Lewis left the room and walked down the corridor. Anna Chang was in the linen cupboard and he went into it and stood behind her and put his hands on her midriff and slid them up across her breasts.

"Today?" he murmured.

"No. Not today."

"Why not?"

"We are driving up to Tamsui this afternoon."

"We?"

"Two or three of the nurses. A swim and a meal."

"Don't go in the sand dunes."

She laughed and turned.

"When are you off duty?" she asked.

"Eight."

"Perhaps then."

"Will you phone?"

"If we get back early."

She kissed him, held him for a time. Then she said with deep affection: "I'm fond of you, Lewis. I want you to know that."

They embraced again.

"Always to know that," she said.

He sensed the change in her.

"Why so serious?" he asked, smiling.

Rain came with darkness. He could hear the wind, palm fronds scratching at the hospital walls. He was at his desk when the telephone rang. It was seven-fifty. The line was bad and he heard Anna Chang's voice, faint behind the atmospherics. "It's here." The receiver crackled. "Speak up. I can't hear you." He saw through the window the electric blue of lightning. "The junk is here. The junk. The *Shantung*." The voice died, then resurged. "Can you hear me, Lewis? The junk is here. At Tamsui." He stood. "Wait for me," he said. "I'll be down."

Driving through the rise of the land and the gathering storm toward the northwest coast he saw again the two tea chests. What will I do when I reach Tamsui? he asked himself. Are they on the junk? I have to know. Firstly I have to know. He felt his fingers tighten on the wheel, as if he was on the edge of violence. The drive was slow and parts of the road were underwater and it was past nine o'clock when he saw the sea horizon. He took the jeep slowly down into the port and along the waterfront road toward the Spanish Castle. There were craft at all the jetties, black shapes in the streaming rain. The bars and cafés made a line of intermittent light and, passing, he peered into their interiors. There was no sign of Anna Chang and the nurses. With the onset of rain, he decided, they would have returned to Taipei. He drove as far as the fish market, circled it and came back along the waterfront. This time he studied the moored craft. The neon sign of the Shanghai Bar threw color on the pools that filled the road craters. Opposite the bar was a jetty and tied to it were three sampans, a fishing boat and a junk. He stopped the jeep, got out and put on his parka. The junk made a silhouette at the end of the jetty. Its mullioned windows glowed with light. He walked a few paces down the timbers of the jetty so that the first of the sampans would not obstruct his vision. Now he could see the junk's stern tiller and its carved dragon jaws. It was the *Shantung*. Lightning forked above her and it seemed as if the jaws had lunged at the raining sky. The port turned white.

Ellen Mackenna saw the flash from the kitchen window and the plum trees whiten in the brilliant light. Then there was blackness and she bent again across the table. Earlier that day she had stripped two of the trees of their fruit and there would be, she judged, sufficient for a dozen jars of jam. When she had finished the stoning she turned to the big copper caldron and in that moment she heard footfalls on the path and the tap of knuckles on the kitchen door. She opened it. Su-ching stood there in yellow oilskins and her madonna's face framed in a drawstring hood. She entered. Water ran from the hem to the floor.

"You are making a mess," Ellen said. "Take off your coat."

Su-ching removed it and Ellen saw that she had been carrying a parcel inside the oilskin.

"Can I help you?" she asked.

Su-ching gave her the parcel.

"For me?"

"Yes."

She removed the wrapping. It was a large black Bible, its bruised leather cover as familiar to her as her own features. She opened it and the gum cracked within its binding. That sound, too, was familiar. She turned the flyleaves. The inked Mackenna names lay beneath her fingers. Mary Mac- kenna. Died of the smallpox. Cromer Mackenna. Died on the Cross like our Lord. That black old book. She had last seen it on the pulpit in the mission church, in the silence, abandoned. Our black old book. She felt the swelling of emotion and she pressed the Bible against her breast and the tears came and she stood shaking and wet of face and Su-ching put out a hand and held her arm.

"There is a note," Su-ching said.

"A note?"

"Inside."

She found the note. It was written in English. *Ellen, this should be with you and will give you strength.* It was signed *John Chen.* The words blurred. She read them again. Chen? Will give you strength? Fear touched her. She put down the Bible.

"Where did you get this?" she asked.

"It was in Anna's room."

"Anna?"

"Anna Chang."

"Anna Chang," she repeated. She had met the girl at some of the garden tutorials, handsome and sullen under the plums. Aloof and sensuous of hip. They had never exchanged more than a courtesy.

"It was on the table," Su-ching said.

Ellen wiped her eyes.

"I am trying to understand," she said. "Do you share a flat with Anna?"

"No, madame. I have a room in the same house. I had borrowed an egg and I had gone to her room to return it. The door was open. The Bible was on the table. And so were her keys. She had gone."

"Gone?"

"Yes. Everything had gone. Her clothes, her books. Everything."

"Except this Bible?"

"Yes, madame."

Ellen picked it up.

"Do you know what it is?" she asked.

"Yes. I opened it and saw the names. It is your family Bible. I wrapped it and brought it here."

Ellen pressed it to her breast again.

"I am still confused," she said. "What was it doing in Anna's room?"

"I do not know, madame."

"Did you not wonder?"

"Yes."

"Well?"

"I assumed he had lent it to her."

"You mean Dr. Mackenna?"

"Yes."

The undercover was wet with plum juice. She took it to the sink and cleaned it. Then, turning, she said: "Had the doctor been visiting Anna?"

Su-ching looked away.

"Answer me."

"Yes."

"For how long?"

Su-ching was silent.

"Weeks?"

"Months."

"Were they professional visits?"

Su-ching shook her head. Ellen tapped the Bible.

"Was he converting her to Christianity?" The sarcasm trembled on her tongue. "Was he?"

"No, madame."

"What then?"

"They were sweethearts."

"Sweethearts?"

"Yes."

"You have the wrong word, Su-ching. That is a word of innocence. A word for springtime lovers. It is not a word for dirty sexual acts."

"No, madame."

"Please go."

When the girl had gone she took the Bible into the living room, placed it on the table together with the note. The fear for him had left her. Now there was only anger. The rainstorm was passing and she went out to the path and up the steps that led to the bedroom floor. There she changed her clothes, brushed out her hair and secured it with a *diamanté* coral comb. Then she walked to the square, found a waiting taxi and tapped on the window.

"Nanfangao," she said.

The rainfall was softer and men were moving on the deck of the junk. Lewis Mackenna returned to the jeep and, standing behind it, watched the men climb from the rail onto the jetty. There were seven of them and they came through the rain, crossed the road to the Shanghai Bar. Six of the men entered and the seventh stood for a moment in the doorway and removed a gunnysack from his shoulders and shook it. His face turned into light and Lewis saw the wisp of straw switching within his teeth. It was the junkmaster. He, too, entered. Lewis crossed to the sidewalk and then to the flank window of the bar. He stared inside. Music had begun. The rear wall was a painted coconut grove and a girl with rouged nipples was performing a ribbon dance. The bar was full and across from the girl was a zinc counter with bowls of fish, meat and rice. The seven men were bent over the steam and he watched them ladle food and take the plates to a table. He left the window, walked through a drizzle of rain to the jetty and then went slowly down its length toward the junk.

He stopped in the shadow of the fishing boat. Ahead of him the *Shantung* pulled on the swell against its mooring ropes. The cabin lights had been extinguished and there was only the amber glow of an oil lamp inside the

crew shelter. How many men had been left on watch? He walked from
the stern and its two tiers of mullioned windows and high-pooped cabin
to where the cargo hatches were battened down, stopped again at the
waist. The shelter, too, had been closed against the rain. He could hear
voices, the chink of coins against metal; two voices, he judged, perhaps a
game of fan-tan. He walked farther toward the bow sweep. The sea sucked
at the wooden piles beneath his feet. When he reached the bow he turned
and looked back. Nothing moved. He climbed over the rope rail onto the
foredeck. He stood with his back against the side of the turret cabin and
the rain gentle on his face. He looked down, seeing again on the area of
deck a pair of goatskin shoes, a purification jar, Shameen's prostrate figure.
I killed a man at prayer. Would those words never leave him? He turned
to the windows of the cabin.

The interior was in darkness. But then, staring through the pane, he saw
shapes emerge in the faint reflected light from the night sky. A pallet bed,
a chart table, a cupboard with an open door, two chests. Chests? I have
to know. He stepped around the angle of the cabin. There were two central
doors, secured to each other with a catch that fell into a screw eye. He
lifted it and entered. He had begun to sweat and he stood in the half-
darkness, listening for sounds. He heard the lap of water, a groan from
the junk's timbers. But that was all. A scent touched his nostrils, the scent
of lemons. He crossed to the chests. Now he could read the Long Jing
stencils, even see the discoloration at the base of the tea chests that had
come from the rising waters of Ogre Lake. He removed one of the lids,
peered inside, inserted a hand. His fingers touched a mass of whiskery
roots. The chest was filled with them. He lifted out one of the roots. It
had a stem and pointed leaves, a cluster of dried berries. It was a ginseng
plant. He removed the lid of the second chest. There was a layer of straw.
He plucked it out and explored with his hand. He felt an object. It had
the shape and texture of a doll. He held it up. It was the Jack-in-the-box.
He stared into its painted face, that face that had grinned down at him
above her writhing hips. That lemon scent. Fear seized him. He dropped
the Jack-in-the-box, ran to the door and onto the deck. The hatches were
opening and men were emerging from the holds, running toward him. A
tholepin struck the cabin. Glass broke. He jumped across the rail to the
jetty. The junkmaster and the six men took shape in the darkness, hunters
coming through the rain. He ran down the length of the *Shantung* toward
the bows of the fishing boat, leaped onto its deck. A hand grasped the
back of his parka. The cloth tore and, twisting free, he crossed the deck
to the farther rail. He could hear their boots behind him, a man slipping,
an oath.

He jumped.

When he surfaced, the water noisome in his throat and nose, he felt his
cheek rasp against the encrustations on the hull. Pain ran. He swam toward

the stern and into the space that lay between the boat and a sampan and then between the piles of the jetty. Boots thudded above him. Someone shouted. Seaweed stroked his flesh. He pulled himself through the timber structures until he was in blackness and the water at his chin. Music from the Shanghai Bar came faintly from the shore. He heard the junkmaster's voice directly above him. Then the boots marched away toward the seaward end of the jetty. He did not move and he closed his eyes, buoyant in the water and the cold of it engulfing him and the hurt of the abraded cheek commingling with the nausea from the swallowed water. The music stopped. A woman screeched with laughter. Then he heard the splash of oars, saw a bloom of yellow light. The junk's sampan came slowly past the piles. The junkmaster was standing in its prow and he held a lantern chest-high so that its light danced beneath the jetty. Lewis moved behind the central pile. He watched the lantern grow small and disappear. Blackness came again. Then the yellow bloom flowered near to the waterfront and grew larger as the sampan returned and he saw the prow and the junkmaster and the upshine from the lantern yellowing his facebones. The sampan passed. He did not move. He held to the pile and listened to the sounds that were coming from the junk. He heard them lifting the sampan to the deck, men calling, the order to cast off. He waited until the spars thrust against the jetty and the bow sweep creaked. Then he climbed from the water.

When he reached the lip of the jetty the *Shantung* was under way. The lugsail was pale in the night and when the oil lamps began to flare he saw the pattern of its bamboo ribs. There was a light now in the turret cabin. A figure came to one of the windows and a face formed behind the rain-smeared glass. It was Anna Chang. She watched him until the junk was gone.

The rain became heavy on the east coast highway south of Suao and the driver stopped the taxi. When the storm had passed and they could see the ocean and the road they began the descent to Nanfangao. Ellen Mackenna watched the first moonshine reveal the canal and the harbor and the steeple of the church. The taxi braked on the quay. She got out and paid.

"Wait?" the driver asked.

"No," she said, smiling. "What I have to do may take a little time."

She crossed the road. There was a light in the vestry at the side of the church and when she rapped on the door it was opened by a young Chinese woman with a flower in her hair.

"The Father is not here," she said.

"Where is he?"

She pointed seaward through the line of the breakwater.

"Working," she said. "On the boat."

Justine was moored between two trading vessels. A lamp was burning on her deck. Jethro was bent across the engine housing. He turned his head and stood upright when he heard her heels on the jetty and when she walked into the orbit of the lamplight he smiled and climbed from the boat. He was stripped to his shorts and she went to him and stood there without speaking and her hair stuck by rain to her cheeks and neck. She could smell the sweat and engine oil. He ran his hand up his chest so that she saw the wet curls spring.

"I told you you'd come to me," he said.

It was daybreak when Ellen Mackenna returned to Crooked Pond. The jeep was outside the house. She entered and went into the living room. Lewis was asleep in a chair. He was wearing a bathrobe and there was a bloodstained towel on the floor. She picked it up, stared down at him. There were lacerations on his right cheek. She folded the towel and put it on the table. The Bible had been opened and Chen's note lay on its pages. She heard him stir and when she turned she saw that he had awakened.

"What has been happening?" she asked. She touched the note. "What does this mean?"

"They tried to take me."

"Take you?"

"Shanghai me."

"From where?"

"Tamsui."

He rose and came to the table. She caught his fetid odor.

"You smell," she said.

"Seawater."

"Tell me what happened, Lewis."

"A long story."

"Tell me."

"They got me aboard. I jumped. I hurt my face. I escaped."

"Is that all?"

"It's all I want to say."

He touched the Bible.

"Strange to see it again," he said.

"Yes, strange."

He dabbed his face with the towel.

"What made you go to Tamsui?" she asked.

He did not answer. She saw the caution in his eyes.

"What made you go?"

"I was lured."

"Lured?"

"Yes."

She watched him, his secret eyes.

"By a woman?"

"By two tea chests."

"Is that a joke?"

"No joke. It was Chen's trap."

She felt a surge of anger.

"For God's sake," she said. "Those damn chests."

He stared at her.

"There was a time," he said, "when you would never have said that."

"I know."

"And not so long ago."

"Well, I've changed. Both of us have changed."

"Yes."

He bent to the Bible.

"A strange man, Chen," he said.

"Very."

"He thought it would comfort you."

He began to turn its pages.

"How did it get here?" he asked.

"Someone brought it."

"Who?"

"Su-ching. She found it in a room. An empty room. A room you know."

Now his hand was unmoving on the Bible's pages.

"Anna Chang's room," she said.

He did not look up.

"Dirty," she said. Now she was shaking. "Dirty of you."

"No. Not dirty."

"Yes, dirty."

"She was Chen's agent."

"Does that excuse it?"

"In a way."

"She seduced you?"

"Yes."

She laughed with derision.

"She's gone now," he said. "She was on the junk."

"You should have gone with her," Ellen said. "You could have forni-
cated all the way to prison."

She walked into the kitchen. The crudity was like a sourness in her
mouth. She went out onto the path.

"You were out all night," he said behind her.

"So?"

"Who were you with?"

She reached the outside stairs.

"Who was it?"

She began to climb.

"Was it Erich Brandt?" he said below her.

"Mind your business."

She stopped on the iron landing. She could see the sunrise color in the plum trees.

"Answer me."

She turned and looked down at him.

"Let's just say we're quits," she said.

She opened the bedroom door. She turned again.

"What was it about her?" Ellen asked. "Her youth?"

"Her voice."

"Her voice?"

"She had only to speak."

Three days later he stowed his gear and some provisions in the jeep. He had arranged a leave with Kodaki's, he told her, and he would go to the gorge, as he had gone once before, for a period of aloneness. But four days after his departure Dr. Winter handed her a letter. He had been asked, he said, to deliver it on this precise date. Lewis, it seemed, had not gone to the Taroko.

> *When you receive this I shall be at sea and bound for the south China coast. I cannot say too much since the safety of others is involved. Indeed it would be better if you burned this letter when read. You would recognize the boat. You sailed in her on the escape from Swatow. J. is my partner in this venture and has brought the boat down to the little harbor west of Taichung where she can be refueled. From there our destination is only about 150 miles. J. says that to allow for weather and wind we should reckon on 200 miles a day. So in thirty or forty hours we shall be there. There is danger, but not perhaps as great as you would think. After all the boat was built and registered in Macao, and J. is a Portuguese national and he has supplied me with papers that identify me as a Canadian with a Hong Kong domicile. What is it all about? A long story. Escape and return, you could call it. Or two idiots in search of a fortune. Yes, idiots. For I know in my heart that there is more than a grain of folly in it. Because even if the risk is tiny it should not be acceptable. We have so much here. A beautiful island. Freedom. My medical work, although ill paid. We even have each other, if we truly want that. We can forgive. It began with an elderly woman living on the mainland who yearns to join her brother, who is here in Taiwan. A common enough story. But the difference is that she has in her possession an antiquity of astounding value. And the reward for getting her out is a share in it. Of course we made inquiries. We took trouble. We were reasonably convinced. I knew, liked and trusted the*

brother. But finally we decided against it. As J. once said to me the effect is to get me back to China and this is what Chen wants. His shadow was there. We could always hear the tumblers clicking in his head. But then came this business with Anna Chang. Chen had sent her. We were looking for some complex trap, not something as violent and unsubtle as a shanghai. So it tipped the balance. With Chen the State must be served and if a simple act of force would best serve its interests then Chen might use that way. Of course it could still be a strategy, moves, pieces on a board, a gambit. But our own minds wearied of it all. Something was driving us. We had to go. A message has gone to the lady by a quick and secret route. We are on our way.

All that morning the patrol boat had watched them. Sometimes it went into mist or grew smaller. But it always returned. At noon it anchored between *Justine* and the shore. They could see the yellow of its brass stern gun and beyond it an expanse of dark-blue water and, distant, the island of Amoy and the harbor. They had fished since early light. "There is nothing more innocent," Jethro said, "than sportsmen catching fish. Let them get used to us." But they had not caught many fish and when, through the telescope, Jethro saw a covey of flying fish leaping from the water he took the boat toward them. "Where you see them coming out like that," he said, "it can mean there are real fish beneath." And so it proved. By midafternoon the hook and the pork rind had brought them three striped tuna of a respectable size. There were four hundred pounds of ice aboard and Jethro gutted and packed the fish. At an hour before sundown the patrol boat came alongside.

The officer was efficient. He spoke in careful Cantonese. He asked many questions and he checked the registration and the documents of identity and then he and one of the crew inspected the boat. They went slowly from bow to stern. They looked in the water tanks, in the bilges, in every drawer and cupboard; and finally in the icebox.

"They are good fish," the officer said.

"Yes."

"Good eating."

"Yes," Jethro said. "And you shall have one."

"One?"

"Two."

Jethro wrapped the two fish in some Macao newspapers and presented them to the officer and the officer handed them to the sailor.

"Will you go ashore?" he asked.

"Perhaps."

"If you go ashore you must obtain port clearance before you leave. Understood?"

"Yes."

But they did not go ashore. The appointment with Tan Lailan was for the early hours of darkness of the following day. "Could not be better," Jethro said. "They know us now. And all day tomorrow they'll see us sitting here." In the morning the patrol boat came from the island and alongside *Justine*.

"Did you go ashore?" the officer called out.

"No."

"You should do so. It is an interesting place."

"We are here to fish," Lewis said. "We are not tourists."

"Nevertheless you should see Amoy. It was once an International Settlement. There are fine buildings and a good beach at Ku Lang."

"No," Jethro said, smiling. "Fishing is a very serious business."

The officer and the sailor came aboard.

"I regret," the officer said, "that we must search."

"Again?"

"It is the rule. You were here overnight. Who knows what you have done?"

"We ate the fish."

"And so did we. They were excellent."

The officer pointed and the sailor opened the engine hatch.

"Do not be alarmed," the officer said, "if you hear artillery." He gestured at the open sea and the five offshore islands that were strung across the channel. "As you know they are held by the Nationalists. We fire an occasional shell to remind them that they are only tenants." His face went sullen. "We can of course take the islands whenever we choose."

"Of course."

"But Peking decrees otherwise." He looked behind him, as if official ears were listening. "Such a battle, Peking says, would drive Taiwan into further isolation." He shrugged with contempt. "Let us search."

Lewis followed him. Once again he explored; probing with practiced fingers in the stowage and the drawers, in the folds of sails and oilskins, under the generator. In the cabin he released the frame of the let-down bed so that it descended to the sail locker. He turned the mattress, shook the pillow. An object fell and he retrieved it from the floor. He held out his hand. A coral comb with *diamanté* prongs sat on the palm. The officer smiled.

"Is the lady aboard?" he asked.

He gave Lewis the comb and he put it in his pocket and kept his hand there, feeling its shape, the prongs that had once pinned her hair.

"She was aboard," he said. "But not now."

In the evening *Justine* headed for the open sea. They passed the patrol boat and the officer saluted and the crew waved and clapped their hands politely. At nightfall Jethro brought the boat back to Amoy. Tan Lailan lived at an address on Ku Lang, an island in the harbor. They could see the light reflections that were thrown from the houses onto the dark water, the silhouette of the causeway. There were many junks and sampans and cargo ships. Docks were under construction and Jethro moored at a wharf that lay in the shadow of a crane. Lewis got out.

"We can still spin a coin," Jethro said.

"No," Lewis said. "I'll go. Give me one hour."

Ku Lang was a tiny island, no more than one square mile. Lewis began to walk. A line of old mansions, preserved since the days of the Settlement, faced the beach. "She lives in a house that was once the American Consulate," Tan Haifeng had told him. "You can still see the crest." He heard a girl's soft laughter on the beach, music from one of the ships. He passed a mansion with a Red star on its door, flowering trees, a wall on which was pinned an execution notice. It depicted the body of a man and the crime committed. Lamplight fell on the lettering. *Stole a boat while attempting to escape across the Taiwan Strait.* He felt a pulse of fear, stopped and looked behind him. Nothing moved. Wind came and tree shadow flickered on the notice so that it seemed that the body jerked. He began again to walk. Another building, this one with an old field gun on its forecourt. A burned church and an angel's wing standing like a fin in the timbers. A mansion with a nameplate on one of its entrance pillars. The Fukien Institute of Oceanography, it said. And then a larger mansion of two stories. Most of the windows were lighted and diffused light touched the front door and the carving that was set above the lintel. Was it a crest? He walked up the short driveway. He could hear voices inside the house. Not much was left of the American crest. The eagle had been smashed off but there were still the stone talons sunk in sheaves of wheat. The voices became louder. Feet scraped behind the door. He walked back to the roadway and watched from behind a tree trunk. The door opened and a party of people emerged. They were young men and women and they carried files and parcels of books and they came chattering and laughing up the drive and when they reached the road they turned and waved and called goodnight to the woman standing on the threshold. She wore a blue Mongolian gown and the light in the hall made a halo around her thick white hair. The door closed and when the voices had died in the night he walked back to the door and knocked.

The woman opened the door.

"Madame Tan?" he asked.

She beckoned and he entered.

"Are you the doctor or the priest?" she said.

"The doctor. Mackenna."

"I am Tan Lailan."

She closed the door and stood there smiling. She had clear candid eyes, a lined brown throat. She carried some roses and a pair of scissors and behind her, across the hall, was a corner table and on it a vase that contained a few of the same roses.

"Did you see my young people?" she asked.

"Yes."

"Students. Every week they come. Tonight was our last period of study. It hurt me when they left."

"Yes, madame."

She put the roses to her nose and took their fragrance.

"These too," she said. "The last time." She crossed to the table and he followed. "I shall arrange them and when I am gone their scent will still be here." She began to snip and set them in the vase. She had beautiful hands, as smooth and perfect as those of a young girl. "Roses were always my passion," she said. "Through my work I have sent many a Chinese rose to English gardens." He watched her fingers move like fragile wands in the clusters of purple and pink blooms. "The ancient roses are best. These are Gallicas. They were first grown more than two thousand years ago." She turned to him. "As old as a certain animal. Do you understand me?"

"Yes."

"You must tell me what that animal is."

"It is a tortoise."

She laughed. "Yes, a tortoise." Then, seriously: "Amoy is a humid place. It has been in hibernation behind one of the old bread ovens, where I hope it kept dry."

She went to the foot of the stairs, turned.

"I shall get it. My bag is packed." She pointed at a half-open door and a lighted room. "Safer to wait in there, Dr. Mackenna. I have to change. Please give me a minute."

She climbed the stairs and he walked through into the room. It was a large study and the light from a bronze table-candelabra illuminated book-shelves, a central desk, a small table at the far end that was set for chess, another vase of roses, walls with prints and paintings. He looked at his watch. Twenty-five minutes had gone. He went to the nearest painting. Women, bent in sun, were winnowing rice. A voice spoke suddenly in his mind. It was that of Tan Haifeng. *She has arthritis in her hands. Her fingers are as knobbled as an old oak.* Those hands, those elegant hands. Fear came. Those straight and graceful fingers. He left the painting, went to the desk, turned, stared at the room. He could hear the beating of his heart. A shadow from some object made a serrated line on the wall that was like the jaw of an iron trap. He walked to the chess table. The pieces were carved from jade and they sat on squares that were formed from a marquetry inlay. There were two chairs placed at the table and on one of them was a round tin. He bent across it. It was a shortbread tin and its faded lid presented a view of Edinburgh Castle and Princes Street Gardens.

The table, the chessmen, the tin that had contained incense sticks. He touched the lid, as he had touched it once before in that veranda room in the Fusan camp. He heard steps on the stairs and in the hall. The door opened.

John Chen entered.

In the car and Chen seated on his left and another man on his right Lewis watched the ruts in the causeway road running into the light from the headlamps. A second car was parked ahead of them. The interior light was on and when they passed he saw men in the car and Jethro's face turn to the window.

"Why?" he said. "Why the elaborate plot? They could have taken me away in the junk."

Now the second car was following.

"I wanted both of you," Chen said. He was silent for a time. Then: "Greed, Lewis." Contempt had edged his voice. "Greed was your downfall."

They did not speak again and when the cars reached the Changchow airstrip soldiers came out of the darkness and Chen got out and walked away toward the army huts. A light rain was falling and the soldiers surrounded the cars. There was no plane on or near the strip and Lewis sat in the car and waited until the sound of engines grew behind the rain.

Chapter 15

From the cell window Lewis could see the distant tongue of water that was the northern shore of West Lake.

"Strange to be in Hangchow again," he said. "We used to have picnics on that lake. The mission isn't far." He turned. "Our mission," he said with affection. "I wonder what happened to it."

Michael Tsang looked up from the papers that were spread on the little table.

"Do you want me to find out?" he asked.

"No," Lewis said. "I'd rather not know."

"You are in Hangchow," Tsang said, "because the alleged offenses were committed here. You will be tried here."

"When?"

"I don't have a date. And I don't yet have an indictment." He produced a fountain pen and smiled. He was young with clever eyes. "Are they treating you well?"

"Yes."

"Enough food?"

"Yes."

"Let me introduce myself. Michael Tsang, as I told you. I am a member of a law practice in Hong Kong. I am American born, but I have lived and worked in Hong Kong for the past eight years. I have Chinese parents. I am a Christian. I will try to understand you and to give you a strong defense."

"I have no money. Who will pay?"

"That has been arranged."

"By whom?"

"Wiser not to say. We have the funds. It will not assist your case if the authorities know the source."

"Please tell me."

"Leave it."

Michael Tsang wrote something.

"Dr. Mackenna," he said, "you must realize that all this is highly unusual. A public trial, a professional defense, court rules. This is a Western concept. Today in Communist China the State is infallible. If it arrests a man it is deemed to have the evidence. Ipso facto the man is guilty. He may not even know his sentence. He may go to an execution post. He may be shut up for a year. Or perhaps for twenty years. But you, Doctor, will be granted the formalities. The prosecutor will be John Chen Yuchang. He is the deputy director of the Public Security Bureau. A power in the land and no doubt he has his reasons for requiring an open trial."

He stood and collected the papers.

"We've met," he said, smiling. "And it's good to know you. When I have the detailed charges we'll meet again."

He went to the door and knocked on it. Then, turning, he said: "Do you have a Bible?"

"No."

"Shall I apply for one?"

"No."

Three weeks passed before Michael Tsang came again to the cell.

"Are you well?" he asked.

"Yes."

"Is there anything you need?"

"Exercise."

"I'll make a request."

Tsang sat, took papers from a briefcase. Lewis went to the window. A boat had appeared on the lake. It was small at that distance and he could not see its details. But its prow and oars would be intricately carved, he knew, and there would be lace covers on the seats and lotus parting under the prow. Two people and a child sat in the boat. A family. Remember? Tears blurred his eyes.

"Is the view important?" Tsang asked.

"Very."

Now the boat was passing out of sight. The father (was it the father?) was pointing down at the water, as if at a fish.

"Who arranged this cell?" Lewis asked.

"Arranged?"

"This particular cell. Was it Chen?"

"I don't know."

"It might be Chen."

"A kindness?"

Now the boat was gone.

"Perhaps a kindness," Lewis said. "Perhaps not." He watched the water, but the boat did not reappear. "Sometimes I cry when I see that lake."

Tsang shrugged.

"You have a view," he said. "Be grateful. Please sit down."

Lewis sat.

"I have been in Hong Kong," Tsang said.

"How pleasant."

"With a man you know. A senator."

"Nathanson?"

"Yes. And three of his colleagues. All of them from Washington, U.S.A. They are deeply interested in your trial." He searched in the papers and placed three documents side by side. "They have given me copies of attested depositions by yourself, by a Lieutenant Pu and by a Dr. Cao Hai. They provide testimony to the atrocity in the Fusan camp. The senators' concern, of course, is with the deaths of two hundred Americans, not with your personal fate. But paths have crossed, and the trial will give them the stage they need. The world, now, will watch and listen." He found another document and slid it across the table. "This is your indictment. Please read it."

Lewis stood and took it to the window. It was written in Chinese and in English and it had been issued under the seal of the Hangchow Higher People's Court in the Province of Chekiang.

You, Lewis Robert Mackenna, Defendant, one-time Pastor of the Edinburgh Presbyterian Overseas Fellowship at Dragon Well Lane, Hangchow, will answer Charges as listed hereunder.

1. *Acting as agent for the traitor Chiang Kai-shek and conspiring with other traitors of China.*

2. *Plotting to subvert the Chinese people's democratic regime and sabotaging the patriotic movement.*

3. *Harboring and sheltering imperialist spies and other enemies of the State under the cloak of hospital treatment.*

4. *Leading a counterrevolutionary clique under the cloak of religion and involvement in subversive meetings with Christian groups in China.*

5. *Acting as paymaster to agents of Chiang Kai-shek and operating escape routes for enemies of the State.*

6. *Wounding by firearm while escaping arrest Lin Sheng, Under-officer of the Ministry of Public Security.*

7. *Sundry acts of espionage and plots against the Communist party.*

8. *Attempting the unlawful export of antiquities.*

Lewis read again the charge under item six. Wounding. Not killing. Lin Sheng was the young man's name. I did not kill him. I did not kill him. Relief flooded. He felt the burden lift. Thank you. He wiped his eyes.

"For what?" Michael Tsang asked.

Lewis turned and stared.

"You said thank you."

"Did I?"

"Yes."

Lewis sat and put the indictment on the table.

"Dr. Mackenna," Tsang said, "you have to be truthful with me. Are you guilty of these acts?"

"I am."

"When did they begin?"

"On my release from Fusan."

"Not before?"

"No."

"Why then?"

"You have read the depositions."

"Many times."

"That night," Lewis said. "That final night. That night of the burning. I saw the face of the Devil in those flames." How odd, he thought, that I can talk of the Devil but not of God. That night. He saw again the excavator, the iron mantis that had lived in Compound One, stretching up from the sea of fire. Had that been the Devil? His risen shape?

"A priest should fight the Devil," Michael Tsang said.

"Yes."

"That is his purpose."

"Yes."

"Let me get this straight, Doctor. Was it that terrible atrocity that set you on your path?"

"It was."

"Then clearly that is your defense."

At dusk of the following day the cell door opened and two men entered. They had thick bodies and empty faces and one of them beckoned and he went out into the corridor and the men walked with him between the lines of cells and down a stairway and through a guarded door and into the prison yard. A car with a Party flag was waiting and he got into the rear and the men sat on the left and right of him, their arms so thick and hard that he felt his elbows crushed against his ribs. The car left the prison and drove through the city and he sat there afraid and the sound of the bicycle bells in the boulevards ringing in his ears.

The car stopped at the flank of a concrete building. He could still hear the bells. The men got out and knocked on a door and it opened and he went with them down a corridor to another half-open door and one of the men touched his arm and pointed and said: "Go in." A sudden fear made him gasp. His mind leaped back to the camp and a door like this and a hand pointing like this and Lieutenant Pu murmuring the same invitation. "Go in." He could not move. That bamboo hut and the two waiting men and the shaved Mongol heads. Don't let it happen again. Please don't let it happen again. He felt a hand push against his back and he entered. The door closed behind him.

A single bulb burned in the room. There was a small barred window, a single chair, naked walls with stains. His legs were weak and he sat and closed his eyes. He crossed his arms and enfolded himself and began to rock. Time passed. How long? A minute? An hour? The door opened. He heard a distant chatter of voices, faint chords of music. Hands were clapping. He opened his eyes. The figure on the threshold beckoned.

"Come, Lewis," John Chen said.

In the corridor, Chen at his side and the two men behind, the music grew louder. A man in a medieval costume approached and passed. Another door. Chen pushed it open, stood back and gestured. Lewis stepped into a perfumed half-light, into rainbow color and the sound of strings and gongs. It was the side aisle of a theater. Faces turned from the crowded rows. Four vacant seats made a square on the aisle and Chen gestured again. They sat; he and Chen together, the two men behind. Dancers were spinning on the stage against a painted backdrop of mountains and temples. The fear in the room had left its waves of sickness and he saw only the blurs of silk and velvet. He had been here before, in those distant days when there had been Western dramas and Western concerts and on festival evenings the children had come from the mission to enact the demon plays and there had been sweetmeats and the smell of fried doughcakes. Chen gave him a program. The light was dim and he could read only the headings. *The Hangchow Theater of Classical Performing Arts,* it said. *A Visit of a Company from the Shanghai People's Art Theater.*

"All amateurs," Chen said. "From the factories, the shops, the hospitals."

He watched. It was in the style of Peking Opera with song, mime and dance, lacquered faces, exact movements of the feet.

"Why am I here?" he asked.

Chen did not answer. The artists were leaving the stage. The last of them, a woman in black and red pantaloons and astride an imaginary horse, rode into the wings. The music stopped.

"Now for the Traditional Play," Chen said.

This time there was a backdrop depicting a throne hall in the Imperial Palace. Onstage a gong hung on a spiked frame and a trio of blind musicians tapped softly on lizardskin drums. A Manchu emperor sat on a golden throne. To his left stood his daughter, the princess; and to his right a young courtier (played traditionally by a girl) stood with downcast face. A warlord in leather and steel waited downstage and the shadow of an executioner's arm and axe moved ominously on the extreme of the backdrop. It was an old story, drawn from legend, that Lewis had seen many times before; the princess and the lowly courtier joined in an impossible love, the weak emperor who had promised her to the rich and powerful warlord in return for a share of plunder and the allegiance of his army. The drums, now, were like distant thunder. The emperor pointed at the courtier. "Renounce him, daughter, or he dies." The shadow of the axe lifted slowly. "Answer. Do you renounce him?" Lewis listened. That dry thin voice. It seemed familiar. The emperor leaned forward. The long whiskers quivered like wire filaments. The finger went to the courtier. "Do you renounce her?" The courtier's face turned into light. It was oval and olive-skinned, as vulnerable as that of a child. "I would rather die than renounce her," Suching said. The emperor shook his head in anger, pointed at the axe. "Then die you shall," Tan Haifeng said. The warlord removed his helmet and flung it to the floor. Lewis stared at him. He had last seen that cropped head and birthmark under an umbrella of varnished paper on the deck of *Cathay Moon*. "Let his head fall and roll like that helmet," Kenneth Choy said. He kicked the helmet so that it rolled toward the throne. The drums grew louder. One of the musicians beat on the gong. The program fell and Lewis bent to retrieve it.

He heard her voice.

Once our love was singing, singing
Where the waters flow
Once we lay and watched the willows
Swaying to and fro

Upright now he saw her move across the stage, heard in the silence of the theater the swish of the brocaded gown. She turned and the tassels of her headdress swung and the embroideries of pearls and jewels caught the light. Her cheeks and nose glowed with colored pastes and it seemed momentarily that they slid against his face and left their taste upon his lips.

Now the trees are weeping, weeping
Where the waters flow
Once we lay and watched the willows
Swaying to and fro

There were silk strings and silver hooks beneath that gown. He felt a faint pressure in his loins. Then it was gone and he looked into Chen's face and gave him the program.

"Enough?" Chen asked.

"Yes."

They stood and went into the aisle. The two men followed. Anna Chang walked to the center and turned. Their eyes met. She held out her arms to him and the horseshoe cuffs hung from her wrists and did not move. Chen waited and when the arms slowly fell they went out into the corridor and began to walk. He could still hear her voice.

The yellow leaves are dying, dying
Where the waters flow
Once we lay and watched them falling
That was long ago

Chen stopped.

"Would you like to meet the cast?" he asked.

Lewis saw the irony in his eyes.

"No."

Outside the theater and the night wind warm on the face he entered the car and the men got in. Chen did not follow. He closed the door, then bent to the open window and offered the program.

Lewis shook his head.

"Take it. Her name is in it. Her real name."

"No."

The car started. He saw Chen step back, shrug, drop the program to the road. It turned in the wind.

Two weeks later Michael Tsang entered the cell.

"Good news," he said, smiling. He put his briefcase on the table and came to the window. "Good, good news."

Lewis waited.

"The charges have been reduced."

Tsang went to the table and spread papers. He picked up a document and cast it aside. "That," he said, tapping it, "is the old indictment." He picked up another. "And this is the new." He laughed with pleasure. "Much shorter, Doctor."

He brought it to the window and Lewis took it.

"As you can see," Tsang said, "you are now charged with only two offenses. Firstly with attempting the unlawful export of antiquities. Secondly with wounding Lin Sheng. These of course appeared in the original indictment. The remaining six charges have been withdrawn."

Lewis returned the indictment.

"Why?" he asked.

"Let us sit."

At the table Tsang wiped his eyes.

"I am so pleased for you," he said.

"Yes. But now tell me why."

"I've been back to Hong Kong, Doctor. There have been more discussions. Senator Nathanson and his three colleagues were present as before. But this time there was another party. A very important man. A man from Washington. A man sent by the Secretary of State himself. The affair has moved to the highest level. Since the Korean War the U.S.A. has had no real diplomatic links with China. But, as we all know, contacts between nations are never entirely lost. Emissaries meet, talk, bargain. Yes, bargain. With politicians there is always a bargain." He laughed. "You, Dr. Mackenna, have become a small fish. And like many small and lucky fish they are going to throw you back."

"Release me?"

"Let me explain. It is more than a year since the war in Korea ended. But to this day there are many thousands of American servicemen in Chinese prison camps. Mainly in Manchuria. Washington, of course, is pressing through intermediaries for their return. There is public concern for the men and the last thing the administration wants is a public trial at which a group of senators will throw the ashes of an old atrocity in China's face. Peking, too, does not want that. Life may be cheap in China and no doubt the Politburo would regard the burning of Fusan as no more than a spark from the fires of her terrible history. But the world is realigning itself. The Russians are massed on the Mongolian border. Already there is talk of the coming war between China and Russia. But could the U.S.A. stand aside? Who will she support? China is asking these questions." Tsang laughed. "Yes, politics. Always the politics. And perhaps an ancient fear. China is stronger than the Soviets only in population. She will need an ally." He laughed again. "There have been stranger bedfellows." Then, seriously: "So governments have whispered. You will plead guilty to the two charges. There will be a light sentence. Do you understand?"

"I understand."

"Fusan never existed. Is that clear?"

"Yes. But what about Nathanson?"

"He accepts it. Stubborn at first. He went out onto the hotel terrace and stared up at Victoria Peak. 'Twelve hundred men,' he said. 'Among them two hundred Americans. And among those my son. They deserve better than this.' He came back into the room. 'But they are all dead,' he said. 'The prisoners are living. If this will help them then so be it. Chen won't be exposed for what he did. And that is wrong.' Then he smiled rather grimly. 'But there is always the handyman.'" Tsang shrugged. "I don't know what he meant. Some Americanism, perhaps."

"Perhaps."

Tsang stood.

"If the atrocity is mentioned," he said, "you will be in peril. They will reimpeach you and charge you with the six grave offenses. So it never happened."

"No."

"Say it."

"It never happened."

"Good." Tsang returned the papers to the case. "I have had a conference with John Chen. He was quite cold with anger. Mackenna is guilty of acts against the State, he told me, and should be severely punished." He went to the door, knocked on it, then turned. "Father Jethro was tried last week. For transporting fugitives. Guilty, of course."

"What did he get?"

"Twenty-five years."

He awakened. This was the night before the trial. He had no watch but he sensed the hours of darkness that lay before him. He turned and slept again and when he came abruptly from sleep he was wet with sweat and the window was still a black rectangle and the dreams were still there, divinities with black wings, black cells in other places, Jethro lying in blackness and listening in desperation for the crack of sailcloth, a bell. He sat up. A bell. He could still hear it. A church bell? He got up and went to the window. The sound came on the wind, not a peal but a single note. *I know that bell.* The bell was distant, mournful in the night. *That is my bell.* There was a time when it had been joyous, even when it had called for the sacrament of death. He had listened to it as an infant. Ellen had listened. His sons had listened. The sound died, then returned with the wind. That empty mission church, the ropes tied beneath the belfry. Whose hand was pulling on them? Our bell. Joyous then because there had been no lies, no deceit, no infirmities of the spirit. Whose hand? It was ringing now across Dragon Well Lane and Ningpo Avenue and the Hangchow roofs, reaching for him. He clutched the lower bars of the window and held to them and let the grief possess him. When it had passed, this grief for that which had gone, he went back to the pallet bed. The bell was silent. He would wait for the light.

In the morning there was the People's Court.

"State your name," Chen said.

"Lewis Robert Mackenna."

"Have you read and understood the indictment?"

"Yes."

"Are you an ordained minister of the Presbyterian Church?"

"I am."

"Do you have medical qualifications?"

"I do."

"What are they?"

"I am a Doctor of Medicine. And a Fellow of the Royal College of Surgeons, Edinburgh."

"Edinburgh?" Judge Liang Fen said. "Where is that?"

"In Scotland."

Liang wrote it down. He was the presiding judge of the tribunal. He was flanked by Wang Hung-wen, a judge from the lower court; and Chou Piao, a judge from the Shanghai Higher People's Court. Chou habitually wore a peasant towel around his head. It proclaimed his peasant origin and it was as if he had just come sweating from his work on the land. The court was crowded. There was a bench for the press and among the nine journalists there were four European faces.

"Where is Scotland?" Chou asked.

"It is a country in the north of Britain."

"Where did you graduate?" Chen asked.

"Edinburgh University."

"And from there?"

"Royal Edinburgh Hospital."

"Were you ordained in Scotland?"

"Yes."

Michael Tsang stood.

"Dr. Mackenna," he said, "were you born in Hangchow?"

"I was."

"In the mission?"

"Yes."

"Did you return there when qualified?"

"I did."

"And remained there?"

"Yes."

"To practice medicine?"

"Yes."

"And to preach the gospel?"

"Yes."

"Did your forefathers work in the Hangchow mission?"

"Yes."

"Practice medicine and preach the gospel?"

"Yes."

"How long ago?"

"More than a hundred years."

Judge Liang tapped in irritation.

"Is this material?" he asked.

"Yes, sir," Tsang said. "I wish to establish that the accused and his family before him gave their working lives to our country."

"His family are not on trial."

"No, sir."

Tsang sat.

"Proceed," Liang said.

"The first charge," Chen said, "is that you, Lewis Robert Mackenna, attempted the unlawful export of antiquities. How do you plead?"

"Guilty."

"I ask permission," Chen said to Liang, "to produce an exhibit."

Liang nodded and Chen pointed at the door that was to the left of the judges' dais and an usher opened it and went through and they heard his voice. Then he returned and two soldiers followed. They were carrying a tea chest and they set it down on the floor in the center of the court. Then they left the court and returned with a second chest and placed it by the first. Lewis stared at them. He could read the Long Jing stencils.

"Do you recognize them?" Chen asked.

"Yes."

"Were they your property?"

"They are my property."

"Wrong," Chou Piao said. An ear of the towel had fallen and he tucked it back. "The State has confiscated."

"I think he owns the chests," Wang said mildly. "It is the contents that are forfeit."

Chou frowned.

"Dr. Mackenna," Chen said, "will you leave the stand and go to the chests and remove the contents and describe and identify each object as you do so?"

Lewis crossed the floor to the first of the tea chests. He pulled out a mass of straw, then a piece of earthenware. He held it up.

"A dragon vase," he told them. "Tang period."

He placed it on the floor, fished again in the chest. He lifted out a round box of brilliant color.

"Cloisonné enamel," he said. "Two parrots on a peach branch. Ming."

He set it down, found another object. More straw fell.

"A brushwater bowl," he said. "Song."

Another dip with his arm.

"A pottery tortoise. Northern Wei."

Another.

"A silver stem-cup. Tang."

His foot knocked the vase.

"Careful," Chou said softly. "Be careful with our property."

When the chest was empty he dipped into the second. He held up a figurine of straw-glazed glass.

"A tomb figure," he told them. "Tang."

Now the floor displayed a treasure of jade and bronze, ivory and porcelain and marble, half-buried in a thicket of yellow straw. He produced the last object.

"A bronze lion. Shang."

He stepped back.

"That's the lot."

"Return to the stand," Liang said.

From the stand Lewis looked down at the floor and felt the anger grow.

"Are these works of art?" Chen asked.

"They are."

"Of considerable value?"

"Yes."

"You pleaded guilty. Were you aware that it was unlawful to export antiquities from the People's Republic of China?"

"I was not."

The first lie. He saw the contempt in Chen's eyes.

"Were the antiquities stolen from you?"

"Yes."

"While escaping the country?"

"Yes."

"Were you accompanied by your family?"

"I was."

"A wife and two sons?"

"Yes."

"What were the circumstances of the theft?"

"A part of the journey was by junk. The master landed us and kept the tea chests."

Chen turned to the tribunal.

"The junkmaster was subsequently arrested," he said. "And the antiquities recovered." Then, to Lewis: "Did you in fact reach Taiwan?"

"Yes."

"Did you obtain employment?"

"I did."

"As a doctor?"

"Yes."

Chen pointed at the antiquities.

"Was it your intention to sell them?"

"No."

The second lie.

"Are you sure?"

"Yes."

Michael Tsang stood.

"Dr. Mackenna," he said, "are you a lover of ancient Chinese art?"

"I am."

"When did you start collecting?"

"Twenty years ago."

The third lie.

"And over that period the collection grew piece by piece?"

"Yes."

"By purchase?"

"Sometimes."

"And at other times?"

"Gifts."

"By grateful patients?"

"Yes."

Chou Piao leaned forward and stared down at the floor.

"You must have saved many patients."

Someone laughed.

"Dr. Mackenna," Wang said, "did you demand payment for your services?"

"No."

"Did you invite payment?"

"On occasions."

"From whom did you invite payment?"

"From those who could pay."

"The rich?"

"Some were rich."

"And what happened to the cash?"

"Not all of it was cash."

"Explain."

"It could be cash. It could be produce. It could be goods."

"In cash or in kind?"

"Yes."

"And what happened to these payments?"

"They went to the mission."

"Did you ever charge the poor?"

"Never."

"But you preferred to attend the rich?"

"Of course he preferred to attend the rich," Chou said. "You would not expect a dying peasant to present him with a pair of Tang vases."

Again the laughter.

"Answer the question," Liang said.

"I went to those in need," Lewis said. "Rich or poor."

"But you hoped for a payment?"

"Yes."

"Was the mission poor?"

"All missions are poor."

"And the missionaries? Are they also poor?"

"Of course."

"Why of course?" Chen asked. "You have told us that you purchased works of art."

"Yes."

"Can a poor man purchase works of art?"

"If they are bargains."

"And you could recognize a bargain?"

"Yes."

"I have heard enough," Liang said coldly. "The accused has pleaded guilty to the charge. There will be a sentence. In mitigation he pleads ignorance of the law. He asks us to believe that he was unaware that the export of antiquities was illegal. But plainly he is lying. Consider the facts. He admits that he was able to recognize a bargain. But ability of that order presupposes knowledge. The knowledge that comes from twenty years of acquisition. During that time he must surely have become expert. The world of fine arts, I imagine, is one of continuous fascination. There would have been publications, museums, exhibitions, talks with scholars and other collectors. He would have walked in that world, or at least on the fringes of it. And because of that involvement it is inconceivable that he would not have known the law." Judge Liang drank a little water. "Let us ignore the laxity of the law until 1949. Let us concentrate on that year of the liberation and the years that followed. It was common knowledge that the traitor Chiang Kai-shek stole the best of the imperial treasures and shipped them to Taiwan. It was also known that great quantities of artworks were left behind in secret stores. To this day the search continues. The law was strengthened. Penalties are severe. There is a watch on our shores and frontiers. Everyone knows there is an absolute embargo on the export of antiquities. It has been known since 1949. And above all it is known in the art world." Liang pointed a finger at Lewis. "I say he is lying."

"Yes, lying," Chou said.

Wang nodded.

Liang's finger moved.

"And what do you say, Michael Tsang?"

Tsang was silent.

"Answer."

"As you say, sir," Tsang said miserably, "he had become a collector. That strange, obsessed creature that only another collector could understand. It was fired by that first distant acquisition. One rarity. One thing of beauty. And after that the hunger for the next. And the next and the next. When the time came how could he leave them?"

"Is that your defense?"

"Yes."

Liang grimaced.

"I am a collector," Chou Piao said with menace. He gestured at Lewis.

"A collector of collectors." He unwound the towel, sighed with fatigue, wiped his face. Surely since dawn he had ploughed a dozen hectares? "A peasant could work in the fields for a lifetime and his total wages would not buy the smallest of those pieces." He rewound the towel. "For him the only beauty is a dish of food."

Wang nodded.

"Dr. Mackenna," Liang said, "do you have anything to add?"

"No."

"We will try the second charge tomorrow." He pointed at the pieces. "Now put them back."

Lewis went to the chests and began to pack them, cradling each piece in straw and the court watching in silence and the task so slow that it became a humiliation. He looked up once and Chou was smiling with malevolence. When the chests were filled he straightened. Judge Liang shook his head and pointed at the floor and the wisps of straw that were strewn on it. He bent again, began to move, crouched low, retrieving straw until the floor was clean.

John Chen walked through the shadow of the pear tree and sat on the stone tortoise that faced the entrance to the mission church. He sat there until the evening sun was gone. Then he stood, unlocked the door and entered. He could smell the dust. There was also the scent that came to all abandoned places. He walked down the aisle to the altar. The painted Christ still suffered on the wall behind it. But the yellow cloth had gone and the screen lay broken on the floor. The piano stood against the wall by the vestry door and he went to it and lifted the lid and looked down at the keyboard. Hymns, nursery songs, children's voices. For a moment those sounds of innocence seemed to fill the church. He tapped one of the black keys. It was dead. He reached out for the lid and let it fall and the echoes flighted in the rafters. Then the silence came and he went to the corner and looked up into the belfry. The ropes had been untied and were hanging. He could see the clapper in the throat of the bell. Ring it, he had instructed. Ring it in the night, remind him. He too had heard the bell, listened in the darkness as Mackenna must have listened. Ring it now, implant yourself again in Mackenna's mind. He took the ropes in his hands and pulled until the bell called and called again across the city sky. He let go the ropes. The bell was still. When the ropes no longer swung he looked up once more into the belfry. Nothing moved. Even the bats had gone.

He went to the front pew and sat, locked his hands so that he might think. He had sat here once before, coming to the deserted church to feel the essence of the man he was about to hunt. That hunt had ended. But there was still no victory. The politicians had murmured in Washington and Hong Kong, had struck their squalid bargain. There was a bigger stage than the People's Court, it seemed. Yet he was party to that bargain. He was a servant of the State, and the State had directed. It was not his responsibility if the State, for political reasons, had elected to take less than its due. But the self-disgust would not leave him. It was growing. Why was a man's estimate of himself forever at his side? During this day of the first of the charges he had listened to Mackenna's lies. He had seen the sense of injury flicker in his eyes. It was like watching a man wound himself. Did Mackenna yearn for truth? He heard his voice in that moment, crossing the Fusan camp at the time of the typhus deaths, coming faintly on the Gobi wind from some graveside service. ". . . and to walk in Thy truth." They were the words, all that he had heard. To walk in Thy truth. Truth. That one immaculate word. Think. Consider the aspects of truth. You and I, he said to Mackenna's face, we are both growing smaller. Tomorrow, the second day of the trial, a part of us will die, like that essential black key in the piano. Us. Tomorrow on that corrupted stage. We are linked, he thought. Why should I care what happens to you, a man once ordered in the Church of Christ? He stood, stared around him at the pulpit, the stripped altar, the nailed limbs. Why?

He left the church.

The glade of azaleas was in deep shadow, the gravestones pale and gripped by weed. He could not read the inscriptions. There had been a time before when he had walked between the stones. "I'll bring him back," he had told the nurse with the big starched body. "He'll get his patch of Chinese earth." He crossed the courtyard. Do I want that now? he asked himself. His death? He shook his head, evading the answer. The State must prove his true guilt. The State must punish. There could be nothing less. He followed the path that skirted the mission house. Another path led from the rear of the house to the little hospital. Think. Tomorrow is the endgame. Clear your mind. Think. Our game. That courtroom with the sixty-four squares that only you and I can see. One move. He reached the hospital. It had been unused since Mackenna's flight. Inside was dust and darkness, perhaps a faint persisting smell of disinfectant. One final move that will excavate the truth from that divided mind. Think. The entrance door was locked and he walked around the flank and looked through the central window. It was a small ward that might at one time have accommodated six beds. It was empty now, except for one iron bedframe. He turned away, began the return walk to the house. Think. One move. One piece. If truth were a chess piece, he thought, it would be so white and fragile within the fingers. He stopped, went back to the window, stared through it at the bedframe. It had no spring and the tiny swiveled wheels were missing from two of the legs. A pallid light from the moonrise touched it and he watched it grow in definition.

In that moment he saw the shape of the final move.

*   *   *

In the morning there was the second charge.

"You are charged," John Chen said, "with wounding by firearm Lin Sheng, Under-officer of the Ministry of Public Security. How do you plead?"

"Guilty."

"What kind of firearm?"

"A magazine pistol."

"Do you usually carry a pistol?"

"No."

"Where did you obtain the pistol?"

"During the journey."

Judge Liang tapped with impatience.

"Chen Yuchang," he said, "you go too fast. There are three aspects to every journey. A reason, a route, a destination. Let us consider those aspects. Begin in Hangchow."

Chen bowed.

"Dr. Mackenna," he said, "what was your reason for leaving?"

Liang tapped again.

"Yesterday," he said, "there was a different word."

"Yes," Wang agreed. "Escaping. That was the word."

Chen shrugged.

"It is the same," he said.

"No. It is not the same."

"In this case it is."

"Was he not pursued?" Liang asked.

"Yes."

"Then he was escaping."

Michael Tsang walked to the stand.

"Dr. Mackenna," he asked, "did you and your family quit the mission in June of 1954?"

"We did."

"Five years after the liberation?"

"Yes."

"Were you among the last of the Christian missionaries?"

"I was."

"Did you in those five years continue to tend the sick and dying?"

"Yes."

"And provide spiritual comfort?"

"Yes."

"Did you maintain a mission hospital?"

"Yes."

"To which all could come regardless of belief?"

"Of course."

"Did you maintain a mission school?"

"Yes."

"For young children?"

"Yes."

"Did you provide an elementary education?"

"Yes."

"And did you," Chou Piao said with sarcasm, "indoctrinate their minds?"

"I opened them."

"Opened them?"

"Yes."

"To what?"

"To the love of Christ."

Chou made a face.

"I thought," he said, "that Christ had been deported."

Wang laughed.

"Yes," Michael Tsang said seriously, "one could say that Christ had been deported. Certainly he was an outcast in the land of Chairman Mao."

Chou frowned.

"Take care," he said.

"I am putting a case."

"Nevertheless take care. You are not in Hong Kong now."

"I am putting a case. I am defending a Christian priest. I was chosen to defend him because I too am a Christian. That means I understand him. I used a form of words. But in a sense they are not my own. Christ was an outcast. Who can deny that simple fact? Who can deny the pressures under which the defendant lived and worked? Picture him in that dying mission. The vanished flock, police surveillance, around him the hostile streets. So much had gone."

"Yes," Chen said drily. "Even the church bell."

"Dr. Mackenna," Tsang said, "how would you describe your work in those final days?"

"As a priest?"

"Yes."

"Futile."

"Was that why you left?"

"Yes."

The fourth lie.

"The only reason?" Wang asked.

"Yes."

"Why were you under police surveillance?"

"I do not know."

Another lie.

"All Christian priests are subject to surveillance," Chen said. "Chinese or foreign, that is the rule."

"No specific reason?"

"No."

Lies, Chen thought, are contagious.

"Tell me," Judge Liang said to Lewis, "did you apply to the authorities for permission to leave?"

"I did not."

"Why not?"

"Because permission was not always given."

"Are you sure of that?"

"Yes."

"But did you not state that you were among the last of the missionaries?"

"I did."

"How many missionaries were at one time working in China?"

"I do not know."

"Thousands?"

"Yes, thousands."

"What happened to them?"

"Some were imprisoned. Some died. Most of them left or were expelled."

"Was it government policy to be rid of them?"

"Yes."

"In one way or another?"

"Yes."

"Then why should the government refuse you?"

"My client cannot speak for the government," Michael Tsang said.

"It is all very obvious," Chou Piao said wearily. "It is nothing to do with frustration, with a missionary who had no mission. He was not merely a priest. He had his work of healing, his hospital. That, surely, is a mission of a kind." He turned a hand and stroked with his finger the callus that made a bony armor on the palm. The plough left its mark on a man's flesh, did it not? "It is all to do with the antiquities. He owned this treasure. He wanted to get it out. He was under police surveillance and he knew that a request to leave the country would at once redouble that surveillance. Perhaps he and his family would have received an exit permit. Who knows? But he could not present himself at a port of exit with the two tea chests. He could not risk a search and confiscation and a criminal charge." Chou slid a hand up under the folds of the towel and scratched. Was it a louse? "So he made his plans. It is all so obvious."

"Yes, obvious," Wang said.

Liang wrote something.

"So we have the reason for the flight," he said. "And we know the destination." He put down the pen and looked up. "Let us now retrace the route."

*   *   *

In midafternoon sunlight struck across the courtroom and touched the pages of the atlas. Judge Liang ran a fingertip through Hangchow Bay toward the city.

"Proceed," he said.

"Dr. Mackenna," Chen asked, "did you leave Hangchow in the mission truck?"

"Yes."

"South through Chekiang?"

"Yes."

"What was your immediate destination?"

"Ogre Head Lake."

"Where is that?"

"On the Liao River."

Liang bent to the map.

"I have it," he said.

"Why Ogre Head Lake?" Chen asked.

"An appointment."

"With what?"

"A raft."

"A raft?" Wang said.

"Yes," Chen said. "The accused and his family and the tea chests and personal possessions were put on the raft. The raft took them downriver to a second appointment. Tell us what that was, Dr. Mackenna."

"It was a junk."

"And where did the junk take you?"

"Into the River Shih."

"A moment," Liang said. The finger moved. "It is not marked here."

"No," Chen said. "It is no more than a narrow branch." Then to Lewis: "Did the junk land you at a point twenty kilometers down?"

"It did."

"What happened then?"

"I have already told the court."

"Tell us again."

Chou Piao laughed.

"The chests were stolen from him," he said. He began to shake. The towel uncurled and he wiped an eye with the fringe of it. "I find that very droll." The laughter shook him again. He pointed at Lewis. "Was it a punishment by the Christian god?"

"Why should it be? It was my property."

"Did you not steal it from the Chinese people?"

"No."

"Let us proceed," Liang said.

"From the Shih," Chen asked, "did you then march to the mountains?"

"Yes."

"Did you have guides?"

"Yes."

"How many?"

"Three. A Hakka and two Fukienese."

"And mules?"

"Three."

"Quite a caravan," Wang said sourly.

"And was it in these mountains," Chen said, "that you shot Lin Sheng?"

"Wait," Judge Liang said. He tapped the map. "Let us complete the journey. We can then return to the scene of the offense."

Chen bowed.

"Dr. Mackenna," he said, "were you traveling to the coast?"

"Yes."

"Where?"

"Swatow."

"How far from the mountains?"

"About ninety kilometers."

"How did you cover that distance?"

"By truck."

"Who drove it?"

"I do not know."

Another lie.

"Was it a Sister Tai?"

"I do not know."

Chen turned to the bench.

"It was in fact a Sister Tai," he said. "She was a nun from a religious Order known as the Swatow Central Mission, one of the four remaining Sisters. All four were subsequently charged and punished." He turned to Lewis. "Will you now recall the name of Sister Tai?"

"I will not name another party."

"As you wish. Were you then taken from the Swatow Central Mission to a coastal village named To-kuei?"

"I will not answer."

"Was there a Catholic mission at To-kuei and was it administered by a Macao Father named Francis Jethro?"

"I will not answer."

"And did he transport you and your family by boat across the Strait to Taiwan?"

"I will not answer."

Chen turned again to the bench.

"Father Jethro," he said, "was later charged and sentenced in the Swatow People's Court."

"What was the charge?" Liang asked.

"Transporting fugitives."

"In the plural?"

"Yes."

"Let me be clear. Are you telling the court that the charge did not relate specifically to Dr. Mackenna?"

"I am."

"Were other fugitives on the boat?"

"No."

"Then what are you saying?"

"That the charge of transporting fugitives also embraced a previous period."

"How long a period?"

"Since 1950."

"Were the four nuns also charged in Swatow?"

"Yes."

"What was the charge?"

Chen did not answer.

"What was the charge?"

"This court is concerned," Chen said, "with Dr. Mackenna and the second charge of wounding. It is not concerned with cases tried and adjudicated in another court."

"Wrong," Liang said coldly. "It is concerned with whatever I say it is concerned. Is that clear?"

"Yes."

"I am the presiding judge and I will ask questions and I will have answers. Is that clear?"

"Yes."

"I ask again. What was the charge?"

"The nuns were charged with harboring fugitives and assisting their escape."

"Again in the plural?"

"Yes."

"Since 1950?"

"Yes."

Judge Liang wrote.

"Chen Yuchang," he said, "how would you define the word fugitive?"

"One who flees."

"From what?"

Chen considered.

"From an enemy," he said. "From danger. From a situation. And of course from the forces of the law."

"Which had been broken?"

"Yes."

"Or seemed to be broken," Wang said.

"Yes," Liang said, nodding. "It is good to be accurate." Then to Chen: "A crime can be committed against a person or against property. Do you agree?"

"Of course."

"Is there not another classification?"

"I do not follow."

"I think you do. There is also crime against the State."

"The worst of all crimes," Chou said.

"Yes," Liang said. "Or so we are now taught. The crime may be treason, or subversion, or an act of counterrevolution, or adherence to the State's enemies, or even disloyalty. We describe these as political offenses." He stared again at the map. "Obviously, in the years since the liberation, the nuns and the priest Jethro were accomplices within the operation of an escape route. And since the members of a religious Order and an ordained priest are unlikely to have assisted the escape of common criminals it follows that those assisted were political fugitives." His finger moved across the map. "By truck, by raft, by junk, by mountain march, by boat." The finger pointed at Lewis. "You and your family, Dr. Mackenna, were taken down an escape route. So answer. Were you a political fugitive?"

Michael Tsang rose.

"I object," he said.

"On what grounds?"

"The question is improper."

"A strong word."

"Yes. For a strong objection."

"I have told this court," Liang said, "that I will ask whatever questions I choose to ask. Surely you heard me?"

"Yes, sir. But there are either rules or no rules. I repeat that the question is improper." Tsang held up the indictment. "My client is not charged with a political offense."

"He is charged with shooting a Public Security officer, is he not?'

"Yes."

"Is not the work of such an officer concerned with political offenses?"

"Yes."

Chou leaned forward.

"Then is it not a political offense to shoot him?"

Wang laughed.

"That is dubious law," Tsang said. "As dubious as the trial rules of this court."

"Rules, rights, objections," Chou said with contempt. "You are not pleading in Hong Kong. You are in China in a court of the people."

"Of that I am well aware."

"Michael Tsang," Liang said, "do you see a jury in this courtroom?"

"I do not."

"No, you do not. You see a tribunal. We listen. We observe. We question. We think. If we give voice to our thoughts how is that detrimental to your client? There is no jury to be influenced."

"This is an open court," Tsang said. "Journalists are present. Proceedings are recorded. That record will be studied in the event of an appeal."

"Appeal?" Chou said.

Wang smiled.

"Did you hear?" Chou asked him.

"I did."

"Have you ever heard that word before?"

"Never."

Judge Liang sipped some water.

"Proceed," he said to Chen.

"Dr. Mackenna," Chen said, "were you aware that you were moving down an organized escape route?"

"No."

"But you agree it was organized?"

"Of course."

"Did you organize it?"

"No."

"Who then?"

"I will not answer."

"A person of power?"

"I will not answer."

"A subversive group?"

"I will not answer."

"Perhaps," Chou said with sarcasm, "it was a grateful patient."

The sun, low now, made grilles on the courtroom floor.

"You told us," Chen said, "that you acquired the pistol during the journey."

"Yes."

"Where were you at the time?"

"In the mountains."

"Did you buy it?"

"Yes."

"From whom?"

"From the Hakka tribesman."

"Had you owned a pistol prior to that?"

"Never."

"Or fired one?"

"No."

"Are you sure?"

"I am."

Chen looked at his papers.

"Dr. Mackenna, were you not in Shanghai at the time of the Japanese invasion?"

"Yes."

"And in Nanking at the time of the massacres?"

"Yes."

"They were dangerous times?"

"Very."

"Was it not a common practice for Europeans to carry guns?"

"It was."

"Yet you did not carry one?"

"No."

"Why not?"

"A priest should not take a human life."

He looked away. The words had struck like the tholepin on Shameen's neck.

"But seventeen years later," Chen said, "you were prepared to carry a pistol."

"Yes."

"And to use it."

"Yes."

"What had changed?"

"I had."

"What happened to the sanctity of human life?"

He did not answer.

"Why did you need a pistol?"

"To protect my family."

Chou Piao laughed with scorn.

"You needed a pistol," he said, "to protect your wealth."

"No."

"Yes. Protect your wealth. Isn't that what the rich always do?"

Michael Tsang stood.

"Dr. Mackenna," he said, "did you acquire the pistol before or after the theft of the chests?"

"After."

"So you had no wealth to protect?"

"None."

"Was it wild country?"

"It was."

"And did the theft remind you that there were dangers in that lawless place?"

"Yes."

Tsang sat.

"Dr. Mackenna," Chen said, "you admit to a sense of danger."

"Yes."

"What were the dangers?"

Lewis reflected.

"Nomads."

"And?"

"Bandits."

"Anything else?"

"No."

"Did you know you were being pursued?"

"I did not."

Another lie.

"Was not the real danger the pursuit by the security forces?"

"I have to object again," Tsang said.

"On what grounds?" Liang asked.

"The term has a certain connotation."

"Which is?"

"Political."

"Not always," Wang said.

"The security forces are concerned with the security of the State," Tsang said stubbornly. "And that is political."

"We are searching for the facts," Liang said. Then, sourly: "When you address me, Michael Tsang, you will stand up."

Tsang stood.

"Thank you. Now sit."

Tsang sat.

"I will ask you again," Chen said to Lewis. "Did you know you were being pursued?"

"No."

"Do you hear me clearly?"

"I do."

"You are not going deaf?"

"Deaf?"

"What is this about?" Liang asked.

"It is about a helicopter," Chen said. Then to Lewis: "Did you on that day of the shooting see or hear a helicopter?"

"No."

How many lies was that?

"Is that not a lie?" Chen asked.

"It is not."

"What helicopter?" Chou said. "We have not heard about a helicopter."

"It came on request from Army Base Five."

"Where is that?" Liang asked.

"Near to Pai-shang."

Liang bent to the map.

"On the Han River," Chen told him.

"I have it."

"It was boarded by myself and Lin Sheng and two soldiers. It flew on a course to the mountains and was landed at a point very near to the accused's party."

"Did you see the party from the air?" Wang asked.

"No."

"How do you know it was near?"

"Because the accused's son and Lin Sheng wandered a few hundred paces from their positions, and met."

"Proceed."

"Dr. Mackenna," Chen said, "the helicopter quartered the terrain where you were located. It flew low. It was painted with a red star emblem and an army numeral. Once again I ask you. Did you see it?"

"I did not."

"It flew through a terrain of cliffs, peaks and granite rock and the noise it made must have filled and echoed in that wild place. Once again I ask you. Did you hear it?"

"I did not."

"An obvious lie," Chou said.

Judge Liang nodded and made a note.

"So," Chen said to Lewis, "you had the pistol. Was it in a holster?"

"In my belt."

"I see. You had the pistol. You would not hesitate to fire it. And you did."

"Yes."

"What happened?"

"One of my sons had strayed from the camp. Night was near and I went in search."

"Which son?"

"Joel."

"How old?"

"Ten."

"Did you find him?"

"Yes."

"Where?"

"In a ravine. But he was not alone. A man was with him."

"You say that night was near. Was the light failing?"

"Of course the light was failing," Chou said with irony. "We expect him to say the light was failing. He intended to fire a warning shot. But because the light was failing the bullet struck the man. Isn't that so, Dr. Mackenna?"

"That is exactly so."

"An accident?"

"Yes."

"We knew it must be an accident."

Wang laughed.

"Continue," Liang said.

"You entered the ravine," Chen said to Lewis. "Tell us what you saw."

"The man and my son were standing in a stream. The man had taken hold of his arm."

"Detaining him?"

"Yes."

"Was your son resisting?"

"He was."

"Describe the man."

Lewis hesitated. Chen moved nearer. The lustrous eyes searched him. He knows your thoughts. There was a feeling that Chen could see the images that were marching through his mind. How can I describe him truthfully? he asked himself: that young man with the smiling lips and the good face and the trousers rolled above his shins and the boots hung around his neck. Only the innocent paddled in streams.

"Describe him."

"I cannot. Not with accuracy."

"The light again?"

"Yes, the light."

An evasion to add to the count of lies.

"And what did you do?"

"I drew the pistol and fired."

"How many shots?"

"Three."

"Three warning shots?" Chou asked.

"Yes."

Tsang rose.

"Were you near to him?" he said.

Lewis hesitated again. Three short paces and he could have touched the young man's face.

"No," he said. "Not near."

"How far away?"

"About fifteen paces."

"Not less?"

"Certainly not less."

"Perhaps twenty?"

"It could have been."

"Would you say that nervous tension and fear for the boy's safety caused you to draw and fire the gun?"

"I would say that."

"Do you contend that distance, poor light and your total unfamiliarity with guns resulted in one of the shots striking Lin Sheng?"

"I do."

"Was there anything in Lin Sheng's appearance to suggest he was a government officer?"

"No."

"Did you believe your son was in danger?"

"Yes."

"Of what?"

"Of being taken away."

"Did that justify the shooting?"

"At the time."

"Do you regret it?"

Lewis was silent.

"Answer," Liang said.

"I regret it. But I had no choice."

"Dr. Mackenna," Chen said, "you had fired three shots."

"Yes."

"And then?"

"The man fell. I went to him. He was bleeding profusely from a wound in the head."

"Did you help him?"

"I sat him up."

"Why?"

"A matter of hemorrhage. He was better upright."

"Is that all you did?" Wang asked. "You, a doctor?"

"I would have treated him. But a soldier appeared."

"So you took your son and ran?"

"Yes."

"Did you not fire at the soldier?" Chen asked.

"I did."

"How many times?"

"Once."

"Was the soldier injured?" Chou asked.

"No," Chen said. Then to Lewis: "You stated that you were fifteen or twenty paces from Lin Sheng when you fired the three shots."

"Yes."

"Are you sure?"

"Sure."

"You will not revise that statement?"

"No."

"Very well. Fifteen or twenty paces. Could you, a man who had never before fired a pistol, be confident of hitting a target at that distance?"

"I was not firing at a target."

"You were firing wide?"

"I told you that."

"The warning shots?"

"Yes."

"Up in the air?"

"No."

"Where?"

"To the right of Lin Sheng."

"You say that Lin Sheng was holding your son's arm?"

"Yes."

"With his left hand?"

"Yes."

"He was very close to your son?"

"He was close."

"So you chose a target and fired?"

"I told you. I did not fire at a target."

"But you fired at an empty space to the right of Lin Sheng?"

"Yes."

"Isn't that a target?"

"Of a kind, I suppose."

"I will ask you again. Could you be confident of hitting a target at fifteen or twenty paces?"

"No."

"So one of the shots struck Lin Sheng?"

"Yes."

"Who was standing close to your son?"

"Yes."

"Does it not follow that in firing the shots you were endangering your son?"

"It does."

"You might have killed him?"

"Yes."

"If they were warning shots why did you not fire up into the air?"

"It was a reflex action."

"A reflex action?"

"Yes."

"You are a doctor. Tell us the precise meaning of that term."

"An involuntary response."

"You drew the pistol, you released the safety catch, you took aim, you fired. Would you describe that sequence as an involuntary response?"

Lewis did not answer.

"Chen Yuchang," Liang said wearily, "where is this leading us?"

"To a conclusion."

"And that is?"

"That the accused did not fire from twenty paces. Or fifteen paces. Or even ten paces. On his own admission he had no skill with a pistol. He would never have fired from a distance and put the boy in danger."

"Agreed," Wang said.

"Dr. Mackenna," Chen said, "do you still claim they were warning shots?"

"I do."

"Did you not run to where Lin Sheng and the boy were standing?"

"No."

"And when you reached them did you not from close range and with intent fire three shots at Lin Sheng?"

"I did not."

Chen turned to the bench.

"Yes," Liang said. "We agree with you. They were not warning shots."

He wrote again.

"But there is still the same unanswered question," Chou Piao said. "Why were the security forces in pursuit? It is an offense to export antiquities. But how does it endanger the State?"

Chen did not answer.

"We are waiting," Liang said.

Chen touched the indictment.

"Two charges," he said. "They are all that concern us."

"I think you should answer."

"I will not."

"I could clear the court."

"Even then I would not answer."

"Do we sentence this man without full knowledge?"

"You do."

"Why should we?"

"Forbidden areas."

Liang stared at Chou and then at Wang.

"Chen Yuchang," he said, "you disconcert me. With those two words you cast away your lawyer's ribbon. You stand there now as a State policeman." He sipped from the tumbler and the sun struck it and sent light across his cheek. "Forbidden areas," he said with distaste. "Why do those words offend me so much?" He set down the tumbler. "There is of course an undercurrent here. I feel it as a swimmer feels it. I am told there was a prior indictment, that its charges were reduced. None of us has seen it but I have no doubt it would have explored a political landscape to which, it seems, this court has no entry. But, then, the courts have no power. The power resides in men like you. There are so many questions. Why should you, an officer from the highest ranks of the Security Bureau, pursue a man from this city to the coast? Why should you, Chen Yuchang, enlist the aid of soldiers and an army aircraft? Why should you step into this provincial court and play the prosecutor's role? And why has not the injured party been called to testify? So many questions." Liang passed his fingers up across his corded neck. "I am old now. I can remember a time when the law, for all its defects in the age of mandarin rule, did not make its judges into puppets. A time when intellectuals" —he looked sideways at Chou Piao— "did not sit on judges' benches pretending to be peasants. Like the accused I was born in this city and I can recall the Mackennas, their work and their benefactions." He smiled. "Shaped and hammered, one of them said, on the forge of faith. It gives me sorrow" —he pointed at Lewis— "to see this man, a Mackenna who once had a spiritual dimension to his life." He bent to his papers and squared them. Then, looking up, he said to Chen: "Does that conclude your case?"

"No. I have a witness."

"His name?"

"Lin Sheng."

The usher left the court. Lewis watched the doorway. He heard the usher's voice, a reply, footsteps. Something bumped in the corridor. He felt the tremor in his hands. This was a moment, such a moment, a response to endless but unarticulated prayer, this moment, to see him, just to see him, his young and pleasant face, the stream and the young man and the slender shins brown in the water and the bootlaces around his graceful neck, such a moment, to see him, to hear his light and springy step, to see him enter, to see him walk through that sunlight shaft, to see him. He looked at Chen, smiled and nodded and smiled. The footsteps came nearer. The front of a wheeled bed appeared in the doorway and the bed passed through the sun shaft and the sheet and the face were white in the shaft and the soldiers pushed the bed to the center of the courtroom floor, locked its wheels and left.

The room was silent. The figure on the bed was unmoving. The face seemed to sleep. Judge Liang leaned forward, stared down at it, then at Chen.

"A witness, you say?" he asked.

"Yes."

"But he cannot speak."

"In a way he can."

Chen went to the bed.

"Dr. Mackenna," he said, "please come here."

Lewis left the stand and walked to the head of the bed, looked down at the pallid face. The right temple was disfigured with scar tissue.

"Do you remember him?" Chen asked.

"I do."

"He is in a coma."

"Yes."

"He has lain like this since the injury."

Lewis bent across him. One of the arms lay outside the sheet. He caught a faint antiseptic scent.

"Could he emerge from it?" Chen asked.

"He could."

"Time is passing. Is there a crucial point?"

"Six months."

"And beyond that?"

"It becomes unlikely."

"Are we near that point?"

"Yes."

Lewis reached out, let his hand rest on the forearm. It had the feel of a cadaver.

"Speak his name," Chen said softly.

"Lin Sheng."

The syllables seemed to brush across the face. He could not weep but something in him was released. Help him, he said to his god, help him, help him. He closed his eyes, held Lin Sheng's arm within his fingers as if he might find and not lose his ebbing life. Have pity, he implored his god, have pity on this man I harmed, have pity, have pity, have pity. He felt Chen move near to him and he opened his eyes.

"A lie or a prayer for his life," Chen whispered. "You cannot have both."

He stood there in silence. Then he took his hand from Lin Sheng's arm and turned and looked into Chen's eyes. Was there compassion in them? Chen waited, willing him to purge himself.

"Yes," Lewis said. "Time for truth."

"Return to the stand."

From the stand he saw Liang lean across to Chou and murmur something. Michael Tsang was staring down at his hands. Lin Sheng's profile was as cold as the marble effigies that lie on tombs in churches and watch the rafters. John Chen looked up at him. There was no triumph in his eyes.

"Dr. Mackenna, have you told the full truth?"

"No."

Chen pointed at Lin Sheng.

"Do you admit wounding with intent?"

"I do."

"Were you an agent for the traitor Generalissimo Chiang Kai-shek?"

"I was."

"Did you receive antiquities in payment for your services?"

"I did."

"Are you guilty of subversive acts against the State?"

"I am."

"Will you tell the court how this began?"

He saw the strain in Chen's face. Was he too in need of expiation?

"It began," Lewis said, "in a place called Fusan."

From the interior of Erich Brandt's shop Ellen Mackenna could see across the road to the mud-and-dung wall and the coiled snakeskins that were pinned to it or decorated the ground at its base. A youth in an orange turban sat among them.

"Where is the old man?" she asked.

"Dead."

"Dead?"

Erich Brandt came to her side.

"He got bitten," he said.

She watched the youth coiling a skin around the spokes of a bamboo cross.

"He was very old," Brandt said, "and he didn't see well. If you are going to catch venomous snakes it is wise to have reasonable eyesight."

They laughed.

"We shouldn't laugh," she said.

"He wouldn't mind."

"He was nice."

"Yes."

"I never painted him," she said. "We talked about how you would do it. Remember?"

"I remember."

"I wanted to. But I never did."

"The talk stopped you. It all came out on your tongue instead of the canvas."

"Can that happen?"

"It can."

He put an arm around her.

"It's a month now," he said. "A month into his sentence."

"Yes."

"Do you think about him?"

"Of course."

"That's all there is," Brandt said. "Just memories."

"Yes, that's all."

He turned her.

"Live here," he invited.

"No."

"Why not? You want to."

"Yes, I want to. If Lewis had returned I'd have come to you. But he hasn't. He's in a prison somewhere and he'll need something to hold on to. Every day he'll see three faces. The twins and mine. So I have to keep faith."

They went to the door.

"You too have needs," Brandt said.

She picked up her handbag from the surface of a cabinet. A newspaper lay on its glass and Brandt pointed at it.

"Have you seen it?"

"No."

"There's a piece about John Chen."

"What about?"

"The chess match. In Manila."

"Who is he playing?"

"The Armenian."

She went outside.

"Then God help the Armenian," she said.

She crossed the road to the wall. I have to keep faith. She looked back and Erich Brandt was standing in the doorway and the sun was lighting up his beard. I have to keep faith. She turned. Or try to. The youth smiled up at her. It was a good head and the beauty of the smooth tan cheeks was enhanced by the orange silk. He would sit here, she knew, until his skin was as old and mottled as the old man's. She would attempt the painting and she would think of his fading sight when she came to the youth's black and lustrous eyes. She gave him some money and chose one of the skins, began to walk. She stopped when she reached the fruit stalls and turned. Erich Brandt was watching her. She could see a shoulder of the mountains and the forests on the ridges and the flame that was the turban. The day was turning vivid in the early sun and she felt a sudden hunger for the color and excitement of it, for this now, for this present. She began to walk again. The past was another country.

William Maggs rested the rifle on the tripod and made some adjustments to the sight. John Chen's head came into focus and across from it the face of the Armenian. He could see their black leather chairs, the stage and its blue carpet and, blurred beyond the definition of the sight, the auditorium and the mass of intent faces. It was a new hall and could be used for a variety of games and tournaments. There was a smell of damp concrete and new upholstery and the Filipinos had covered the circular wall with a frieze of advertisement posters. Up here in the little storeroom there was the silence that he needed for his concentration and he could hear his own breathing and the rustle of his shirt cuffs when he moved his arms. He shifted his eye from the sight and looked down into the well of the auditorium. He could see in the sixth row from the stage the empty seat for which he had purchased a ticket. They had given him a pamphlet with the ticket and he had read the histories of the players and some information about the game. He did not play chess and he had learned that there were more than seven hundred openings and variants on such openings and that grandmasters like these two men were capable of memorizing them and then, as if that were not enough, to a depth of three subsequent moves. He returned to the eyepiece. Chen's shapely head appeared. Dissect that skull, he thought with a sense of wonder, and you will never identify the miraculous bit of tissue that holds within itself such unique powers. He watched Chen move a bishop (or was that piece a knight?) and the Armenian's suffering face. Chess, the pamphlet concluded, was the cruelest game of all. Now Chen's head was still. Maggs made a final adjustment so that the shell would smash through the occipital bone. He did not agree with the pamphlet. Without doubt the game of government handyman was the cruelest. He pressed the trigger.

During the first weeks of his captivity there were five faces that Lewis Mackenna saw continually in the darkness of the hut. They came and went in dreams or on the edge of dreams; Lin Sheng and Shameen, Joel and Gerard and Ellen, floating away down unnavigable rivers of the conscience. Then, as the season changed, it was Lin Sheng who was his close companion. The comatose face was always there. He prayed for his return, that whatever door it was that locked him in would open and release him. At first there were many forms of prayer, familiar words, dug up from the past, that seemed to perish on the tongue. Then they were gone and there was one simple prayer, the old Gaelic blessing that he whispered to that white unmoving face. May God hold you in the hollow of his hand.

The prison camp was built in a brown and barren land and, now, the winds from the Gobi had begun to feel around its contours. The huts and compounds were enclosed by a breastwork of upright stakes. They were crowned with coiled barbed wire and beyond the stockade were villages and cultivated land. A dirt road followed the line of the stakes and often there were walking people and army and commune trucks. They had taken his boots when he entered the camp and in the beginning it was painful to move on the sharp earth and one of the guards had laughed at his limping feet and, with malice, had quoted the Buddhist saying: "Have mercy on me, O Enlightened One, I was angered for I had no shoes. Then I met a man who had no feet." But now his soles were callused and he could walk the compound without pain and every day he went to the fence and watched the road and its curve into distance. Someone would come down that road, if his prayer was answered. May God hold you in the hollow of his hand. John Chen's voice always spoke behind the prayer. "If Lin Sheng comes back to us," he had said at the end of the second trial, "you will be told.

That is my promise. Someone will come and tell you." Every day he watched the road.

At times there were children on the road. They were accustomed to the sight of political prisoners and mostly they did not even turn their heads to stare. A few might cross the open ground and stand at the fence in silence and provided they were small the guards would not wave them back. One of those who came frequently to the shadow of the stakes was a boy with starved cheeks. He never spoke or smiled and perhaps, Lewis thought, he was fascinated by the condition of captivity. He always carried a bamboo cage with a lark inside and when he walked he swung the cage so that the bird beat its wings in desperation. A caged bird, carried about like a toy, was a common sight and Lewis did not know at first why he should be affected by it. But the plight of the lark became unbearable and one day he said to the boy: "Set it free."

The boy shook his head.

"Please."

The boy held out his hand.

"I have nothing," Lewis said. He pointed at his naked feet. "Not even boots."

The boy shrugged and left. But on the evening of the following day he came again to the fence and this time he swung the cage around his head, again and again until the bird rattled like a ball of feathers on the bamboo ribs.

"Please stop," Lewis said.

The boy set the cage on the ground and held out his hand.

"I have no money," Lewis said. "No watch, nothing."

He saw the boy's eyes go to his throat and he put up his hand and felt the chain and Father Tsai's silver fish. The ball moved and spread its wings. His eyes blurred. He felt the pressure of related pains; Lin Sheng imprisoned, he imprisoned, the bird imprisoned. He took the chain from his neck.

"Set it free," he said.

The boy opened the cage. The lark soared and Lewis watched it lift on the wings of the wind. The boy put his hand through the stakes and took the fish and hung it around his neck. Then he picked up the cage and walked back to the road.

In the morning Lewis left the hut. The sun had not yet risen and darkness lay on the camp. He went to the center of the compound. There was a freshness in the air and when he turned his face to the sky he felt a moisture touch his skin. He held out his hands and the palms took a sheen of wetness. He smiled and began to walk. He did not believe in the dew of heaven. It was a feature of the Old Testament and its soft rain fell throughout the pages from Genesis to Zechariah. The old chroniclers had given it a divine origin; and certainly a little light rain on the arid lands was a kind of blessing. But he did not believe it was a bestowal from God or that the absence of it was a curse. But it was good to walk in it and feel it on the flesh and taste it on the lips. At the fence he watched the sunrise and the road emerge. He felt an uplifting of the spirit. A messenger might come down that road. Please let him come.